Bloodless
Book Three: The Binding Tenets Trilogy
G.J. Terral

Copyright © [2025] by [G.J. Terral]

All rights reserved.

No portion of this book may be reproduced in any form without written permission from the publisher or author, except as permitted by U.S. copyright law.

Contents

Dedication	VI
Acknowledgements	VII
Left Map	VIII
Right Map	IX
1. The Thaw	1
2. Drums of Hope	4
3. Drums of Bone	16
4. Drums of Hate	35
5. Drums of Blood	50
6. Desperate Hope	64
7. Desperate Bone	74
8. Desperate Hate	92
9. Desperate Blood	105
10. Denied Hope	117
11. Denied Bone	131
12. Denied Hate	144

13.	Denied Blood	158
14.	Delayed Hope	172
15.	Delayed Bone	185
16.	Delayed Hate	200
17.	Delayed Blood	216
18.	Daring Hope	226
19.	Daring Bone	237
20.	Daring Hate	250
21.	Daring Blood	263
22.	Disastrous Hope	277
23.	Disastrous Bone	291
24.	Disastrous Hate	312
25.	Disastrous Blood	324
26.	Dirge of Hope	337
27.	Dirge of Bone	351
28.	Dirge of Hate	362
29.	Dirge of Blood	374
30.	Dying Hope	383
31.	Dying Hate	395
32.	A Dawning Tapestry	402
33.	The End	416

34. The Crystallium Depths	417
Definitely Not A Secret	421

Dedication

Bloodwoven was for my wife.

Bloodbound for loved ones.

Bloodless is for me, but I hope everyone else enjoys it too.

Acknowledgements

There are far too many people who have supported, encouraged, and inspired me to list them all but I must give special consideration to my wife, mother, grandmother, and my best friends. Each and everyone has told me I could do this, and each and everyone helped to ensure I would do this.

I want to express my deepest thanks to Cristiana "Cru" Leone for once again bringing my vision to life on the cover, I think all the covers have been stellar but she really captured the villain on this cover. I must again thank Jack, for designing the map used throughout the series.

A huge shout-out to the Secret Scribes; A collective of wildly different authors who've banded together to make the experience that much more bearable. (They're listed at the back!)

Calm's Peak

Lyre

Fallo

Duchy of
ERROND

Orekinsburg

Lakewatch Lake

Elswood

Duchy of
ELMORE

Wakewatch

Fentis

The Duchies of
DANICA

The Thaw

A signed accounting from recently elevated junior scholar Denro.

Once more, I find myself accounting the trials and actions of a man dear to my heart, a man that has done his best and given his all to rescue a child many might say he had no business chasing after. My time with the Scholars has taught me as much about myself as it has the Fentians, and in doing so I've found a small semblance of forgiveness, both for him and myself. I'll do my best to recount events, but much of it is a recounting afforded me by others and not Lindel. Much of what occurred in Ladrica I learned from others, as the time I saw him once he returned was far too short lived, and something I regret as I pen this.

It is true, we were confined as the Fentians decided which side of the war they'd land on. It is undeniable they took extra precautions to limit Lin's more dangerous capabilities, feeding him a restricted diet and limiting what tomes he had access too. Ultimately, Pael, a crotchety ally of Lin's, rescued us. But in our captivity, Mellyr was spirited away by a Ladrican Emissary. Aemun was a rot on Danica, his corruption spread far beyond the initial corpse he left behind. It came back to me through Anya, sweet stoic Anya, that Aemun had offered his child's hand in marriage to the Ladrican King in hopes of uniting the people. Uniting their old *bloodlines*.

Lindel failed to prevent Mellyr from being stolen and chased her north with Pael and I in tow, though to say I was reticent at this point would be justified. But it was clear to me, even then, that something needed to change. Danica as a whole couldn't survive a war. We didn't have the supplies, the funds, the *people*.

From the time between Lin's departure at Wakewatch and his arrival at the Ladrican fort, I have very little information. It is clear many dark things occurred, awful things that Lin wouldn't go into detail on other than admitting he feels he is unraveling. Untethering from the Grand Tapestry and going mad.

Though there has been word of continued problems related to untethered, and I fear Lin's obstinate silence and doubt is related to this somehow.

His arrival at the Ladrican Fort, Fort Talmsdale I believe, would've been the first documented case of a militant attack on Ladrican soil since the War of the Siblings back before the Accords were drafted. He survived and even rescued a quite young Ladrican lad who now follows Anya like her shadow. Tests, tests explicitly *breaking* the Accords were being conducted at the Fort and this has been confirmed in reports from High Scholar Anya in her official capacity.

This part is where I'm most proud of Lindel. Not for saving the lives of the gathered leaders when the talks eventually failed but for trying to reason with those who violence would never sway. Glimmers of excellence were reported from not only Anya, but several of the world leaders. He wasn't eloquent. He wasn't the speaker who could begin to sway their minds, but he touched their hearts. Of that I'm left with little doubt. He survived, coming back with Mellyr in the custody of Anya and the scholars. But more importantly, he bought Danica time. Three months to prepare an argument against the current state of things, though it seems King Lodram may not stay his hand. Time will tell, but ships have been spotted off the coast. All I can say, truthfully, is that I'm happier to be penning this versus my documentation of the Fall. I'm sure this was less detached, less unbiased, but when recounting the tale of a hero, personal feelings should have merit. And while I'm displeased with the Fall and how that was handled, I couldn't be more proud of Lin for the steps he took during the Thaw. I just wish he had said goodbye before departing for the Ferrucium.

Drums of Hope

"War is never something one should rush easily into. Let resolution be bloodless when possible, bloody when necessary, but never let it be rushed."—High Scholar Anya of Fentis.

Lin couldn't stop himself from staring at Denny. Ever since he found her in Townsbridge, she'd carried herself like nothing had happened between them. No shared kiss. No awkward denial of feelings. Just *nothing*. And it ate at Lin more than the leeches had when taking his tainted blood.

"Two more days," Denny called over her shoulder.

They'd arrive at the Ferrucium in two days and see if King Lodram's threats had been idle or not.

Lin itched at his scars and watched the way Denny moved. Lithe and nimble. Everything the mad woman did seemed natural, even when she was sprinting faster than a non-Binder could. Lin kept up thanks to his own Inlays and he was sure if anyone with the Sight saw them rushing along the well-worn path they'd think them untethered.

Maybe they were untethered. It wasn't long ago in Lyre he would've assumed the same. Back when his red cloak and Ferrucium steel sword were his only two constant companions. And Nebra, of course. But... But now it was him, the Inlays, and his madness.

Since the leeching, Aemun's voice had been mercifully silent in his mind, but Lin could feel it there as if it were a figure standing just outside the ring of light provided by a campfire. All it waited for was a flare-up of sparks to cast light on its shadows.

Denny raised her lone arm, signaling Lin to slow. Her eyes, lined with so many Inlays it was a marvel she could see past the glow, locked onto his and held them for a long moment. He wanted to look away, but she deserved better. *More.* And he couldn't give it to her. What fairness was it in life to promise a life he couldn't give her? He *was* untethering and not even her lips could save him from himself.

"Fire," she finally whispered.

Lin scanned the thicket ahead of them. A burning fire's light would seep through the thick-pressed dark forest, but none did. Then a whiff of smoke— burned wood, thatch, and worse— carried on the breeze.

Fear gripped his heart. He'd considered what it would mean to actually find Ladrican soldiers, to fight them and worsen his untethering by Binding. The goal was to use as little magic as possible, but if there were Noosemen or even those heavily armored bastards, what choice would he have? Lin had to fight. Had to save the Danican people who couldn't save themselves.

Like Mellyr. Leaving her was the hardest thing he'd had to do, like leaving Nebra with Alderman Pryor at Lyre. Even if it was to keep them safe, why did it hurt so much to leave behind the ones you loved?

Lin sucked in a breath and drew the Ferrucium steel sword he had at his waist. Binding as little as possible meant relying on his sword skill. Not that he was the most competent, but Gods knew he could stand on his own in a fight.

Denny moved like the breeze, not entirely silent of course, but wholly natural sounding. Each step like the rolling of a leaf as it skittered across the forest floor. Her boots didn't kick up sticks or rattle brush and Lin followed her steps as best he could. She stalked forward, pressing away branches and brush until she drew up to a stop and nodded at the knee-high stone wall in front of her.

All the villages in the northernmost parts of Danica had short walls like these that encircled them, but he couldn't recall ever seeing one this far past Townsbridge. Villages past the Telms River just didn't seem to hold onto true Danican traditions and Lin was sure the Ferrucium was the cause.

"Stone shroud." Denny kept her voice low and knelt in front of the wall, studying it. "Recently built."

Lin's brow furrowed as he stared. Smoke still hung in the air and now glimpses of smouldering remains drew his attention. "Stone shroud?" he asked.

Denny smiled at him, all mischief and mocking. "You wouldn't know about them, but I bet your priestess might. It has something to do with the old religion, Velkath and his kin. Keeps out bad omens and worse. Supposed to anyways."

Tylle. Thankfully it was night, so his blush wouldn't be quite so clear. Something about Denny bringing up Tylle made him uneasy as if he'd done something wrong by either of the women. And maybe he had.

Seemingly without effort, Denny hopped atop the wall, took three steps, and jumped down to the other side. Her grin only deepened Lin's unease and soon he crossed over the stone shroud too. An action he'd taken countless times while thinking the small, useless walls were anything more than decoration. Lyre had one, and Fallo too. And both had been beset by untethered. Omens didn't get much worse than an untethered attack.

All through the village, fires died. Campfires, by stacked stones and dirt-covered ashes. Footprints, bare and booted, stood out in the path. A force of five, maybe six, people had been through here and seemingly left in a hurry.

Like most of the smaller villages across Danica, a center path cut through the stone wall encircling it, and the homes were grouped off the pathway a fair bit. Trees grew inside the village perimeter, something the northern villages didn't abide by for whatever reason, and one lone tree rested at the center of the village proper. Spring was nearly upon them, but the leaves hadn't returned to the long-limbed, dark-wooded tree yet and it looked more like a black hand clawing at the night sky than anything else.

"Fuck," Denny said.

Lin followed her stare and noticed the bodies. Dragged there by the sticks, leaves, and dirt stuck to them. Bindings pinned their wrists to the bark of the tree and it looked like they were alive when it happened based on the fresh blood still seeping from the wounds. *Innocent citizens.*

"Worst thing is... After everything we saw in Ladrica, I don't know if this was untethered or the damned Ladricans."

Lin spun in a half-circle. He'd heard a snapping sound to the west. Nothing stood out against the dark buildings.

"I don't think a Nooseman would do this. And Ladrican soldiers don't Bind." Denny stood beside the bodies and cocked her head to the side. "These bodies are still warm."

That was true. So it was untethered. Every time he took his mind from the untethered for a moment, it seemed they came back to haunt him. Fallo. Drekinsburg and that odd coordinated assault. The strange occurrences in Northern Danica Tylle had wanted him to look into.

Untethered had been the worst thing he had to fear for so long as an Escorter, that once the threat of the northern kingdom materialized, it was too easy to let that take his focus from the monsters that had always existed in Danica's shadows.

A snarled howl carried from the pocket of woods to the west and they moved in tandem, Lin taking the lead despite Denny being the quieter of the two.

Limbs were scattered through the brush—pieces of bodies that hadn't been fit for the tree for some unknown reason. It had been too long since he'd seen wanton violence like this, too long since the reminder of Fallo had been seared into his mind. Scenes like these were nearly bad enough to make him consider King Lodram's intolerance with a more open mind.

Lin winced as his sword caught on a spry branch as he cleared the thicket.

Three untethered circled a fourth. Dingy Inlays covered their pale flesh and the mix of washed-out gold from the Inlays and a ghastly green hue from the hand of the tallest untethered made Lin's stomach knot. Green meant *stasis*. Green meant pulling on copper. Flashbacks to the tree where he'd tested the more obscure Bindings on that near-dead untethered surfaced like a clawing hand ready and able to drag him down into the foul memory. Now with a mind cleared from the leeches, perhaps that moment was the bell rung signaling his true untethering.

Howls and kicks came from the untethered in the center, sounding more like a wounded animal than the human the monster had once been. Where it had hair, it was in knotted tangles, but patches were missing and it bore a long gash down its scalp that ended near its cheek. Dried blood crusted its mouth and hands but the other three untethered looked fine. Normal even, like Carine and her people. Except for the antlers the tallest one had sticking from its temples with a faint green glow.

Like the one attacking Dreckinsburg.

The only difference Lin could tell was that each one had a green Binding writhing just under the surface of their brows, save for the mad one.

Denny was beside him, making herself known by a gentle tap on his shoulder. Her eyes, despite the golden glow of Inlays set in them, reflected the sickly green light the tall untethered held to the struggling monster's temple. The point of the copper Wieving shifted, and then the green light pierced the temple and wriggled under the sickly flesh like a burrowing grub.

A Thorn, blossoming from the seed of stasis.

In two breaths, the untethered calmed, limbs stilling and howls dying as the magic brought some semblance of sanity back to the creature.

"Jo-Jollan... He... He won't be pleased," the newly sane untethered whined. Features of rage and fury had shifted to fear and remorse.

"The Horned King has little worry over southern citizens who only recently built a shroud. He will forgive, as is his way."

Denny had apparently heard enough. She rushed in, Binding Blade at her side as she swept past Lin like a gust. In one quick motion, she took the head from the tall, horned untethered and sent a Weft scything through the air toward the trio.

Lin moved just behind her. His first instinct was to send a Weft out to compliment Denny's, but he held back his magic and closed the distance with his sword leveled.

Crude, brittle bands of magic soared toward him and broke against the Ferrucium steel he carried. Rust and death traveled on the air in such a suffocating wave that Lin gasped and covered his mouth.

"We— We can talk this—" The untethered's words died as Denny's Blade thrust through its throat. Her breath puffed out in heavy clouds and she turned to the remaining two monsters.

One tried to flee, spinning and rushing to the north, but Lin cut it off. Binding met Lin's sword's edge and broke, over and over. There was a rhythm to fighting the monsters that Lin had missed in the north, a dance that Lin couldn't achieve against Nooseman and the Ladrican soldiers with their damned Bound Metal batons.

Lin harried the creature, slashing and striking at every chance until a well-placed strike took its left leg out from under it with a crunching chop.

Gods.

It cried. Velkath's Sigil glowed in bright lines across its chest, Stitched into place befouling the Grand Tapestry. If such a thing even existed. Lin didn't care if Velkath and his kin had been people before, good people even. These monsters now used his symbol for wicked, terrible things. And it certainly didn't help that when he was slipping down the slope of madness, he'd seen the damned symbol burning bright where no symbol actually rested.

Denny moved to him, breathing far heavier than she would've if they hadn't been injured during their incursion of Ladrica. She held her side, her Blade already unraveled into motes of light and drifting away on the wind.

"P-please," the untethered begged.

"First time I've seen one of you talk," Denny whispered.

The monster shook its head, eyes searching from Lin's face to Denny's. "S-spare m-me and we won't pass the Telms a-again."

"There are more of you?" Lin growled.

A chuckle churned from the untethered. He'd likely been a thin man once and now was a thinner monster. Gaunt face and sharp nose not helping with his pallid complexion. He sat up on his elbows as he wiped his eyes. "Family. A path for those like us."

Denny kicked his arm out from under him and the monster fell to an elbow. He laughed harder, shaking his head. "We aren't like *you.*"

Lin winced at the words. How many times had he worried over that simple statement? How close was he to that fate? If things had gone differently, he could've been like this bone-bare untethered, begging for his life.

"See the Thorn?" Lin asked as he pointed the tip of his sword at the untethered's brow. "Let's them regain their mind somehow. Who is the Horned King that your companions spoke of?"

"He would accept the both of you for who you are. The true children of Danica."

"Who is he?" Denny snapped. She'd formed her Blade again and leveled it near the untethered's arm that still supported him.

"Velkath Reborn. And he will love you—" Denny's Blade took him across the throat. And she kept slashing as the untethered died choking on his blood. His hands desperately worked to close his wound, blue magic flaring to life as he drew on zinc for healing. The slash nearly puckered closed fully before another vicious arcing blow reopened it and took the untethered's hands from his wrists.

Denny snarled and when Lin dropped his sword and hugged her to calm her, she shrugged him off and nearly attacked him. Her Blade raised, then lowered, then broke apart like embers shooting off from a burning log. Her voice was so weak, that Lin struggled to hear it.

"We aren't like *them.*"

"I've seen untethered like them attacking a village. Second time seeing one with fucking horns. Would've thought it was the same I saw if we didn't just learn there was another bastard out there calling himself the Horned King."

That name itched something at the back of Lin's mind. Like he'd forgotten the name of something and knew if only he could think a little harder, he might recall it.

"Fuck them. If they're attacking innocent villages when they should be working with Grovetender and the new Ferrucium to defend Danica, then fuck them. Don't care if they talk or not. Don't care. Not one fucking bit." Denny turned, hawked a glob of spit onto the dead untethered, and stalked back to the path without a look back.

There were plenty of times he'd been scared of Denny, especially early on, but this was different. Even not fully recovered, even exhausted and running for the better part of the last few days, she was still the scariest fighter he'd ever seen. Save Dennick perhaps. That Nooseman had been a monster made of ice and ire. A hatred for Danicans so devout that words couldn't reach him. But... watching Denny stalk away now, wasn't she the same?

No. She was passionate. Fierce in her feelings and beautiful because of her blemishes. And she was mad at him. Furious even, though she wouldn't put voice to thought. That was the only reason he could imagine for her behavior.

Blaming her was something he couldn't bring himself to do. He'd resented Tylle a bit when she'd declined him, hadn't he?

Maybe it was for the best. It meant if he did untethered, she'd kill him all the easier.

Lin retrieved his sword, wiped the blood from it, and sheathed it as he followed Denny's trail back to the path. Denny had broken the Weaves holding the corpses to the tree but left the bodies where they were. They didn't have time to bury the dead or build a pyre, so instead they'd rot and feed the wolves. Though this was a much smaller scale, it really was Fallo all over again. Except this time Lin hadn't almost died.

Once they'd left the village behind, they took to a route just off the main road. By his judgment, they were close to the Ferrucium. Another day at most and they'd be to the farmlands and barren fields that separated the stronghold from the rest of Danica.

"Do you want to talk?" Lin asked. They'd slowed as they crossed through a hilly area. Inlayed limbs were great for additional speed and strength, but an ankle could roll all the same.

"About?"

"I don't know. You just seemed upset back there and—"

Denny wheeled on him, her lone arm gripping a thin tree that swayed from her weight. "Did I? Let me guess, you think it's about you? An entire village massacred, talking untethered claiming you and I are like them, and you think I'm upset because you'd rather die a hero than run away and *live* with me?"

When she put it that way, it did seem rather silly to assume she was mad at him and not at what they'd just witnessed. He'd seen and survived Fallo, of course, this remote village hadn't struck his heart as hard. Lin blinked. Did she think he was a hero? Him?

A grin broke across Lin's face despite himself and Denny's eyes widened.

"You really think I'm being heroic?"

"I think you're the most heroic idiot I know!" Denny shifted her weight and used the tree to turn herself back around. "And utterly hopeless without me."

Lin couldn't say it, not knowing how near he was to untethering, but he wholeheartedly agreed. Without her, he'd have died in Ladrica.

Drums of Bone

"War can be many things... But from my experience, it is a catalyst of change. Take the violence, ash, lies, hope, and lives, and allow all the reagents to mix and you're left with the outcome. I suppose it sounded grander in my mind but my point still stands. War is alchemy, and the survivors are something magical." —Erias Wellgrove

Since the devastated village they'd stumbled upon a day ago, the trip had been uneventful. No more signs of untethered, intelligent or otherwise, and not even a whiff of a Ladrican invasion force. Lin had half expected the southern part of Danica to be overrun, but if they'd assaulted the Ferrucium port, the Ladrican ships were being kept at bay.

Denny hadn't said more than a word or two toward him and Lin felt the tension growing taut like a stretched thread. He almost preferred the way she'd been before the village as if nothing had happened between them at all.

Now they'd been stopped for a brief moment, just long enough to catch their breath, sip from their nearly empty waterskins, and not much else. Lin gasped as he adjusted the compress around his ribs. They'd loosened during the fight at the village and now it felt like something in him had done the same.

"What's wrong?" Denny asked.

Dark circles under her eyes suggested she felt as bad as he did, exhaustion not caring whether they were Inlayed or not.

Everything. "Nothing," Lin lied.

Denny's eyes flicked to where his hand fiddled with the wrap and she closed the distance between them in a blur. Before he knew it she was behind him, lone arm draped across his shoulders as she pulled at his tunic.

Confusion and curiosity warred within him and then sharp pain cleared both from his mind as Denny tightened the compress. She pulled the loosened bandage so tight that dots of light exploded in Lin's vision like a shattered Binding. After a moment, the sudden pain lessened, and a dull throb— more comfortable than he'd been with the loose wrap— took over.

"Better?" She asked, more than a hint of a smile to her tone.

Lin shrugged away from her. It was fair for her to be upset, but to take it out on him and take pleasure from his pain wasn't. He wheeled on her and saw her faltering expression. Pain in her eyes and worry at the slant of her thin lips, the bottom just a bit fuller.

"Yeah," Lin managed. "Should be a good sign we haven't seen any Ladricans, right?"

Denny shrugged and forced a smile. As quick as she'd taken his top from him, she helped slide it back on. She patted his chest twice, fingers lingering as she pulled away. "Speaking of, you still didn't say how it went with that Nooseman and her Bludwieve."

It hadn't come up. Or rather, they hadn't talked about Fentis since Lin departed the tower.

The truth? Well, the removal of Gritt's Bludwieve went well. Surprisingly so. But it was what came after that made him want to keep that morning to himself, tucked away like a grievous wound he had allowed to fester. Lin *was* untethering. His blood sickening him from within. Sure, Denny and he had made jokes about cracking and going mad, but how was he supposed to tell anyone, even Denny, the truth if it meant he had to sit in the tower and hope everyone else managed the upcoming war without him?

"It went well."

Denny frowned, bringing all her uneven Stitches across her face nearly level. She waggled her ring finger where her own Bludwieve twined a bloody crimson. "So well that you decided not to do the same. Despite all the talk of eventual removal?"

Lin grimaced and took in the deepest breath he could manage. "We didn't have time. And the recovery would've made me miss out on all this. Let's go. If we press hard we can get there before nightfall." He hated not being honest with her, but ever before spotting the massacred village, everything had felt wrong. Even before that, something had felt *off* as if the leeches had taken more than blood from him. Their shriveled, dead forms had consumed his hope too.

As he rushed ahead, not waiting for her reply, he was thankful to be in Danica and not in the cold, icy north. This far south, the weather was cool and comforting, not biting and harsh. Notes of winter still hung in the air, but spring was well on its way, breathing a fresh life across their embattled country. Only Nebra could have made it a perfect moment. No voices from long-dead enemies. No sigils in his peripheral to haunt him. Just him and the land he'd called his home all his life.

By the time they slowed again, night had taken the sky. The moon marked it's territory, coloring the nearest clouds like piss in snow. Not his most poetic thought, but Pael would still enjoy that analogy. Maybe. Denro, considerably less so. A pang of regret pulled at him like a loose stitch at the fact he hadn't told Denro goodbye. Hadn't told Mellyr either, but of the two he doubted she would have very strong opinions on his abrupt departure.

"Thinking about me?" Denny asked. She stood beside a boulder that had seen better days, a terrible crack running along its southward side.

She wasn't far from the truth, as much as their kiss had taken prominence in his mind. He felt his cheeks blush and was thankful for the clouds and trees filtering the moonlight.

"I..." Lin started.

"I'm messing with you," Denny laughed in short little manic bursts, her eyes large and bright.

Lin smiled and shook his head. "I'm just nervous."

"Nervous to see her again? Is that who you were thinking about?" Denny, always quick to attack from his blind spot. Gods, she excelled at catching him off guard.

Tylle. Lin flushed deeper at that. With everything happening, he hadn't stopped to consider she might be at the Ferrucium. "No."

Denny shook her head and her smile shifted to something a wolf might wear before attacking prey. "But you just did think of her, or you wouldn't have known who I meant."

Shit. The last thing Lin wanted was to hurt Denny, to upset her more than he'd already done. Even if she wouldn't admit it, something bothered her and it *had* to be his fault. Lin sucked in another deep breath and shrugged. "I was thinking about everything. All of it."

Gods. The way Denny stared, it was like her eyes pleaded with him for honesty. The trek to the Ferrucium hadn't been a hard one save for dispatching the untethered, and it was far easier than the last time he'd come east, but Lin had let silence fill the soft spaces between them ever since their shared kiss on the balcony.

What was he meant to tell her? There weren't words for it. Of all the people, she alone had rushed to his aid at learning his plans, she alone had fought and struggled and made it back from Ladrica. But she couldn't be a part of his future because *he* didn't have one. Gods willing, he wouldn't have to Bind, but if he was meant to fight back the same caliber of soldiers as what he faced in the north, he wouldn't have a choice. And that was without even considering the untethered threat that refused to be quelled. Every turn he made there was a reminder of the taint across Danica. The untethered problem was like mold that had spread and not been excised properly, growing worse for having been ignored. Even if he hadn't *meant* to ignore it. And now some Horned King, undoubtedly an untethered, was causing more problems?

Lin looked down at his boots, breaking eye contact. "Can you make me a promise?"

"What?" She whispered.

He looked up and saw how intently she stared, how hungrily she waited for his question as if it might feed whatever turmoil was starving within.

"If something happens, and I untether, kill me. Please. Before I can hurt anyone I care about." Lin wouldn't give her a chance to pry open the wound at the heart of his request. "Please."

Denny nodded, tapping her chin as she did. She held up her hand as if she just had the grandest idea. "And if I untether," she said with a lop-sided grin, "Inlay your bits for me. As a way to remember me."

Lin forced a smile. He had hoped she would take him seriously. "I mean it, Denny."

Her smile faltered and she leaned in. "So do I. Deadly serious."

Lin wanted to grab and hold her, but instead, he only held the emotion back. If he managed to get through this to the other side with her, they'd hold each other then. But not a piece of him thought he'd make it, not if things were as bad as they seemed.

"Do you think we'll make it by daybreak?" He asked.

A chuckle escaped her, followed by a puzzled look as she pointed past the tree line. "You don't see them? The tips?"

Lin squinted. The night sky was clouded, and even with the moon's comforting glow, the horizon was nothing more than a dark blur. He squinted harder, wondering if perhaps Anya's warning of his worsening sight was coming to fruition. There had been plenty of times he could think of late when his sight failed him.

"Even if you can't see them, you can taste the salt in the air, no? Shouldn't this feel like home to you?"

There was no way Denny could know how painful those words were. The night didn't smell like anything to him. And it certainly didn't feel like home, even though it should.

Lin followed silently as Denny picked the path forward. They'd avoided the main roads so much up until now that walking on the well-worn path felt strange. A sharp bluff rested to the right and the sound of the sea, vast and hungry, carried up over the cliffs. If the waters by Fentis were known as the Pellic Sea, what sort of name did these waters hold?

Lin's failing eyes finally made out the looming red brick walls of the Ferrucium and, thanks to the moon overhead, the scattered ships struggling to make landfall on the rocky coast below.

"Shit," Denny spat. "Ten fucking ships."

Lin was tired of squinting and took her word for it. He'd seen six, maybe seven. As if losing his mind wasn't enough, he was losing his sight too. "But if they haven't docked, that's a good thing. No?"

"Three are pretty damned close," Denny hissed.

At full sprint, they could get to the walls before the moon dipped in the west. Running injured was never a good thing, but Denny was a woman possessed and Lin couldn't let her rush forward alone. It could be, hidden at the docks they couldn't see, that the ships had already docked. The Ferrucium fallen. But Denny didn't seem to think so as she rushed headfirst towards the place Lin had called home for so long.

As they neared, a percussive explosion shattered the stillness, followed by rumbling and a column of fire from one of the nearer ships. Ladricans. An invading force. Just as King Lodram had promised.

Lin gritted his teeth and pushed through the burning in his side.

Soldiers clad in the crimson cloaks and livery of the Ferrucium looked to be standing guard. Six of them, and when they noticed Lin and Denny, crossbows and spears were pointed at them. One must've possessed the Sight, as they quickly shouted, "Untethered or allies?"

"Could be lying, either way. But friends," Lin called back through gasped breaths. He took his eyes from them and stared out across the black sea, flames reflected on the surface from the burning wreckage.

"Grovetender's people?"

"Yes," Denny shouted.

What Lin had always known to be empty fields, killing fields if it ever came to it, with brush and a wide path ended up being lined with intermittent barricades of sharp sticks and heavy stones and ballistas, the latter firing onto the approaching ships with little to no coordination.

Lin studied it all, doubtful it was enough to cause a ship to catch fire. Doubtful it was enough to repel an invasion.

Lined up along the cliff, teams of Binders stood twisting magic into existence. Some were clad in Ferrucium reds, but most weren't. But they worked as a team, whipping together disparate Wefts into larger ones. Working in tandem to perform greater magic— something Lin hadn't thought possible.

"Not sure what help two people can give, but the fools on the ships have tried to moor once or twice to no avail, skiffs have attempted landfall and have been pressed back once they hit the runbacks. Figure at the rate they've been going they'll run out of supplies before we run out of soldiers."

Lin nodded at that, half-listening. In truth, he was watching what he thought to be one of Carine's people form the largest Binding he'd ever seen. Others worked alongside him as if they helped shape it.

Denny gasped beside him. "Jun."

That was his name, the one with stripes across his torso and a bald head— the one who'd been partnered with the one who'd betrayed Carine for Aemun's plan. His flesh shone with Inlays and a layer of sweat made him glow even brighter, bare-backed as he was.

The Binding was shaped like a cone, a sharp-tipped, thick-bodied bolt. It was longer than it was wide, and far larger than anything Lin thought one person capable of forming, let alone wielding. And with a mighty thrust from Jun, it flew like it had wings. The magic flew like a bolt too, spearing the nearest ship's hull. Wood crushed, the hull pierced, and screams carried on the wind. Arrows peppered the ground around them and the ones that nearly found purchase were cut from the air by watchful Binders.

"I taught him that," Denny said. Gods. She sounded proud as she formed a Binding, a smaller, thinner twin to the massive one Jun had just launched. "Except you know, they made it bigger. The flat ones are great for cutting, but these ones? Only Ferrucium steel, like the armor they wore in the north, would stop it if it's made right. Hard to control though."

A pointed Weft. Essentially what it was if Lin tried to wrap his mind around it. His fingers itched under the flesh, like an urge to conjure a Weft, Weave, Inlay, whatever just to feel that spark of creation. What was the last binding he'd formed? The strange blue healing thread? All he needed to do was—

"Lin, we need to move!"

His attention snapped to Denny and her bright eyes. If looks could cut, she'd slice to the meat of him with a glance. "I'm sorry, I've never even considered forming Bindings like that."

"You and your Ferrucium people. Too worried about the Tapestry to think of ways to ruin it." She cackled. "Now, stare any harder and your eyes might cross. We need to move. Erias and Azhura should be up ahead, near the outer wall. Come on."

Denny was right. Even after taking techniques from untethered, he hadn't considered making up any of his own. If there was some madman out there calling himself Velkath Reborn, perhaps Denny was Vellia reborn, the way she seemed so capable all the time.

Lin followed as more of those large Binding Bolts ripped through the air. Ones that missed ships stuck out from the water like discarded spears.

They neared the southeastern walls of the Ferrucium. Shouts and cries sounded from a slew of tents with mossy-covered tarps, plenty of soldiers, and two bickering individuals. A command center of sorts. How they'd sorted out that the invasion would be from the southern sea and not the northern pass was beyond Lin unless perhaps Erias Wellgrove and Weaver— Ex-Weaver Azhura— had better tactical acumen than Lin imagined.

Erias appeared as poised as the last time Lin had seen him in the man's lair at Wellgrove. He carried himself like a duke, even if it was his brother who held that esteemed title. His dark hair was still slicked back and cropped, but his formal, nearly regal, clothes from what felt like a lifetime ago had changed for armor in the dark greens and browns of Wellgrove. He wore a sword at his hip sheathed in a scabbard that looked made from the night sky itself.

The soldiers in the immediate vicinity watched Lin and Denny with suspicion in their eyes, no matter if they wore Wellgrove or Ferrucium colors. Lin didn't blame them. If Lin and Denny looked anything like how he felt, it wasn't the best look.

"A valid point, but if we give up the Ferrucium Hold, more than the blow to morale that will give all *our* remaining soldiers, it will be a true boot to the neck of our people. You know, that boot you're always on about. We only have the one port if we think Fentis will continue to flounder." Azhura's raised voice lowered as she noticed Denny and Lin standing there.

Seeing the two leaders standing together brought a strange emotion bubbling under Lin's surface. Resentment, maybe. Hope, possibly.

Erias frowned and shook his head. "We don't receive imports anyways. What is the loss of a single port."

"Ha! You think I don't know about the Elodian's little skiffs of aid? Hmmm."

Erias exhaled through his nose and rubbed his temple as his hard gaze took in Denny and Lin with one sweep. "Lindel. Hero of the Fingers. Denny. Glad to see you've returned to us wholly intact."

Denny nodded at him, matching his stare with her chin held high. "Of course, should've known the cowards would attack as soon as I left."

Erias waved her comment away. "We had—"

"Where is my great-granddaughter?" Azhura interrupted. Her loveless eyes were focused entirely on Lin. Her thin painted lips were drawn into a tight line that made the wrinkles around them all the more severe. Where Erias had changed for battle, Azhura looked much the same as when Lin last visited the Ferrucium. Her hair was bound in ornate, silvered braids tied into weaving knots and her top was sheer, silken scarlet, though this time she wore golden wrappings underneath.

The words didn't want to come. Not because Lin was ashamed of his decision or was scared of her reaction, but because he hated that he had to leave her. When he'd last seen Weaver Azhura, he'd simply been a custodian of the newborn. Now? He was her father, for better or worse and leaving her with the Scholars of Fentis had taken all his resolve.

Lin cleared his throat and said, "Mellyr is with High Scholar Anya. She will be kept safe, I have assurances."

More explosions sounded from the shore below the Ferrucium, resounding off the cliffs. Flashbacks to the island he'd only recently returned from crashed across his thoughts like the percussive explosions rebounding from the sheer cliffs. He wouldn't wish that horror of sizzling Wanderer's Ore on anyone.

"Safer than she would be if brought back here to this conflict anyways," Lin added.

Azhura made a noise that seemed a mix between a purr and a growl and crossed her arms. Rings glittered on three of her fingers, silver bands accenting finely cut rubies the size of an eye.

"A conflict we wouldn't—"

"We wouldn't have if your grandson hadn't brought it about," Erias interrupted Azhura. "Thank the Six our troops were slow to train and mobilize or they'd all have gone north with the others. Now, you two have returned, doubtless with information?"

Watching the Grovetender, the man responsible in no small part for helping orchestrate the Fall of the Ferrucium, bicker with Weaver Azhura was a sight Lin couldn't help but grin at. Each of them fed off the other, both too high and mighty for their good but somehow, amid the chaos and divisiveness, it *worked*. These two had managed to get the Ferrucium and soldiers prepared for the battle to come.

"What other troops?" Denny asked.

Erias turned and gestured at the table centered underneath the tawny tent. A map, very likely the same one he'd had in his room back in his room at Wellgrove, was unrolled and weighed down by chunks of narrow Wanderer's Ore at three of the corners, and an unsheathed dagger at the fourth.

"At Pael's return, we sent him and a contingent of Holbrook's men, and some of my brother's men of course, to the northwest. Exploratory mostly. Some few thousand men. When you went through there, on your way up to Ladrica, did you see any of Duke Errond's men?"

Lin frowned. "No, actually."

"We fear—"

"That Duke Errond in the north has either sided with Ladrica, ignoring all summons from the other dukes, or has been besieged without our knowledge." Azhura's lips twitched into a smile at being the one to interrupt her contemporary. She stalked over to the map and knocked a grouping of upright purple blocks over.

Erias tsked and moved to stand just beside her. He adjusted the blocks as he shook his head. "So, Pael went to investigate, and since then..." He glanced at Azhura, and when she didn't interrupt, said, "Nothing."

Lin chewed at his lip and looked at Denny. She leaned against a pole, caught him staring, and shrugged. If she had left at Pael's arrival as she claimed back at the northern pass, she would have known that more of Erias's people were on the way. Perhaps not for Lin, but they would have been near enough. Lin bit back his questions and nodded. "For my brief time in the north, I saw no signs of Ladrican troops. Though... I witnessed one coordinated attack by a group of untethered."

Azhura nodded at that, a smile coming to her wrinkled face. "As I've been saying, reports have shown the untethered problem worsening!"

"And there were some a day out, Stitched villagers to a tree in the center of the town." Denny's voice was soft and her eyes were trained on the ground.

Erias crossed his arms and looked at the map, studying the array of small villages that dotted the expanse between Townsbridge and the Ferrucium. The last map Lin had seen didn't have even a third of the villages listed on it. Perhaps that was the difference between Ferrucium maps and those acquired through the Erias's rebellion.

"We're aware of the growing concerns but... In preparing for enemies from without, there is always the risk of ignoring the ones from within. We've had a succinct lack of recruits. That was why Tylle went ahead of him, to see if she could request aid from any of the small pockets who still share the oral histories of the old ways."

Lin tried to imagine it... Surviving a Ladrican assault only to have the disease of untethered eat them from within. Gods. Thinking about those monsters who'd almost killed him in Fallo, he wasn't sure he'd best them now, even improved as he was. Especially if he wasn't Binding.

"And the status here?" Denny asked. Her eyes drifted away from the map, half-lidded despite the explosions and sounds of battle scaling the cliff far easier than the Ladricans were. Perhaps she'd grown tired of the conversation. Gods knew Lin's teeth ached to do something— anything.

Knowing that allies fought below as he stood here having a conversation with two leaders too scared to dirty their hands bothered him. Or perhaps that insidious itch just under the surface had spread to his teeth. A fiending for more. He'd traded hearing Aemun's voice and seeing Velkath's Sigil for a constant, unnatural urge to work magic. And he knew the cost.

Lin clenched his hands at his side and paled as he looked out over the harbor. Two more ships were aflame, but the Bolts Jun and the others threw had slowed in volume and shouts carried on the wind.

Azhura cleared her throat and nodded to the southern portion of the map where larger wooden blocks lined the coast. Twenty blocks. *Twenty* ships. "Truth be told, we hadn't anticipated an assault from the sea."

"At first," Erias said with a grin. He rubbed his chin, the Bound Metal ring on his hand pulling Lin's attention like a lodestone. "But we received puzzling words from a foreign interest. Northern passes not in masses. Only Binders avoid open sea, believe."

"Mostly nonsense with no real backing but with Pael and that contingent already heading north we hedged our bets. And having dealt with King Lodram and his people in the past, I didn't believe they were half so clever as to make us commit to staying south with intentions to come through the northern pass," Azhura said.

Erias nodded, letting his eyes linger on Lin. "Denny. We have some messages that could be run, if you're willing. Azhura, care to relay the recent tidings to her?"

It was clear neither of the women regarded taking orders from Erias well, but both moved reluctantly to appease the man. They didn't leave the area altogether, but Erias beckoned Lin to come closer, putting plenty of space between him and Denny.

Lin eyed Erias. "Did you need something from me?"

Erias's grip on Lin's shoulder lessened, but he didn't pull his hand away entirely. "Lin. Hero of the Fingers. It pained me not to have the chance to speak with you after the Fall occurred. After news of Aemun's death reached me, I'll admit, I was rather cross. And before I knew it you were squirreled away to the Scholars to speak for our cause." Erias shook his head. Far below them, the sounds of combat had stilled, but a wind had picked up and the scent of smoke clung to the air. "You wouldn't have been my first choice, but I resolved to trust Carine's judgment."

"I wouldn't have been my first choice either," Lin replied.

"And I want you to know I reprimanded Pael for his actions at Fentis involving the child. It is certainly for the best that she survived."

"What do you want?" Lin asked. "With all due respect, I should be down there aiding the soldiers. Or... If you think I'm not needed here, I should be heading north to aide Pael and Tylle. What I shouldn't be doing is wasting time discussing things best left for the past."

Erias brought his slender fingers up to his chest as if he'd been wounded. "You feel this is a waste why? Because you have so little time left?"

Lin tensed and pressed closer to the man. The scent of pine and citrus tickled Lin's nostrils and throat. "What do you know of the time left to me?"

Erias took Lin by both shoulders and pushed him back as if evaluating him. Then he raised one hand and waggled his ring finger. "Bludwieves and Uethes are odd magics. We are entwined. If you were ever lost, I could find you, like tracking a trail of yarn through the deep forest. At the same time, it is like a shared vein. I feel, to a small extent, what you feel. And you, my friend, are frayed at all ends."

Lin smacked his hand away, glaring the entire time. A sharp pain, reminiscent of the sensation he felt when attacking Aemun for touching Nebra flared where his Bludwieve rested.

Erias opened his mouth to speak when a loud, echoing horn sounded. One prolonged burst preceded two shorter ones.

It was like the world had frozen, everything slowing to a crawl. If Lin focused hard enough, he could see the sweat beading Erias's brow. He could hear the irregular sound of a whistle. Gods, it reminded him of Dreckinsburg to a degree, but there couldn't be untethered this close to the Ferrucium. Not true ones at any rate. *Could there?*

Everything snapped into focus at once and Lin drew his sword, slashing toward Erias and catching the shaft of an arrow that very nearly caught the man in the soft spot of his neck.

"Ladrican soldiers!" A lookout behind one of the nearest palisades shouted as more arrows whistled toward them.

Lin pushed in front of Erias. To the Grovetender's credit, the man had already drawn his blade. It wasn't a standard-issued Ferrucium sword, but it was Ferrucium steel, folded on itself many times over to give it a strange rolling wave look.

"Get behind me. You shouldn't fight if you're so close to untethering," Erias hissed.

Lin shook his head and pushed in front of the man. "I knew what choice I was making when I left Fentis. My blood *is* already poisoned. I might as well die making sure Danica is safe for Mellyr, and all the children like her. Can't do that if you die before you have the chance to speak at the conference."

Another flurry of arrows peppered the earth and tent, shattering an amber bottle and sending up chunks of broken debris.

Lin blocked two more arrows with his sword and was forced to from a Weft to slash through three more once he saw the angle they dropped from. Fucking archers. Ferrucium soldiers and men clad in Wellgrove's colors swarmed from the main gate on the northwestern side. "Come on. Get your lot to safety and then I'll show these bastards what happens when you come to my home and attack *my* people!" Lin growled the words, a grin breaking on his face despite the anxiety roiling within him.

He'd wanted to sound confident to Erias, to prove whatever magic powered the Bludwieve was a lie, but Gods, he *was* frayed. Like a knotted thread he'd worn ragged by trying to loosen it.

A single Weft and already he noticed a faded, flickering visage of Velkath's Sigil.

Drums of Hate

"Never be fooled to think that time is your ally. It has never, and will never, benefit the cornered, broken, or harried." —Duke Errond

Seeing fields he'd always thought would keep any would-be attackers at bay filled with screaming, raging Ladrican soldiers unnerved Lin. How had they managed to get so close? The soldiers sprouted up from behind the barricades and crested the trenches in waves as the horns announced their arrival.

The stretch from the Ferrucium walls to the tree lines to the north and further east was a barren field of mostly rocky soil unsuitable for farming. Natural slopes informed where the trenches had been dug out but the Ladricans moved confidently through the space. Barricades meant to keep them back were now spaces they hid from the archers on the walls.

Ferrucium steel armor and swords glinted with moonlight. At least it wasn't a damned moonless night. Counting them felt like trying to count the waves on the ocean's surface during a storm and Lin quickly gave up. *Too many.*

Wefts sparked into existence intermittently among the encroaching soldiers. Binders in service of Ladrican.

Lin swallowed against the tightness in his throat. This force likely had a Nooseman and Lin's hands wouldn't stop trembling. He'd survived worse.

Arrows peppered the approaching force, but many of them carried shields, and the pings of the arrows being rebuffed set a cadence as they marched forward. And arrows returned fire from the backlines.

"They're fools!" Azhura yelled. "They'll be in the open and at our mercy!" She drew a bright blade from the wrap at her waist and held it above her as if she might stab the sky. "Drums!"

At her command, a steady dum-dum sounded from the walls.

The way the Ladrican force moved set the Danicans to shame. Lin had thought himself a soldier, but the Ferrucium had never gone to war, never attempted battle formations so far as Lin knew. The more he studied the approaching force and the defenses the Ferrucium clung to, the more he was sure *they* were the fools, not the Ladricans.

Losing the advantage of stopping them at the barricades and trenches seemed terrible. A blunder if Lin compared this to King's Castle— a game Denro enjoyed playing. Surely Azhura and Erias had placed scouts to watch the northern fields?

Arrows whistled through the night sky, and soon Wefts flew from both sides. The Ferrucium had pure, golden light arcing but the Ladrican's magic looked rusted and foul. Vials. They had to be using vials of Danican blood to make those Wefts.

Drawing a Weft into existence to join the fray would be so simple. He didn't even need a focus, he simply needed to—

His attention snapped into focus as Denny jostled past him. She was a blur as she joined the force of soldiers spilling from the

Ferrucium. A smear of black amid the press of crimson and olive tones.

Erias pointed his gleaming blade at the approaching troops. He shouted something unintelligible as Lin jerked him to the side, pulling the man off-balance.

"Not you! Or Azhura for that matter. I need the both of you safe or everything I did to push back the meeting between our enemies will be wasted!" Lin hoped the man understood what he was saying. If Erias died, Lin's pending untethering and death would be a waste.

"The troops need to see—"

"They'll see *us* fighting. Your hand-selected people. The soldiers will find strength knowing the people you have trusted to fight this war are alongside them. Now go!"

Erias appeared ghastly, with gaunt cheeks and sunken eyes exaggerated by the flickering war between torchlight and Wanderer's Ore. "I will take Azhura into the hold. If it can be avoided, don't overdo it. There may be hope for you yet." He meant don't Bind. Don't untether.

Lin nodded and covered Erias's retreat into the Ferrucium's outer wall. Erias and Azhura were flanked by three soldiers who looked more than ready for violence.

Azhura turned and locked eyes with Lin. Her blade was drawn at her side and a fire lit her eyes from within. "If they're this close, they've already killed several of our scouts. Horns further inland should've sounded long before our men on the walls spotted them. Make them pay a bloody price for their greed."

Arrowheads bit into the wall beside them, steel tips sparking against the red stone. The Ferrucium's archers had lined the pathways over the gates, sending back volleys from the advantageous height. This was the folly with a headfirst attack against the Hold, and why Lin had snuck over the walls so very many months ago.

Lin froze. What if that was the point— send expendable soldiers to distract the watchers on the wall and have a Nooseman attack from within? Lin was far from the sharpest strategist and even he'd been able to come up with that plan. He rushed up to the parapets as he took the steps two at a time. His side ached but he caught his breath as he staled behind the archers and the wicker baskets of arrows beside them.

The portcullis grated closed. Inside the outer walls, a mob of soldiers waited. Reinforcements readying their weapons. And in the heart of the hold, innocent Danicans would be sheltering. The Ferrucium had been the safest place in all of Danica a season ago, and now it had been under siege twice. Red stone stained by the blood of the fallen.

Torches lit the walls and were spersed every so often, casting shadows along the entire stretch of the wall. Despite the dancing shadows, none looked out of place or made from more solid, dangerous things.

Lin wanted to be down in the melee, to call on the magic itching to be woven into existence. So he calmed his nerves as he walked the perimeter. Every moment he wasn't out there fighting was wasted, but he couldn't risk letting the Ferrucium be caught unaware.

"We've got watchers on the walls," a soldier, clothed in faded Ferrucium crimson, said. "Can't risk it after what happened last assault."

Real fear laced the young soldier's words and looking at the boy he couldn't have been much older than Herm from Lyre. His hair even had a curl to it like that large young man's. But this boy's shoulders seemed barely wider than his hips and his hands shook on the spear he held.

"You were here?" Lin hoped the guilt he felt didn't taint his voice.

"Yes, sir."

"And you survived?" Lin lowered his voice. Of course, chances were none knew it had been him, masked as he'd been and clothed in the tattered robes of the Nooseman.

"Was a message runner. Nooseman didn't see me, hid in a barrel. Watched the Ladrican monster slaughter everyone. Helped convince me to do more. That and the bonus pay."

"Focus up. Keep a sharp eye on the walls then. And remember what you fight for." Lin put a fist to the boy's chest above his heart. Make it through this one alive too."

The young soldier saluted Lin and swallowed audibly, returning to his task of patrolling the parapets.

It hadn't occurred to Lin that none of his fellow soldiers knew who'd been behind the slaughter, behind the mask. He was sure Azhura had known or perhaps blamed it on the other Nooseman who'd infiltrated the Ferrucium just behind him. But all their speculation in the world wouldn't take the blood from his hands on the matter.

More rumbling sounded from the bay and dark plumes of smoke rose from several more of the ships. The drumming continued near the front gate but shouts of fear interrupted the steady rhythm, accenting like an off-beat tempo. Screams, shouts, wails. *Gods.*

Lin rushed to the front. Gods. The soldiers, many of them armored in at least half-plates of Ferrucium steel, had already pushed far further than expected. With shields held overhead, they nullified the advantage of archers along the walls. They'd crossed the field, past the barricades and trenches, and were pressing into the defenders.

And if their progress wasn't bad enough, their numbers made Lin's stomach twist. There were at least a few hundred. A paltry sum compared to the scores sitting in the bay attempting to make land, but more than enough to bleed the Ferrucium's nose.

The last count he had, the Ferrucium had numbers in the high hundreds, but that was before the Fall, before Lin had personally dispatched the ones allied with Aemun. Either way, it looked like the Ferrucium had the higher numbers, but the Ladricans still pressed in. Their armor and coordination beating out the numbers.

Lin spotted Denny. She was deep in the sea of Ladrican soldiers, disrupting their formations as she flashed in and out of view. Her Inlays looked as if they pulsed, the way she came up for air before diving back into the fray. Alone, she seemed worth an entire army.

He couldn't be sure of her expression from this far, but he was sure she smiled.

She needed his help, but Lin couldn't move his legs. He gripped his hilt tight in one hand and rested the other on rough stone as archers all around fired futile into the back lines. Binders had joined them now, launching Bolts similar to what Jun had thrown at the ships, but smaller. The magic crashed into the Ladricans, knocking them back and slowing them but apparently weak to the steel same as the arrows.

Lin had come up to the tops of the walls under the pretense of checking for Nooseman and had his worries assuaged. Now what was his excuse? *Fear.* Even as his hands itched to make Bindings, he knew that if he dropped down there and fought, he'd lose himself. Even the briefest of tastes earlier had set him on edge.

A snarl tore from the mob Denny was in and she leaped into the in a spiraling flash of Bindings and blood, howling like a wolf at the moon.

Lin flew from the wall before he could make another excuse not to, his sword stabbing into the rocky soil and soldiers falling away to the side at his arrival. He'd do as much as he could without Bindings and if he had to call on his magic, so be it.

Sweat, smoke, and the scent of piss, shit, and death filled the immediate air. Suffocating and stifling. Even injured, the speed and strength Lin possessed from his Inlayed flesh became immediately noticeable compared to the waves of allies and foes around him. Denny was somewhere far ahead, carving her way through the enemy and Lin was intent on bridging his way to her.

Somewhere in the sea of foes, various Bound Metal weapons pulled at his pulse. But not every enemy soldier carried one and in the melee, surrounded by friendly soldiers the weapons didn't affect, their potency seemed hindered. Not all Danicans were Binders after all, and steel worked just as well to kill as sorcery.

Slowly from the walls, they were pushing back the Ladricans. Barricades and palisades would be pressed into their backs. Azhura's words echoed in Lin's mind. *Make them pay a bloody price.*

What if there was no Nooseman? What if these troops had overcommitted thinking the majority of Danica's defenses would be near the north?

Lin was in the press and blocked an ambitious sword aimed at his neck. Using the arming sword in the melee was difficult, but a Wellgrove soldier with a spear came in and took the Ladrican attacking Lin in the throat, blood spraying from the wound as another Ladrican stepped in where the fallen had just been. Denny's fluid fighting style meant she could slip between the slow enemies and use the confusion and chaos of battle to her advantage.

It was chaos. A frantic, fevered assault to repel the invaders. Lin regrouped and whirled, his sword slashing at the nearest Ladrican he could see but he wasn't making progress. He needed to fight like Denny, and that meant he needed a Binding Blade. Lin formed one, a shudder rocking him as he did. He kept his Ferrucium steel and carved his way back into the cluster of soldiers vying for control.

Blood and viscera coated him and it took several corpses falling behind him to realize he'd strode forward killing until he was surrounded by enemies on all sides. Of those immediately around him, three glinted with full armor.

A trench dipped just behind the enemies ahead and behind Lin, the Ferrucium walls looked distant. They were pushing the invaders back. Step by step. Body by body. Dead Ferrucium soldiers stared up from the ground, crimson cloaks matted with blood and mud.

Lin parried a thrust, swept his Blade across the attacker's throat, and took a Bound Metal baton to his ribs for his trouble. Too many. He'd overcommitted and now he would be the one to pay a bloody price.

An arrow took his attacker through the eye, knocking them back into the Ladrican behind them who raised a shield to defend. A spear tip jutted out behind it and a wall of Ladricans pressed toward Lin.

He gave up a foot, dodged a slash from his side, and nearly lost his nose to a separate chop from his right.

Untethering would be the least of his problems if he died here.

Lin formed ten Wefts into existence and made them circle him like the cocoon he'd made several times before. More enemies near him must've possessed batons. Many of the Wefts were pulled from his control and flung wide, but most found purchase, biting into unarmored flesh and cleaving meat from the bone.

Corpses and the injured piled around him. Spotting two of the baton wielders Lin ran the first through with his sword, shifted his weight to avoid the other's counterattack, and slipped in the mud and guts. Before he could stand, a boot crunched into his nose.

A shield edge nearly cracked into his temple, but he rolled and stabbed his sword to the inside of the attacker's leg, blood flowing like Lin had spigoted a tree for sap.

Incoherent shouts came from behind. Lin hazarded a look behind and saw the walls even further away.

Despite wanting Erias and Azhura to get somewhere safe, Erias stood on the wall in his fine armor. He stabbed his sword into the air and it looked everything like it had been cut from the cloth of the night sky itself. Say what one wanted about the Grovetender, he had a way of presenting himself in such an imposing light. But up there, he made himself a target for more than one aspiring archer; he needed to get down.

Lin did his best to block incoming sword strikes with steel, not Binding. The last thing he needed was to discover that more than one of those daggers existed, capable of melting steel and cutting through Binding.

Another, nearer, rumbling explosion sounded from the bay and Lin wondered if someone *had* managed to sabotage the Ladrican fleet much the way Royce had used Wanderer's Ore to explode the ships moored at the island. A terrible hissing death would await the soldiers if that was the case, but so be it. More worrisome was the fact it was closer. Far closer, possibly even moored or close enough soldiers could swim the rest of the way.

The press of bodies had been too much to bear long before this point, but try as Lin might to catch his breath, the enemy wasn't willing to accommodate. He pressed his Blade into the space between an enemy's armored plates, the magic grinding until it caught bone and dropped the enemy.

Two more Ladricans attacked, stepping in and swinging in tandem. Lin attempted to dodge backward, but the enemy he'd just downed grabbed Lin's Blade with a gauntleted hand and rooted him in place. Lin swung his sword, crashing steel on steel but the soldier's grip didn't loosen.

A quick upward slash took Lin across his forearm, his Inlays sparking against the Ferrucium Steel. He gritted his teeth against the bone-bruising force and was nearly stabbed in the kidneys by the flanking opponent when Lin broke the Blade into Wefts, tattering and tearing into any exposed flesh around him.

Lin rolled with the force from the blow against his arm and used it to propel him over the back of the lunging soldier. He grabbed the crevice on the soldier's backside where their helm met their chest plate and sent a Weft within.

The soldier collapsed instantly.

By the time Lin finished with the crashing wave of soldiers, he was covered in bruises with several deep cuts along his back. His tunic and compress were ripped, blood-soaked shreds, and hung from him in grim ribbons. His Inlays and Stitches along his torso were exposed making it clear to any enemies with the Sight where they should aim to injure him.

Lin sucked in several deep breaths. There wasn't a piece of him that didn't ache. He'd pressed past the barricades and trenches. He was nearer now to the northern pocket of trees than he was to the

Ferrucium and most of the Ferrucium soldiers had pulled back to regroup.

Even further ahead, glimpses of Denny's Inlays shone through the enemies ranks. How she had managed to get herself so surrounded was bewildering, but with his path cleared, Lin found his next target. He formed a Weft and compressed it as Denny had done to demonstrate what it was Jun and the other Binders were doing A Bolt. Not quite the length of a spear, and thicker than most Bindings.

Lin backed up, spun, and ran forward as he hurled the Bolt like a javelin. Velkath's Sigil swam in his periphery. He saw it on the bodies of the dead and dying, in the patterns of the clouds that allowed the moon's light to leak through.

It was *everywhere*.

The Bolt looked like a dying strand of lightning, the brilliance of color long lost to the storm that summoned it. Already, one battle in, his spul was nearing its limits.

Two enemy soldiers, one in a plate of Ferrucium steel and another in a simple gambeson took the Bolt through their torsos, pinning them to each other and bowling over another one of the heavily armored combatants.

Lin rushed toward Denny and was in the opening his Bolt created nearly immediately. Blade, colored like a patch of dirt kissed by the sun, slashed swathes of the nearest, unarmored soldiers as his sword did the same.

More enemies pressed in from all sides, screaming, shouting, swearing, cursing, fighting like they weren't the invaders. Even out here, the ground was littered with corpses, many of them clad in Ferrucium crimson and the deep green of Wellgrove.

Gods, his fears when encountering the armored troops in Ladrica had been proven right. Danicans as they were now had little hope of keeping armored attackers at bay. Another symptom of Ladrica's long-running disease that kept Danicans shackled.

"Lin!" Denny's voice carried over the press of clanging steel and cursing soldiers.

Lin thought he saw a flash of her face, overly pale under the skewed Stitches and smears of blood. He dodged a slash, sunk his Blade through the attacker's throat, pivoted forward with a spin, and chopped at the back of an attacker facing away from him.

Three more fell to his attacks but he was flagging. Despite his Inlays, his arms and legs trembled. Sweat stung his eyes but he had to keep them open, thankfully, the dried, crusted blood helped. Making any sort of forward momentum felt impossible. If the living didn't block him, the uneven corpses did. But with a final, exhausting push he made it to Denny. She was surrounded by bodies, piled up around her like an ant mound.

Fear sparkled in her Inlayed eyes.

"There are too many. Where the hell is the Ferrucium group Carine and Tylle had been training?" Denny shouted above the surrounding din of combat.

It was like she was the center of a storm made from Bindings and blood. He moved to stand back to back with her, fending off the Ladrican soldiers pressing in from all sides. In all the fighting, he hadn't considered that there weren't any other fighters matching his and Denny's prowess. *Shit.*

If Lin lunged to strike, she was there behind him like a protective shadow. If she pivoted, he was there. It was how they should have fought from the beginning but he'd been worried about the walls they'd left far behind.

The steady drumming from the Ferrucium walls continued like a faint heartbeat in the back of his mind, but a horn, loud and demanding, blew out from behind the enemy ranks. Perhaps they meant to—

Lin's thoughts fled him at the overwhelming scent that wafted to him from behind the remaining enemies to the north. Icy, mint-laced rust. Lin spun, Denny pulling away and standing shoulder to shoulder with him.

Soldiers clad in Ladrican gambesons and garb all readied weapons and looked like they planned to press the advantage. There were far fewer than there had been when the battle had begun, but there were still too many of them.

Like an arrow loosed from a taut string, a figure zipped through and over the ranks of soldiers. A pocket of Wellgrove's men had come to Denny and Lin and kept the Ladrican troops from flanking entirely.

A Nooseman was at Lin's face in an instant, a long slender Blade wielded in both hands slashing horizontally across their body. A fluid, decisive motion that would have taken Lin's neck if Denny hadn't knocked him aside and blocked the Nooseman's Blade with her own.

The flat, metal mask the Nooseman wore had only a single slit, and from it, a bright, Inlayed orb stared back.

Drums of Blood

"War doesn't cause casualties. The peace between times of war does. The friendships and connections— people to be used. Those are casualties and most, if not all, are acceptable. But some things will never, ever be acceptable losses and as a leader, you must make that distinction before war is upon you, for after it has begun, it is far too late to decide. My war started when I was old enough to learn we were treated as cattle and I hope your war comes far later, dear daughter." —Excerpt from Aemun's letter to Azhalia.

Lin flinched his sword up, ready to square off as his boots slipped on the uneven terrain underfoot. He stood beside Denny, matching her pace as they struggled to fight off the Nooseman.

Each of the bastard's strikes bled into the last. Fluid slice into a shoulder press into a sharp upward cut. The Nooseman made his own rhythm, unconcerned with Denny and Lin's counters.

Binding Blades didn't clash like metal swords and this monster used that to his advantage, slashing and following up like it was the most natural movement a person could have. The Nooseman pressed forward with each chain of their barrage, a brutal overhead blow nearly taking Lin's sword from his hands.

Lin had thought the King's Noose a monolith, but after meeting Gritt and now this one-eyed fuck, that idea scraped away with each swing of the bastard's long Blade.

"How many of you monsters are there?" Lin screamed. He pivoted away from a thrust, turning to spot Denny attempting to flank but getting swarmed by three Ladrican soldiers wielding Bound Metal batons in their off hands.

"Soon your sword will break. Then your will. Where is she?" The Nooseman's voice was soft and cold. Calm even, despite the ferocity of his attacks.

She?

Lin had seen Ferrucium steel ruined by the dagger, he'd even recently witnessed it chip against an untethered's attack, but it had never broken outright. As powerful as the technique was, a Blade was still just a Binding. But the Nooseman's words rattled him as much as the powerful strikes did. Fatigue was setting into his bones as deeply as bruises.

Something needed to change.

Denny snarled from the side, flickering in and out of Lin's periphery like Velkath's Sigil. She'd killed one of the baton-wielding soldiers and seemed to be getting the better of the two remaining. More Ferrucium soldiers bolstered the push, coming in from the reprieve they must've had nearer to the walls.

The Nooseman swung wide, his momentum easily kicking aside corpses.

Lin saw the opening, darted past the man's Blade, and stabbed at the blind spot created by the over-commitment. Lin's sword sparked against the Nooseman's flesh and, true to the monster's words, the Ferrucium steel sword Lin had taken from the soldier shattered into four shards. A broken edge was left near the hilt and rattled as Lin's hands trembled.

The thick black cloak covering the Nooseman fluttered revealing the hole Lin made. Despite the enemies and allies he'd met since Lyre, Lin had never seen a torso so consumed by such bright Inlays and Stitches. Not a piece of the man's flesh could be seen through the tear not illuminated by the golden glow of Bindings.

A counterstrike nearly took Lin's arm. Proof the man had anticipated Lin's attack or had overcommitted purposefully to lure Lin out.

Lin managed to sidestep to the left as a gouge of hot pain raked up his side. The Nooseman's Blade was slightly longer than it had been just a moment before.

"Where is she?"

The man either meant Mellyr or the Nooseman Gritt— and Lin didn't think his intentions for either of them would be good. Luckily, they were safe in Fentis with the Scholars.

Lin winced as he formed a focus and dipped into the cerulean current of healing from within, ripping the power from just under the surface and coating his side in a thin, crystalline blue Binding. His digits numbed at the touch of the power, and he blinked away the image of two Noosemen where one had been a moment before.

More percussive booms sounded from below the cliffs. Distant, another battle entirely. Lin steadied on his feet. They hadn't brought enough to take the Ferrucium. A good number of soldiers had likely died to the ocean and Bolt's Jun and his people launched.

Surely this Nooseman didn't think he could turn the tide of battle all on his own?

"You can't beat us," Lin growled. Not all of them and not by himself.

The Nooseman froze, cocking his head to the side.

If something didn't change, chances were he wouldn't have to worry about untethering and going mad. This One-loved bastard would kill him before then.

Yes. Accept death and let everything until this point be moot.

Gods. Anya had warned him, but Lin hadn't thought the voices and visions of Velkath's Sigil would come on so damned quickly.

When the Nooseman didn't reply, Lin shifted his stance, leveled a Blade of his own, and gasped out, "She?" His Blade was speckled like rusted steel compared to the vibrant hue of the Nooseman's.

"Don't play me the fool." The Nooseman sprang forward, breaking Lin's Blade with a heavy horizontal strike. He gave chase as Lin attempted to roll away, his Blade gouging the earth and corpses alike, grinding against occasional pieces of Ladrican armor.

Lin tripped. He stumbled and caught himself on a still-warm body. A weak groan escaped the dying woman as Lin grabbed her armored arm and rolled her a bit, letting the steel of her bracer take the blow. Blood-slick hands made grabbing the dagger from her belt difficult, but he managed it.

"To think any of my brothers and sisters lost against cowards like you. To think you bested and stole away Gritt is laughable." His voice was flat and he accented each sentence a screeching slash against the Ladrican armor.

Well, that confirmed it. At least this one-eyed monster wasn't after Mellyr. But letting him get to Gritt was effectively the same thing. This man would be like a fox in a henhouse if he entered the Tower of Fentis. No doubt about that.

Lin tensed to lunge up, but a shrill scream sounded and Denny was on the Nooseman in a blink. The two armored soldiers she'd been dealing with were lost in the piles of corpses. Blood blurred the Stitches across her face and matted her curly hair to her scalp. Her cheeks were gaunt, her lips drawn. She looked like death as she moved and her movements, as ferocious as they were, had slowed drastically.

They'd overextended.

Lin wanted to move and urged his legs into action to aid her, but rolling waves of exhaustion crashed across him. He could give up. Let someone else fight. Let others survive. He'd had better luck than most and the weight of it all was too heavy. When it all becomes so heavy that even eyelids refuse to stay open, wasn't that a sign that the burden was too great for one person alone? Couldn't someone else fight?

Denny's growls snapped Lin's eyes open and he sucked in a desperate breath, jolting the body atop him to the side. He used the back of his arm to wipe sweat and blood from his eyes, making it worse, before blinking as much of it away as he could. Lin struggled to his feet, the dying Ladrican still grasping at his tattered clothes.

The Nooseman pressed Denny the same as he'd bullied Lin, and all around them, the soldiers from either side continued to fight. Those who strayed too close to the fight quickly added to the death toll, Denny and the Nooseman uncaring for the colors the soldiers wore.

Lin rushed in with the dagger in his offhand and a weak-hued Blade formed in his right. He matched his pace to Denny's, pushing himself. She had to have been wounded, considering Lin was able to match her cadence blow for blow. As a pair, they harried the Nooseman, pushing him back. This was how they should've fought him from the beginning but those damned soldiers had split her off.

Denny pivoted to flank into the Nooseman's blind spot, her Blade colored like the sun dipping below the horizon.

Another counter, seemingly planned, came crushingly swift. The Nooseman kicked Denny's leading leg out from under her and she tumbled, rolling over bodies and terrain alike until she crashed into a mound of the Ladrican dead. A few feet to the right she would've impacted the front of a palisade.

Lin jerked forward in response. Striking at the Nooseman with the dagger while he swung up with his Blade.

The Nooseman ignored him, weaving away from his blows as if he anticipated each strike and where the next would be. A Weft formed in a blink and sliced the air toward Denny. It was the first the man had thrown and was as bright as a full moon. And then a barrage of five Wefts cut the air in quick succession, all zipping past Lin as the bastard avoided his strikes.

"I'll ask one more time. Where is Gritt? Locked away?" A cold voice with flat inflection. The Nooseman wasn't even breathing hard.

Lin howled and let his Blade explode into strands of a dying sun as he tackled the Nooseman. Or tried to. When he slammed into the man's body, Lin couldn't budge him. Lin thrust up with the dagger, and his arm was caught and nearly twisted out of the socket. Lin had been outmatched before, *survived* before. Tears stung his eyes and he would've taken a Blade through his throat if Denny hadn't launched a flurry of Wefts from the man's blindspot.

The Nooseman pivoted, kicking Lin to the ground as he did, and broke the Wefts with his bare hand, crushing them into rusted embers.

Nothing worked, Blades or Wefts. Lin was sure they'd said Dennick had been the strongest of them... But this man was something else. Though, Dennick had only been bested by all of Carine's people and Tylle. Lin wasn't on par with them, no matter the Inlays or how hard he pushed himself. He was just an Escorter, playing at something more.

"She... She isn't here!" Lin bellowed as he formed a Bolt at his side. He'd started lying out a snare to trap the monster like he had Dennick, but he was too weak, and his Bindings were too frail. "She's with the Scholars at Fentis!"

"Then when we finish—" Whatever the Nooseman was about to say was cut out by the arrival of two figures charging past Lin, one landing a flying kick straight into the blind spot caused by the mask's design. The blow forced the Nooseman to shuffle back as he swung his Blade to retaliate.

Finally, I suppose they didn't leave you to die. This time. Though, they should've.

Lin's jaw clenched at hearing Aemun's whispered words in his mind. Worse than Velkath's Sigil burning at the edges of his vision, worse than his poor eyesight and brittle nails, he loathed hearing Aemun's mocking voice.

Jun, shirtless and striped in Inlays, shone with a layer of sweat and deftly avoided the Nooseman's counter. He pressed the masked monster back, attacking with swift unarmed strikes that sparked like Bindings when they made contact. The second figure clarified into Carine, tall and rough-looking. She stood at an off-angle sending a flurry of fresh golden Wefts in arcing paths at the Nooseman.

Soldiers clashed, and fled, and jostled as an uneven half-circle of combat and chaos surrounded the magical melee.

Even outnumbered and pushed back, the Nooseman seemed to maintain composure, though those masks made it damn hard to tell if he was searching for an escape.

Denny limped up beside Lin. Clouds puffed out from each heavy breath she took and she bumped his hip as she rushed past. She let out a battle cry as she flitted into the space opposite of Jun, harrying the Nooseman from his blind spot and gouging a scar across his mask with what had to be one of the brittlest looking Blades ever conjured.

The Nooseman spun with the slash, black tattered cloak lined with crimson stitches billowing and hiding his movements until his Blade came out in a flash and looked to nearly catch Denny across her stomach.

Lin planted his feet and sent the Bolt like a javelin, the edge of the Nooseman's Blade caught it and split the magic into strands of smouldering light.

Denny had stumbled back, clutching her stomach and shaking her head. Her eyes shone like wild embers in a dry pasture, ready to burn it all away.

Carine had slipped into the pocket Lin's Bolt had created and her and Jun's assault pushed the Nooseman back but the bastard wasn't quitting. Wasn't tiring or flagging compared to Lin, and now Denny.

Lin struggled to evaluate the battle. Drums continued to pulse from the Ferrucium walls. They hadn't fallen yet. He hadn't heard an explosion in a while, but they also hadn't been overwhelmed by Ladrican soldiers coming ashore.

No horns. No reinforcements. Just the Nooseman.

They were doing it. The Ferrucium was winning and beating back the Ladrican assault. An assault that, Lin had to remember, that technically broke the Danican Accords. Even if Aemun and the Fall had started it, King Lodram still hadn't gotten approval for the invasion.

Jun moved like he hadn't fought at all yet. Carine was swift and decisive with each strike, but Jun was a powerhouse. From their movements, it was clear the Nooseman was the better of the fighters, but he was one man— one monster— matched against two other monsters.

Lin formed another Bolt. He just needed to catch the Nooseman off guard. Each step forward, each throbbing of bunched muscles and split flesh, made the world around him pulse. He launched the Bolt. For the briefest sliver of a moment, Lin thought he'd hit the Nooseman.

It had only happened once, twice maybe if Lin pressed his mind to recall, but the sensation of magic being ripped from his control was like a grinding, aching sensation deeper than his bones. Not painful, but wholly uncomfortable.

And the Nooseman ripped Lin's Bolt out of his control.

A bright, blinding light formed in the sky. That was his magic, thrown into the sky, and exploded like it had near the Ferrucium outpost so long ago. A Bloom. Light flared, expanding like a miniature moon before shattering into cold embers of broken magic.

The world tilted and Lin stared into the eye's of a dead man. He was a mass of pain and confusion and hands raised him. He was half awake as he was dragged into the shadow of the Ferrucium's outerwalls.

Lin blinked, struggling to clear the spots from his vision. He'd passed out. Briefly, but he'd lost a moment there after his magic was stolen.

Clips of sentences made sense but hearing them and understanding them weren't the same thing. "He retreated northwest.... Injured, hanging on by a thread.... Goodbyes.... Jun, don't chase him...." Carine's voice. Calm and passive the way Lin remembered it being, but there was something else to the tone. Pain.

Lin swallowed and tried to stand, but his legs didn't want to listen. Every where he looked, he saw flickering spots and Velkath's

Sigil danced around his periphery, taunting him. Even wounded and weak, he felt far from hanging by a thread.

From the multitude of grim, battle-worn faces around him, this was where they'd moved the injured. Bodies were being moved from the trenches. Clearing the battlefield to mount another defense.

Physikers in bloody aprons moved along the lines, carrying wounded into the walls. Something felt broken inside Lin, like he couldn't catch his breath despite himself. He hung his head and pressed his palms to his temple, staring at the rutted earth under him. Tears started and they didn't stop as he rocked back and forth. He squeezed his eyes shut. Opening them meant dealing with what came next. Dealing with the untethering and he couldn't do that right now. Didn't want to deal with it when there was much else he still needed to do.

A rattling wheeze pulled Lin up for air as he glanced to his left. A boy, barely a hair on his upper lip clad in the greens and browns of Wellgrove sat against the wall. Wheezing. A hopeful, gasping breath in, a mournful rattle of a wheeze out. Blood stained his chest and he held a bloody hand to the wound there, doing little to stop the blood.

Lin and the boy were both drowning. Lin on madness, him on blood. If the boy knew he was dying, he didn't make a fuss about it. Lin steadied himself. Steadied his heart.

For as bad as it had been during the battle, the commotion after felt flat. It was somehow too silent, as if the survivors were concerned with disturbing the dying.

Lin winced as a weight settled onto his right shoulder. He looked down, the top of Denny's head a welcome realization. Sweat matted the curls to and dried blood coated the visible side of her face.

"We made it. Kept them back," Lin whispered. "And you said... You said Erias thought you couldn't fight anymore. Showed him, didn't you?"

Denny didn't respond.

Lin reached for her hand before embarrassment crashed across him. She didn't have a hand on this side for him to hold. Even if she did, what right did he to that small comfort after keeping his madness from her? Knowing her, she'd say they could grow mad together, but she deserved more. He sighed and settled his hands across his lap.

It wasn't often that he noticed Denny's touch, the way she drifted around like a spirit, light as a breeze, silent as starlight. He was sure the few times he had noticed her, it was solely because she wanted him to.

Lin smiled at the thought. They sat there for a long moment, Denny silent and Lin the same in case she slept, like she had done after storming the island. His heart beat in his chest and the brokenness he felt before hadn't gone away. The longer they sat there in silence, the longer he watched the people picking through the aftermath, the worse he felt.

They'd run out of wood building all the pyres for the dead.

"Denny?" Lin whispered.

He glanced down again.

Lin sucked in a deep breath and shifted to lean her fully against the wall. She was limp and, now at this angle, her Stitched face was pale. White. He pulled her to his chest, feeling for breaths, feeling for life. She was cold and stiff and her cloak stuck to her with clotted blood and worse. A gash across her stomach showed parts of her he'd never wanted to see.

Tears blurred it all.

"P-physiker!" Lin shouted. "Physiker!"

When no one came, he drew on zinc, weaving a glossy strand of deep blue, nearly black, magic to pull her flesh back together. He pressed his ear to her cold lips. No breath.

Sobs racked him as he pressed bloody fingers to her neck. "No.... No... No. S-stay with me."

Lin grabbed her and lifted her up. Gods, she was so light. As he struggled to carry her into the main gate where they'd set up tents, a woman with her hair in a tight bun and an apron smeared in blood came. Her expression was unreadable.

"S-she's a hero. Save her!" Lin screamed, spittle flying from his mouth as he did.

A man came, hands twisting a bloody rag as he stared at Denny's face.

"Friend... She's gone."

"The One whisper your damned name she's *gone*. Save her! Use the blue thread! The blue Bindings! Do it!" Lin shook, not from the weight of holding her but from the screaming and soreness and all of it.

Confusion was clear on their faces. And everyone just stared at him. Stared and did nothing to save her. Stared and did *nothing*.

"We can get you some root to help the shock from battle. You need rest and look like you may have received a blow to your head." The woman reach a probing hand up to the side of Lin's head.

Lin would've slapped her hand away if he didn't have Denny in his arms. He pressed his brow to her's, pulling her up as sad, silent tears flowed from him. "We need... we need to warn Fentis that a Nooseman is coming for Gritt. *I* need you."

She offered herself, no? A real man would've taken her, a real man would've protected her. Margaret, Mellyr, now her. Who else will you fail before you finally admit you're no hero?

"Shut up! Enough!" Lin snarled. "If you won't do anything to save her, I will!"

Desperate Hope

"Some might wonder at the defensive fortifications of the Ferrucium. Not months after the failure that was the Fall, a contingent of Ferrucium soldiers and Danican Blood Wievers held back a force far larger than any considered possible. War is bloody enough without pushing soldiers into a mess of sharpened sticks and fangs."—Steward Bodrose of the Ladrican Kingdom.

Lin gently set Denny on a cot in the nearest physiker's tent. He pressed his lips to her knuckles, kissing them despite the dried blood and coldness.

A rag, fresh water, and a bundle of three cork-stoppered vials were set wordlessly beside him. Without smelling it, he recognized the fluid's sheen. Greedily, he drank them all. Gritty fluid dribbled into his beard and his stomach immediately ached, but that was the cost to replenish his spul.

His head throbbed as much as his limbs and his eyes stung as he forced back his tears.

All around, physikers and aides moved about. They tended to those they thought they could save but kept far from Lin and Denny, occasionally glancing his way and quickly averting their stares when they saw him glaring back.

Corpses were taken out. Wounded groaned.

Lin grasped the rough fabric of the cot and squeezed as he put his lips back to her hand. As gently as he could, he took the rag, dampened it, and wiped away the build-up of blood and mud and worse from her flesh. It only took one wringing of the rag for the bucket to cloud.

"Excuse me, but you really shouldn't be in here. The dead have a way of—"

"I need something," Lin snapped. "Then I'll take her and go."

Lin told the physiker, the same one who'd already told him there was nothing to be done for Denny then stared at him like a fool when he mentioned the zinc healing, what he needed.

Sitting there, lips to her knuckles, the water beside him ruined and bloody, Lin stared at Denny's pale face.

Lin exhaled. "You didn't...." He paused, his throat aching. "*We didn't survive Ladrica just to die here. Please.*" Lin leaned up and brushed the hair from her face, staring at the uneven horizontal Stitches across her face.

Steps came from beside him; Carine. She crouched beside him, Bound Metal baton across her lap. Her dark eyes studied him, then Denny.

"Lin. She's gone. Died a warrior's death. It's the death she would've wanted." Carine's voice didn't waver but was soft.

Lin frowned and glared at her same as he had at the physikers. She didn't know what she was talking about. Carine might've known her longer, but she didn't know that Denny could still be saved. She had to survive. She had to.

"No," Lin spat. "She wanted to run away from all this. And where were you?" He leaned over, getting an inch from her face, eyes level with hers as he yelled.

"Jun and I ensured the ships didn't land. We arrived as soon as we could."

"It wasn't soon enough!" Lin snarled. "At all. We... we... couldn't fight him off alone. I was... I... All this time and I still couldn't do *anything*."

Carine took the yelling, staring at him with pain painted in the slight wrinkles around her eyes. "The two of you ensured he didn't overrun the Ferrucium."

Knowing she was right and accepting it were two different things. He wanted to lash out. Strike her. Worse, maybe. But instead, he turned from her and put his lips back to Denny's hand.

"Is that for me," he whispered.

Carine shifted and tapped the baton's tip against the ground, thudding dully. "Why did you want this?"

Lin reached for it and she pulled it away. He needed that Bound Metal. If Denny was dead like everyone kept telling him, then he'd preserve her until he found a way to bring her back. Save her now, where he had failed before.

"Please, just give it to me," Lin begged. With Bound Metal and pulling on copper, he could keep her as she was.

"You did everything you could. She charged in recklessly and the bastard got her. Denny knew what she was doing."

Lin shook his head. No. She was a fighter; a survivor. "I need that. Don't make me take it."

Carine didn't blink, didn't look away at all. She tapped the baton on the ground again and let it fall. It rolled over to Lin, bouncing off his knee before rolling back and stopping.

"We lost her, I don't want to lose you too."

And if he'd lost himself long ago?

Lin placed the baton in his waistband and scooped Denny from the cot. After downing the vials, his strength had somewhat returned. Denny was lighter than ever, like a bird whose bones were all hollow.

"Lin!" Carine raised her voice but didn't move to stop him.

Lin continued walking, staggering past the odd person watching him as he carried Denny through the layers of the Ferrucium. He wept as he walked, unable to keep the pain from leaking out of him. How was it fair? They'd survived Ladrica. Just the two of them. *Outnumbered.*

Guilt washed over him. She'd only been there because of him, was only wounded at this fight because of him. He'd pushed her away when she'd been the only one to come to his aid. All because what? He was untethering and hadn't wanted to hurt her.

But the thought of Ladrica, that cold unwelcoming place, was what had given birth to what he was about to do. Even if she'd already joined the Great Tapestry, Lin could change it. Stitch her body to the world and leave it as it was, unmoving or changing. He'd seen it done. He could do it too.

When he finally arrived at the baths, he wasn't surprised to see them empty of others. Soldiers were far too busy reinforcing their defenses and tending to those they deemed able to be saved to worry about cleaning themselves. He wasn't even sure they'd caused a full retreat. If anything, more Ladrican soldiers might be pressing in around them now and a selfish, pitiful piece of him hoped they were.

Mellyr didn't deserve that thought. Tylle or Denro either. But if Lin could die here, fighting as Denny had, maybe he'd feel better. *Maybe.*

"I'm sorry I was so cold to you... After the kiss we shared. You scared me. The future scared me... a-and I-I d-didn't think I'd s-survive. So I pushed you away." As he spoke he slid her into the bath and laid out several towels beside the large basin.

Lin kept his ruined clothes on but removed hers, cleaning her flesh with a soaped towel as best as he could. He'd never seen what remained of her arm and the stub was a gnarled network of red, stitched flesh, both magical and mundane. She had scars over most of her bare skin and where there wasn't a scar, an Inlay or Stitch showed.

He worked as tenderly as he had when bathing Mellyr that first time, but he didn't have Carine or anyone else to help him.

"It's funny," he whispered. "The first time you came to me, I was the one floating. Scared me half to death."

Lin wiped his eyes with the back of his hand. Soap stung, but he didn't care.

Same as the bucket in the tent, by the time he was done the water was a hazy, muddied mess. He had tried to brush her hair, but too many curled strands came out on his first attempt. She'd been sicker than she led him to believe. Perhaps she had been untethering after all, bad as most of her Binder's ailments presented. Brittle nails, frail hair. Gray patches of flesh. She'd been so full of energy, he'd never dug deeper.

Try as he might, he couldn't get all the blood out from under her nails without breaking them. So he stopped and lifted her. He wrapped her in the towels he'd set aside sooner and held her for a long moment.

"I'm sorry that I couldn't save you," Lin said, again pressing his brow to hers as he laid her flat on the cool, damp tiled floor.

Lin grasped the baton and steeled himself for what had to come next. What *he* alone could do. Carine said Denny was gone but if they were all part of the Grand Tapestry, and Wievers could affect it, why couldn't they repair a person's snapped thread? All he could think about since realizing she'd died, was stopping such a horrible thing from happening.

Denny barely looked like herself. Removed from her cloak, hair washed and wreathed around her face, she looked so peaceful. Lin blinked as the tears assaulted him anew, and he nearly tossed away the baton but as he sobbed he squeezed the handle tighter. If threads could be snapped, why couldn't they be fixed?

Lin grunted as he stabbed the tip of the Bound Metal into the wound across her abdomen. At the same time, he formed a Thorn, planting it at her temple in the hopes of freezing Denny as she was now. Dead, but not decaying. *Dead.*

Forcing the baton through the wound proved harder than he expected, the magic and flesh resisting up until something tore with the sound like a pierced tarp.

Lin gasped, nearly threw up, and pressed it deeper into the abscess. He ignored the sounds, and scents, and looked only at her eyes. Even her Inlays had lost their glow like the fire of her soul was snuffed out.

Steps echoed through the bath chamber and Carine came into view, much like she had when he'd bathed Mellyr, but her expression was far grimmer. Far less forgiving. "What do you think you're doing?" Her voice peaked and dipped, shaking in her anger. She was on him before he could turn.

Lin struggled to cover Denny with a towel. "Leave us!"

"No! I let you take her— let you mourn because I had other things I needed to see to, but this? This is unbefitting of the warrior she was, the *person* she was. That…" She gestured at the baton's hilt rising out of Denny's abdomen. "Is *wrong*!"

Wrong. The word echoed, rebounding off the walls in the nearly empty chamber as if mocking him.

"I don't care. It will keep her as she is until we can find a way to—"

"To what? Raise the dead? That was beyond even the reach of Vellia and her brothers. Verbanth wouldn't have needed to be "Wrathful" if it was as easy as snapping your fingers and bringing back a snapped soul. As much as it hurts. She's gone. War is messy. We lose the ones we love, we lose *ourselves*." She moved to kneel beside him and brushed a strand of Denny's hair away from her face. Her hand drifted down until she touched the hilt of the baton. "We can take it out together, but this *thing* is coming out of her."

Lin's breath wouldn't catch and his free hand dug into the towels around Denny. She shouldn't look so cold, so lifeless. It wasn't what she'd been made for. She *was* death but it didn't suit her to be of the dead.

Worst of all, he knew the truth. Had felt it in his bones when consciousness found them both there against the wall amid the dead and dying. She'd died before he even healed the terrible wound that had opened her from navel to ribs. "I can't..."

Carine squeezed the hilt tighter. "You can. We'll do it together." As her hand shifted higher on the hilt, she narrowed her eyes. "What... What were you trying to do here?"

After he finished telling her about the staked untethered in the northern pass and the way they'd confirmed that the green threads of magic, Thorns, imparted a sort of stasis when combined with Bound Metal, they both stared at the baton forced into Denny. Neither one of them had removed a hand from it and Carine's head shook slowly.

Tenderly, Carine put her other hand on Lin's. "She—"

"I know she might not want this... but... but what if there is a magic that can bring her back? What if there is a way to keep from untethering? What if there is something we could do? The world is far vaster than I ever could've dreamed before the Fall."

"And far crueler, it seems. I've found that hope in something unreachable can be far crueler than even a despot's reign. I feel your pain, but I can't allow you to keep her as she is. And if it was truly meant to keep her from deteriorating, then your magic already fails. Look."

Lin frowned and studied Denny. True enough, the wound wept, but it wasn't the vital scarlet of fresh blood, and her flesh had gone from a milky white to a ghastly gray. He panicked and with Carine's aid, pulled out the Bound Metal, again ignoring the sick squelch. He shifted Denny and placed an ear on her chest. Only the steady thrum of his Thorn buzzed from her temple.

Denny's Inlays looked like old scars, all hint of glow gone.

Lin swallowed, throat tight, and sniffled. He wiped his nose and eyes with his palms and realized he hadn't gotten all the caked blood from the lines of his hands.

Fresh sobs racked him, and he shuddered as he clutched Denny's corpse. "I— I failed her. She wanted... we... she talked about running away from all of this."

"You need to compose yourself. I need to meet with Erias and I'd like to have you there with me to recount some of the things you've told me about... All this."

"The One can have Erias," Lin snapped, curling his fingers in the towels under Denny.

"The One will have us all someday, but Lin. Think of Mellyr and Tylle."

Lin forced himself to breathe. He wasn't being rational. Denny had loved fighting and had avoided death on more than one occasion. It just wasn't fair; another life he'd failed to protect.

"Please give me a few moments. I'll join you briefly. I promise."

It was plain in the way she carried herself, Carine hadn't come out of the battle unscathed. It was also apparent she was a good leader, likely better than Erias thought of himself. Of course, she'd come to check on Denny. *On her corpse.*

Lin shifted to the pool of clouded water and scrubbed his hands, digging under the nails, feeling the hum of energy from the Stitches along his left hand. He wept as he worked, playing the battle over in his mind countless times. Lin might not have inflicted the wound, but his weakness, his fear of pressing himself deeper into madness had helped cause it. When he finished, his hands were as raw as his eyes, and his throat felt tight like he'd been strangled for the better part of the night. He rose on shaky legs and moved back to Denny's corpse, the lack of life unnatural for someone so terrifyingly full of it not long before.

"I'm sorry. You terrified me when we first met. But you always came to my aid. *Always*. And now you've left me alone. I don't know that anyone else will understand what I'm feeling as I slip towards madness. But I hope I'll see you soon if our souls are truly stitched to the Great Tapestry." Lin fell to his knees, leaned forward, and kissed her brow. "And I'll avenge you and break every bone in that damned Nooseman's legs. Just for you."

Desperate Bone

"The Mourning Ballad is taught to all Danican children. We are taught young to mourn."—Tylle

Acknowledging she was gone made Denny's corpse far heavier than her lithe frame should've allowed. It was like her body, so light and nimble in life, had turned to stone, cold and unmoving. Not through the green magic, as Lin had intended, but through the cruelty of death.

Carrying her felt wrong, as wrong as leaving her there in the baths for someone else to find, so Lin did it. He must've appeared grim, like a walking specter to anyone who looked at him, the way they turned their eyes whenever he met their gaze.

Soldiers clad in washed-out colors moved like ants crawling across a carcass. Perhaps their fight was a lost cause. If Danicans were ants, surely Ladrica was a vulture, ready and able to pick apart the last bits of carrion from Danican soil. Consuming the ants as it did.

When Lin had first been marked by Tylle's magic, stitched and saved, he'd bemoaned his fate. Now, seeing what they were up against, he wondered how any of them could've bested monsters like the Nooseman without Inlays. Without befouling the fucking Tapestry.

Every single Ferrucium soldier Lin passed seemed frail. One kick, one Weft, and they'd die so easily. It was true some few had Inlayed their flesh, but it was too little too late if more of those Nooseman bastards attacked.

The heavy scent of a pyre tickled Lin's throat before he noticed the smoke curling into the sky. As he exited the Ferrucium proper and stalked his way through the congested streets, he wondered at the fact that none of the enemies had slipped over the walls or gotten through the gate. If they had, it would've been a massacre not dissimilar to what Lin had helped Erias achieve. It was impossible to think of it as a small blessing considering Denny's corpse in his arms.

Erias. Even after all they'd been through, there was still something about the man Lin didn't like. Some nagging thought at the back of his mind. Aemun had struck a deal with him, Ladrica, and the Scholars. Aemun had played all these people off themselves, but Lin didn't know what he'd promised Erias. Carine, Pael, and Tylle all seemed to regard the man highly, but what had he done for Lin and what did the man have to gain from all this?

Lin blinked and fought to keep his throat from tightening. He was tired of crying. Tired of feeling frustrated and powerless. If he was meant to go mad and die, then he needed to do so after giving his all to save those that he still could. He couldn't take any more failures. He passed the outer walls, stomach growling at the scent of stew coming from the various tents lining the walls.

"You there," a nasally-sounding man called from the nearest tent. The tent looked a bit like the one Erias and Azhura had been meeting under, but the makeshift desk was far less cluttered. He was built like a pestle resting in a mortar and hadn't glanced up from the papers he was shuffling. "Bodies to be burned need to be lined up along the cliff. Too many, so sea burials were ordered for our people and the Ladrican corpses to be thrown over the cliff into the sea."

"But... But who will sing the Mourning Ballad?" Talking *hurt*.

"Waves have a certain rhythm to them, do they not?" The man chuckled, then looked up and blanched.

Several ships still floated far out in the water, well past any reasonable threat of a trebuchet or Bolt. Lin squinted, wondering if his eyes were deceiving him.

The man followed Lin's gaze and managed to stutter out a string of words. "A-ah y-yes, the cowards have waved a white flag for now. They've got a rowboat coming to shore—"

Each word the man spoke grew more confident as if he expected Lin to be placated.

Lin stared at the man, said nothing, then turned around and walked away from the southern cliffs.

If Lin fully untethered this instant, he'd still not let Denny be sent to sea. She hadn't hated the water as he had their time aboard the boat, but Denny hadn't loved it. What sort of end was that? Even their enemies deserved more respect than being tossed off a cliff to pollute the sea and shore below.

Most importantly, Lin didn't care to hear the man speak anymore. The pompous individual sounded as if he had some personal involvement in bringing the Ladrican fleet to a treaty. Still, his unblemished clothes and skin said everything about the man that Lin needed to hear.

Lin walked northward across the battlefield. Fresh ruts and gouges carved out by Bindings made the earth uneven. He walked so far north that blood no longer stained the soil. He carried her and fought back the tears that came at the thought of her. And he couldn't stop thinking of her.

He wanted to carry Denny to the river she'd first spotted him in, but even the stone they'd had their second meeting at was too far away. So he settled for the fields of wheat he'd rushed through when he'd realized Carine's group might be walking into a trap. It felt far enough from the Ferrucium that its shadow couldn't touch her resting place.

Lin set her body down gently, dry stalks crunching from the weight of her corpse. He was a constant failure. He couldn't even send her away correctly as he realized he hadn't brought anything to burn.

The moon hung heavy in the air high above, free from the blanket of clouds that had obscured it throughout the battle. *Why?* Terrible things were meant to happen on moonless nights, so why was the damned moon up there looking so pleased with itself?

Lin knelt in silence with her body for a long moment, shivering at the cold cliffside breeze that still managed to haunt him despite the distance he'd carried Denny. The wind carried the scent of burning wood. Perhaps a pyre had been started somewhere to burn the bodies after all. He sighed and stared at Denny among the dried bits of grass and grain. Grass crunched as he grasped the narrow, brittle blades and stabbed his palms.

The only solace was the lack of Aemun's mocking voice as if the madness pitied Lin.

Steps sounded and two shapes clarified against the darkness.

Carine and Jun stalked across the field. Stacks of timber were piled in a carrier on Jun's back and Carine held two thick bales of straw tucked under one arm and an amber bottle in the other hand.

"Grovetender sent us to find you. His attendant at the front said you refused to take her to the sea burials."

"Denny wasn't of the sea. She was open fields and dark woods. S-silent as a breeze and...." Lin looked away from Carine and back up at the traitorous moon as he wiped away the tears wetting his beard.

"And a dependable friend," Jun said, shifting so the wood tumbled to the ground. "Find some rocks. If you don't mind. Last thing we need to do is raze the fields when the idiot Ladricans didn't."

"Could always blame them for it though," Carine said. She grinned, the slight smile falling away as her eyes shifted across Lin's face when she thought he wasn't looking. "Either way, Denny deserved better than to burn with so many other bodies. So we'll do this. I bet Hugo wished he was here to see this. They had a running bet... which one of them would die first."

Hugo had been the mountain of a man the mute one had murdered when she betrayed Carine and them. "She never really mentioned him," Lin whispered.

"She wouldn't have, being it was a personal wager between *friends*. Didn't tell us much about you either, whatever way that makes you feel," Jun said.

"Jun," Carine chided.

"What?" Jun snapped back before turning to point at Lin. "He knew her for how long and gets to mope like a child who lost his favorite doll? She is the... She is the third companion we've lost to this damned war. One of them the mother of my child, the last piece of her I had!"

Lin rose to his feet and stepped toward Jun. "Just because I didn't know her long doesn't mean—"

"Long? I doubt you knew her at all! Where was she born? What foods did she like? She was our *friend*. What was she to you? Really?"

"Watch it," Lin growled. What hurt more than the hurled words was how accurate they were. They hadn't had a chance to talk about the small things— to learn more about each other.

Carine shook her head and began building the pyre, setting the logs and timber Jun had hauled and stuffing the straw into the gaps.

"Or what? Did she ever even tell you about the Stitches across her face or why she was so off-kilter about her eyes?"

Lin unclenched his fists and shook his head. "I... I barely knew her. Is that what you want to hear? She wanted to know me more, she tried to open up to me... and I was afraid of what that might mean, so I kept her at arm's length. She aided me time and time again...." Lin nearly stumbled, his voice raising with each forced breath. "And I couldn't save her!"

Jun was on him in an instant.

Lin flinched but instead of a Binding or blow, two solid arms wrapped Lin in an embrace. Jun smelled terrible and his stripes of Inlayed flesh hummed against Lin's own.

"She cared about you. And clearly, you cared about her. That's *all* that matters in moments like these. We aren't ever guaranteed the next day, so appreciate those around you while you can. Mourn now, but know, understand, she wouldn't want that. She'd want you to make them pay, but also to find happiness. And if one doesn't bring the other, she'd be alright with that.

"Now gather those stones before we use yours," Jun accented his words by breaking off the embrace and tapping Lin's stomach with the back of his hand.

Lin wiped his eyes and went about the task. Stones were few and far between, but he managed to find enough to make a broken circle around the spot Carine had built. Stone by stone, Lin calmed. When he realized the stones wouldn't be enough to circle the makeshift pyre, he used a Blade to cleave ruts into the field. Soon, Denny had a pyre all of her own, and she rested atop it.

Carine took a heavy pull from the amber glass she'd carried, then poured a bit on the straw she'd already laid out. In a moment, the field was lit by the crackling fire as it took Denny.

They shared a moment of silence, letting the sounds of a burning body fill the air. *Six above, Faceless Weavers, watch over your daughter as she takes her place among the Grand Tapestry you've woven for us.* Lin wanted to pray more, but he'd run out of things to say that felt genuine. Even those words had struggled to escape him and only managed to do so because Denny had once said she preferred her Gods to be Faceless.

Lin hummed the Mourning Ballad and Jun joined in, his voice a smooth pitch as he sang crisply. As he sang, he put his arm around Lin's shoulders and squeezed.

"Here." Carine leaned over and pressed the amber bottle to Lin's chest. "*Drink.*"

Lin took it, sniffed it, and coughed hard at the potent brew. The sort of strong brew that wouldn't take away his pain, but would take *him* away from it, if briefly. Belanisian maybe. But as he took a swig it became clear this drink was made from ash and smoke, not berries and a breeze. Lin coughed several more times to Jun and Carine's growing amusement. He passed the bottle to Jun who, despite his chuckle moments ago, couldn't stifle the cough churning up from within after his swig.

Another stretch of silence carried as the fire devoured Denny. Lin struggled to take his eyes off the flames.

"What was Ladrica like?" Jun asked, clearing his throat.

"Cold and gray," Lin said. He reached back for the bottle but Carine snatched it.

Carine tipped the bottle over so that the contents spilled onto the grass beside them. She repeated the slow, intentional action several more times and when she seemed pleased with the amount of liquor gifted to the worms, she took another, long pull for herself.

"And worse than both those things, I saw the hatred fed to even the children of Ladrica."

"You mean like the way Danican youth are taken and taught by the Ferrucium?" Carine asked.

He hadn't considered it that way, but of course, it made sense. Though, somewhat different, the intent was the same. To make people fear Danicans. To make Danicans fear themselves. Lin couldn't help but smile.

"What?" Jun asked.

"You just reminded me of my time spent with Tylle." Lin sighed and watched a group of embers dance among the smoke, pieces of Denny drifting to her final rest.

"Tylle is an interesting woman. I was surprised when she declined to join our little group outright. Of course, she wanted to aid in the restructuring, but to say she wanted little to do with the rest of us might be painting it in a kinder light than it deserves. She couldn't wait to leave after we took the Ferrucium."

Lin nodded at Carine's words. His mood had shifted small strides towards stability. It was as if an ember from Denny's pyre had found kindling within him to warm him with. Though his stomach was likely warmer for the beverage's potency than anything else. As much as he hurt for Denny, something was welling inside him for the thought of Tylle. Of seeing her again. Of the chance that perhaps she'd been eager to leave the Ferrucium to reunite with *him*.

If that sharp-boned bitch wanted to be with you, she would've been the one to go to Ladrica, not your mad little cunt burning now.

Lin leaned over and pressed his fingers into his temples as if that might stop the spread of Aemun's vile words. Words that shouldn't exist. Words capable of cutting so deep only because they came from within him. Not once had he considered that Aemun's spirit truly haunted him. No, Lin knew he was untethering and every wicked, awful, cruel thought came from his inward doubts. It had to. "Have either of you had experience with a person untethering? Going mad." Lin asked.

Jun burst into a full-bellied laugh and took the bottle from Carine. "This war is fucking madness. Now if you mean the honest-to-goodness slavering monsters that people become? No. I've been fortunate enough to never see it. Or at least never notice it."

Carine seemed to watch the bottle, eyes lingering on Jun's lips as wiped them with the back of his hand. "I have," she said. "A friend of mine. We were young and Erias had just taken us in. His rebellion was a dream more than anything else and what would eventually become my little bedlam band was just a hope. My friend... She overdid the Inlays. Started exhibiting all the worst signs of Binder's ailments. Brittle hair, nails, teeth. You know what I mean. Then she started hearing voices. Her father's. He'd died in an untethered raid years prior. Said she saw things too. Horned monsters dancing at the edges of her vision. One day she ran off. No note or anything."

Horned monsters, like the untethered he and Denny had seen. Lin nodded and shivered despite the flame. He'd brought it up, but now he wanted nothing more than to change the subject. From every source knowledgeable on the matter, he was untethering. Losing himself day by day, moment by moment. He thought back to the untethered he'd tested at the tree, cutting and healing, each bit of magic drawing him closer to the monster he'd been hurting.

"It can be undone," Carine said. "If you stop now. It's not too late."

Lin squinted and dug at the dirt and blood under one of his nails. "I can't."

"Nobody would fault you if you did. You've done more for Danica than most anyone," Jun said. "Erias told us he'd received a bird from a... Well, an unlikely ally. You're the Hero of the Fingers and all that. Saved the Ladrican king's ungrateful life. Helped see the Fall to fruition. Gave Denny hope." He shifted where he sat and cocked his head and in moments a figure Lin hadn't seen or heard clarified into a rider on horseback.

Lin rubbed his eyes. Like it or not his vision was failing. Why was nothing ever easy? People feared Danicans for their gifts, but they didn't have to experience losing themselves piece by damnable piece.

"Grovetender is requesting your presence. An envoy is coming from the ship and should be to shore shortly, he wishes to have all of you attend in the case of subterfuge."

"We'll head there right away," Carine assured the Wellgrovian soldier. The man nodded and turned back to head into the flickering shadows of the moonlit night.

Lin made to stand, but Jun passed him back the bottle.

"Denny was... She was a madwoman. Strong. Passionate. She had a hard life before meeting us and lived an even harder life after. But she loved deeply and cared about those she chose to care about so, so fiercely. Anyone she loved, I can't help but do the same."

Carine nodded at Jun's words. "We asked her not to go, as telling her not to would've done no good, but she knew was made to do more than deliver messages. I'm sure she reveled in whatever occurred in Ladrica. It might seem like a waste to see her gone now, but she avoided death so many times Wicked Tel'Myr was bound to have her sooner rather than later."

Wicked Tel'Myr. "Venya," Lin whispered. "It's a long story, but Denny and I learned the One's supposed true name."

"Venya?" Jun scoffed.

"Mhm," Carine grunted and rose. "I shouldn't have mentioned anything. Bad enough we're burning a friend, we don't need to bring the One into it any more than it's already involved."

As strong as the two were, it was odd seeing them put so on edge by the mention of the One, or rather the One Shadow's true name. "Denny would've laughed at the both of you."

Jun offered his hand to help Lin up, a smile spreading on his face. "I think you're right."

***

The boat, a small quick thing built for several rowers and not much more, touched land surrounded by several torches stuck into the shoal-coated beach. Most of the torches were askew, the rocks offering little stability as the boat was pulled on shore by three purposefully unarmed soldiers. The envoy was dressed the same as the bitch who had stolen away Mellyr, armored lightly underneath dark robes. He was a petite man completely hairless save his brows. The white flag the man carried never stopped waving, though the speed with which it waved flagged once he was firmly ashore.

Lin hiccuped, the brew besting him as he stared down the Ladrican. He wondered if he'd seen the man in the north, but he couldn't have. Not if he was getting off a ship that had been sailing this way when Lin was on the island.

The thought of this man amid sailors made Lin giggle, which he regretted as Erias spared a sharp, irritated glance his way. Perhaps he'd had too much to drink. "Or perhaps Erias, in all his Grovetender glory, needed *some*. No reason a strong drink couldn't unclench Duke Wellgrove's upstart brother. Grovetender. As if he'd ever spent a day seeing to the groves."

"Shhh," Jun shushed Lin, a smile half-formed on his face.

Oh. Had Lin said that aloud? He sucked in a deep breath and attempted to steady himself. Either the waves were moving the shore with each pulsing surge, or Lin was growing more intoxicated with each passing breath. He had doused the ember within with more heavy pulls of the beverage. And he hadn't even coughed the last few swigs. A raucous hiccup escaped him, followed by several more in quick succession. Lin covered his face, decidedly sure he'd have given nearly anything to have a Nooseman's heavy mask hiding the embarrassment on his face.

The envoy cleared his throat and picked his way across the shoal to stand near one of the slanted torches. "You are the esteemed—"

"Save it," Erias interrupted.

Lin flinched back at the Erias's tone, suddenly reminded of the time he'd been struck by the man's ring. He gingerly touched his cheek where the scar dimpled his flesh.

Erias rubbed the bridge of his nose and glared at the envoy before speaking. "You and yours—"

"*You* save it," The petite man interrupted back, pointing the flag's rounded tip at Erias's chest. "Me and mine have come to make you acutely aware of *your* situation. Now will you allow me to speak with no further crude interruptions?"

Lin didn't think he imagined the look both men gave him as he swayed. He licked his lips and then Jun was there, letting Lin lean on him. The man might've been shorter but felt as solid as the ground underfoot. More solid, actually, considering the rocky shore.

Erias glowered, looking as incensed as he had the day Lin challenged him in front of Aemun. The entire exchange looked silly, though that could've been the drink clouding his mind. Grovetender, tall, armored, and imposing towered over the petite, armored but mostly robed envoy.

But, that was what Erias liked doing, wasn't it? Looking like a leader, that was. Giving the impression of power and control. Spending so much time away from the man had softened Lin to the hard truths he'd already known about the bastard. Erias and Aemun were cut from very similar bolts of cloth.

"Please continue," Azhura said, bowing slightly toward the envoy. Even beside Erias, Azhura managed to look noble. Say what one wanted about the Weavers, they were well-kempt. She wore her hard lines with confidence and kept her shoulders back. Whatever arrangement the two leaders had, Azhura was the more poised one. Perhaps it was her years of *actual* leadership working alongside the other Weavers while Erias always conducted himself in the shadowed boughs of Wellgrove.

The envoy smiled with all his teeth, an act that would've looked wolfish from any of the others gathered around but because of his wide mouth and near-set eyes, he looked more like a toothy fish. "I am Lucin, envoy of Ladrica, mouth for the kingdom in this matter."

Lin chuckled. He'd need to tell Denro about this man being the *mouth* of Ladrica.

"As I'm sure you've noticed, we've pulled back and are offering an armistice, of a sort. There will be no further Ladrican action until the council reconvenes, unless, of course, the duchies of Danica instigate. Enjoy the freedom until that time."

Until that time.

Erias sighed and rested a lazy hand on the hilt of his sword. "Message received."

"And Erias Wellgrove and Weaver Azhura. The two of you have been granted... attendance to the council and amnesty for your crimes while in attendance. King Lodram eagerly awaits your meeting which will be held in the assembly hall of the Fentis Tower."

"Yes because they are famously neutral," Erias said.

"They, and others, are the only reason this little resistance hasn't been ground under heel. Consider yourself fortunate. Oh, and one other thing. News arrived with the orders to stay our hand— more untethered have been sighted in the pass leading to Ladrica."

"We have the untethered... problem... under control," Erias said.

Lucin snorted and looked over his shoulder to the rowboat waiting to ferry him back to the main ship. "Be that as it may, a friendly bit of advice," he said. "All of you are monsters. Tainted blood, tainted minds. You can't possibly win a war with us while battling yourselves."

It seemed the envoy, finished with everything he'd intended to say, didn't wish to be on the shore any longer than necessary.

Lin couldn't help his grin. All considered the meeting had gone without issue and, using Jun as support, he waved at the petite man as the envoy climbed back into his little boat.

"What has gotten into you?" Erias snapped, wheeling on Lin.

Jun's hands twitched and he gave Lin's shoulders a reassuring squeeze, but nobody else moved save for the soldiers rowing away. Erias stood inches from Lin, expression twisted with disgust and irritation.

"Me?" Lin asked back, voice rising above the lapping tide. "You heard the man. It was basically all thanks to *me*. I stayed Ladrica's greedy fingers. I... I... I break myself over and over and over again and now that I'm fully fucking broken, what? Am I too broken for you to bear? Like Denny was when you wanted her to just run messages? I don't owe you fealty. I don't respect you. I don't—"

Erias's hand flashed out, Bound Metal ring glinting with torchlight, but Lin caught it.

Lin leaned in and whispered, "I've saved your life. Don't make me end it."

With a jerk, Erias's arm came free. "You could try. But you swore an Uethe. That Bludwieve wouldn't allow it."

Lin chuckled but kept the truth of it to himself. He could remove the magic, and cut it with the dagger he'd left with the Scholars. "Also... while I'm thinking about it... if you ever... *ever* think about allowing Mellyr to be targeted again. I will find a way to end your life myself. Grovetender or not."

"Excuse me?" Azhura chimed in. She'd been watching off to the side, a sly smile on her wrinkled face. But any hint of humor had disappeared like it had been pulled into the sea by the tide.

"I never—"

"Pael claimed he made his choice based on what you'd want. You sending a man like that is like pointing a crossbow and being surprised when the bolt launches." Lin stifled a hiccup and would've staggered a bit if not for Jun.

He blinked as he took his eyes off Erias and realized the man had been doing something with his Bound Metal ring. *Bastard.* No wonder Lin suddenly felt extra nauseous.

Erias shook his head. "Leave us all of you."

And they did, all save Azhura. Carine patted Lin's shoulder on her way past and took Jun with her as she left. He hadn't noticed her until now, standing just outside the ring of torches. The guards hesitated but started the long uphill walk back to the Ferrucium proper. Lin swayed there, glancing between Azhura and Erias.

"If Pael tried to harm Mellyr, I'm sorry."

Azhura's hands trembled. "I'm growing far too old for these games Erias. Unlike Lindel, I'm not beholden to a Bludwieve. If anything— No, look at me— Anything at all happens to my great-grandchild not even the Six could save you. I've aided you and yours as best I could to see that this remains as bloodless as possible. Do not make an enemy of me." She didn't wait for Erias to speak before taking slow measured steps up the hill, leaving Lin and the man he'd berated alone by the sea.

"Leave me," Erias whispered. "Leave me and tomorrow we will discuss what I need you to do. I will forgive all this, but you've wounded me."

Lin didn't believe any of it. The only thing wounded was the man's ego and perhaps whatever trust he'd been building with Weaver Azhura. Not that Lin cared. A poor decision or not, his chest felt a touch lighter having gotten those feelings out.

Desperate Hate

"Not many wars can claim to be caused by the death of a single woman, but those that are often seem to be the most costly. Vellia's death was one such and led to the eventual creation of the Danican Accords." —Gritt

Morning light cracked over the Ferrucium's walls like slow oozing yolk from an overeager egg.

Lin burped and fought to keep the bile rising in his throat. He leaned against the tallest part of the Ferrucium, a thick pole built to support the large flag of the double-headed hawk. Or was it meant to be an eagle? Wrapped around him like a blanket, it was hard to tell and he'd never paid much attention to what sort of bird it was before. Either way, the cloth was rough and weathered from years of beatings from coastal winds.

Truth be told, he couldn't recall scaling to the vantage point last night, but he smiled as he stared out over the horizon. Denny would've loved the view, and would likely have made the climb look easy.

Bits and pieces of the previous night clung to him. He'd told Erias off. Mourned Denny alongside Carine and Jun. Perhaps made a soft ally of Azhura. Though, she wouldn't be too happy to learn he'd taken the flag as a blanket. He leaned forward and rubbed the bridge of his nose. Maybe he was being a bit generous with himself.

Sleep would've treated him better, but he hadn't wanted to sleep. Hadn't wanted to chance at having terrible dreams. So instead he'd stayed awake counting stars. Wondering at their beauty and if, somehow, they really had been Stitched up there so long ago. And when he eventually spotted the harbor where Tylle had taken her vengeance on Aemun, he replayed those moments. Over and over.

Lin stayed up there as the sun fully broke, rising to take its place among the clouds. Gulls cried and Lin wondered if the two-headed bird of the Ferrucium was meant to be one of those loud pests. He shifted around the pole to glance down at the Ferrucium. He couldn't see the northwest fields from his vantage and he was thankful because it gave the impression that the Ferrucium, this place where he was raised and trained and lied to, was still an ideal, peaceful place.

The scent of frying eggs and cooked meat snuck up to join Lin before drifting away to tantalize the birds and clouds above. He needed to move, needed to sleep really, but he sat motionless, body doing neither.

The breeze rustled the edges of the flag and for a still moment, Denny was up there beside him, wondering at what he was doing. And when he looked, she was gone. Perhaps, if he was lucky, Aemun's haunting voice would change to hers. Even if all he heard was awful things it would be better than that bastard lingering in his mind.

A sharp whistle sounded from the outer walls below and Lin spotted Carine as she waved at him. She was too far for her words to carry but it was clear she wanted him to come down. Lin sighed and unwrapped the flag from his shoulders, tying its tattered ends around the pole so someone more suited to mending things might be able to fix the mess he made of it.

"Erias and Azhura would like to see you." Carine studied him, her eyes lingering on his once he'd finally vaulted down.

"I'm surprised they didn't climb up and join me if it was so urgent they sent you," Lin said.

Carine chuckled. "The old lady might've if you refused to come down. They're down in that big chamber talking with some of their commanders."

The Chamber of Judgement. A flash of fear rushed through him before blowing away like the breeze.

"And why aren't you with them?" Lin asked.

"Because I was sent to find the drunkard and drag him back if he was unwilling. You aren't unwilling, are you?" Carine offered a half-smile but she stood in a bladed stance and seemed ready to fight.

"One bad night and suddenly I'm treated like an enemy— a threat?"

"Any of us are one bad night away from being an enemy," she said as she tapped the side of her head. "And sometimes we're our own worst ones."

Lin sighed. She wasn't picking a fight and even if she was, Lin didn't have it in him to argue. "Would they object if I bathed first?"

Carine shrugged. "I doubt it. Not many likely would."

Lin ignored the slight jab and looked down at the milling people. Message runners darting between stalls and people alike. "If you're heading back to them, please let them know I'll be there shortly."

The walk to the baths was an echo of the trip from the prior day, except this time the only thing he carried was guilt. A stain still rested where Denny had lain and Lin stepped around it, instead letting his eyes rest on the water's surface. He dipped in, the chill water causing him to shiver. They had ways to heat it, and normally he would've, but a warm bath wasn't what he wanted or deserved.

Ungently, he scrubbed himself. Once he was soaped, he submerged himself entirely and floated there for a long moment, breath held.

Lin was a blade, broken and reformed. He was a blade tempered and shattered only to be made again. With a kick, Lin pushed himself to the surface and wiped away water and strands of hair from his eyes.

Toweling off took little time and he regretted not thinking ahead to what clothes he'd wear. What he'd worn through the night was a jumbled mess of tattered, ruined cloth. Wrapping the towel around his waist, he moved through the halls until he found the room he'd been looking for. An armory of sorts, though, really, it was where the Ferrucium uniforms were kept. He found underpants, trousers, and a tunic that fit well enough, lacing everything like he hadn't gone months without wearing the familiar outfit. The last piece he donned was the crimson cloak, warm enough down here in the bowels of the Ferrucium. By the faded hues of the dye, it was a cloak well worn by its owner before being recycled to the ranks of cloaks for eventual soldiers. Normally the swords would be kept down here as well, but it seemed with war coming to the coast, they'd been moved. He wasn't even sure if they'd let him keep wearing the red, or if Azhura would request that he remove it.

Lin ran a hand across his cheek, dragging his nails through the unruly stubble. It didn't seem that long ago that he'd shaved. He walked through the halls as if he still belonged there. As if he wasn't so far removed from the man he'd been the last time he'd worn the Ferrucium soldier's uniform.

No soldiers stopped him as he made his way to the looming doors of the Chamber of Judgement, a name that seemed so unfitting compared to the grand castle off Ladrica's shore that had belonged to Velkath and his kin.

Two guards, Enforcers by the sigil on their armor, opened either half of the double doors. In the smoky light of the hall, they could almost be mistaken for Ladrican armored soldiers. Except their armor was old and worn-looking despite possessing the sheen of Ferrucium steel.

When Lin entered, the three conversing in the center of the room looked his way. Azhura, clad in a sheer white top that left little to the imagination, looked down from her seat as if Lin had slapped her. "What do you think you're wearing?" She'd risen from her seat and the indignation across her face couldn't be clearer.

Lin bowed his head as he approached, kneeling beside the man who'd been speaking to Erias and Azhura. It was the short, rude man who'd told Lin to give Denny a sea burial. The man harrumphed and cast more than one side-eyed glance in Lin's direction. Whatever conversation they'd been having couldn't have been that important considering the way Azhura had pivoted her focus onto Lin.

"We can continue this conversation at a later date, but for now see that a group repairs the coastal defenses," Erias dismissed the man with a wave and settled his dark glare onto Lin. "I thought my disappointment for you couldn't dip lower... and yet you arrive to us hours later than requested."

"And clad in stolen clothes," Azhura added.

"I spoke out of turn last night," Lin raised his chin and met both leaders in the eyes. "In a manner unbecoming of one dubbed a hero. And for that, I'm sorry."

"And the uniform?" Azhura asked.

Lin shook his head. "I beg you to remember that long before I went to the Scholars, I had been a Ferrucium Escorter. And it was either this or I walk through the room to meet you in the nude. And while the former is unwanted I imagine the latter is doubly so."

Erias seemed to brush the thought away with a wave and shifted in his seat. "Rise. One drunken night doesn't remove your name from the deeds or songs, *Hero of the Fingers*."

As Lin rose he looked at the tapestry behind the platform. Since he'd last seen it, someone had repaired the ruined parts, attaching the swathe that had been sliced away and mending the hole caused by the Enforcer's spear. With the memory of the great tapestries from the castle, it was easy to imagine this one alongside the collection there, or at least woven by the same creator.

Azhura rose and stepped down from the dais, silken top fluttering open and revealing her bare chest. "I don't know about the two of you, but I'm tired of this war. And it's only just begun. In all my years sitting as a Weaver, I never had to worry about invasion. Hadn't thought I needed to worry about rebellion."

"We've exhausted this at length. The Dukes didn't rebel simply to form a new council of boot-lickers. Waving the flag now at the first internal hiccup... That is a surer way to chains around our throats than resisting by half. They'd kill us and replace us with more pliable minds." Erias rose and several attendants sitting along the wall rose with him.

From that alone, it seemed however the power dynamic had shifted after the Fall, Erias "Grovetender" Wellgrove held more sway in the Chamber of Judgement than Azhura. Lin wondered if the same could have been said if Aemun had stood there as opposed to his grandmother. Though from what Lin recalled, Aemun hadn't planned to stay with Erias or the Ferrucium. He'd meant to flee Danica altogether.

"If I may... you two have a real chance to change the tide of things. A chance to show the people of the world that we aren't monsters. Aren't *only* monsters, that is. I may have bought us time in Ladrica, but I'm no speaker. No leader." Lin looked down, studying the grooves in the tiles that so often ran with the blood of the condemned.

"You say that... but we have entire sections of Danica gone silent," Azhura turned to bore her cold stare into him. "Silence from outposts. We also excommunicated several noteworthy members of the Ferrucium for refusing to swear allegiances. So turning a tide as heavy as what drowns us isn't as easy as it might sound."

Lin winced at the snap in her voice.

"Yes. Silence. Silence from Duke Errond. Silence from scouts. Silence consuming us from within while we are attacked from without." Erias looked as if he appraised Lin before directing his stare to the space just behind him.

"You mean to say there still hasn't been any word from Tylle and Pael."

"Among others," Azhura said. She walked until she was beside Lin, hand resting on Lin's shoulders, tracing the veins of humming power under his clothes. She smelled slightly of roses, but sweat undercut the aroma. "So the untethered must be dealt with."

"And our concern is that I've never known a bloody nose to keep a tyrant from reaching avaricious hands into a pot that isn't his. Even if others demand they don't. If we could focus wholly on one or the other, we'd win without fail." The words, as passionate as Erias spoke, sounded well-rehearsed.

Lin was silent as Azhura's hand fell away and she stood beside him staring up at the tapestry.

"We thought, before you'd left for Ladrica, that you might be capable of handling the untethered problem. Well, truthfully *Tylle* thought you capable. Are you?" Erias turned to glance at the tapestry, shook his head, and pursed his lips. What he wasn't saying was clear enough. Was Lin capable of doing this task *while untethering*?

"I am."

"Good man," Erias said quickly. He looked as if he was about to say something else when Azhura raised a lone finger.

"But the untethered... I have reason to believe they might be organized," Lin said.

Azhura had begun walking back to the dais but turned and stared into his eyes. "What?"

"Denny... Denny and I came upon a village past Townsbridge, assaulted as Fallo had been. We killed the monsters we thought responsible, but they mentioned a Horned King. And Aemun... Aemun's letter to Mellyr mentioned not bowing to any king, fanged or horned."

"My grandson was many things, but he wouldn't have worked with an untethered," Azhura said.

"I didn't say he did. But... Aemun had dealings with *everyone*. Ladricans. Erias. The Fentis Scholars, Elodians, and probably others. Who is to say he didn't have some sort of understanding with an untethered king?"

"Speak his name again, and I'll take the tongue from your mouth," Azhura hissed.

Lin shook his head and stared up at Erias.

"I will ask more pointed questions to my contacts about this... Horned King. Where there is a power void, there will be those who seek to fill it. What better time than to organize an assault from within, than when the defenders are all facing outward?" Erias said.

The three of them, and Erias's attendants along the wall, sat in the silence for a long, painful moment. Lin had thought he'd made progress with the old woman, but—

"Before anything else is said... I want you to know, as little as it matters, that I *am* sorry for the mess you found yourself in. Weaver Danur was in charge of approving final assignments for Escorters. It could've been anyone from your branch tangled up in my grandson's web.

"But it ended up being *you*. And you were marked by magic which you knew to mean death. And you fought and struggled and most importantly, *survived*. Do so again. Survive and show the others, those scared few who refuse to see this new way of things, what we Danicans are capable of. No matter what happens from here, I'm proud of what you've achieved."

Azhura turned her back on Lin and settled onto her pillowed seat on the dais. Erias shifted, the look in his dark eyes showing that he was processing what she'd said, looking for hidden meanings, but if there were any, Lin hadn't caught them. Despite all the time that had passed since he last stood before Weavers in a position to be judged within the chamber, he felt warm within. As little as it mattered, he'd been found *deserving*. Lin blinked and hoped his eyes weren't as watery-looking as they felt.

Erias cleared his throat and shifted uncomfortably. He could wear all the ornate armor and ostentatious gowns, groom his hair, and manicure every detail about his appearance, but he couldn't force Azhura's respect and it seemed it was something he'd been struggling to obtain.

"There was another matter that Tylle broached with me before she departed." Erias fished through the folds of his cloak and pulled loose a scroll, sealed with a scarlet wax sigil of a branched tree. "Please take this."

The scroll felt light as Lin took it, wondering at the aged look of the material. Before Lin could ask what it was Erias smiled. "At our first meeting, you made it abundantly clear that you were Stitched without consent. You since then have worked Inlays, but I'm sure the sentiment from that time is likely the same. You wish to remove the Bindings lining your flesh. That will tell you how."

It was as if the scroll suddenly became too heavy to hold without his hands trembling. Anya had said... she'd claimed that it wasn't possible. Yet here was a scroll, far older looking than the journal Lin had lost, that claimed to know how to undo them.

"I... I can't," Lin croaked.

"What?" Erias asked.

"I can't." It hurt to say those words after finally having the means to achieve what he'd sought for so long. "I've seen the untethered plaguing the north. Fought them. Earned scars and Stitched flesh from some. If I undo my Inlays... how can I possibly hope to stop them?"

Erias clasped his hands and shook his head, his shoulders making a nearly imperceptible shrug.

"You could undo the magic in your flesh and we could send someone else," Azhura said. "You could retire to the Scholars and live the rest of your days attending to my great-granddaughter."

Lin forced himself to breathe. Erias looked unworried but Azhura's expression was so intense and genuine-seeming. She truly meant what she said. But if not Lin... Who? There wasn't anyone else with the experience Lin had gained. He knew what these monsters were capable of. "I can't leave Tylle and Pael and *all* of Danica at the mercy of these monsters. I know they have some level of intelligence despite what we were taught. Some of them anyways."

"Fine. Then take the scroll and when you have a chance at respite, do what you must with it."

Lin shook his head. "I'm *dying*. High Scholar Anya said as much. Not to mention going mad. I'm hearing and seeing things that aren't there and I think if I held in my hands the option to stop that... I would. I would take it at the cost of everything I've fought for. So no. Thank you, but I can't take this with me."

"Then how about this. I will hold it for you until you can return to us."

Lin nodded. "High Scholar Anya has been an ally of sorts, I think she would very much like to know what that scroll holds." Odds were, he wasn't ever returning to the Ferrucium. Even now, not having worked a Binding since the day prior he saw Velkath's Sigil flitting around at the edge of his vision. No wonder untethered seemed drawn to forming the damned thing, as often as they likely spotted it. If this was what they even saw. Lin twitched and refocused on the two staring down at him. "So I'm to follow Tylle and Pael's trail?"

"And with any luck, find no trouble," Azhura said, though her voice faltered. The way she'd blanched at Lin admitting he was untethering seemed evidence enough that she hadn't known he was going mad.

Erias's expression remained neutral aside from the slight pinching of his brow.

"With any luck," Lin agreed.

Desperate Blood

"A silent knife is worth its weight in silver— It is one of few things that can effortlessly begin and end a war." —Pael Hollander

The straps of Lin's pack dug into his shoulders. It was weighed down with provisions; dried meat, honey-caps, and other staples in a Binder's diet. Erias had attempted to give Lin the scroll two more times, the man's frustration growing with each declination, but ultimately Azhura had told the Grovetender to let Lin be. And, surprisingly, the man listened. It amounted to a pack burdened with everything needed for a trip to northern Danica. Everything except the one thing he'd sought since Lyre. Lin couldn't trust himself with the scroll if it detailed how to remove Stitches and Inlays, not if Pael and Tylle were in danger. Not if he was *needed*.

A sense of detachment, bittersweet and painful, haunted him through the Ferrucium. There was a good chance this was the last time he would ever step through the echoing red-stone halls or past the protective inner walls that shaped his youth.

Lin ran his hand along the rough stone of the main hall, grooves and pits catching along the ridges and callouses of his fingers, as he stepped out from the Hold and into the inner square. But it didn't smell like home, that honor would always belong to the wilds of northern Danica.

"Might I walk out with you?" Weaver Azhura's voice caught Lin off-guard and he spun to see her looking at him from the side of her eye. "You are leaving, are you not?"

Lin licked his lips, noting that she'd changed from her sheer, silken robe to something sturdier and padded. It looked nearly like a gambeson, but the material wasn't quite as thick. "I am."

She inclined her head and Lin noted her hair. What had once been complicated braids woven along her scalp in symmetrical patterns had been brushed out and cut. Her hair was shorn, styled nearer to High Scholar Anya's nearly bald head than the elaborate spiraled twists she'd had just that morning in the Chamber of Judgement.

Lin considered his hair and frowned. He'd washed it in the bath but hadn't done anything beyond that. Even if the braids looked a mess, it was one of the last things he had to remind him of his time with Tylle and was the closest they'd been... Aside from the still moment beside the docks.

Azhura lowered her chin and faced Lin fully. "So, may I?"

It felt odd, leaving the Ferrucium side by side with a Weaver, especially considering how unbothered those clad in Ferrucium garb looked at seeing the elderly woman beside him. In six or so months, they'd taken the ruling powers, fierce and unknowable, and turned them into people. If that was any sign of things to come, perhaps there *was* hope for Danica once Lin was gone.

"You seem more pensive since the Fall," Azhura said.

The Fall. The day the Ferrucium fell. He'd heard the Scholars call it that but hadn't known the name had spread back to the Ferrucium.

"I don't have much to say," Lin said. He nodded at the guards who stood idly by the path from the inner Ferrucium to the outer holdings. The scent of meat from the morning had only intensified as the merchant stalls, seemingly unbothered by the looming threat of invasion, opened in earnest.

"Are you hungry?" Azhura asked.

"No, but I'm sure you didn't ask to walk with me simply to see the stalls or offer to eat with me."

Azhura nodded and a spark in her wet eyes caught the afternoon light. "I wanted to ask after Azhalia. I believe it's clear enough that Erias has no real concern for her."

"Last I saw *Mellyr*, she was well." Last he saw her, she'd been bundled up and safe back with the Scholars. A sentiment Lin couldn't have had before his time in Ladrica. Not that he fully trusted her with anyone, but Anya had seemed as if she was being so honest, so damned deliberate in the way she handled everything.

Together they wound through the crowd of civilians being tasked by a man clad in Hollander's livery. Shouts of rebuilding and some such. He let his eyes linger on a pair of youth clutched tightly by a haggard-looking woman. They pushed each other playfully, but their hands were just as dirt-stained as the older individuals gathered.

Everything was for them. For the children who didn't know any better. For those who would walk after them. All the pain now was so they could have a better life later. Velkath's Sigil flicked between the press of bodies. Always dancing in his periphery.

Once they were to the outer wall and it became clear Lin didn't plan to offer up any other thoughts on Mellyr, Azhura slowed her steps and sighed.

What was it that she wanted him to say? It should be obvious he meant to see the child protected and cared for. See her safe. It was the least he could do for Margaret. It was why he'd fought so, so hard to get her back. Driving himself untethered to do so. "What?"

"I've made mistakes. Lost most of my family and that child," Azhura gritted her teeth, jowls shaking, "*Mellyr* is all I have left. I didn't ask to be the last living Weaver but soon my role will be cut, my duties swallowed, my heritage and legacy *lost*."

Legacy is something a bastard like you would know nothing about. Aemun's snide voice condescended from the depths of his mind.

Azhura's voice shook as much as her jowls as she spoke, her eyes the closest to tears he'd ever seen them.

Lin steeled himself and met her stare. "Some legacies should be torn down. You and yours helped oppress our people, bettering your stations in the process."

"My family and the other Weavers, Six watch over them, helped *save* our people." Azhura stumbled forward. "Our ancestors did the best they could with the paths they were given."

There was grief in her eyes. Her colleagues, no matter how she felt about them, had been murdered beside her. Her life was only spared because of Aemun.

Lin clenched his fists and snorted. "Sometimes... Sometimes a person must make their own path. And sometimes when they do, they might find it already existed and had just been grown over. There is nothing wrong with struggling. *Fighting*. But giving up? Letting the Ladrican King not only convince the world but also our people that all of us are monsters? That is what can't be forgiven."

Azhura took another step and stood within arm's reach. "Sometimes you sound just like him."

Lin flinched. *Denro, his father, Aemun?* If it was the latter, he'd be sick. "If you don't mean the father I can't recall or Denro, don't speak a name. Any other comparison will make me wish I hadn't spoken."

Some passersby had slowed, watching the scene before a Ferrucium soldier acting sentinel at the outer gate moved them along. Apparently, being a Weaver still held some merit to some.

When Azhura didn't speak, Lin pressed on. "Did you know them? My parents? Denro said they were Ferrucium soldiers."

Azhura narrowed her eyes and a frown settled onto her face. The pivot of the conversation left her mouth slightly ajar as she studied his face. "Do you have their names?"

"Denro didn't say," Lin admitted. And possibly worst of all, Lin hadn't asked.

As if letting sand slip through her fingers, Azhura spread her hands. "I understand we played our roles well, making it seem like we saw and knew everything, but you could be Velkath's own son and I wouldn't know it without his name."

"They fled from the Ferrucium. Abandoned their roles."

Azhura's lips became a tight, thin line and she shook her head. "For what it's worth, I'm sorry. If it was in my power to tell you about them I would. I'm not sure I can ever truly forgive you for taking my grandson from me, but in the end, he'd become someone I couldn't recognize. He despised me. Wanted me dead." She looked at her hands and gave a slight shake of her head before balling them into fists. "And I think he wouldn't recognize who either of us has become. He was always a smart boy, sharp as a honed blade, but there was a cruelness to him... A rottenness we didn't cut away because of his cleverness. Thank you. For saving me that night. I know you didn't have to and you did it to keep some potential semblance of peace. You're a sharper man than Erias gives you credit for. I understand why Aemun requested you to be his Escorter when submitting the approval to Weaver Danur, he likely thought he could use you rather well."

It was as if the woman, frail and brittle, had somehow crushed his chest. "Requested?" He managed to say.

"I... I thought you knew. My grandson specifically requested you. Weaver Danur had to approve it, which of course the fool did. I always had a not-so-secret policy that anything Aemun requested had to be run by me, but on a request so simple, he chose to ignore the policy." Azhura shrugged as if she hadn't somehow changed everything with her words. Perhaps to her, she hadn't. Just because Aemun requested him didn't mean it was for something even remotely close to this eventual outcome. Except the man had penned and sent a damned letter regarding his death to Anya. Lin wasn't positive about what reputation he'd made for himself if not that of a fair, *good* man. A man who would do anything he deemed correct. *Fuck.*

"Did you know, he had Mellyr set up to be a princess? Safe until she came of age to be married off to a Ladrican lord. Peace between our lands."

Azhura scoffed and stepped closer to the stone wall, leaning on it after a moment to the hovering soldier's chagrin. She looked him up and down and shook her head. "That is very nearly the same as what happened with the Danican royal family. Venya, the sister, was married off to the Ladricans and became the first noose."

A laugh escaped Lin, followed by another nearly throaty chuckle as he noted Azhura's incredulous expression. "Aemun had the Ladrican king and Fentian scholars convinced he was descended from Velkath. So that would mean he was orchestrating something similar?"

Azhura leaned and whispered. "It's true. Mellyr, she *is* descended from Cunning Velkath."

It's true. Words that made Lin rethink what he'd already rethought. If they were related, then they were Gods in their own right, no?

"But Velkath and his kin are treated as Gods."

"And monsters," Azhura sighed. "Oral traditions are funny things. Now hush. I don't have much more to say on the matter, but we've seen how that plays out. Even if they say it means freedom and peace and prosperity and all the bullshit they spout, don't let them take Mellyr. Swear it."

Lin had likely never seen a person look quite so sincere. "I never planned to. Even if it kills me, I'll keep her safe."

Azhura leaned forward off the wall and brushed her backside clear of dust. She stood on her tip-toes and whispered into Lin's ear. "I'd watch you die a hundred and one times if it meant seeing my great-granddaughter again safe and sound."

The palm of her hand was icy as it caressed Lin's cheek.

"So would I," Lin said.

***

Denny's grave marker didn't do her spirit justice.

Stones had been stacked, those and the burned earth marking the spot she'd been sent to the heavens. But the stones were too straight, too orderly for a place meant to remember the force of nature that was her.

Regret over her death was something Lin would carry with him forever. If he'd just done things differently... He shook his head. Lingering on thoughts he'd already scrubbed away couldn't do him any good.

Lin knelt and prayed. Prayed as if it might help her find peace despite knowing one set of Gods was made to hide the truth of Danica's past, and the other set wasn't ever actual Gods to begin with.

Not unless it meant Aemun, Azhura, and countless others had the blood of Gods in their veins, which was doubtful. It was Tylle who'd said if they can bleed, they aren't Gods.

When Lin felt his prayers were useless, he begged. Not to nameless, faceless Gods or their named contemporaries, but to Denny.

"I keep wanting to not think about you, but how can I not? I failed you plenty of times, in plenty of ways. I can only hope you find a way to forgive me if you're still capable of that. But you need to know, I need to say, I wouldn't change anything. So please, please, please forgive my failures. Because I can't, and one of us has to."

Lin inhaled, smelling the char of the area as he attempted to steady his breaths.

"What if we hadn't gone to Ladrica? What if we hadn't come back so hurriedly? What if I'd taken you up on that offer to leave Fentis? I've gone through so much these last few months but I know your life was hard. It was etched in the way you carried yourself. The way you smiled and showed your teeth. I hope… I hope that Mellyr grows to be half as fierce as you."

Lin sat there in silence, letting the moment linger. He couldn't rid himself of his feelings, but what would come next was just as important as what had come before. Danica needed him. Tylle and Pael, as capable as they both were, might need *him*. Lin rose and kicked the stones over. Denny wouldn't want such an organized stack. And fuck anyone who—

"Didn't much care for the way I stacked those?"

It was the second time in the day that Lin had been surprised by a person's voice. Jun stood angled a good bit away on one side of him, Carine on the other.

"I don't think Denny would've," Lin said, opening his eyes and steadying his breaths. Of course, he hadn't heard them, as loud as his heart had been while praying for Denny.

"You're probably right," Carine said. She stepped around Lin and put a hand on Jun's shoulder while giving a slight shake of her head. "I'm glad we caught you. Didn't relish the thought of chasing you while a Nooseman might be out there."

"Chasing me?" Then Lin noticed the packs strapped to their backs and the three horses grazing nearby. "You're coming with me? What about defending the Ferrucium?"

"Erias is many things, but he's not a fool. You were injured in the battle, as much as you've ignored it. And if there is a group of untethered coordinated as they seem to be... Even we may not be enough. The threat of some untethered king leading them *is* serious."

Carine spoke flatly, her words stated so matter of factly that Lin believed her despite seeing what she and Jun were capable of. Lin always thought himself a capable fighter, but he was in over his depth and didn't possess nearly the frightening prowess either of them did.

Jun, for once, was wearing a shirt. The material was thin like Azhura's sheer top, the fit loose, and the front open in a V cut so low his Inlays were visible across his well-defined chest.

Lin nudged one of the larger stones with the tip of his boot and shook his head. "But what about the Ferrucium?" he asked again.

A grunt escaped Jun and he shrugged. "They can make do. We've trained those we could the best we could. And besides, scouts in the fields suggest the Nooseman retreated alongside the other Ladrican troops. You bought the Ferrucium time. That is all the defense they need for Grovetender and those wiser to make a case for Danica's freedom."

Lin let the thoughts slide around in his head before speaking, slithering and knotted like a coil of lustful serpents. It sounded like fair points. Noone would argue Lin couldn't use the help. Especially if it was a force like what had taken Fallo or that nearer village.

"Be honest with me," Lin said. "Does Erias not trust me?" It was like one of the serpents had broken free and bit the edges of Lin's mind. He'd allowed Tylle to go alone, hadn't he? Pael was many things, but he wasn't a fighter capable of withstanding untethered.

Jun opened his mouth but Carine pulled her hand from his shoulder and twitched her finger, stopping whatever the man was about to say.

Lin pursed his lips and Carine stepped toward him. Her eyes narrowed and she looked him up and down. "Honestly, he does. Or he wouldn't be sending you at all. You've built quite a reputation for yourself. But with the Ladricans on ceasefire, everything running smoothly between the old regime and new, and the lack of fresh trainees to *train*, we might as well make ourselves useful. This is *your* task, consider us complimentary."

"And we've seen enough of our people die. Hugo. Denny. Prish. I don't need to hear about how you or Tylle died fighting these monsters. The burden is on the Ferrucium, but the fault is more complicated. For instance, what if the untethered problem has only worsened because of the war?" Jun shook his head. "Things to consider. But I mean it. Denny wouldn't want you running off to die and she'd be threatening to rip herself free of the Tapestry and come kill me if I allowed it."

Lin glanced down at the burnt earth and scattered stones. Jun was right. If not about it all then at least about the fact too many lives had already been lost. His mind wandered to Royce, the Ladrican soldier who'd been working with Julius. It didn't matter that the sun was beaming down warm and unblocked by clouds, a shiver took Lin. There were still forces out there wanting to use Danica but before that could be dealt with, they needed to handle this internal threat. They'd ignored it for far too long.

Lines like Wefts dashed across Lin's periphery, sending his hair on end. But when he chased them, they were gone, darting away. His eyes stung. They'd felt irritated all morning and he'd assumed it was from crying, but it felt as if something was lodged in his right eye, like a splinter but duller.

They don't trust you. Why should they? Why would they? You've failed every mission you've been sent on since Lyre. Margaret died. I died. You don't have Mellyr.

Lin rubbed his eyes, digging his knuckles into his eyelids in an attempt to sharpen the pain, hoping it would dull the voice within. When he stopped he watched purple stars flash across his vision. "All fair points. Let's go before we lose the daylight."

Denied Hope

"Boats. A tool of war that any island nation must have to succeed. Danica, while not truly an island, might as well have been, surrounded on all sides but one by the sea. It was fortunate many supplies came from within. If they didn't, an embargo would've crippled Danica's rebellion before it began."—Duke Hollander

They rode at a pace Lin knew Nebra could've handled easily, but of the three horses Carine and Jun had acquired, only one was Ferrucium trained, and even that one needed rest more often than Nebra ever had.

Riding this other horse felt wrong somehow.

After Denny and Lin had rushed on foot from Fentis, he learned how much ground they could travel using their Inlayed legs at full speed. Driving these horses to exhaustion when the trio could manage the distance and pace was unnecessary, and cruel to a certain point. As much as he missed Nebra, he was glad she wasn't with him now.

When Lin brought up his concerns, Carine's counter-points seemed valid. They might need to conserve their strength, especially if there was some untethered king, and the horses were more than capable of covering the distance at pace without harm.

Lin sighed. He did miss Nebra fiercely. He'd left her in Lyre with the Alderman, hoping she'd be safe. But if Errond's holdings, Northern Danica, were at risk, so was she. Leaving her behind hadn't been a choice, just to be sure she was living a good remainder of her life.

Days passed with the fields, giving slow way to the creeks and forests more familiar to central Danica. Homesteads, warm and inviting, dotted the hill-speckled horizon. Not so welcoming that they intended to stop, but enough so to give confidence in the fact that no Ladrican or untethered forces had come through the peaceful land. After the battle at the Ferrucium, seeing the land so at peace left Lin uneasy.

Soon enough, spring would be on them in full force and seeds would be sewn to be harvested. With the tensions along the southern coast and the multitude of threats in the north, it seemed unfair the heart of Danica was so unbothered. Good, but unfair.

Lin sidled his horse alongside Carine's. What words they'd exchanged since leaving the Ferrucium were sparse and it seemed that the tension of their mission was eating at her and Jun as much as it was Lin. Like a starved serpent coiling around them and unhinging its jaw to consume them.

"You're leading us too far north," Lin said. If they continued along this path, they'd cut closer to Fallo and the northern pass than strictly necessary.

Carine ignored him, watching the road ahead for any sign of Jun. The bald man was scouting, something he seemed to enjoy.

"More northward than I expected, I mean. I assumed we'd cross Townbridge and cut north from there." If this was truly his mission, as he'd thought it was before setting off, he would've led them across the bridge there that cut over the Telm's river, and taken them up through Elswood.

"A fair route to take. Nothing wrong with it. Nothing wrong with the way we're going either. And besides, if we're meant to follow Tylle and Pael, I'm sure this is the route they took. What if they were waylaid along the way?"

Lin narrowed his eyes. To start, he hadn't been given that information. And he certainly couldn't imagine much of anything waylaying them except... He swallowed. Except untethered. "Then we'd find them on this route."

"At least it isn't in the full heat of summer," Carine said. "I hate riding in the summer."

They continued eating at the stretch of road for quite a distance before Jun came back into view. He pulled along the side of the path, resting under a tree with branches dotted with budding flowers. His tunic was open to the breeze and he slumped back in the saddle as if he were well worn out.

"Well?" Carine asked when they were pulled up beside him.

"No sign from here to Riversbend. They may have continued northward but odds are they took the ferry across and cut up from there. Peaceful. The main road that is." Jun shifted. He looked from Carine to Lin, and finally to the road.

"We continue then. To Riversbend," Lin said. Perhaps it was imagined, but he didn't like the sensation of mounting tension between them. He'd thought they'd been on good terms when leaving, but they acted like Lin was a cumbersome inclusion and not the one who'd originally been tasked with this.

Before either of them could reply, Lin dug his heels into his mount and took off. It felt good to feel the wind whipping, catching, and pulling the tail of his cloak. This horse was no Nebra, and Carine and Jun certainly weren't Tylle and Pael, but if he closed his eyes for a moment it was almost like he was back at the beginning, before the Fall and before he'd truly Inlayed his flesh.

Before you—

Lin tuned out Aemun's snide voice. Instead, he focused on the wind in his ears and the sound of Carine and Jun pushing their mounts to keep up with him. He considered standing in his saddle and jumping. A foolish thought to be sure, but he could jump and land and then *run*.

By the time he slowed his horse, he'd made it to Riversbend. A hard ride, one that the steed had taken well enough, building up a slight lather. Jun and Carine weren't on the road behind him, but that didn't matter. He'd wait for them.

Riversbend bustled as the bell for the ferry rang and hawkers sold wares by the water. It wasn't quite as raucous as the festival taking place the last he and Tylle came through the town, but there was a frenetic energy about the city that grabbed Lin and refused to release him. He recalled thinking that the gaudy perfumes, over-excited citizens, and bright-colored flags had made Riversbend as un-Danican as a city could be. But seeing how it was now, similar but toned down and tamed, made him reconsider.

The Danica Lin had grown up knowing, living in, and defending, hadn't ever been the nation he thought it was.

A smile broke across Lin's face. If Riversbend wasn't a representation of freedom, nothing else could be. Of course, he'd prefer the wild, untamed north to the cities stuffed with people, but places like this were worth protecting.

The horse parted the crowd easily enough. Children pointed at Lin as he rode by. His cloak. They saw the colors of the Ferrucium and *ran* from his stare.

"Thought you might be trying to leave us altogether." While Lin was taking in the city, Jun had walked up alongside him, bridles in hand.

Lin shook his head. "I don't leave allies behind."

No, you just let them die. Lin tensed at that one and swatted the air as if it would rid him of the dancing Sigils or Aemun's damned voice.

Jun scoffed and nodded at Carine as she forced her way through the crowd. "Great timing, let's catch the ferry. Likely won't get another one until daybreak."

Lin dismounted and led his horse through the thinning crowd to the simple dock. Undecorated, the dock still looked like a splinter shoved into the side of the colorful town, but the ferry had a fresh polish and seemed well-kept. Solid as it was, and large enough to barge a few decently sized wagons if needed, but aside from a handful of people who looked like they'd fared well in the market based on their lack of wares and how tightly they held their coffers, the boat was empty.

"We'll keep the horses to the back."

The wood creaked underfoot but held and Lin settled against the rail to stare out across the slow-rippling water. The way the sun danced on the surface made him feel far safer than he had on the open waters heading back to Fentis. It also helped that this ship was wide and low and not at all something that seemed intent on making it off the river.

Lin craned his neck and watched as Carine whispered to Jun. The more time he spent around her the more he was convinced that she wasn't intentionally taking charge of this mission. Leadership just came naturally to her. Like the quiet confidence she carried, and the polite smiles she gave anyone who looked her way. She was nearly the opposite of Erias, and perhaps that was why they worked so well together.

Carine eyed him and noted his lingering stare. "Come here please," she said with a wave of her hand.

The operator of the ferry moved like he had a life-long cramp in his left leg and undid the mooring that kept the wide boat attached to the old pier.

"I've been thinking about the blue and green threads you mentioned. If you don't mind, tell us about the other Wievings. Please."

Lin frowned. She was being too polite as if she was worried he might snap even though she and Jun had been the pair acting odd the past few days. "I'm far from an expert but...."

A shake took the boat as the ferryman pushed the ship with an oar so long it likely reached the riverbed.

"Just the basics, like what you mentioned to me."

Lin leaned fully against the waist-level rail and stared at the sky. "We have the basics we're all familiar with. You both have the Sight?"

They nodded, confirming what Lin long thought. Lin formed a Weft. It looked everything like a shard of broken glass catching the sun. "So we have the golden threads. Versatile. Flexible or rigid. Sharp or dulled. Pointed even, as I recently learned." Lin shifted the strand of magic with each expression of it. "And I'm sure other variations I never thought to imagine."

Jun crossed his arms across his chest and crinkled his nose. "Not to be rude, but I'm more interested in the others ones."

"Right," Lin whispered, shattering the magic into motes that drifted away on the breeze. "Then there are the blue threads. The book... There was a book. From the Scholars. I lost it in northern waters. But the book claimed it was magic that drew on Zinc. A mineral in our bodies. Finding the core, as you'd do with a normal Binding, felt like snatching a fish barehanded from a flowing current. And it was capable of healing most wounds, though much the way standard Wievings would darken and become brittle and wasted, so too would this."

If anyone else on the ferry cared what the trio were about, they didn't seem like it. Not one even looked their way. Some few were entangled in conversations with themselves, and a pair of youths seemed to be taking the trip solely to whisper sweet things to one another. Guards stood near one man who looked like he wore more wealth on his finger than the rest had collectively. Especially now, one could never be too careful.

It was hard to imagine even the most remote locales not having at least heard about the potential war. Or the rise in untethered activity. Danica was a land beset.

Seeing that noone paid them much attention, Lin pulled aside his cloak and raised his tunic to show the dark, twisted flesh along his ribs.

"Gods," Jun said as he leaned in. "May I?"

"Sure." Lin shrugged. He hadn't rewrapped his compress but aside from a dull ache, he felt mostly alright. He hadn't quite known what Jun was asking to do, but it became clear when Jun's deft fingers ran along Lin's ribs, tracing the wound. It tickled and itched all at once.

"The tissue... nearly necrotic. But not quite somehow."

"I should've known that would interest him," Carine chuckled.

Jun stepped back, looking a bit ashamed at his excitement. "I studied with Duke Elmore's people to be a physiker at one point. Seems like another life now, but still these things are fascinating."

Lin lowered his shirt. It was hard to fault the man, even if it had been a bit strange. "Tylle once said we draw from our spuls to Wieve. Pulling the blue thread is similar to the gold, but it is far easier to overdo it."

"And the green?" Carine asked.

Lin stared down at his feet. Green. Copper. The magic of stasis and when done to the mind, rejuvenation to an extent. He didn't retell the story about the northern pass... or recount his time at the tree with the Bound untethered. He'd already told Carine about the one and didn't think Jun would react well to what Lin attempted with Denny's corpse. He looked up and studied Carine's face, hoping to see a hint of anything in her eyes. Patience and pain were there, but no reproach and no hint that she'd mentioned any of Lin's darker failings to Jun.

"The tome said we also pull on copper. It creates a green glow. I haven't experimented much with it, but it seems capable of slowing down the wear on things. The mind included. The first I'd heard of anything like that was from Tylle, actually."

"She is an odd one. I sometimes wonder if she knows more than she shares," Carine said, absently stroking the nearest horse's neck. "I know how you feel about her and I don't mean to imply she isn't an asset or welcome... But for someone so young, she is *steeped* in the old ways."

"She's a *priestess*," Lin retorted. It sounded far too defensive and he raised his hands, showing his palms. "I'm sorry, that came out wrong."

"My question, that I never got an answer on, was where she learned it all from. Erias knew her and her sister from a young age, but he won't speak on it. Treats her differently. And neither she nor her sister were ever pulled into our little group. Margaret, I understood... As he sent her off to infiltrate the Ferrucium. Her and others, though the others didn't fare quite so well."

Lin shook his head and turned to face the water, casting a wary side-eye at the ferryman still pushing along the boat. This was how it was talking with them. For some reason with Tylle and Pael, and even Denny, there were no moments of feeling like he had to step around shards of broken glass. They'd become friends and allies quickly enough, but Jun and Carine seemed distant. Or perhaps he'd become the distanced one, not wanting to let them in. Overreacting at the slightest comments. He ran his hand along the rail, fingertip catching on a rough, splintered piece of wood he now pulled at. How many others might've been sent to disrupt the Ferrucium from within? Lin sighed and broke the splinter entirely.

"Finish about the green threads. Please." She spoke like she was trying to coax something from a toddler. It seemed she tacked the pleases onto the end of her requests just to guilt him into speaking.

Lin tossed the splinter shards overboard and squeezed the rail. "Preservation might be a better way to describe it. It felt like a seed just under the surface, eager to bloom, and drained out just as fast as the threads of blue. The Tower of Fentis has green and blue Wievings worked around it into the stone. So, like our standard magic, I believe it is capable of being versatile once understood. It's just much harder to work with."

"Fascinating. And you said there was a book, with notes?" Jun asked. He'd moved to stand directly beside Lin and leaned on the rail the same as him, coming up to Lin's shoulder.

"There was. I went overboard on a ship and lost it and some other important things."

"And yet here you are!" Jun smiled.

"Hmm?"

"Leaning on a rail, staring at the water, unafraid that you might go in again. That marks you as a braver man than most." Jun chuckled and knocked into him. The action, while far more friendly than how Denny usually did it, made Lin think of her. She should be here with them.

Lin hung his head and leaned further onto the rail. He'd seen brave men— brave people. Denny had been fearless. Tylle too. Royce even, the Ladrican traitor, had met his death bravely. Lin though? He was constantly terrified. "No. I'm just more foolish than most. Anyway, the magic is there and I wouldn't be surprised if there were more threads than just those three. I read notes on something called mercury. They called it quicksilver. A liquid metal thought to be powerful, but causing madness in leaps and bounds."

"Sounds fanciful," Carine said.

Jun frowned. "No, it's very real. Naturally occurring like the other minerals he's mentioned. But I can't imagine imbibing the stuff."

Lin shrugged and straightened his back. "The notes said it drastically accelerated the symptoms of untethering. Based on that book, I wouldn't do it. Once this was all done... I wanted to maybe try to recreate the book for future Danicans."

Jun nodded. "Really? Didn't take you for much of a scholar."

A snort escaped Lin and he ran his hand along the wooden rail, feeling for more splinters to break away. "I'm not. But the world is a big place and I wanted to note everything I've seen and learned."

"Learned like what?" Carine asked.

Lin waggled his fingers much the way Pael often did when imitating magic. "For one there are other magics in the wide world.

Saw some myself. Elodians are capable of putting people to sleep with dark, twilight-colored threads."

"Really? And you're sure it wasn't some sort of hypnotism?" Jun had perked up at the mention of other magic and stared intently at Lin. "Straight to sleep and it still resembles threads? Surely there is some relation to our Danican magicks."

Carine shrugged. "Who cares? The world is a big place as you said. Whether that empire has actual blood ties to us or our humble plot of land or not, honestly what does it matter if we are still shackled?"

"To be fair, it could explain why they aid us," Jun whispered.

"No," Lin interjected. "They aid us to hurt Ladrica. That's all." Or at least that was all Julius had made it seem like. He'd even wanted to kill Lin to make him a martyr.

"The enemy of my enemy is my friend," Jun said softly.

"No," Carine whispered the word at the same time Lin snapped it.

"If I've learned anything," Lin said, tapping the rail and watching the slow rippling wake left by the boat and the oar that pushed it along. "It is that we don't have any allies in the wide world. Some want us shackled. Some want to use us. Both groups are afraid of us. And the more I see and learn about the truly mad untethered. The less I blame them. But I'm tired of being used."

"Agreed," Carine said. She looked as if there were more she'd considered saying but at hearing Lin's piece chose to remain stoic. To be fair, it was a look that went well with her sharp, lean features.

Jun shrugged and sucked his teeth. "We survived the Fall. We survived the Ladrican siege. I'm not all that worried about rabid wild animals baring their teeth."

"But they aren't *all* wild. I thought I mentioned it, but I've seen them coordinated. First at Fallo, where Tylle saved my life. Then on my way north to Ladrica, they assaulted a village. And even on the way to the Ferrucium from Fentis this most recent time. It was brutal but also as organized as a hunting party. Truthfully, if Duke Errond has gone missing and his holdings silent and the northern woods have become a haven for untethered... The three of us alone might not be enough."

Jun shifted where he stod, as if reading something on the wind, and turned to follow Carine's stare. All Lin could see was the blurred horizon, green-glass rippled river surface blending with the orange-streaked horizon.

"What?" Lin asked. At first, he thought they were choosing not to speak about Fallo or the fact that what they might be approaching could be anything more than wild monsters needing to be quelled, but as they continued staring, a worry settled over Lin. "What is it?"

"Ship," Jun said.

Several of the other passengers moved to look in the same direction, some of the closer ones clearly having heard the conversations they'd been having and looking unsettled. Not that it took much to unsettle the average citizen as things were.

"Ladricans?" Lin asked. He squinted, but nothing clarified. If he'd had any doubt his vision had begun failing, this settled it. *Damn.*

"Probably. Too far to tell but the ship is downstream, closer to where the Telms might let out. Probably reckoned they'd come up this way and found as deep and wide as the Telms is, it isn't for war boats." The ferryman's words came slow and steady, a slight lazy drawl clipping at the end. "Wouldn't be the first I've seen. Likely won't be the last."

The rest of the trek across the Telms went by in a tense silence that never quite broke despite the few attempts from Jun.

Lin tried to see into the distance, squinting and frowning. Even the far shore, much closer than the ship would've been, seemed an undistinguishable blur. He rubbed his eyes with his knuckles and considered what it might take to fix his failing vision. If Denny had worked Inlays into her eyes to restore her natural vision and grant her Sight, he could do something similar, couldn't he?

Denied Bone

"We were safe, for a time. War was a looming threat, but never something that felt inevitable. But of course, it was. Inevitable. Coming for all of Danica well before any generation of Danicans had been born. And it will happen again." —Uncredited Priestess of the Six

The pier on the western bank of the Telms made the old, shoddy one by Riversbend look brand new, and the disgruntled boards underfoot groaned from the weight of the horses and carts. The forest rose above dark hills, much of the light of day wasted and spilled across the Telms's surface. To some, to many most likely, the forest no doubt appeared unwelcoming. The way it loomed timelessly, branches and boughs eager to catch any warmth not wasted across the river. But Lin smiled at the bird calls, clacking of limbs, and rustling of underbrush. And through it all a well-worn path was tread into the soft earth looking every bit like a rough-hewn continuation of the pier. The bank continued to the south and north, thick foliage making it hard to see much of anything except for the slow-moving waters.

"Think you'd seen a river nymph the way you're smilin'," The ferryman said. He laughed and made a little whistling wheeze as he did.

Jun and Carine had moved off to the side of the road, eyes scanning the brush-coated hills and lingering in different directions along the forested backdrop.

"Nymph?" Lin asked.

"You'd know one if you'd spotted one. Though, I s'pose you might not if you hadn't seen one before. Bawdy things. Big-breasted little beauties. Even the men," he cackled and returned to untying the rope he'd moored the ferry with and whistled as he worked.

Lin had expected the man to live on this side of the Telms, but he was already preparing to depart and make the trip back.

As an Escorter it hadn't been uncommon to hear tales meant to scare children, tease men, or explain some local phenomena. But lately— these last few years really— all tales had slowly shifted to warnings of untethered. Humans who moved like animals and brought the stench of ruin and death with them.

But he'd never heard of a nymph. Maybe Denro, or even Tylle, had. He'd have to ask.

"Have you ever seen one?" Lin asked before the man could push his long oar against the bank.

"No, actually. But my grandpa swore he had. And my nan didn't argue with him. Said I'd know it if I ever saw it. Did see a man with horns more than once. Odd that." The man leaned on his oar and pointed a gnarled, sun-darkened finger at the curved northern bank. "Stood as tall as two men and had a rack on him— antlers mind you not like the nymphs— about yay wide." He was slow to move but brought his hands up and squinted at Lin through the wide space he'd formed between them. "Luckily I was in the middle of the river and it's common knowledge spirits and the like don't cross running water."

"Even river nymphs?" Jun asked, coming to stand beside Lin. He wore a huge smile and nudged Lin with his elbow. Apparently, he'd heard it all.

"They're the exception. Can't get to running water, get behind the stone shrouds." The man tapped his nose like Pael so often did when imparting what he felt was valuable information.

"Stone shroud?" Lin asked. Denny had called the low walls that, but, why? They didn't keep *anything* out. Weather or worse. Not much of a shroud if it doesn't hide something or protect it in some way.

"Oh... You'd know one if you saw one!" The ferryman shouted, pushing the boat away from the pier with his oar.

Lin watched the man slowly make his way back across the river. "I think he's seen untethered. Like the ones in the village with the horns. Have... Have you ever seen them?"

"Can't say I have," Jun said, patting Lin's shoulder and turning him around. "But there are many and more things I'm sure I've yet to learn. Like the Elodians' magic for example." Jun chuckled and let his arm drop.

But there *was* more magic. Whatever the broken dagger he'd left in Anya's possession was, there was no doubt in his mind that it was some different form of magic. Capable of cutting right through any and all types of Wieving.

Lin just hadn't wanted to share that with anyone. He stared down at his Bludwieve, the crimson band still twining about his finger in slow serpentine spirals. "As a Physiker, did you ever see things that didn't make sense? That seemed like magic?"

"Ha! All the bloody time. The flowering leaves of the vivanticus plant for instance... Poisonous in most doses, medicinal in others. What is that if not the magic of nature? Or venti seeds. When eaten whole, they are foul, bitter things a person might break a tooth on. But charred, grounded, and inhaled? Suddenly you have something that will ease even the worst fever."

"If you let him continue, you'll never find his tongue stilled."

Jun beamed and nodded at Carine's words. "Few paths I've walked in my life have not been born of necessity. But I do love the pursuit of knowledge. I like to think I'd have made a fine Scholar if joining them had ever been a true option."

"Why wasn't it?" Lin asked.

Carine climbed into her saddle and urged her mount forward a step. She listened, but her shoulders looked tense and she kept scanning the treeline.

"Prish. When we met, we were young and in love. But she was sick, so I studied medicines to aid her. Then she was captured by the Ferrucium and I had to... Well, suffice to say I had to rescue her. She was never the same afterward and that viper Aemun had tainted her somehow. But in the process of saving her, I met Carine and knew I had a larger purpose than just expanding my knowledge. Oh... And raising our child of course."

Before Lin could speak Jun raised a hand and shook his head. "The child, Fenna, was sickly like her mother had been. She passed the summer before the Fall." Jun took a deep breath and continued to shake his head. "I'm sorry. I didn't mean to ruin the mood."

Lin reached out and placed a hand gingerly on Jun's shoulder. Words wouldn't come but Jun seemed to understand and patted the back of Lin's hand twice, lingering on the third strike.

"I'm sorry for your losses," Lin managed after a long moment.

"So you can excuse me when I excite over the small things?" Jun smiled again and looked over his shoulder at Carine. They were the last three near the decrepit dock and the faint glow of torchlight brushed the trees from over the hills.

"I can." In truth, Lin's heart ached for the man. Mellyr wasn't Lin's child, but he couldn't imagine a sickness taking her. And he certainly couldn't imagine being betrayed by the woman he cared about. He pictured Tylle, sitting there with her back against the wall working her Bludwieve in Fallo after she'd saved him. Then lying there, near to death after staving off the Noosemen. But the image truly burned into his mind was of her stabbing Aemun, over and over and over again.

"We better get going before Carine decides to leave us behind for good," Jun said loudly from behind his hand as if he'd intended to whisper.

Lin hoped Tylle was well but more importantly, knowing he was likely to die or truly untether, he hoped she would be willing to reconsider raising Mellyr now that time had distanced her from the pain of her sister's death.

Mellyr deserved a family, someone to look after her when Lin was gone.

Ahead, Carine waited at a crossroads. The north-running road was well-maintained and clear of roots and brush while the west-running path curved off around a low rise of earth that seemed perfect for sheltering from the wind. Wind and worse, considering what they were potentially riding towards.

"West or north?" Lin asked.

Carine shook her head, eyes never settling anywhere for a prolonged stretch. Lin wasn't the only one on edge. As much as the thick forests of Danica felt like home, there was no denying the creaking branches overhanging the road seemed more sinister now than they'd been before. A strong breeze rattled the branches and the slight tang of rainstorm carried through.

"North," Carine finally said.

"North reminds me," Jun started pulling up alongside Lin's mount. "What was Ladrica itself like?"

"Talk and ride," Carine ordered, angling her mount northward as she spoke.

It didn't take long for them to overtake the lone farmer who'd headed this way as soon as departing the ferry. His wagon was bare save for scraps of fluttering tarp and two bales of hay. He barely offered them a glance as they rode past.

"It was cold," Lin said. "Inhospitable, and not just because of the people. Even the children saw me as a monster. Would've killed me if they could've." He thought of little Leo and wondered if the boy had settled into his role with the Fentian Scholars. That boy had been infatuated with Anya up until Lin left, and he couldn't see anything having happened in the last span to change that. He hoped Leo was happy. Or at least happier than he'd been running messages at the fort. "They're taught we're monsters through and through."

"Are they wrong?" Carine asked.

Lin sucked his teeth. He still didn't have an answer for that, not one he fully believed in anyway. Not once when he was an Escorter had he thought Danicans were monsters. Untethered? Absolutely. But he had to hope not all Danicans were doomed to the fate of going mad. There were plenty of elderly Danicans. Azhura for one. Denro. The oldest being some he'd met in his travels as an Escorter. "Of course they are."

"You say that but I haven't heard any other nation of people going mad and violent," Jun said. "It is a feature unique to Danicans."

"Feature?" Carine scoffed.

"I mean in a clinical sense. A trait. Is that better?" Jun said.

Lin shook his head. "I think... I think our people's madness is just harder to hide. Not one group out there has any lesser capacity for violence than we do. Not one."

They rode in silence until only faint moonlight marked their path and when Lin thought they'd stop, Carine urged them onwards. A cold wind rustled the leaves overhead. In many ways the chill air felt like winter's icy claws desperately clutching to keep its hold on Danica, knowing full well its time was past.

Lin yawned and finally, mercifully, Carine waved a hand from in front to slow them. When he dismounted he spotted the game trail she'd likely seen. It was narrow and led to a clearing with knee-high grass. It was wide enough for the three of them and their mounts, though if they'd had a fourth it would've been a tight fit.

Carine made a pit and soon a tiny fire sprung to life. Shadows were cast from the center and danced all around. Owls made their presence known and the steady sounds of small animals skittering through the undergrowth brought Lin comfort. There was something so fierce about the northern parts of Danica. Fierce and *untamed*. His heart sank as his thoughts drifted to Denny. If any person embodied northern Danica, it was her. Wild and fierce and... Lin pulled his knees to his chest and stared at the flames. He would miss her for as long as he lived but he needed to find a way to stop dwelling on it. At least while there were other things he could focus on.

"What can I help with?" Lin asked.

"So near a game trail, wouldn't hurt to see what you might catch," Carine said.

"I'll go. I want to stretch my legs anyway," Jun said. There was a small to the man's soft features and he headed silently down the trail. In two breaths he was gone from view and not a sign nor sound of him made it back to where they rested.

"He seems to be in a mood," Lin said softly. He stared after the shadow of the man until the individual branches and brush melded into one dark, hungry blur. His vision was worsening, no doubt about it. The dark of night made it even worse.

"Black pot, kettle calling," Carine said as she took a seat beside the firepit across from Lin.

"How do you mean?"

"I mean you've been kind, then distant, then irritated. If I didn't know any better I'd think you were one of the most dangerous men I've met."

"Because I'm untethering?" Lin asked. The question came out far angrier than he'd intended.

"Because you clearly don't know how to process your emotions. If you're going mad, that's one thing. But being an ass is an entirely different problem."

If. Lin shook his head. He *was* going mad. Hearing things. Seeing things. And now, losing his sight. Carine was right. His moods seemed to shift nearly as badly as Pael's always had and now that she'd called him out on it, his cheeks flushed and the embarrassment rising within him made him want to lash out. "I never would've had the sort of thoughts I'm having now when I was an Escorter. I'd never have sat here and doubted myself so much."

"Do you think Jun is a happy man?" Carine asked.

The question caught Lin off guard and he turned to stare into the dark forest again, the sound of crickets greeting him in response. "He seems well enough."

"But does he seem happy?"

Lin rested his arms on his knees and shook his head. "He smiles enough."

"I told you, we've lost so many friends. But in a fairly short period, he lost his child, his Bound partner, two dear friends, and countless acquaintances."

It felt wrong tallying up the number of people Lin had lost, but when the numbers came down to it, it was only Margaret and Denny. And any acquaintances from the Ferrucium. But really, it was two people, who on the scale of those he'd known, he'd barely known. "So you're saying he isn't a happy man?"

"I'm saying he's a man pained. But he takes it all, the grief, sorrow, and remorse, and turns it into a weapon. Sometimes that weapon is a blade. Other times it is a shield made of a smile."

Lin frowned at Carine. She didn't share Tylle's abrasive cadence, the tone and bite to her words that were meant to batter Lin's resolve into belief. No, Carine had a calming cadence, a rhythm meant to soothe but not convince. "You're saying..."

"I'm saying that perhaps you're untethering. Maybe you'll go mad and—" She laughed and shook her head, bringing her hands up to the sides of her skull and splaying out her fingers. "—put antlers to your head like an unhinged monster. But maybe... just maybe you're growing old and your body has already been through so much. Your mind too. Either way I think sometimes saying you're untethering is just a fancy way of saying you're losing yourself. The good news is you can always follow the thread back to who you used to be. *Always*. And perhaps your foul mood feeds itself. Give us a chance. I know we aren't Denny. But neither are you. And Jun won't say it, but you and I can both admit we'd each prefer the other. Fair?"

"Fair." Lin nodded.

"Now, let's talk about sweeter things while we wait. How is the child, Mellyr?" Carine leaned back on her hands and looked up to the sky.

"It wasn't until you came into the baths when I was with Denny, but I'd forgotten you'd been there, helping me clean Mellyr," Lin whispered. "But last I saw her, she was good. Safe. Loved."

"If it were my child, I'd have done the same as you. Torn the world apart to get her back."

"I... I'm still not sure I made the right choice. But she's with the Scholars now and well cared for. She's a princess of sorts. Promised to the Ladrican King as a sort of peace treaty. And she's got the blood of Cunning Velkath running through her veins if Azhura is to be believed."

"A princess. Sort of like a duke's daughter, but bigger, eh?" Carine looked surprised. "That Aemun... hard to put a pin on him. Didn't like him, but the man nearly seemed like he could see into the future, no? Those last few days on the road, when you were following us, he seemed like a man condemned. Like he knew he wasn't making it out of that exchange unharmed."

Even thinking about Aemun was enough to make Lin worry he'd hear his mocking voice, so he ignored the path Carine was trying to lead the conversation down. "Do you think I made the right call with Mellyr? Leaving her behind."

"Absolutely. The road is no place for a child even if we don't find Duke Errond's estates ransacked and swarming with untethered."

Lin chewed at the inside of his cheek and his stomach rumbled as he hoped Jun would return soon. "That's why I left her. That's why Tylle didn't want to stay with her and me. I think. I don't know."

"Tylle is a strange one. I couldn't get a real feel for her and besides her going off and doing something for Grovetender when she was younger, I don't know her story. Erias never did tell me and Tylle was as tight-lipped as Prish though her lips weren't Stitched shut."

"She was a priestess. Or that's what she claimed. And she told me about the histories of Danica, which at this point all seem to have been true."

Carine clicked her tongue and rose to her feet. She stretched her arms and hinged at her hips before crossing her arms. "I never said I didn't believe any of that. What I don't get is where she learned it from. I don't know if you've noticed, but Danica isn't exactly a repository for ancient secrets. Even if she learned it from traveling and speaking with old priestesses, how did she learn to do so in the first place?"

It was hard not to feel defensive, but Carine brought up good points. Tylle *could've* learned it from the Scholars, but he knew she hadn't. That meant either someone high within the Ferrucium, like Aemun or someone else with the lost knowledge had shared it with her.

Lin rose with her as he heard shifting from the path Jun went down. In moments, Jun appeared with one of the largest rabbits Lin had ever seen hanging lifeless at his side. He smiled warmly, then pushed the dead hare into Lin's arms.

"Skin it, cook it, and wake me when you're done." Jun pat Lin on the arm and whispered something to Carine before he laid down with his back to the opposite side of the fire.

Jun had moved so quickly that Lin hadn't had a chance to react other than grabbing the dead creature and mumbling as Jun lay down.

Lin sighed and started working on the task at hand. Maybe he *wasn't* going mad, maybe these two could become friends. He watched Jun's heavy breaths turn into soft snores as he peeled the hide from the hare. *Maybe.* If only it really was as simple as laying a thread and following it back. Lin looked down at his Bludwieve.

Or maybe it's all hopeless, Escorter. Maybe you're a fool who bit off more than he could chew and now chokes on the repercussions of it all.

Lin nicked his finger as he sliced at the remnants of the hare's fatty skin. He hadn't known many of the bastards to have fat the way this one did.

Denied Hate

"Let them wail about inequality. Let them rail about their rights. But let them not infringe on our land or people. I'd rather die ten times over than let a tainted blood Danican sip the marrow from the bones of good Ladrican people." —King Lodram

Carine raised a hand to slow them. Lin had been paying more attention to the fog clouds than the road, so to see the short, knee-high stone walls of one of the northern villages surprised him—a stone shroud, whatever that actually meant. Silence carried, not even the clucking of chickens breaking the dense, rolling cloud.

Taking no time, Carine slid from her mount and knelt beside the wall.

Lin did the same, taking his sword from the strap near the horse's rear and following to crouch beside her. He tried to picture this village on the map, but like most of these small, secluded places he wasn't sure if he'd visited it before. Maybe seeing the layout would bring it back to him, but he couldn't be sure as he knelt and smelled the mossy stones and fog.

Jun was last to move but did so nearly as silently as Denny would have and was to them in a blink. He gestured at the wall and put a finger to his lips.

Like most of the knee-high walls dotting the northern villages, this one was composed of flat stones, gray in color, with lichen climbing to the top from the forest floor. In the near-evening haze, the top of the wall glistened.

Lin pressed closer and narrowed his eyes. *Blood.* The wall was coated in *blood*.

"If this is the work of untethered, I didn't think they'd be this close to Elmore's holdings. We aren't even in Errond's territory yet." Carine's face scrunched and she leaned closer to the wall.

But that wasn't right. They'd even crossed the river already, massacring the village near enough to the Ferrucium that it could've been meant as a message. The untethered didn't care.

For a moment it seemed Carine might sniff the stone wall, but she pulled away and shook her head.

Not a sound carried from the village and even the surrounding wood was silent. Not a twig snap, leaf crunch, or babble of a brook. *Fallo*. But Fallo had been different, stained with the scent of rust and death sharp on the air. That's what made this scene all the worse, there hadn't been any indication of—

A lone figure appeared within the village's boundary, a shaded lantern casting an arc of light toward them. The figure slowed to a stop, near enough that his hard features clarified. "If you're thieves, we've nothin'. Save the arrows aimed your way. State'cher business skulkin' about."

Lin rose despite Jun's hand trying to keep him crouched. "We're about the business of the Dukes... and the Ferrucium if that matters to anyone here."

"Sure, sure," The man said. His hair looked like it hadn't been brushed in years and dirt caked his clothes. "But what're ya' doin' skulkin'?"

Carine rose, her hands up with her palms out. "We saw the lack of lights and the blood smeared along the wall and worried we were heading into trouble."

The man nodded and squinted as he raised the lantern a bit. "Blood on the stone shroud, eh?"

Lin looked down at the wall. Nearly thirty years, most of which he'd spent as an Escorter, and he'd never know these useless walls to have a name. He shook his head. If he used that as an excuse for things he hadn't known, he'd die a fool. What he did know was that every single village he'd visited in this stretch of Danica had one of the low, easily passable walls. "What does blood on the wall mean?"

"We've been marked. Not that it means much to the Reds. Haven't seen a Red come through in some time. Or Duke's men for that matter." The man shuffled a few steps forward and opened the hood on the lantern wider. The light cast shone six individuals, all with weapons, but only two with bows. "Might as well come in. I'm... Alderman Joff."

From behind the line of gathered men and women, children and some of the more elderly folk appeared. If Dreckinsburg had looked like a symbol of survival, this village seemed like one content with a slow, steady death.

Try as he might, he still couldn't place this village on the map. As small as it was, it likely *wasn't* on any of the maps. Though Creekside had been, hadn't it? "Alderman Joff," Lin bowed slightly. If Lyre's Alderman taught him anything, it was to give more grace to others, even if they don't seem to give it to themselves. "Does your village have a name?"

"Many," Joff said dismissively. He waved the lantern and frowned. "Why hasn't your friend gotten up?"

Lin glanced at Jun who shook his head.

"He's injured. Took a tumble earlier today. Do you have a physiker?" Carine kept her voice even, but with her hand at her side she made a series of gestures that Lin didn't understand. Jun motioned back, so clearly it was a way to communicate.

"We do."

Noone in either group moved. Hard, tired faces stared back at Lin. They looked hungry. Exhausted. *Worn-down*. If any of them had Stitches or Inlays, he'd think they were all untethered by their appearances. Even some of the children wore dull, vacant looks. Velkath's sigil danced in Lin's periphery and there was a scent of something sweet in the air. Over-ripened fruit.

Carine nodded. "This is your one chance to tell us the truth."

"What do ya' mean?" Joff spat.

"Are you bandits?"

Lin blinked. His eyesight was worsening at distances, but he doubted he would mistake a group of frail, worn-down villagers for bandits. Then again. All Alderman he'd ever met were proud of it. Proud of their villages all in their own way. There was no symbol of office hanging from the man's thin, dirt-crusted neck. Was this what the North had come down to? Bandits taking whole villages?

Perhaps it wasn't untethered wreaking havoc but *people*. Normal people. Somehow that thought brought a shiver down Lin's spine.

"Was born and raised here in Tellmer," Joff said, swinging the lantern around to shine brightly on the others gathered. "We had a hard winter and..." the Alderman blinked and wiped his eyes with the back of his arm. "And look. We're just tryin' ter survive same as any others. Either come into Tellmer or be on yer way. Don't have the patience to play games. For all we know, you're the bandits."

Lin moved past the stone wall. He could practically feel Carine's eyes boring into the back of his skull. Nobody had time for games and Lin certainly didn't have the patience for this odd stalemate. Either these people would attack him and pay the price, or they'd give him a place to rest for the night. There were of course in-betweens but anything would be better than the tense stand-off they were facing. It brought back memories of the time Tylle stopped the Ferrucium Evaluators along the roadside.

Jun rose with Carine's aid and limped along into the village. "Physiker?"

"Well... unfortunately I lied."

Lin tensed, but the man's voice wasn't the slick tone of a man who'd tricked someone. He didn't grin or give any indication he'd played them.

The lantern lowered as the man coughed and said, "Guinn, Tellmer's physiker left moons back."

"A physiker abandoned you?" Carine asked.

More people than the Alderman spoke up, cursing the physiker who'd left. There were very few villages Lin had visited that *didn't* have a learned man. And of those that didn't, they tended to have wise men and women familiar enough with herbs to claim the title.

"Is there a place we might rest?"

The villagers moved aside and the walk to the home was short but tense. Not one person met Lin's stare, not one whispered a hello. All of them, old and young, watched Lin from the corner of their eyes the way a cornered animal might.

Inside the home was mostly empty and smelled of stale dust and sweat. "I wouldn't wish my worst enemy a night in this place," Lin whispered. The place was more a shack than a home and seemed constructed by the same builder who'd made the shed he and Tylle took refuge in at Fallo.

"They're odd, no?" Jun asked. Once inside he quit his feigned limp and shook his head. "And you," he walked to Lin and shoved his shoulder. "Walking in. What if they had a trap?"

"Better to spring it on our terms than let them catch us unaware."

"Shh. Come here and lower your voices. We wait a stretch, then leave. None of us sleep. Try not to even blink if you can help it."

"Agreed," Lin whispered. "As if the blood wasn't bad enough, there is something strange going on beyond that."

"Wow," Jun said with a grin.

"What?" Lin asked.

"I just don't know if I've ever met someone as perceptive as you."

Carine exhaled and shushed Lin's irritated response as she nodded to the door. In moments a knock sounded and, without waiting for a response from within, the door opened. Alderman Joff shuffled in, his lamp down by his waist as he led a petite woman.

"This is—"

The woman pushed past him and folded her arms as she took in the three of them. Her hair was cut shorter than the Alderman's and looked better cared for, if barely. She didn't look clean, not the way an average person would, but streaks along her face and arms made it look like she'd at least tried to wipe herself clean. A pocketed apron was tied tightly around her torso and she patted the pouches uneasily. "Name's Leisha. The closest thing this village has left to a physiker. So what's the matter?"

Jun had, on their entry, laid down along the far wall. He held his stomach and groaned as Carine answered for him. "His stomach is killing him something fierce."

"I thought you said he took a tumble," Joff said. He raised the lantern and squinted toward them.

Carine nodded and looked up with such a sincere expression that Lin would've certainly believed her if it were up to him. Eyes large, bottom lip quivering. She even brushed a strand of hair behind her ear on the unshaved side. *Terrifying.* "He did, and since then he's had a limp and he's clutched his stomach like he's worried it might leave him entirely."

Leisha sniffed the air and hunched closer to Jun than seemed necessary. "Don't smell like shit, which is a start. I can mix him up something for the pain, to ease it that is, and should be able to help keep his insides, inside."

"Oh!" Carine exclaimed. "That would be wonderful."

The Alderman and the woman exchanged a glance, the former giving a slight nod to the latter. Then he wheeled around, lantern blinding Lin for a brief moment. "I'll be back shortly."

Lin's instincts told him to follow the man, but boots sounded on the gravel path outside and two of the younger villagers stood by with weapons lowered. Sent to watch them, likely. He moved to rest against the wall in the sight of the villagers stationed to watch him. Lazily, he let his hand fall to rest on the sword's pommel.

As tense as the situation was, with the not-quite-a-physiker tending to the not-quite-ailing-patient, Lin was thankful to at least be dealing with normal people. No Ladricans. No Noosemen or untethered. Just bandits at worst or scared town-folk at best.

A horn sounded in the distance, so far off that it could've been imagined. But everything approaching the village had been so silent. Unnaturally so.

Blood coated *the wall. Do you truly think they're* only *scared town folk?*

Lin twitched, bending his neck, and focused on the soft conversation being held across the room from him. It wasn't often that the voice did anything but belittle him.

Jun's eyes had grown wide as Leisha crushed various ingredients— mostly wild herbs by the scent now in the room— she'd pulled from her pouch. Focused on her task, she seemed not to notice the hand signs Jun made to Carine.

Lin yawned, stretched, and sidled up alongside Carine where she knelt adjacent to Jun. She shook her head but said nothing. He shifted and tapped his foot several times before looking at the pulverized mush of fragrant weeds. The smell was familiar. Over-sweet.

Carine nodded at Jun, tapped the side of Lin's leg, and nodded at the woman. Whatever notice she had attempted to give him hadn't been enough as Carine and Jun moved in a blur. Jun grabbed the woman's hands, stilling her process, and with nearly no resistance twisted her arms and forced the mushy concoction of weeds and herbs into the woman's mouth.

It was all so swift that all Lin could think to do was move closer.

Leisha grunted, twisting in Jun's firm grasp. She was working her jaw, desperately trying not to swallow the mess. Dark green saliva dripped from the corners of her mouth. Her groans were muffled and if not for the worried look on Carine's face as she helped hold the woman, it would've seemed like the two were murdering her. Leisha groaned and convulsed. The heels of her feet slammed hard on the wood-paneled flooring and Lin moved to grab her legs.

Convulsions turned to twitches, verdant ooze into a murky sea-green foam, and eventually, she stilled.

"She wanted to kill me. Recognized the rusch leaves right away." Jun twitched and wiped his hand on her apron. "Bad for a person in the correct doses, let alone what she was trying to muddle for me."

Carine rose and leaned to the side to glance out the doorway. "We need to go."

"I'll get the horses," Lin whispered.

"Assuming they didn't kill them," Jun growled. "Meat is meat. No idea what they had planned for me if I was actually injured. Think... They assumed I was in pain and weak. I take what she mixed for me and start convulsing and die. They offer to burn me for you, and when you go, who knows what they'd do with my corpse."

"Monsters," Lin managed. It wasn't that he doubted them capable, it just seemed too plausible. A pang of worry stabbed him. What if this was the current state of all the small hovels and villages? He couldn't be sure Nebra was safe in Lyre.

"No. We move as a trio. Be ready. Wicked Tel'Myr can take me if any of us are dying here to these bastards," Carine said.

All of it could've been speculation but it quickly became clear it didn't matter. As they moved from the shack, the two posted guards moved at once, as if they'd been expecting trouble. Unwieldy, untrained, sword chops flashed at Lin and Carine.

Whatever the guards' goals had been fell short as the weapons broke against Lin's Blade. The metal sizzled and cracked before shattering into a spray of sparks. Both attackers snarled and cursed as his Blade drew a dark, straight line across their throats. They choked as they stumbled, rage wilting to shock as it bled from them. A shout carried through the night and the village was upon them, crooked arrows sailing through the air. Most went wide, but Jun broke any that cut close. Alderman Joff was visible in the dark, his lantern painting arcing sections of the village in splashes of dull orange light.

It seemed a sea of darkness, save for several torch flames that sputtered in the cool wind. The fog hadn't fled and obscured the darkness beyond the stone shrouds further.

Carine took the lead, passing Jun, and shot toward the horses. She threw two Wefts, one each at the attackers foolish enough to push her direction.

Arrows thumped dully into the dirt around them and Jun continued slicing them with sharp, precise Wefts.

Seven villagers had already died, counting Leisha, but those that remained pushed towards them with fervor.

An eighth villager fell to Lin's Blade as her poor, worn sword met his magic and failed where Ferrucium steel would've held.

"Why?" Lin shouted. It wasn't that he expected any of them to answer, even if he wished they would. Ladricans, he understood. Untethered, he understood. But Danican citizens attacking each other? All for what?

"If... if we don't... we all get punished," the eighth attacker he'd struck gasped.

Lin slowed, dragging his feet. He wasn't sure if Carine and Jun had heard the dying woman's words, but whatever she meant confirmed his feelings. There was no way the Danica he knew would see citizens attacking each other like this. He clenched his jaw.

Carine and Jun had left a trail of death between the shack they'd started at and the knee-high stone wall.

Lin pressed ahead, rushing past dead and dying villagers, pulling up alongside Jun as he ran.

"See that?" Jun asked.

Before Lin could reply, Jun was gone. The short man had raced forward far faster than they'd already been dashing. Lin only saw the brief, dying outline of the man's visible Inlays.

Then Lin was to the horses and Carine.

Alderman Joff was hunched beside the stone wall sniveling, the lantern shaking with each intolerable, shuddering breath. In, shake. Out, shake. But despite the sniveling and tears, Lin felt no mercy. Not a drop. Even if Joff had anticipated something nefarious from the three of them that didn't mean he was allowed to attack them and certainly not poison Jun. How many travelers had been waylaid by these monsters?

"P-p-please..." Joff gasped.

"Why?" Carine asked. Her voice had an unsettling distinct lack of emotion. She had no intention of sparing the man. And Lin agreed. Whatever the reason, forced or not, "necessary" or not, he'd *never* do to someone else what they'd tried to do to Jun.

The horses hadn't been lamed or killed. Not that it made a difference in Carine's actions as she shifted to lean over Joff. Her forearms tensed and it looked like she was a sneeze away from taking the man's head from his shoulders.

Part of the reason Lin was so irritated was a touch irrational admittedly, but it was the fact that he'd decided to quit judging people as much as he had back in Lyre... And this bastard ended up being more than deserving of the cross-judgment.

"Tell us," Lin said. "Why should we spare you?"

"We—"

Jun jumped from the darkness. His Inlays were barely visible through the shawl of blood he now wore. And he formed the closest thing to a crater Lin had seen caused by a single man. The unfortunate monster under his foot writhed, coughed up rust-colored blood and stilled. It looked like most true untethered often did, stringy patches of hair nearly falling from their scalp. Gray skin was highlighted and accented by strings of nonsensical Stitches. It struggled in vain, a lone arm clawing ineffectually up at Jun's boot. Antlers studded the flesh on either side of its head and Velkath's Sigil was emblazoned across its torso.

"Th-them, those monsters. They've been attacking us. Raiding. But if w-we put out an offering t-they leave us be." Alderman Joff sobbed as he spoke, his beady eyes darting from Carine to Lin, and back. Often if a man has to search for mercy, he should close his eyes for that still darkness is the closest thing to mercy he'll find.

Carine didn't draw out the man's end, as she slit his throat in a single decisive motion. She took his lantern, unhooded it, and threw it against the nearest home's thatched roof. The thatch caught aflame quickly but the fire was slow to spread. "And that one?" she asked as she nodded at the untethered.

"A scout of some sort," Jun growled. "Tried running from me, routed it back this way. Seems to be a basic mind-addled monster."

Lin moved beside Jun and looked down at the monster's hand. Its fingers curled like gnarled roots and it clutched uselessly trying to gouge lines into Jun's boot with broken, jagged nails. "Do either of you know why it is that every single one of these monsters I've encountered has had a Bludwieve?"

Jun shook his head and as the monster tried raking his flesh, he pressed down with his heel. A muted snap sounded and the untethered's arm dropped and its groaning ceased.

"If this village is any indicator of what to expect, I think we may need to consider the chance that the untethered are organized. At least in some small way." Carine mounted her horse and nodded at the road that cut through the village. "Let's go."

Lin stared at her. It seemed she'd ignored his question, but perhaps she was just eager to get away from this awful place. *This terrible place.*

Denied Blood

"War is the path we've always been on. From our first, forced breaths to our faltering, final ones, it is the dust kicked up from the path of war that we breathe."—Denro

Tellmer didn't make sense— not the attack, stone shroud, or untethered lurking in the forest. None of it did.

Lin had ridden in silence, mulling over what it all might mean. An untethered scout? Was that what had attacked him in Lyre so many moons ago? But that beast hadn't had horns or Velkath's Sigil shining across its chest.

Northern Danica was wild and untamed compared to the central stretch and the farmlands and sprawling Duchies of the east. The wild aspect was what made him fall in love with his escorting role— that and the idea of helping people. But now, that same raw wildness was what allowed oddities like this to occur. Untethered were organizing. Following some false king.

Something larger was at play. From the coordinated attacks, the scout-like untethered, and the use of the stone walls as ways to mark certain villages, something was wholly wrong across Danica. And it had taken Lin this long to realize it. Or maybe he'd always known. He had listened to Tylle after all. After she saved him back in Fallo. Lin rubbed his left hand's knuckles, the comforting thrum of the Stitches easing his mind.

And you never thought it was odd that she was woundless? And... Why was it that she just then formed a Bludwieve? I've known you're a fool, but it seems you're finally starting to realize it too.

Lin drew his hand away from his Stitches as if they were hot coals burning his fingertips. Since they'd left Tellmer, he'd seen Velkath's Sigil everywhere. He'd look to the clouds and notice the brilliant lines drifting on the winds. His sigil was formed by branch and bough and the absence of them. Even the ground conspired against him, the few ruts in the road looking everything like the symbol snaking up from the raised, ruined earth. At this point not even closing his eyes saved him from seeing the symbol. Any semblance of sleep saw it branding his dreams, marking him and everyone he cared for in the fierce golden glow. So sleep came and went in fitful bursts.

Now they approached another village, this one blanketed in the warm rays of sun shining through the treetops, and Lin expected they'd go wide around it. But Carine dismounted and walked forward with a straight back.

Lin yawned and hesitantly followed her lead. The path was silent, the clipping notes of songbirds carrying in the early morning light.

Unlike Tellmer, the soft quiet wasn't an ominous lack of noise, but a familiar serenity found only between the northern villages.

Soon, Jun was beside them nonplussed and covered in dried blood that started near his navel and stained his entire torso. When he caught Lin frowning Jun nodded in agreement. "Why do you think I'm eager to stop? Might mean a bath." Jun raised his eyebrows and matched Lin's expression.

Fair. But still they had enough provisions to make it further to some of the villages Lin was familiar with. Like Lyre.

"This will be a good test to see if all the villages here have been affected evenly," Carine said. She kept her voice low and her shoulders back. "And we will get to the bottom of this."

Confidence dripped from her like the beaded dew from a flower in a field. Natural, easy, the sort of stuff that made a leader. As much as it seemed she and Jun didn't like Lin, he couldn't help but respect the woman. But there was a chance the ghost of Aemun's voice echoing in the cavern of his mind was making him paranoid. Tylle had saved him after all, why doubt her just because of an offhand comment from Carine, a woman who barely seemed to tolerate him? *No.* That wasn't fair. She was a leader, he'd just considered as much and she treated him like a captain would a footsoldier.

Lin stifled another yawn and scratched his chin. His eyes darted from the trees to the clouds and finally came to rest on the ground just in front of his feet. Everything he looked at threatened to pull his focus.

The road narrowed until it became a path, weeds and brush encroaching on the edges in clumps that the horses eagerly sniffed. Nebra would have stayed more on task. Though, there was a good chance she'd grown fat and happy in the care of Alderman Pryor. If anyone had earned a good, deserved rest, it was Nebra.

Ahead, the stone shroud came into view. Flowering vines bearing petals colored like fresh Bindings hung from the top of it, striking in the sun's light. Lin squinted to be sure he wasn't imagining the vibrant hues. The vines were a dark scarlet, like veins from some creature too large to possibly exist. *Or the intestines of people, strung about like banners and stabbed through with Bindings shaped like flowers.* Lin shuddered at the thought and his stomach turned.

A breeze blew and the petals shifted. Delicate. Bindings couldn't— Bindings usually didn't move like that. They approached nearer and Lin's breaths calmed. Flowers. Just flowers and vines, beautiful but not Bindings.

"Amazing," Jun whispered. "For a moment I feared they were something worse."

Carine grunted and knowing he hadn't been alone in his worries eased him further.

A cloud shifted and the sun caught fully on the petals, adding to their luster. The leaves rustled, revealing intermittently placed deer skulls. Antlers and all.

As they passed the wall, Lin let his fingers brush the nearest flower. It didn't hum and felt as delicate as it looked. But on closer inspection, unlike certain mosses and the honey-caps, these flowers didn't glow as Bindings did.

A well, coated in the same vines and flowers, rested in the center of the village. Nine homes, including what appeared to be a physiker's medicinary and a House of the Six—though it was missing the stained glass windows most possessed— were spaced out around the rolling green turf. Most of the northern villages had an ancient feel to them like they'd been there since the founding of Danica. However here, some of the wood used for the buildings smelled freshly cut and still looked a bit green in some places. The paths were used, but not worn aside from the main one cutting through the village. A newly constructed settlement then.

Loud enough to wake the dead, a horn bellowed. It was pitched low and carried for a long moment.

"The lungs on that bastard, eh?" Jun said with a smile.

Lin grunted and looked around. Villagers had come out and one middle-aged woman carrying a basket of linen approached them, eyes narrowed and hard jaw set. She had a slightly hooked nose and a streak of gray hair that framed her face. "Welcome to Vole," she said.

"Vole?" Carine asked.

The woman nodded and searched their faces. Her eyes lingered on Jun and brushed a loose strand of hair behind her ear. In moments a tall, tired-looking man approached. He looked to be about the size of a house and moved like it. A horn so large it had to be carved from a beast as large as the man, dangled from a worn leather strap around his chest. "Can we help you strangers with something?"

Carine recounted the events in the village prior, leaving out the fact that they'd set a home to flame.

Lin half-heartedly listened, watching the villager's faces. They looked horrified, concerned, and then as if they might be sick. Then, they explained who they were. The basket-holding woman was Anne and the large man was her cousin Burt. She was more or less an Alderman, though they hadn't held any elections and as of yet, had paid no tithes. More than one person eyed him and when he looked down and feigned to brush dirt from his tunic he knew it was due to the Ferrucium clothes he wore.

It was as if he was fated to never feel comfortable again. Didn't matter if his Inlays were covered or bare, or what clothes he wore. Lin couldn't feel welcome. Not as Velkath's Sigil flickered between the peoples' hard expressions. Eventually, they'd stare at him for being a gangly, gray-skinned untethered. Lin licked his teeth and stared at the ground.

"So that's how Vole came to be. Duke sent no aid. We grew tired of fending off attacks at Dreckinsburg and found a path to build our own little haven. No attacks. No threats of attack. We've got a river not too far, enough fields for the goats, and hunting is pretty good," Anne said. She'd sat her basket down at some point and now gestured to each of the things she mentioned.

"Sounds nice," Lin said.

"It is." Burt scratched his chin. "And there are enough of us to stop an attack if it were to happen." The man shifted as he spoke and showed the large ax slung over his back.

"Right—" Anne was interrupted as a group of five children chasing a chicken rushed past them. As they ran the children half-hummed, half-sang a melody. When they noticed who it was they rushed past, they nearly all tripped over each other to get back to Burt. The large man knelt down and half-heartedly fought them off as more than one of them tried to lift the horn hanging from his chest.

"Children, children please," Burt said with a chuckle.

Lin watched silently. He'd likely never see Mellyr reach that age. Never hear her first words or see her walk on her own. If he kept worrying the inside of his mouth he was bound to make it raw but he couldn't help it. All he could do was hope to make Danica a place fit for her to grow in.

"Where is the river you mentioned?" Jun asked, waving at his torso.

"Small creek more-like, just up the western path. Don't stray far though, wolves haven't been the kindest in the area," Anne said. She certainly looked worried as she spoke, but anyone would if they'd just noticed the copious amount of dried blood coating the man.

Jun's excuse to leave was a good one, and Lin didn't blame him. He'd lost a child after all, and seeing the group playing couldn't be anything but painful.

Carine stared after him with a sympathetic smile on her face. "Have you seen any soldiers passing through? Or perhaps a woman about my height and a much shorter man?"

"He'd have been wearing a hat far larger than necessary for his size," Lin added. He gestured, bringing his hands wide around his head.

Burt and Anne shared a look and both shook their heads.

"Can't say we've seen anyone come through here recently. Certainly hadn't experienced anything like what you're saying. But it sounds like you had a time of it." Anne picked up her basket and waved a hand, shooing off the children. After a moment, they listened and rushed away in a fit of giggles.

Lin stared at the basket. At the woven reeds that made it and the linen within.

Anne shifted it to her other hip and cleared her throat. "What I mean by that, is if you three need a place to stay, our church has more than enough space to house travelers for a night. We've got meat to cook from the latest hunt and I'm sure the children would enjoy stories of adventure, if you've any to tell."

A kind offer. But something about the village had begun nagging him as much as Tellmer's people had. He glanced over his shoulder at the knee-high wall. "I wouldn't say no at a chance at prayer."

"And Velkath wouldn't listen even if you did," Anne said, her voice hushed.

Carine nodded and smiled. "You believe in the old ways?"

"When the new Gods fail us, why not give ear to the old?" Burt asked. He'd risen to his full height and stretched, looking everything like an exhausted bear that had missed his chance to hibernate.

"If we do end up staying, I'd hate to think we were a burden... Could I help with anything? Folding more linens perhaps?" Carine offered.

Anne returned Carine's smile and leaned over to her, covering her mouth but not speaking quietly enough to hide her words. "You can tell me all about the shaved-head man in your company."

"C'mon, we'll leave them to it and I'll show you the church."

They left the horses grazing at the front of the village and Lin followed just behind the large man.

The village might have been recently built, but for the most part, it felt like all the rest. Something about it was just as wild, just as— They rounded the corner and Lin saw a patch of burned earth, charred logs of a pyre stark against the otherwise verdant backdrop.

"Ah. Wounded before Vole was founded. Peace like ours comes at a cost, not one paid in blood but in privacy and seclusion. We don't have a real physiker and couldn't aid them as the infection spread. We prayed of course, but it seems all manner of Gods are selfish at the best of times."

"Well said," Lin said, staring after the pyre as they walked past it. With everything he'd learned about Mellyr's bloodline, he wasn't sure that he believed in *any* Gods. Not the Faceless Six or Velkath's kin, or... Anything. He licked his lips and hung his head.

"Can I ask something?" Burt slowed as they approached what looked to be a House of the Six despite the missing glass. More of those beautiful vines crept along its exterior, clinging to the sides of it and trellising up the slanted roof. Fewer flowers bloomed on these, but those that did were so vibrant that Lin's breath hitched in his chest.

Burt followed his gaze and nodded. "Never seen them myself before either. Anne says they're a blessing. Helps keep us and Vole protected."

"I've traveled all over Danica and I've never seen flowers quite like those. Or the deep red vines they rest upon...."

"Hmm. Strange times we live in. Are you... Are you actually a Red? A Ferrucium soldier, I mean."

It was likely unintentional but the man had rested his hand on the strap his ax hung from and had bladed his stance a bit. Burt was missing two fingers from the wide hand, right at the knuckle.

"Honestly? I don't know. I was. I still think they can do more good than harm, but..." Lin raised his hands and dropped them. "I didn't know things had gotten so bad that our people had to vacate their homes and start anew." Which wasn't entirely true. He had witnessed an untethered assault on Dreckinsburg. He'd been hearing reports before he escorted Aemun and Margaret.

"We all lose ourselves sometimes... But I've found faith. And you look like the sort that could use with some belief. And if I can be saved, anyone can." Burt let go of the strap, the full fingers left to him strumming across his chest as he offered an exhausted smile.

Of all the people he thought might try to persuade him into faith, Burt hadn't looked the type. The man hummed, the same odd-noted tune the children had done. He turned and opened the church doors.

It smelled like fresh-cut wood, and a cloyingly sweet scent hung in the air alongside more of the vines worked into the trestles of the ceiling. They draped in woven patterns the length of Lin's forearm and only had one flower a piece. Where a House of the Six would have stained glass showing the six aspects of man, this building had walls with carved cutouts in patterns eerily similar to Velkath's Sigil that allowed for light and a steady breeze to enter.

Lin slowed his steps as he noticed the altar at the front. Candles lined its edges, wax build-up at the base attesting to their use. Centered on the raised top was a skull similar to the ones that rested on the short stone wall. Stripped of flesh and made white by the sun, with antlers as large as he'd seen. Each horn had six points and thin strips of scarlet ivy draped through them. It might have been beautiful if not for the way the tendril snaked through, like a reminder of the Ladrican's heraldry eating at the carcass of what was Danica. No. Even with that thought eating at him, there was something else nibbling at the edges of his mind.

The hanging vines shifted with the breeze as if the building breathed. And the wooden floorboards creaked with each of Burt's steps.

The large man rested an uneasy hand on Lin's shoulder. "Nice looking, eh? Still can't believe we managed all this," Burt whispered.

"The church?" Lin asked, keeping his eyes on the empty sockets of the fleshless skull. "Or Vole?"

"Both." Burt chuckled. He squeezed Lin's shoulder, nodded, and looked around. It seemed the big man had assumed Lin's apparent unease was due to reverence. "Well... If you want to grab that end, we'll move these pews aside and give you three a place to lay."

They worked silently, the pews lighter than the thick carved legs suggested. When it was said and done two pews a piece were lined along the side walls.

"It's Burt, right? Who exactly do you worship?" Lin nodded at the altar and waved a hand at the cut-outs that gave an obscured view of the children running outside.

"Velkath." Burt furrowed his brow.

"Of course," Lin said as he feigned a smile. "I figured."

Lin unloaded his pack from the horse, watching the villagers the entire time. Carine seemed at ease speaking with Anne and even managed to look natural hanging linens on a line. She smiled and waved when she caught Lin staring.

By the time evening fell, Lin's mood had soured sufficiently enough that he stayed within the church as Jun and Carine mingled with the villagers. If there was nothing going on here, then they'd wasted a day they could have spent traveling. If there *was* something, then these people hid it well enough.

Jun stumbled in, cheeks flush. Someone, likely Anne, called out his name and he giggled in the doorway as he turned and waved. Then he fell back, chuckling the whole way down as he let the door shut.

"You're drunk?" Lin leaned up and glowered at the man.

"You're a sourpuss," Jun yelled louder.

As he did, he raised a finger to his lips and seemed to sober up from the floor, shaking his head. He made his way to Lin, not standing up entirely. He smelled of strong drink, and his eyes were a touch bloodshot, but his actual breath barely had a hint of odor. "Here is what we know and what we've surmised.

"They haven't lied to us. They all came from various villages and there are no signs of attacks, scouts, or violence taking place on this land. They are enamored with Carine, but there is someone they venerate. A traveler that they say is Velkath Reborn.

Lin tensed. He couldn't recall telling Carine and Jun about that specific moniker.

"And before you say anything, I know how strange that sounds, but it is what we've gleaned."

Jun straightened his posture a bit and crawled to his bedroll. "Carine will tell us what she'd like to do when she joins us."

Velkath Reborn. The Horned King. Lin shifted and swallowed through the tightness in his throat. The antlered skulls, the Sigils etched into the walls. How could a man, revered as a God or not, be reborn? And if Velkath were reborn, what did that mean of the man's lineage running through Mellyr? Through *Aemun*.

The door thudded open and Carine stepped in.

Lin flinched and formed a Weft that hummed with taut energy.

"We're good for now," Carine said, lowering her voice. "But you look terrible. Have you been closed off in here all day?"

Lin broke the Weft, the magic glimmering like pollen from the bright fluorescent flowers on the vines above. "If things are good, I don't know why we've stayed."

"Because," her voice had gone so low she was whispering. "We have a lead. But you have to remain calm."

"Calm?" Lin asked. He did his best to match her tone but the more placid she acted the more worked up he felt.

Carine nodded and signed a string of things to Jun who returned it. Them and that damned language he didn't understand. If they trusted him, why did they keep things from him?

Lin laid on his back and glared up at the lone flower dangling above him like a star plucked and placed on a vine to hang in this church. Every time it felt like they were coming together, understanding each other, these two found new ways to drive him away. Did they not want him on this journey? Did nobody want him? He was the Hero of the Fingers and they treated him like some poor tagalong, not worthy of knowing anything. A failure.

Delayed Hope

"Good men aren't always the ones who make it to the end. Sometimes, they die. Sometimes, it's horrible. But always, they leave behind those who loved them. I'd like to think he was well loved." —Alderman Pryor of Lyre

Lin jolted awake at the sound of the bellowing horn. Low and long it cried out. *Burt.* Lin rose, wiping the sleep from his eyes. He'd only fallen asleep to spite the others and his dreams had been foul and filled with vines intent on strangling him.

Jun was the first thing he noticed, hovering beside Lin, dark eyes locked on his. He held a lone finger to his lips but was soundless.

Nothing seemed out of place within the church. Vines still hung, though their flowers were pale without any light illuminating them. The candles that lined the altar were unlit and the shadows cast from the cutouts in the walls put odd lines of light across the skull.

Lin stretched his back. Carine was gone. He turned back to Jun and narrowed his eyes. This had to be something they'd planned in their silent language, but to not mention a thing about it to Lin left a sour taste in his mouth. Every time it felt like they took a step forward, they pushed him back two more. He'd gone to bed in a poor mood and it seemed intent to linger, like a cloud without a breeze.

Jun crept silently to the western wall and waved Lin over.

The village was quiet and still. But through the cutouts... Lin spotted the torchlight at the far side of the village. It would rest just past the short stone wall.

"Carine showed proof she knew of the old ways... Things you pick up being in a rebellion." Jun's breathy words tickled Lin's ear and raised the hairs along his neck. Despite proving he'd been feigning his intoxication, there was the faintest scent of strong drink on his breath.

"And you didn't think to tell me this earlier?"

"She is meeting with the fellow they claim is Velkath Reborn. And had to go alone."

Lin's throat tightened and his breath caught. He'd forgotten about that in his sleep. He clenched the edge of the pew separating him from the wall. Even here in the dimly lit space, Velkath's Sigil taunted him, skirting away from his periphery every time he tried to glance at it.

"That still doesn't explain why you wouldn't tell me," Lin hissed.

"Some Gods demand sacrifices is all she said."

And she knew you wouldn't be able to do what needed to be done. A trend, Escorter.

Lin grit his teeth. It didn't matter what he heard in Aemun's cruel, snide tone. The words were his, from his mind and they weren't true. Carine could've meant she'd have to sacrifice something of hers. Herself even, as unlikely as it sounded.

"And if she doesn't return soon?"

Jun sighed. "Do you not trust me? Or my words back at Denny's pyre? I told you..." He grabbed Lin's shoulder and pulled him closer into a near embrace. "I don't plan to lose any more friends. Not one. If she doesn't return before the moonlight fully touches that wall, we will raze this village to find her. I trust she won't die so easily."

The moonlight cutting in through the carved sections of the wall they leaned upon was only a hand's breadth from the opposite wall. Lin tapped his fingers along his knee, his stare alternating between the stretch of moonlight and the distant torchlight.

"You're an interesting man, Lindel." Jun kept his voice as low as his eyes.

"Am I?"

"A Ferrucium Escorter pulled into a rebellion, a key player during the Fall, and the Hero of the Fingers..."

"But?" Lin frowned up at the man, taking his eyes from the wall for a split moment.

"But for all of that... You seem..." Jun shook his head, what little light there was reflecting off his pate, and looked up at the vine hanging nearest them.

If it were Lin sat from the outside looking in, what would he see? A man defeated, exhausted, dying. *Hopeless.* All Lin could hope to do was make some small difference. Find Tylle and Pael, and ensure they are safe. See Nebra once more if he could. Mellyr and Denro, too.

Mellyr. Lin pulled his hand to his chest and for a moment, it felt like she was there. Pressed right to his heart. But he'd left her behind. He had to, of course. For her safety. Even if he was still an Escorter that wasn't a life for a child her age. Or any child at all for that matter.

"Scared."

"Huh?" That single word pulled Lin from himself. *Scared*. Of all the things, he somehow hadn't expected that.

"For all you've done. All you've been part of. Every time I look at you, you seem so terrified of what's next." Jun had a way of speaking that irked Lin. His tone was kind, but blunt. It was easy to see the man as a physiker in his old life.

Lin glanced back at the wall. The moonlight had barely inched toward it.

"You can talk to me."

Lin ran his tongue over his teeth and squeezed his eyes tight before facing the man. "What do you want me to say? Of course I'm terrified. I... I've lost the one person who seemed to... To care about me for me. Not for what I could give her. And I couldn't even be man enough to tell her how I felt because I knew I was dying. I pushed her away. And I'm horrified of what I'll become. I'm scared of the untethered and these fucking villages I thought I knew. I'm scared that Tylle and Pael might already be dead and now, I'm worried that Carine is out there alone and hurt, and... And I can't save anyone.

"Margaret. Royce. Denny. I even tried to spare Aemun and he *still* died. And your partner..."

"Hugo too," Jun softly interrupted. "He would've liked you. Weak men often can't admit they have fear in their heart."

Lin's fist tightened in the fabric of his tunic. "Strong men protect the people they care about."

Jun licked his lips and nodded gently. "They try. If we die tomorrow, there will be people who pick up where we fell and will carry that torch. Sometimes a torch, as charred and wasted as it might become, can still be too heavy to continue forward with alone. The important thing is you took it as far as you could... And lit the way for others as you did."

"Even after these Inlays. I don't *feel* strong."

"I think you're a better person than you're giving yourself credit for. And take it from me as someone who has lived through the inverse of what truly weighs on your heart. I'd die a hundred times over if it meant my sweet Rallia could have had the chance to live."

"I'm sorry," Lin said.

Jun waved a hand and stared outside. "Look. Our worries were wasted on an uncaring night. They're returning."

Lin followed his gaze out the ornamental slits in the wall and watched as a small group dispersed. Carine walked alongside Anne, appearing no worse for wear.

"Let us lay down and hope that the news in the morning is more comforting than the dreams we might have." Jun touched Lin's shoulder again, squeezing it gently. Lin tapped the man's hand in return.

If Lin understood Jun's meaning, they hadn't told him about Carine's plan because they thought he'd try to stop it if it meant Carine being endangered. His heart raged against his chest, and as the door opened and Carine slinked in, he couldn't pretend to sleep. If anything his breathing would give him away.

"We leave before the sun rises and we ride north. We'll discuss it more on the road." Carine's voice was soft, tired, and shaky. Not that he knew her well, but there wasn't a moment he could recall where her voice quivered. The odor of blood wafted in her wake

Lin rolled onto his side to get a better look at her, but she had already moved to sit beside the door, a Blade conjured and held flat across her lap. She faced away from them, her Blade lighting the corner like a dying candle.

***

Carine led the way and Jun brought up the rear. She'd insisted they leave the horses lest the sound of their riding give them away. They slunk away from Vole under the cover of night, leaving both supplies and sleep behind. It was some small luck Lin had spent a portion of the day resting, even if the sleep had been fitful. Once they'd crossed the stone shroud, they broke into a sprint.

Each possessed Inlays, which meant they ran without faltering until sweat coated them and the sun broke the horizon.

Far off, like the call of some great wounded beast, a horn bellowed. Lin glanced over his shoulder at Jun, but the man didn't react.

Only once the sun towered over the treetops did they slow. Heading north meant wading into deeper pockets of forest and chancing across other, smaller settlements. But Carine led with confidence, picking paths that looked far less used.

When they rested, Lin removed his cloak— folding it and pressing it to the base of a tree he rested against. While they ran his torso, where the strange dagger had slashed through him back at the island, had begun aching. It started as a slight pain then turned into the stinging ache of a fresh wound. Lin slid a hand under his tunic and pulled it away. His fingers were slick, but only from sweat.

"You look pale." Jun leaned against the opposite tree, one arm stretched to rest on the branch above his head.

"Something... Something feels off," Lin admitted. "Why did we run from Vole as we did?"

The brush beside him rustled and Carine stepped through, tightening her belt. Her lips were pressed into a thin frown as she shook her head. "What do you know about Velkath and his kin?"

Lin smoothed the front of his tunic and sighed. He wanted answers, but odds were he'd have a better chance of getting them if he played her game. And despite his misgivings, she hadn't given him a reason to distrust her. Even if she had smelled like blood and looked like worse last night. "More than I'd like.

"At the Ferrucium we were shown Velkath's Sigil. Told it was heretical, a twisted image loved by untethered. Then I met Tylle. She taught me *her* truth. Velkath and his kin were Danica's original Gods. Loved by the people. Each one with a moniker gifted to them."

Carine nodded and started to speak but Lin raised his hand, cutting her off.

"Then I met the Fentian scholars and read old books kept from our people. They weren't Gods, but venerated Danicans. Danican royalty, for lack of a better term. Vellia *did* somehow discover our magic. And as loved as they were for what they gave Danicans, it was their fault everything went to shit with the Accords. Venya and Verbanth and all that."

Not to mention the rumors of Mellyr being descended from them. And King Lodram too, allegedly.

Jun whistled, then brought his arm down and rubbed his nose with the back of his hand. "Going to tell us what all that has to do with Vole?"

A breeze made the leaves overhead chatter like nervous children doing their best not to interrupt.

"I'm not saying I witnessed a God in the flesh last night. But I saw the people of Vole believe they had." Carine's voice lowered, barely audible over the breeze. So soft and light that the wind might take hold of it.

"And we had to flee for that? Leave the horses and all?"

"It doesn't sit well with me either, for the record," Jun added.

Carine stepped forward. "Some Gods demand sacrifice."

"You said as much," Lin snapped.

"Carine. I trust you. We've been through more than most together. But what are you keeping from us?"

"Listen. The person I saw made it clear they were only a messenger of the so-called God, Inlays along their flesh. Velkath's Sigil Stitched into their chest."

Everything they'd been through. Everything he'd fought for already. Untethered were one thing, a very real, terrifying thing. But to think they'd fled a village in the dead of night over potential nonsense. The vein in Lin's temple felt like it might burst— as if one of those damned leeches meant to suck the poison of his blood out had crawled under his flesh and had grown fat since. "You're saying we fled for fear of some madmen pretending at Godhood?"

"Calm yourself and try to understand what I'm saying. The north has gone silent for some time. Untethered, by all accounts, seem to be the cause. You claim they're organized."

Jun straightened. "You're saying that this "Velkath Reborn" *is* the threat?"

Carine nodded. "One village paying tithe goes silent, it could be anything. A second village? That's a pattern and now his people would be on alert for us."

"Tithe?" Lin's anger dropped with his stomach.

"Children," Carine snarled out the word and turned her back.

Children? Just when Lin thought his stomach couldn't twist further it knotted into itself. Writhing within like some sort of twisted serpent. "No. You don't get to walk away after saying something like that." He lunged for her shoulder but Jun stepped in front of him and held him.

"Give her space."

"Fuck that!" Lin struggled in the man's grip.

Jun's arms tightened, easily holding Lin back. "Give yourself the space then. Think, then act. She didn't have a choice."

Lin's knees buckled and he sunk into the shorter man. His first thought was there was *always* a choice. Then, like a weight promising to break him, his past crashed onto him. How many times had he thought he didn't have a choice once his flesh had been Stitched? How he had turned his faith on its head and worked Inlays into his limbs because he didn't think there was a choice?

"Let me go," Lin managed.

Jun released his hold, but let Lin cling to him until he could stand on his own. "I've known Carine a long, long time. I don't expect you to see it... Not the way I do but there is pain burning in her right now and I promise you, she wouldn't have gone along with it if it wasn't necessary."

There was nothing else to say. Carine had helped the villagers of Vole give a child to the messenger. It was like some sick, twisted version of what the Ferrucium had done for years.

Lin stumbled after the path Carine had made, his strength returning at the same pace as his resolve.

"Wait," Jun called.

Lin spun to face the bald man. "Do you trust me or not? Did our talk last night mean anything to you?"

Jun's silence sounded like an affirmation, at least in the way the man stood stark still far longer than natural. It was as if the man intended to stay there at that moment and never move again. His dark eyes scanned Lin and finally, he shook his head and waved him away.

If it came to it, Lin knew the man wouldn't let him hurt Carine. But he doubted the opposite held. What would Denny have done? What needed to be done, of course. Tylle too. Pael also. If it meant seeing them to the end of the mission, any of the people he cared about would have given a child up. Tylle had gone out of her way to take Roge and his sister back to Creekside.

That lone untethered attack in daylight was odd, no? Lin blinked the voice away. Tylle, she'd killed the monster, she wasn't one.

Carine knelt in a clearing, head low, hands held out and trembling. She watched Lin approach, her face a mask of anger and something Lin couldn't place. Fear maybe, but he hadn't ever seen her look anything except strong.

"I reacted poorly," Lin started.

"No... I mean, yes, you did, but no. You acted as a sane person should. Probably why Denny took such a liking to you. Why Jun likes you too." She shook her head and looked away. "If we made them suspicious, it would've ruined anything else we might achieve. I did what I had to do." Her fists clenched and Lin noticed how raw and tender-looking they were. Crushed leaves and strips of ruined bark were piled beside her.

Flashes of the Ferrucium soldiers along the wall he'd murdered surged through his mind. The surprise of those who hadn't seen him coming. The shock of those who had but assumed he was on their side. It wasn't only the Inlays. He'd done plenty of things since that first incident in Lyre he wasn't proud of.

Carine rocked where she knelt for a moment, then made to stand.

Lin held out a hand, his trembling just as much as hers. "Vole told us more than we could've hoped. Some madman is going around claiming to be Velkath, and they're organized and believable enough that at least two villages have been convinced of it. What I don't understand is why Tellmer was in such poor shape compared to Vole."

"Because," Carine said, rising with Lin's aid. "They were willing to play the game. Tellmer must've resisted at least for a while. We've already wasted too much time. If they send someone after us..."

"You act like we can't beat them. You and Jun are stronger than anyone... Save perhaps that crazed Nooseman."

Carine smiled, though it faded quickly. "You're not giving yourself enough credit."

The path was easy enough to follow as Lin and Carine made their way back to where they'd left Jun. He sat there, a tension to his shoulders that looked like it might never drop. "I need to show you two something."

Northern Danica was a mix of tall, healthy trees and thick unkempt brush, save of course where the various villages rested. Which made the sight all the more unbelievable.

Each tree stump was a grave marker for a history that could never be regrown. A sea of dead, ruined tree limbs scattered and broken. It wasn't as expansive as the hills near Wakewatch Lake or the farmlands near the Ferrucium but enough trees had been laid low that two to three villages the size of Lyre could be built where that section of the forest used to stand.

There hadn't been any stretches like this on his way up to Ladrica, but the northern forests were vast and patches like this could be hidden in the thick of it. Worst of all, aside from the bushes and scattered small limbs, the trees were missing. Someone had hauled them away.

"Duke Elmore has been a busy man," Jun said.

Lin shook his head. "Or whoever the fuck this Velkath Reborn is."

"Who's to say they aren't one and the same?" Carine's hands still trembled at her sides and there was a darkness to the circles under her eyes.

Delayed Bone

"Who is he to decide what makes a monster? Are the real monsters the dead-eyed creatures slinking at the borders of our towns, or the authorities who caused them to be there? War is many things, but hardly ever is it simple. Hardly ever is it easy. When good men become as the monsters you fear, then we have failed."—Duke Errond

They kept a wide berth of the deforested section, skittering past the edges in solemn silence, and they didn't come across another stretch nearly as large as that, though the once untamed north was pared down in strips. Without their packs, left on the horses back in Vole at Carine's insistence, hunger soon became a real concern. Days running on foot had left Lin irritated, hungry, and ready for a fight if only it meant he might finally find peace.

He'd always imagined his end would be at the hand of a crazed untethered... Not that his mind and body would betray him to madness. Yet, what was more mad than racing into the unknown without food or guidance?

As they crested a sparsely coated hill the cold, not quite winter breeze of northern Danica prickled his skin. It was so cold he wished he hadn't left his cloak behind, but running meant it had become a burden.

In the distance, hoarding the horizon like some large spined beast, was the mountain range of Vellia's Fingers. They'd come too far north. Cutting wide around the ruined forests had a steeper price than he'd expected. Pael and Tylle wouldn't have cut this far. Shouldn't have anyway.

Much nearer than the looming, snow-dusted range, was a stone shroud. It sat entirely unbothered, needled leaves scattered all around the stonework.

Lin's throat ached at the memory of the place. The thaw just starting the last time he was this far north had finished and left behind a mostly muddy terrain sprinkled with the earliest promises of spring. And as unfamiliar as Vole and Tellmer had been this area— this specific village— was burned into his memory.

Fallo.

Seeing the ruined village brought a burning to his chest that traveled to the deepest depths of his heart. But the thought that truly scorched him wasn't the massacre or even his near death, but the thought of Denny. Of course, she hadn't been in Fallo with him, but she'd been near. She'd come here for him. To save him.

"This place is long deserted," Carine called back.

Lin ran his hand along the bark of the nearest tree and sighed. Months later it still hadn't been rebuilt. Likely, it never would be. Not with the threat of Ladrica to the north with the pass and the terrible attack that had befallen the village. "Fallo. It was where I was attacked by those insane untethered and Tylle saved my life."

"Hmm." Jun nodded, then added. "If it's the same group as that Horned King's, this could've been their first attack."

"Maybe..." Lin paused. He tried to recall them. He hadn't thought he'd seen any horns. Hadn't seen any of the monsters emblazoned with Velkath's Sigil, but each home had one bright and bloody made from the limbs of the slaughtered villagers.

"I mean... This far north. Crazed, super tough, untethered. Maybe this was the beginning of what was to come." Carine said it like it was a statement of fact and not a question.

Lin shook his head, realizing why it couldn't be true. "Impossible. Tylle saved my life and defeated them. Killed them all."

"Maybe she did," Carine agreed. She waved at the short wall as they approached it. Without the scarlet vines and shining flower petals of Vole's, it looked plain and filthy. "But you also defeated a group at Dreckinsburg, no?"

"Yes." Lin stepped past her and over the short stone wall. Perhaps there were more of them. Roving bands of untethered. Coordinated bands of untethered, more like. He walked through the village, shaking his head as he went.

At the center of Fallo, it seemed even the wolves and weeds had decided the village wasn't worth having. Everywhere he looked, he saw signs of the fight he'd barely survived. The crater the untethered had made at landing. Sections of scattered earth. He didn't want to doubt Tylle, but how was it she had slain those untethered alone and as weak as she supposedly was? His memories offered nothing, just a scrap of red cloth floating away and the constant pain when waking.

Like a large headstone commemorating his first of many deaths, the shack Tylle had Stitched him to save his life rose from the ruined terrain. Its door had fallen from the loose hinge it once hung from and the inside looked far smaller than it had when Lin had laid within wounded.

Lin stalked through the village, and Jun and Carine spoke near the outskirts. Her stare was even further north up the slope. If the mountain pass was visible she'd be staring at it. But it wasn't, so perhaps she could sense what awaited up there. Scores of staked untethered, alive but paralyzed by the Bound Metal and copper. When she noticed him looking at her she looked down and continued speaking softly to Jun.

Odds were, they were insulting him. It didn't matter what sweet things Jun might say to his face if shit flowed from his lips once Lin's back turned. They didn't trust him. Didn't want him. Lin's skin crawled. And they disparaged Tylle every chance they got. Was she perfect? Of course not. But she'd saved him, comforted him when he was lost. Fought for Danica.

As hard as he looked, as much as he forced his mind to recall what might've happened, there was no sign or clue as to what might've happened between her and the monsters when he lost consciousness. Last time he was in Fallo he hadn't considered that he should look for clues... But even now he wasn't sure why he felt he had to. Tylle had saved him. Countless times. And they—Carine mostly—were implying Tylle had somehow let the untethered get away? *Fuck her.*

Tylle had saved him. But as he recalled the morning after, she hadn't had any new wounds. And... As she piled the corpses and disparate, maggot-bitten limbs, he hadn't seen any Stitched or Inlayed flesh among the dead.

Lin closed his eyes and looked to the center of the town again. The pyre remains were long gone, but in the place it once rested he was sure he saw Velkath's Sigil in ash and bone. He blinked and it was gone. He blinked again and it was back. He blinked and hot tears ran down his face. When he finally found Tylle, she'd explain herself.

"She wanted me to hunt the untethered," Lin whispered. He spun in a half circle and swallowed as he stared up at the cloudless blue sky. A beautiful day, all considered. "What if she only wanted me to do so, because she thought I'd be gullible enough to fall for her sweet lies again? Get me away from the Scholars, away from Erias's people. But to what end?" A chuckle escaped, then another, until he was laughing and crying and his sides and torso ached with each exhaled breath.

Jun was there in a blink, the man hovering over him like Lin was a corpse and the man a fly wishing to befoul his remains. "Are you alright?"

"I'm fine…" Lin managed. He wiped away tears with one hand and swatted at Jun's proffered hand with the other.

Carine stepped through the village, her lips pressed into a frown as her eyes seemed to take it all in.

"Fallo in all its gory glory, though you didn't see it when the limbs were Stitched to the roofs." Lin raised his hands and spun in a circle as if the gesture might encompass the entirety of the ruins. "And up there is the pass!"

Their expressions proved he was alarming them as much as he was himself, but knowing something felt wrong and stopping it were two very different things.

"I wondered." Carine's voice was flat and she tilted her head to the side. "What are the chances the Ladricans have come down across the border?"

"I spotted some tracks, wagons judging by the ruts and hoof prints—"

"We'd see *signs*," Lin interrupted Jun, grabbing the shorter man by his shoulders and staring hard into his dark eyes. Lin's energy was swiftly fading and the void it left behind would swallow him entirely if he wasn't careful. "I don't think the problem here is the Ladrican army. It's the two of you. Blaming allies. Whispering behind my back!"

Lin turned away before they could say anything else. He didn't need any soft words from Jun or hard advice from Carine. He didn't need them. In fact, this was his task. His duty.

Without giving them warning, Lin sprinted away.

He rushed full tilt westward, running as if a Nooseman chased him. And he knew where he was aimed, like an arrow loosed at the heart of Lyre. To Nebra, assuming the tucked away little village had survived all this chaos.

Thin branches whipped at his face, lashing his cheek. But the pain was freeing. It let his mind focus on what bothered him. Ultimately, he'd turned his life upside down for Tylle. And it was all predicated on the fact that she'd saved him, never forcing her views down his throat but letting him slowly ease into them on his terms.

Lin slowed, passing a pond that begged to be fished at, just visible through the overgrown weeds along the path. Even before Lin got to Lyre so long ago, the roads weren't being maintained as well as they could have been, but as he looked to either side of the path, he noticed the brush at the edges had been pushed down. Like a large wagon had come through this way. As Jun had said.

They'd asked about soldiers coming through— but what if they had? Lin stepped into the rut. Heavy wagons would've made these, the way the solidified dirt crested. Wagons laden with soldiers.

Insects called out— screeching as the afternoon sky, still cloudless, painted everything in bright shades that northern Danica didn't often get. Even the shade from trees seemed less inclined to ruin the light and for a moment, Lin lifted his face to the sun.

Steady sounds of steps came from the weeds and brush beside him and then carried on past him. Lin opened his eyes and watched as Carine and Jun continued forward, both noting the wagon tracks he'd spotted.

When they eventually came to a split in the path, they turned southward. Lin hung at the crossroads, staring in the direction Lyre should rest. Assuming no harm had befallen it. He had to hope Nebra was well. Even if Lyre had been ransacked or massacred, surely an army would need a capable mount like her. With a heavy heart, he followed behind the other two. If he'd had any doubt about his deteriorating health, the more frequently his mood shifted the harder it was to form excuses. His mind at times felt like sand, grains of sanity sieving through the cracks, leaving behind only the worst parts of himself.

Camp was made in silence— a fireless night for the warmth around them. Lin hunted for honey-caps, finding them easily in the dark forest. Not a full meal of course, but if Carine regretted leaving their supplies behind she didn't show it.

"I'm sorry." Carine's voice carried to where Lin sat with ease. A light drizzle had started tapping a peaceful rhythm across the tree tops, so gentle that only the occasional drop made its way to where the trio huddled.

Lin brushed his tongue along his gums to clear the sweet, slightly salty grit of the honey-caps from them. "For?" He asked. Clearly for not saving the child she'd let be taken.

"For taking you through Fallo," Carine said.

"What she means to say is that with everything going on, especially your own concern of untethering, stepping through a place where so much trauma occurred was a poor plan."

Lin narrowed his eyes. "Trauma?"

"Injury and betrayals," Carine said. She held a hand up to Jun before the man could add anything. "And I don't mean Tylle before you get defensive." *Of course, she meant Tylle.* "Aemun left you there to face those untethered alone. You were grievously wounded. Anyone would have a hard time dealing with that and as a leader—"

"You aren't my leader. Grovetender owns my leash, not you." Lin raised his hand and wagged his finger with the Bludwieve. It ever-twined like a garnet-hued serpent. He hadn't told anyone that he knew a way to sever a Bludwieve and as much as he wanted to toss it in her face now, it wouldn't do any good.

"I wasn't trying to argue," Carine said.

"Good, because I wasn't arguing. And I'm not some sort of frail, mind-addled fool that you have to whisper about behind my back."

"We haven't been," Jun interrupted. The man's nostrils flared and he half rose to a crouched position. The pitter-patter had slowed even more and the air was lacking a breeze making the camp feel stifled and humid.

"Don't feed me shit and call it honey," Lin quoted Pael. "I've seen the whispering, the looks."

"How many times must I bear my heart for you to accept the fact that you have a place in it?" Jun clenched his fists. "How many times?"

And they treated Lin like he was unstable, a madman with a fuse burning away. Lin bit back his reply as he stared at the man. Carine hadn't moved, but painted across Jun's tired features was hurt. Real pain in the way his brows furrowed and how he stared into Lin's eyes. Lin dropped his hands and looked down. "I... I think perhaps my mind has been playing tricks on me."

Watching the tension leave Jun was like catching the sun first breaking over the horizon. Comforting, nearly warm. At every turn, the man seemed to prove he was a kind, caring person. *A friend.*

"We all want the same thing. To save Danica. To ensure our people are cared for. If you don't feel fit to continue, say so. We will see you to safety and no one will question your choice." Carine's jaw was set and the way she sat, back propped against a tree, hands hung in front of her, reminded Lin of Tylle.

"I'll be alright." Lin rose, sucked in a deep breath, and shifted. "I passed a small brook when gathering the honey-caps. I'll be right back. Skins need filling?"

"No. Thank you though. Are you sure you want to go alone?" Buried just underneath the question was what Jun *really* meant. *Don't go alone.*

But there was something that Lin felt he needed to do. Something he had to do. And knowing these two, they wouldn't let him. "I'm good. I'll be back soon. Thank you." Lin didn't say what he was thanking Jun for, because again, the two likely wouldn't understand.

Stepping over a fallen log, taking easy steps up a slope then down its opposite side, and finally reaching the brook that looked to be a run-off from a cave set into the side of a hill, Lin made his way through the forest. Alone but not feeling half as solitary as he had before Jun had spoken up.

Untethered were mad. But he'd never seen one slipping into it, and hadn't known what it looked like. Even knowing Velkath's Sigil didn't float feet from him and that Aemun's spirit didn't truly haunt him hadn't kept him from seeing signs of betrayal among his allies. Signs that likely weren't there.

Some might say he was justified. He'd been betrayed before. But taking a step back and looking at his mindset the way he so often examined everything else had told him all he needed to know.

All the breaking he'd done to himself to fit into the shape Tylle required of him— Mellyr needed of him— had caused him to lose pieces along the way. Sanity. Trust.

Lin knelt over the slow trickling water. What little moonlight shone down was hidden behind the trees so the only light aiding Lin's reflection were the Inlays along his hands. He ran a hand over his hair, the braids loose and tangled. One by one he undid them, letting his hair fall to his shoulders. It had grown long, past his shoulders in some places, and had enough grease to start a fire. A brush would be best, but he didn't have time for that.

His hands shook as he reached within, testing his spul. It was like sticking his hand into the shallow brook, raking his fingers across the pebbles and stones hoping to feel something different. But all he noticed were the strands he'd already found thanks to the lost tome. A seed, eager to bloom. A fish, darting away from him. And the most common type of Binding came to him as naturally as breathing.

Do you really think this will fix anything, Escorter?

Lin conjured the green thread of copper, the magic forming into a thick thorn-like barb. In the darkness of the brook, the light it shed was a ghastly, green-gray, making every rock, pebble, branch, and stem of grass look coated in a sickly moss.

Alone beside the water, his hands trembled. He'd seen the magic affect an untethered first hand but seeing it and feeling it would be very different. What if it changed him? Saved him. Ruined him. Lin attempted to steel himself. He was, and always had been,

Ferrucium trained. *Any and all impurities hammered out long ago.* That's what he used to think.

Recognizing his reflection was becoming more and more difficult. Each and every Inlay had been done with the hopes that he might save others. And this? He took his eyes off his reflection and stared at the green Binding. This he did to maybe save himself, or at least stall his decline.

Like forcing a seed into dry, cracked soil, Lin pressed the barbed magic to his temple. A rivulet of warm blood stung his eye as the Thorn sank in, taking root. He screamed and nearly vomited from the pain, as he pushed the last bit of it deeper. He blinked away Velkath's Sigil and the pain. When he managed to open his eyes and see his reflection, there was nothing save a thin line running from his brow to his eye, and down his cheek like a bloody teardrop. There wasn't even a scratch at his temple.

Tylle had said there were magics one could work on their mind and as the seed blossomed under his flesh, he struggled to imagine she meant anything but this.

What bothered Lin the most, was that the magic seemed to eagerly enter the untethered he'd practiced on, but Lin had to force it into himself. Easy enough, all things considered, but not at all as swift and smooth. He stared at the stranger in his reflection for a long, breathless moment before wiping away the blood.

His eyes were next. He'd already decided he needed to fix his failing vision and if he could pull it off, it was another way to remember Denny for whatever time he had left.

Lin licked his lips and leaned further over the water's surface, using the Inlays along his hand as a lone spot of light.

If working Inlays into flesh required specific intention and patterns, as Tylle had shown him, it felt the same should be true for his eyes. He stared at the fine point of ethereal light as it grew closer. Doing this wasn't necessary. In fact, he could stop now and nobody would know he'd even contemplated it. *But.*

But Denny had managed it when she was a child if her story was to be believed. And he'd let her die. He couldn't think of it as atonement— Denny wouldn't want that.

Lin sucked in a breath. Then gasped as pain, sharp and surreal, coursed through his eye socket. The magic stabbed into him. The Inlays along his arms and legs hadn't caused pain but this... This was something else entirely. Each motion stung and the brightness of the magic so close to his eye brought tears, but blinking would mean breaking his concentration. Bile rose and burned his throat as he worked.

In. Out. In. Out. If there was ever a time that Lin understood Wievings as threads, even knowing it pulled on something from within his blood, it was now as the magic and his intention laced into the soft portions of his eye.

When he was finished with his left eye, he lowered his shaking hands and hung his head. He could stop now and be none the worse for it. But as he looked around, his head throbbed with a new problem.

From his left, his vision was so clear it was a marvel he ever thought he'd actually seen the world before. And on the right, once he covered his left, it was as if he looked through a fogged window. Waiting would ease his body too much— make him think the lack of pain was how things should be.

With gritted teeth, he leaned back over the water and worked small, intricate circles along his right eye. Keeping his eyes forced open dried them out and the occasional breeze made things worse. Much like with his limbs in the wagon so many moons ago, the second Inlay came easier than the first.

In his reflection, he saw flashes of the wild woman he couldn't save. In his eyes, of course, magicked and golden. Tears came fully bidden. He'd thought he'd mourned enough, but seeing a semblance of her countenance brought it all back and he decided a person rarely knew how much they were meant to mourn. It was a marvel his tears weren't colored like that of a dying sun, as empty as he felt. He steadied his breath and listened to the forest around him.

Lin cupped water from the brook as best he could and splashed the cool water across his face. Where he touched his temple, it felt tender, but not as if a wound had been there moments before. And his eyes were sore, but closing them brought a comfort and coolness he hadn't expected.

Exhausted, he fell back and let the sounds of nature swallow him. The sounds of home. When he opened his eyes, he felt relieved knowing not much time could've passed, as dark as it still was. The disruption of steady water over jutting stones made for a peaceful rhythm that might've dragged him back to the depths of sleep if not for knowing Jun and Carine likely wondered where he'd gotten off to.

Hopefully, this Wieving would slow the deterioration of his mind. Revert it even. He waited to hear Aemun's snide remark about one failing or another, but none came. And when he looked around, all he saw was the forest, still and dark and clear. No golden sigil shifting from view.

Lin let out a long, slow sigh and rose.

Delayed Hate

"It is easy to blame a faceless king for the woes the weary might face. Blaming Gods is just as easy, but the average person should be more reflective. How many citizens of Danica blame themselves for the current state of things? I think much of this war of the false kings could've been avoided if they had." —Physiker Collier of Lyre

When Lin first returned, neither Carine nor Jun mentioned Lin's eyes, though they both stared intently at him. The first few hours of travel, Lin had intentionally avoided looking at them, even going so far as to shield his eyes as naturally as possible as if the sun was too bright— which at the wrong angle cresting a hill, it had been.

By midday, they encountered several more sections of the forest that had been stripped bare of trees, leaving jagged stumps and thick, unruly brush. There was no discernable pattern, just whole sections of northern Danica ruined as if the errant hand of a furious God had swept away everything in its path. If there was any truth to this Horned King's claims, maybe it had.

"And you're sure you saw nothing like this on your way up to Ladrica." Carine looked over her shoulder northward. She'd tied her hair up in a braid similar to the style Tylle often chose, though Carine's locks were far shorter. In the time they'd been on the road, she'd become nearly as dark as Jun. Though neither was as dark as Pael, likely due to his heritage.

"I think I would've noticed it," Lin said.

"Would you have?" Jun asked. He raised his thin eyebrows nearly up to his hairline where a thin dusting of hair had begun cropping up.

Lin found a smile formed where not a full day ago a frown would've rested. With a chuckle, he said, "My vision may have been failing, but I think I could see the forest for the trees. Or lack thereof."

Jun gently elbowed Lin as he passed him. "You'd hope. Going around the clearing will take even more time. I can't help but think we cut too far north—"

"What other option did we have? Seems every village we've encountered is worshiping this Velkath Reborn," Lin said.

Jun nodded and slowed his pace. "Or have fallen victim to it. If your theory about Fallo bears any weight."

Carine drew close and studied Lin's face the way a hound might try to sniff out a fox, then she took a step back and moved around him. "Have you been teaching him to meditate? You seem calmer."

"Not that I'm aware of," Jun said. "Unless I did so in my sleep."

Before Lin could speak, Carine interrupted him with a raised finger. "You Inlayed your eyes. What else?"

Lin rolled his tongue over his teeth and looked into the dark pits of the woman's eyes. He still hadn't mentioned what he did to the untethered at the tree. Cutting them. Healing. Cutting again. How the green Wieving had allowed the monster to beg for death. He needed to think of a name for the magic, but nothing came to him. Seed perhaps, but something felt *wrong* about that. Thorn had been his second guess, but the magic hadn't pierced him the way it had Denny.

"I... I worked the copper magic into my mind. To slow the effects of untethering."

Jun was a blur, grabbing Lin by his collar and getting so near his face that the sweat on the man's lip would have dripped onto Lin's if the breeze had been a bit stronger. Or the man a bit taller. "Have you lost all sense?"

Lin smiled and raised his hands. "I've found sense. The voices I've heard? Gone. The Sigils floating in my periphery? *Gone.* I should've done this before we left the Ferrucium. If I had, maybe these past days would've been more enjoyable for all of us."

"You don't know what the long-term effects could be." Jun let go of him and shook his head. "But what's done is done. Your vision improved?"

"Like I hadn't seen clearly a day in my life before." Which was true, all things told. He likely couldn't have noticed the birds circling ahead of them or noticed the slight trail of smoke rising.

"We need to keep moving." Carine looked and sounded defeated. "But I don't relish the thought of walking these paths with nothing but stumps alongside us."

Lin smoothed out the ruffled cloth near his shoulders. "Jun may be short, but he is far from a stump."

Carine's mouth hung open at Lin's attempt at humor. She looked from Jun to Lin and rolled her eyes before continuing down the path.

As they walked Jun sidled up to Lin and nudged him with his elbow. "I'm not that short."

Lin laughed, the sound surprising even himself. Try as he might, he couldn't recall the last time he'd really laughed. It was likely through Denny. Or perhaps Pael. But still. Sometimes reasons to laugh didn't exist and a person had to make it, instead of find it. "Of course not. And I'm not nearly so tall, but my point stands."

The path consisted of leaves, ruts, and bits of broken branches. And despite the amount of surrounding trees felled, there was a serious lack of *wood* left behind. Boats. The wood could've been harvested and used to build ships. Another slight giggle threatened to bubble up. Of course, getting them to the coast would be an ordeal in itself but the fact that building a ship practically broke the Binding Tenets seemed ridiculous. Wagons maybe. There'd been more than enough wagon tracks to suggest an entire caravan had cut through the north.

"What do you think of the markings in the stumps left?" Jun asked. The question seemed to come from nowhere.

Lin leaned over and lifted a stick that had seen better days. The knobby thing had probably been a branch on a dying tree and the bark underhand was rough but flaked off easily. Pale wood gleamed underneath. A fine walking stick if he'd ever seen one. Not something he needed but he could see it with either Denro or Pael old as they were.

"Oh." Lin flushed as he noticed the cuts for the first time. Sure— most of the destroyed trees looked broken, with only jagged stumps left. Those were the majority, but tucked among them were cleanly sliced bits of tree. So precise and flat that they could be tables if only they had a meal.

Swinging his stick like a blade he pointed at the nearest smooth-topped stump.

"Miss your sword so much?" Jun asked, eyeing the stick. His comment didn't make much sense seeing how disparate the sizes were.

"I miss many things, but if nothing comes from this and I never have to draw a blade again, I'll be happy." *Nebra. Mellyr. Denro. Tylle,* of course. *Of course.* "But I see trees felled by Bindings. Not all of them. But some. In my experience, some trees are more resistant, like they've got Ferrucium steel in their bark."

"Iron oaks," Carine called back. "Not that they're actually iron, mind you."

Jun nodded and sighed. "Well, that settles it. Binders cleared these swathes."

"It settles nothing." Carine stopped and studied Lin's stick before shaking her head.

"Right. I think it's clear enough that this Velkath Reborn is the culprit, but whether that is Duke Errond playing on some fantasy, or related to the untethered...."

"Or both," Carine said.

Lin licked his lips and nodded. "Or both... it doesn't add anything to what we thought we might know. I'd argue it gives us more questions."

Carine watched him from the corner of her eye, taking him in again as if the circle she'd walked around him hadn't been enough to capture her uncertainty. Fair, Lin supposed. But they'd asked three times now and three times he'd answered. With a sudden thrust, Lin placed the stick into the dirt and leaned on it. They'd shown they weren't above theatrics back in Tellmur. If it helped prove he was well, he could do the same.

Carine remained stoic but a twitch of her left eyebrow gave her flinch away. She was scared of him. Him of all things.

As if it took all his strength, Lin began trudging along. He treated his legs as if iron shackled them and hunched his back so much that the stick slightly bent in protest. If she feared him, he'd show her how unworried she should be.

"What are you doing?" Carine asked.

Lin raised his chin, opened his mouth to form a word, then sighed and just continued onward.

A slight snicker escaped Jun which, like a landslide that couldn't be stopped, turned into a full-bellied laugh. "I see, I see. You're a harmless old man all of a sudden," he wheezed out. He'd doubled over and the sheer intensity of his laughter caused Lin to stop and stare at the man.

"It... It wasn't that funny," Lin said, raising slightly.

"It wasn't funny at aaaalllll," Jun struggled to speak through his gasping laughter. "B-But you tried. Six bless you, you tried."

Carine chuckled and covered her mouth. "Come on you two. And if you plan to bring that stick, it better not actually slow you down."

I'm sure Mellyr would've loved it. There had been times, not many of course, where Denro had acted as a mummer for Lin and some of the other young ones at the Ferrucium. Maybe Denro was just better at that sort of thing, as the man had never failed to make Lin laugh.

Lin weighed the stick. Between the strength and endurance granted him by his Inlays, there was little chance the stick would cause any sort of issue. The stripped section of bark was smooth against his neck and he grabbed either end of it as if he might lift it into the air over his head. Surprisingly comfortable.

A smile failed to fade for the entirety of the day, plastered to his face the same way Jun's tunic stuck to his back. Lin would try to let his face rest, the muscles sore and uncomfortable, but it would just come back. Jun stayed a good pace ahead of him as they made their way along the path, sad, desiccated woodlands around them a poor backdrop as they raced by.

The more he considered it, especially now that his mind felt so clear, so clean, northern Danica was being gutted from within. Stripped of what made this portion of the nation so special. Termites, eating at the wood. Hungry, ravenous grubs. Lin shook his head and kept his eyes on the growing stain at the back of Jun's tunic, glad that even if it wouldn't drop entirely, his smile at least wasn't growing.

When they finally slowed, it was near a patch of plateaued hills dotted by trees with grand, sweeping canopies. The path split a ways back and this stretch had devolved into a glade that may have been walked through recently at one point. Fruits— pears by the looks of them— littered the ground, ripe and rotten, causing a sweetness to haunt the air. It was a far cry from the strangled, overcrowded northern forests, but still a marked improvement compared to the stripped, broken fields they'd crossed through recently.

Jun kicked a pear, then another. He rolled his foot under one that seemed solid and kicked it into the air, juggling with it as he walked. The man looked everything like a child at that moment, the fruit bouncing from knee to elbow, and rolling along the length of his arm.

"Not just a physiker but a juggler as well?" Lin asked.

"Well, maybe your little act inspired me?" Jun's eyes were alight as he tossed the pear to Lin.

With his arms still draped on the stick over his shoulders, Lin didn't have the hands to catch it and the pear thudded into his chest, squelching. He tried, and failed, to bounce it on his knee, nearly tripping for his troubles.

When he looked up he expected to see Jun laughing, but the man was motionless. Carine was further ahead, shadows from the large pear tree beside her covering her like a blanket. And not more than fifteen paces away from her was a group of five untethered.

Lin blinked, wondering if the green Wieving had failed him already. When he opened his eyes they were still there looking like corpses strung through by ochre threads. Velkath's Sigil was Stitched across their chests in large relief. The "V" shaped top resting in the depression at the base of their throats, blazed with a platinum hue. A gold so close to white Lin was sure it must be a different thread of Danican magic entirely.

"Horned ones..." Jun snarled. "Carine! Move!"

Sure enough, horns. He'd been too focused on the ornate Stitches across their chests but as they swarmed toward Carine he noticed the antlered protrusions branching from the monsters' scalps. The base of the bones at their skulls glowed the shade of dying grass.

Lin unshouldered the long stick and dropped it, catching up with Jun in a breath. Even with his vision improved, he couldn't see a reason why Carine hadn't yet moved. The damned monsters were charging right for her and...

The tallest of the five untethered cleared the distance to Carine the swiftest, long gangly limbs letting it move with the fluidity of a beast. The thing had no hair and its flesh was coated in the swathes and bands of Stitches all true untethered bore.

Lin threw two Wefts, formed a Blade, and sprinted. Despite all the previous running, he kept pace with Jun as the man tore toward Carine. Both Wefts found purchase as the tall untethered caught them in open palms. With a clench of its fists, bones showing through taut, gray flesh, the Wefts shattered, motes drifting like blown sand.

"Wait!" There was no hesitation as Carine screamed.

Dirt kicked up as Jun stopped, near enough to sneeze and touch Carine with the air. Lin was further back and slowing down was the last thing he wanted to do. These things— These horned untethered were dangerous. All of them were. But these horned untethered could be the key to unraveling whatever was going on. Lin shivered as he studied the horns and the ghastly pale green glow that held them in place. A glow that *could* mean intelligence.

"Lin, hold," Carine ordered. She still faced forward and hadn't lifted her arms.

Lin leveled his Blade, watching the five untethered for any sign of movement. They'd stopped and stared blankly, hands clenching and unclenching. Their nails were jagged and some of them still had tangles of greasy hair twisting around the antlers like some mockery of the altar back in Vole. Though, these sorts of untethered were likely the entire reason for *that* display. *Velkath Reborn.*

Lin's stomach twisted as the nearest untethered licked its thin, gray lips. This one had been a young man before turning and it stared at Lin's Blade with an uneven grin.

What Lin hadn't ever understood was how an untethered became so strong with random, haphazard Stitches. Since learning what Inlays were— and the intention required— it had bothered him. Did untethered put intention behind every stray, ruined Stitch?

"Why can't we kill them?" Lin asked.

"You can try." The lead untethered hissed and bared its blackened teeth, some of which were missing.

A shiver shook Lin as he watched the monster speak. Velkath's Sigil rose and fell under the creature's throat. He hadn't been sure, but by the voice, slightly more pronounced chest, and style of ruined cloth hanging from it, the monster had once been a woman.

"Delia," Carine whispered. "That was your name once. Do you remember it? An old name."

The monster cocked its head to the side, strips of hair falling between antlers like a curtain failing to hide some macabre thing.

"No. Delia lost herself to the voices many moons ago... But a worthless wretch like her was reborn in the image of Velkath. Reborn like our Horned King." The untethered straightened her posture and grinned to show more ruined, decayed teeth s if she were proud of simply forming the words.

Lin flinched as Carine took hold of the lead untethered's horns, pulling the monster's face down as she brought her knee up. If this was someone Carine had known, she spared no mercy. Each strike was harder than the last. Wefts cocooned outward from the untethered and those jagged, dirty nails bit into Carine's arms but she didn't let go.

Jun exploded from his position, a blur of Inlays as he threw himself into the fray. Lin launched himself forward, blocking the two untethered who lunged at Carine's right.

It was an outright brawl as magic flew in a flurry. All Wefts, no soft, malleable Weaves in sight. As Lin's Blade bit into the arms of the two untethered before him, his mind flashed to the last real combat he'd been a part of. Not the massacre of the villagers wanting to murder them. No. Back to the fight at the Ferrucium where he'd lost Denny. She'd been weak, tired, not fully recovered from their antics up in Ladrica and *his* weakness cost her life.

Lin grit his teeth and pushed the untethered back. The nearest monster threw a Weft, formed a short, crude Blade, and slammed it against Lin's. The monster's Blade shattered in a spray of sparks, reformed, and shattered. Over and over. They might string words together and even have a sentient light to their eyes, but these were still monsters with one-track minds.

A spin sent the one untethered past him, sprawling to catch themselves. The other, arm now free from Lin's Blade, seemed keen to lunge at him. Wefts cut in the wake of their gnarled claw-like hands.

Lin ducked, pivoted on his heel, and drove his Blade through the center of Velkath's Sigil. His weakness had cost him Margaret. Denny. He pulled it free with a clean yank that sent viscera and thick blood oozing out of the wound.

A glance toward Jun showed he had dispatched one of the two he'd intercepted and Carine danced with the leader, stray magic flying and slicing into earth and tree alike. A scenic path turned battleground.

But as Lin rushed to the untethered righting itself, he was thankful they hadn't been caught back in one of those open stretches of destroyed forest. Though, there was always the chance that more of these monsters lay waiting in the shadows. He hadn't intended to let the monster rise, but it was back on its feet. Bright, Inlayed eyes stared back at him. Cloth hung to it in matted tatters and the bands of Stitches across its flesh looked like beams of disparate sunlight cutting through the canopy.

Sinewy muscles under taut graying skin tensed, and the monster lunged. Then pivoted. Two Blades formed in a blink, one in each hand, and the untethered sliced up with one and horizontally across with the other.

"You are no *God*." The untethered's words were harsh and hissed, leaking out through rotten teeth.

Lin stepped back, response dying on his lips as his left boot slid out from under him. For a moment he thought the monster had formed a Snare or one of the other tactics he'd learned through fighting the awful creatures. But as he turned his fall into a tumble that he righted, he noticed the culprit smeared into a streak of browned-yellow shit. One of the festering pears had caught him underfoot.

Like the sound of cracking branches, the untethered before him laughed. Then it was on him, twin Blades swinging at him like he was little more than brush meant to be cut away. With all the force he could put into it, he compressed his Blade into a Bolt and launched it.

Surprise and pain competed to contort the monster's expression as thick, dark blood leaked from the corners of its mouth. It brought its hands up and gingerly felt the edges of the hole caused by the Bolt impacting flesh. Its innards were on display, pale, graying flesh stripped like the skin of a dying fruit to show the rotted meat within.

Lin turned away as the monster collapsed into the pool of its viscera. The other corpse Lin should've left in his wake wasn't where the untethered should've dropped.

Carine and Jun were working together now— both of them circling the tall, lanky untethered. He couldn't imagine how she felt, seeing someone she'd known had become a monster. He'd die before he truly untethered. Letting Denro or Mellyr see him like that wasn't something he could allow.

Like a rotten overripe pear falling from the tree overhead, the missing untethered dropped. A band of crystalline blue magic striped its neck covering the wound and ruining the Sigil's appearance. Wefts followed its descent, chunking the path all around Lin. He formed a Blade and broke those that would've bit into him and was forced back as the untethered assaulted him anew.

To think that the damned monster knew about the other magics to draw on…Though they'd known about the green threads and had worked those into their mind. Someone or something had taught them the other Wievings. Lin shuddered.

The untethered over-extended as Lin pulled back, then lost both its arms as Lin brought his Blade down and imagined the edge as sharp as possible. It sparked for a brief moment against the crude Stitches along the monster's flesh but once it shattered through those simple, ugly magics, the Blade cleaved muscle, bone, and all.

Howls, as ugly and crude as the Stitches in the monster's flesh came from it. These untethered seemed above those he'd encountered assaulting Dreckinsburg, but perhaps the monsters had some semblance of a power structure.

Carine stood over the tall untethered. She hadn't formed a Blade, but Jun had at her side.

The untethered— Delia if it truly was the person Carine had once known— tried to crawl away.

Carine stepped on the monster's legs, the limb severing with a flick of her wrist. "What do you know about Erron's holdings? Why are the trees being cleared?"

"C-cunning Velkath guides us. Sees for the sightless. Speaks for the voiceless. He is the Horned King and he walks among us."

Jun's face paled and he looked around. Even the forest itself seemed to grow darker as the untethered spoke.

"So the Horned King is behind this?" Carine asked. She took another short step, severing the monster's other leg in the process.

Lin swallowed at the violence of it. Not that these monsters deserved any less but his thought went back to the one he'd bound and experimented on at the tree. His stomach was eager to upend itself, but he held it together and stood at Carine's opposite side.

The untethered shed tears, but it did so as it cackled. "The Horned King will kill everyone who refuses to submit. He is loved. He is blessed. He is a God." It was as if the monster didn't even realize Carine shoved a boot into its back. It gouged the earth by pulling itself forward and left a trail of dark, rust-colored blood smearing the dirt underneath it.

Carine knelt fully onto the monster's back, grabbing it by the antlers and pulling its chin up from the earth as it laughed.

Carine's arms tensed, muscles knotting and flexing as she twisted and pulled the horns. A crack sounded, followed by something that sounded like stones grinding on each other, and finally, a pop as the antlers snapped free. The green glow at their base faded leaving behind a residue that looked more like ghostly mold than anything else.

Lin's stomach lurched and Jun turned from the sight.

Carine rose to her full height and dropped the horns to the dirt. Tears streaked her face. "It was her. Delia. She had a birthmark." Carine didn't explain further as she continued forward.

From her expression and the way she didn't look back once, it was clear there would be no burial or pyre for these monsters.

Delayed Blood

"No discussion on the War of the False Kings can be had without acknowledging the terrible state of the Danican nation that led to those circumstances. Fault of which can and should be laid upon the Ladrican kingdom, The Ferrucium, and the four duchies. All of the rungs on the ladder to chaos failed the citizens of Danica. Each and every one of them." — Duke Hollander on the war.

Encountering the untethered on the roadside in broad daylight had taken the potential threat, nebulous and on the outskirts, and manifested it. Of course, untethered existed. Of course, there was proof they were organized and wreaking havoc. But as a group, they'd only heard whispers. Not that they hadn't been real before, as often as Lin had encountered them, but seeing another intelligible untethered who professed a connection to Velkath reborn— The Horned King— that was something else entirely.

Sleep evaded Lin, so he kept watch. They were still among the plateaued hills and he'd walked a tight perimeter around their camp until he was at the highest point. Toward the north, the darkness of Vellia's fingers loomed over the trees like a hand poised to flatten everything. And somewhere between those peaks and Lin was Nebra. The stars looked every bit like motes of a shattered Binding stuck to the sky and he couldn't help but wonder if that beautiful expanse was where Denny's spirit now rested. They'd burned her, sent her embers soaring.

Lin blinked. To his amazement, a scattering of them dropped. For a single still moment, it was as if they really were souls stitched to the heavens, and the weight of all the lives had grown too heavy, ripping the fabric and sending the stars themselves plummeting.

"I can relieve you if you'd like. Though, I don't know how much you're watching over us if you're watching a star fall."

Lin forced his eyes away from the phenomena and shook his head. "When I sleep, I dream of her. And it isn't always pleasant. This at least is."

Jun didn't allow for silence. "I worry for our people if those are the types of monsters waiting to ambush the roadways. I... I think it best if you prepare yourself for the chance that Pael and Tylle might not be..."

"Alive?" Lin asked.

"Alive," Jun whispered.

Lin couldn't help the smile that came. "It would take more than a handful of untethered to kill Pael. His dice are well-loved. And Tylle..." Lin didn't want to put word to thought on her. He missed her. Missed their talks. But Carine and Jun had brought up very good points. Points so good he'd be a whole fool to ignore them. How had she learned what she knew? Oral traditions and practical application aren't the same thing. And as infatuated as he'd become with her, combined with the chaos surrounding The Fall, he hadn't considered how she'd gotten out of Fallo unharmed. Or why she'd only then formed a Bludwieve if Erias wasn't present to do his part. "Tylle is very capable."

"I've heard." Jun sighed. He stared up for a long moment as if counting the myriad stars up in their bruise-colored expanse. "Do you think, once this is all done, that Danica can truly be free?"

"I hope so. If we can just get the world to see we aren't the monsters they think we are."

"Something you already achieved." Jun turned his eyes to Lin. "I'm sorry for how I reacted when I learned you'd worked magic into your mind. It is a dangerous thing."

"All I did was convince them to give us a chance." There was no point in speaking on the second thing Jun had said. The less they talked about the ghastly green Thorn he'd placed into his mind the better. He'd doubted himself when first seeing Velkath's Sigil on the chests of the untethered, but Aemun's ghostly voice had been amazingly silent since working the magic.

A horn bellowed in the distance, rebounding along the hillside. Another one sounded nearer, just beyond the thick copse of trees to the southwest.

Lin squinted. Even with his improved eyesight, it was a sea of darkness. Except for what might be the faint glow of torches.

Another horn, even closer, sounded.

"Get down," Jun hissed, dropping into the ankle-high grass. Lin matched him and buried his hands into the grass. "We could've been spotted already. Staring at the stars and outlined on a hill like fucking fools."

"They could be our people. Or Errond's. Or Ladricans. There's no guarantee it's untethered. We should follow them, no?" Lin whispered.

"Don't move. I'll get Carine." Jun cursed under his breath and began a slow crawl down the opposite side of the hill from the tree line.

Lin waited so long his legs numbed and his arms began to itch. It was already early morning hours and the bruised sky was slowly lightening. The wind rippled the grass in slow waves and Lin shuddered. The sun was a way off from rising, but that could make their position worse. He'd kept himself alert by counting torches and had stopped when it passed a hundred with who knew how many people spanned between them. Too many for it to be people Erias had sent.

Time stretched and Lin scratched his nose. He'd never been good at waiting and as he watched the nearby trees, he noticed more and more movement. Or at least, what he thought was more movement. It was akin to trying to spot ants from atop the walls of the Ferrucium.

Jun still hadn't returned. Sounds of a camp being set carried through the early morning hours. Horses. Wagons. Tents and pans. Shouts and laughter. Screams, distantly.

Lin grasped at the grass and then slowly rose, ripping out blades as he did. It had to be Ladricans. Untethered couldn't be *this* organized, even if they followed some false king.

No sight of anyone coming up the hill from where Carine and Jun should be. There was a shorter hill, more of a slope with what looked to be a steep dropoff on the southern side, nearer to the tree line. Lin fidgeted where he knelt, then sighed. Waiting wouldn't do anything for them. If untethered could be scouts, Lin could too.

Using what Denny had taught him, he moved naturally, in time with the breeze. By the time he'd gotten to the shorter hill, he'd looked behind him no less than seven times. Still no sight or sound of the other two. But now that he was closer, the edges of the burgeoning encampment clarified.

It seemed there were as many tents as stars in the sky. A veritable army hazed by an oppressive fog that had crept in from the south.

Lin flattened into the grass and stared. Another horn— the first in a long stretch broke across the early morning and caused Lin to flinch. The mouthwatering aroma of meat on spits filled the air but there was a tangy undercurrent, like the odor of freshly spilled blood.

Crawling forward, breath held, he made it to the hill's slope. Sure enough, the drop-off he'd noticed was there and steep. Striated bands of garnet-hued earth fell away below in an uneven slant.

"Lin," Carine hissed.

She and Jun were there just behind him on their bellies. She glared but Jun's brows were scrunched together in concentration. They spoke using that hand language they hadn't bothered teaching Lin and crawled until they were beside him.

"I guess when the sun breaks, we'll have a better idea of what we're dealing with." Carine's voice was barely a whisper. "And next time, don't move without us. If these are Ladricans and you'd been spotted, I doubt we'd have been able to save you in time if they had a fucking Nooseman with them."

Lin nodded. Of course, he knew what she meant, but he'd never once been good at waiting. He looked up, the sky shades lighter than it had been before.

By the time the sun's first fingers scratched streaks into the sky above them, he'd pulled out fifty blades of grass and had woven a sort of knot in a similar style he'd worked Nebra's mane in.

Carine looked at it, shook her head, and tightened her jaw.

Lin stuffed the grass weave into a pocket at his side, sure Tylle would've liked it. Or complimented it. Either way, he intended to give it to Mellyr if he made it back to her. *When he made it back to her.*

The lingering chill of night gradually faded, leaving the air to feel crisp with the promise of another warm day. Every time Lin eased himself to relax, another horn would echo across the plains. Whoever these people were, they didn't care to move in stealth. The fog had succumbed to the sun, dispersing to reveal at least five rows of scattered tents and firepits. But for every pit, there were another ten to twenty people not near it.

A staggering total of people, doubly so if they were some sort of untethered army. But it wasn't Ladricans. Not unless they moved without the strangling standard of the twined serpent.

"What..." Jun said, trailing off at a hand signal from Carine.

Carine propped herself up on the elbows, leaning as if the extra inch would clarify her vision. But Lin saw it clear as day, even though the sun hadn't fully risen behind them yet.

Atop a horse as white as bone rode a large man. Tall even if he wasn't saddled to the huge steed. The milling troops moved aside for him. Those who stood knelt, and those who knelt bowed their heads. They treated him the way they might a King.

"Could it be Duke Errond?" Carine asked.

Lin shrugged. It could be. He'd never met the man. He didn't want to take his eyes off the imposing figure, but as the man rode, the camp below lightened with the cresting sun. If there was any doubt whether the group was an army, it was burned away by the sun. Possibly the largest gathered force Lin had ever seen. Rows upon rows and columns of what looked to be people motionless atop wagons. *On wagons?*

The breath in his lungs didn't want to leave. And new air didn't want to change places with the old. Those weren't soldiers on the wagons. Lin rose and Jun tried to keep him down, but Lin couldn't fucking breathe with his chest pressed to the dirt, so he rose and took hurried steps back. Carine let him. "Those are untethered. The ones that should be staked in the northern pass. Rolled about on wagons like immobile livestock."

"How can you be sure?" Carine hissed.

"It's either them, or they gathered up a new bunch and did the same thing to them." Lin steadied his breaths and went prone again, wishing he hadn't let the sight disturb him. "But why?"

"Look," Jun whispered. He gestured toward the section of the standing army where the tall figure on horseback had been last.

The figure had gotten a bit closer, moving through the camp to stand at a pavilion that had likely been built overnight. The individual had dismounted and still stood a good head and a half taller than most around them. A tattered, ruined robe cloaked them and a bright, golden crown rested on their head. By the figure's frame, it was likely a man, but even with his enhanced eyes, making out their features proved a challenge. But what stood out most, now that the crowned figure turned and faced them, were the antlers atop their head.

"The Horned King," Lin said in disbelief.

The untethered hadn't been lying. The ferryman hadn't been spinning tall tales. A small part of Lin, the exhausted piece of him tired of fighting, had hoped it was all a lie. No great untethered threat, just more Ladricans. But that wasn't the case and signs had been there since before Lyre of a larger problem, signs that had gone ignored thanks to the failure of the Ferrucium.

"Shit," Carine spat.

Lin struggled to pull his eyes away from the horned figure. He squinted and the more he stared the more he believed the crown was made of Bindings, and not real gold gleaming in the sun. When he did finally look away, his stomach sank.

Being led to the pavilion was a line of shackled soldiers, clad in the livery of Duke Hollander's colors. Each one was anchored to the next by chains of golden light. The soldier leading them bore no colors but was tall, lanky, and wore a wide-brimmed hat. *Pael's hat.*

"I can't tell if they're untethered or not. The actual soldiers I mean," Lin said.

"What does it matter?" Jun shook his head. "Either way that confirms they've Binders among them."

"It matters because we could probably handle *normal* Binders," Lin snapped.

"No. Skilled or not, these numbers are too great. If they are Ladrican and happen to have a Nooseman among them—"

"They aren't. I mean, that's not King Lodram. So unless they crowned a new king with bone and Binding, and sent him into the heart of Danica, these people *aren't* Ladricans." That much at least Lin was sure of. What he wasn't sure of was the purpose of the raised pavilion.

Executions. The thought was the loudest in his mind. Examples always had to be made. Lin pulled at the grass near him. He was always late. Too damn late.

Another horn, nearer and louder, bellowed from the pavilion. The camp's attention all seemed to focus on the crowned figure. The crowned and horned figure raised their hands, gesturing for those kneeling to rise.

A path was cleared and the imprisoned soldiers, roughly twenty-three by Lin's hurried count, were led and forced down in front of the tall, horned figure, an eerie silence sprawled outward. The pavilion was the epicenter and it was like a ripple of hushes and murmurs crossed through the camp. Even the wind seemed to rest in silent awe.

Lin stared in horror as the figure— *the Horned King* as there was no other explanation that made sense— approached the first of the soldiers forced to kneel. They were too far away to hear anything, but it looked like words were exchanged. Then the soldier jerked and the Horned King glanced down.

"He spit on him," Jun whispered.

A Blade, molten-hued like freshly heated steel blurred into existence, and the soldier's head fell away, cleanly separated from their body. Such a clean, fluid stroke. The intensity of the Blade left spots dancing in the air where it had been.

The Horned King moved on to the next soldier forced to kneel as if the disrespectful soldier had been an errant weed in a curated garden.

Lin tried to lurch to his feet but Jun was ready for him and held him down. "No. The numbers are too great. We need to run and report this to Erias. Now."

What was the point of having strength and magic if he couldn't protect people? *Save* people. Lin blinked as tears threatened to sting his eyes, which hurt all the more for their newfound sensitivity. "But..."

"I know," Jun growled. "I know."

Lin looked back down at the staggering number of gathered untethered, ready to leave, and hoped that wherever this force was heading, Erias and Azhura's newfound Ferrucium could be enough to stop it. Then he saw *her*. Like a pale flower blooming in an ocean of thorns. Tylle.

Daring Hope

"They danced and ate and fucked and fought, but all of them, the king included, were monsters made for war. Made of it, even."—Pael Hollander

*T*yl*le.* It couldn't be anyone else, it *had* to be her, the way the woman walked with a steady, even pace. Her features were impossible to make out but even surrounded, she moved with confident ease, shoulders back and chin up. A single long braid trailed down her spine. Her raven black hair was stark against the white robes that clutched her lean frame.

"Lin," Carine hissed. "We need to go. *Now.*"

Carine and Jun had begun backing away to the northeast side of the hill but Lin was rooted in place, unable to pull his eyes from her. She'd approached alongside the Horned King's mount and had slowly ascended the few steps leading up the pavilion.

Lin waited, breathlessly. She'd done it. Managed to sneak right up beside the Horned King, hidden in plain sight. Tylle was so close that a Needle to the taller figure's spine would be enough to take him down. But instead, she placed her hands on the shoulders of the first soldier the Horned King had spared.

Having doubts, ugly horrible doubts, and being forced to face them were very different things. It didn't make sense. Tylle had claimed to want to free Danica. To save the people. The villages. The children. She'd opened his eyes to so much. But then why?

All along had it been in the hopes that he might join— not Erias and his petty rebellion— the Horned King?

He struggled to recall what Pael had said when they first reunited at Fentis. Tylle had wanted him and him alone to look into the untethered problem. Had she thought him capable of stopping this? A force larger than any Lin would've thought possible as the sun crept higher into the sky and lit the further reaches.

This gathered army, most of which he had to assume were untethered, was vast enough to repel the Ladricans. Enough to conquer all of Danica. If this force had attacked the meeting at the island— the world never would've accepted that Danicans weren't monsters.

The wagons transporting the staked, motionless untethered had finally ground to a halt near the pavilion. Despite the soldier who'd led the bound soldiers to kneel having Pael's hat, there was no sign of the short man among those who'd been lined up on the pavilion.

Lin rose slowly and backed away, not taking his eyes from the display. An occasional distant shout broke the tense silence. Pleas, curses. More of the bound soldiers died. Well over half. But those that didn't lose their heads were left kneeling only for Tylle to move behind the Horned King and touch them. She likely prayed for them. As if praying could save them or bring back their companions who'd been struck down.

What would Vellyr think? Lin shook his head. Tylle had never claimed not to be a monster. She'd even mentioned many times over that she wanted to bring the old ways back to the people. He wiped the tears from his eyes with the back of his arm and nodded.

Whatever was going on, she was being used. Being lied to. There had to be an explanation. The Tylle he knew wouldn't— couldn't be willingly siding with an untethered who wantonly attacked Danican villages.

"We rush back. Split even. I'll head to Erias. You've got a rapport with the scholars. Jun can move with you."

Lin saw Carine's lips move. Heard her words. But it was like all the clarity he'd felt he gained the last two days had seeped away, leaving everything painted in a dull pallor.

"Are you listening?"

Lin nodded as he pulled his tunic off, revealing the lines of Stitches across his torso and the Inlays along his arms.

"Have you lost your mind?" Carine asked. Jun was beside him in a blink, nearly wrestling with him to keep his boots on.

"Three of us," Lin said. "We... we don't even know what this force wants. I'll infiltrate. Try and see what's going on. You two can report back to Erias and try to prepare the scholars, but they likely won't move until it's too late. They didn't last time." Even to himself, his voice sounded distant and flat, but he shrugged Jun off from him and kicked his boots away.

"You'll get yourself captured or worse," Jun said.

Carine paced just down the slope of the hill and off in the distance another horn sounded. "Let him go." She spoke as if she thought she or Jun had a choice in it.

"Carine."

"Jun," she said back.

"I'll stay with him then," Jun said. He kept his top loose-fit and open along the front most of the time anyway, so he slid it off with ease. Striped Inlays shone with sweat.

"No," Lin and Carine said simultaneously.

Lin stretched his back. "At this point, I'm an expert at infiltration. The Ferrucium when I was pretending to be a Nooseman. The Fingers. What is some band of maddened untethered against those?" He grabbed Jun before the man could argue, pressing his brow to the shorter, bald man's. "Go. I'll be fine."

"If you insist on someone staying, then we should trade places. I've lost enough friends. And you've got a daughter to return to."

Not if these monsters decided to continue south. Besides, Lin was going mad. Or at least, he had been before the Thorn worked its odd magic. Who better to walk among the untethered than the man becoming one?

"All the more reason why I need to do this. There is no way I won't make it back to Mellyr. Go. Plus, if Tylle has betrayed Erias, she may be less on guard with me than either of you." Lin pushed the man away.

All the talk had done was steel his resolve. He'd sneak in when next the camp broke, find Pael, and, despite what he'd said out loud, rescue Tylle.

"Get in and get out if able," Carine said, drawing up alongside Lin. "Don't draw attention to yourself. If they continue in the direction their bearing indicates—"

"They're heading for Fentis. Why is unclear, why now even less so, but it's the only thing that makes sense," Lin interrupted.

"Right. We'll get word to Erias and Azhura and see if we can mobilize the Ferrucium."

The small force that remained, anyway. Lin tried to estimate—if the Fentian scholars *and* the Ferrucium's remaining forces fielded together, they might stand a chance. Maybe.

Carine grabbed Lin and pressed her brow to his. Her grip was achingly strong across the back of his neck and she didn't close her eyes, staring into his. "Be safe. Jun isn't the only one who's lost enough friends."

She pushed Lin away leaving him to watch them leave. They quickly passed over the hillside and disappeared into the eastern treeline.

Once they were out of view he waited, alone with his thoughts. He tried to weave together the disparate threads. If he didn't know any better, after everything involving Aemun and Fentis and the meeting that had taken place in Ladrica, he'd assume the Horned King was another errant thread of the dead man's. A rueful smile formed. Of course, that bastard Aemun wasn't done causing trouble.

As he waited, the hill became too warm, the air somehow too stifled. The grass itched his arms and the scent of something bitter tickled his nose. But he had to wait. The camp was stationary save for those running about tasks. What had been the pavilion was broken down, lumber carried away behind the treeline blocking most of his view.

When the sun had reached midday, the camp began breaking. An act that didn't occur all at once and carried on well through the afternoon as the many tents were broken down. The routine passed along with concerning efficiency.

Watching them move, it was hard to imagine that they were all untethered. Odds were, they weren't. Most were likely soldiers, like those who'd been taken in today, forced to serve. Lin had known plenty of soldiers, himself included, and he found it hard to imagine so many of them willingly serving some tyrant just because comrades were slaughtered. Danicans should be made of sterner stuff. Lin looked down at his Bludwieve and frowned.

Perhaps their subservience *wasn't* so willing.

All this time he'd had a yearning to speak with Tylle, to see her again, and now she was down there among the army. Surely there was a reason she'd done all this. Sided with this Horned King for a reason other than the unsubstantiated claim he was Velkath Reborn.

What could a self-named king want with Fentis if that were truly his destination? Lin's first thought was the dagger. But the odds of anyone knowing about that strange weapon were as narrow as a needle's tip. Port of Fentis was the largest across all of Danica—and the trees hadn't felled themselves. Perhaps they intended to leave the isolated land. Good riddance. No. Untethered, organized or not, were a festering, wicked blight. Of all the things the Tenets, Accords, or whatever the histories wanted to remember them as, did, keeping Danicans from leaving Danica hadn't been the *worst* decision. Especially not the bloodthirsty ones.

There was another possibility that nagged him. He could almost hear Aemun's ghostly voice chiding his idiocy for not considering it sooner. For once, having that haunting voice to coalesce thoughts and feelings he might be averting his gaze from felt as if it could be a boon. He waited, but no voice came.

The Horned King could be marching south for Mellyr. One king already had her hand promised to him. What was to stop this monster from thinking the same? Surely Aemun hadn't been so foolish as to work with an untethered.

Lin shook the thought from his head and waited in silence. Waiting for the tail end of the encampment to begin moving would draw more attention than otherwise, so when it seemed that the throngs below thinned out, he made his move.

Crouched among the thick brush, many of which had dark berries that would quicken a man's guts as swiftly as rancid water, he watched. Outliers marched forward as they walked the borders of the camp. He waited, seeing an opportunity when a large wagon laden with more of those staked untethered rolled loudly past. Even with the path well worn by all those who marched ahead, the wagon wheels groaned and struggled over uneven bumps in the field.

He spotted a group— five or so exhausted-looking individuals who dragged their heels as they walked.

Lin rustled his trousers as if he had been relieving himself among the trees and moved to walk alongside the group. He kept his head down, matching his steps to theirs. All of them wore homespun and didn't appear to bear anything that would distinguish them as any of the dukes' people.

"Well, don't you look like a tall glass of warm shit?"

The voice was harsh and Lin shrugged at the speaker— a haggard-looking woman with greasy, bob-length hair and chapped, dry lips. If she thought he looked bad, perhaps she hadn't seen herself in some time. None of the others even looked up at the woman, so Lin turned his attention back to the milling crowd ahead.

Getting an accurate number, even from the hill, was a hard task. But walking among them, he saw most weren't soldiers like he'd expected. At least not in the section he'd joined.

"Think they'll hit another village today?" The man to his right asked.

Shrugs and grunts were all the answers he got. Not keen to talk, at least not to each other.

Lin frowned. "Where are they keeping the ones we just took?" Lin asked.

"Where do you think?" The same dry-lipped woman snapped.

With a shake of his head, the man on the right croaked, "Ignore her. She's pissed we had to go all the way north for wagons of staked, near-dead men and women just to march back south."

"You should be pissed too. Bad enough all the things they're making us do. But all this marching has given me blisters on the bottoms of my feet. And I don't know about you, stick-man, but I've curves that chafe from all this."

"Anyways," Stick-man said. An odd name, but when he studied the man, it stuck. Thin, stick-like limbs and hair colored like shed bark. "I've been with the Horned King for months now. Just before the thaw. All the new.... Recruits are kept close to the center of the force. In case they try to run. Not that they'd get far. Scouts and all." He waved his hand as he spoke, Bludwieve twining on his ring finger.

Would running away cause the magic to attack the body the way it had Gritt? Lin looked down at his own Bludwieve, wondering if Erias could sense where he was from the scarlet thread connecting them.

"Makes sense. Just thought I saw someone I recognized and wanted to go check."

A hand grabbed his shoulder and Lin looked to see the bob-haired woman staring at him. It was hard not to look at her lips and the way the skin flaked from them in places. "Just make sure you're back in time to help us. Lazy bastard. Haven't seen you a single day if I've seen you any."

Lin shrugged her grip loose and licked his lips. He didn't say farewell, instead moving through the throngs of marching people. Sweat and blood lingered in the air, acrid and tangy. Cutting the stench was the odor of saccharine rust. It was thick and pungent and only worsened as he headed toward the center of the army.

Wagons laden with supplies, freshly felled lumber, and the staked untethered rattled along. And walking alongside them were a group of soldiers, gambesons tattered and ruined. They didn't bear any weapons and many of them had swollen eyes and bruises painting their faces. But these weren't Duke Hollander's men based on the colors, instead, they bore shades of dingy brown with no discernable heraldry.

Walking just ahead of them was a lean, horned untethered. Lin couldn't help but stare at the back of the creature's head, their hair matted and tangled. To think there truly had been an untethered army amassing.

Lin sidled up to the nearest soldier, a young man with a gash across his eye that looked to have been made to calm the swelling around the socket. Dried blood coated the side of his face.

"I've no food," the young man started without glancing at Lin.

"Not after your food," Lin said softly. With his arms down at his side, he gestured at the man's clothes. "What force were you with?"

"Oh," the young man looked around. His one good eye darted like a nervous doe's while the other barely seemed to move. "Village militia for Tonburn. Though we couldn't stop them when they came. Too many."

Too many indeed. Even before the incident at Lyre, it had been clear the Ferrucium was short-staffed. If this faction had been operating in the shadows, it made sense why. New, promising Binders weren't being recruited. They were being stolen. Stolen, and not taken for training as the Evaluators did.

"Have you seen other soldiers? Duke Errond's men?"

The young man from Tonburn shook his head, hanging his chin to chest. "You better move along. They see you interested in us and you'll just get hurt. Especially if they hear you asking about any Dukesmen."

"You're a brave lad. That much is clear. Be brave. I've been through worse and made it back out. If we're to be embers, be one that doesn't fear to burn." Repeating and twisting Denro's words had never felt better, leaving an easy warmth in his chest.

No response came from the young man but as Lin slinked off, he noticed the young man's shoulders shifting with silent, strangled sobs.

If Lin had ever been forced to describe himself, he'd have said he was a soldier. An Escorter. A good one at that, at least until the events that sent his life into a spiral. But walking among the filthy, desperate people, like they were on some sort of twisted pilgrimage, made him reconsider. Somehow along the way, like his dreams had implied, he'd been forged into something. Not a weapon, as he feared. Not a fragile dagger to shatter, but a shield. The Hero of the Fingers. The bringer of the Fall.

Him. He'd get answers from Tylle, assuming she had any. And he'd stop this Horned King somehow. Velkath Reborn. The Horseshit King, more like.

Daring Bone

"Do the best you can, when you can, and some'll say you haven't lost the war. That's horseshit. Winning is winning, surviving is winning, anything less and you've lost. Plain and simple."—Carine

Moving through the encampment raised more questions than it answered. All around, untethered mingled with captives. However, calling them captives felt wrong. They ate, moved, and spoke as soldiers mustered for war might and not one seemed eager to flee. Some even laughed amid the monsters.

Even those bruised, like the young man Lin had spoken with didn't have the eyes of someone looking for an escape.

Lin took his time traversing the marching army. He blended in, matching his pace to those around him. He tripped once, drawing muttered words of irritation from those behind him, but adding a decent layer of grime for his troubles. Even shirtless and exhausted from the journey before, he still imagined he looked in better shape than the average person.

Horns bellowed in the distance. Some were so far away that only their echo reached back.

It felt like he'd walked all day and had barely arrived at the camp's edge. The press of bodies was longer than it was wide, but the sun had already begun setting.

People were more scarce here, at least those that looked like they'd been conscripted against their will. Untethered, some hornless and chained to the wagons, marched forward like they were a breath away from death.

Lin kept his distance, slowing to see the wagon's contents. Supplies. Barrels of fruit. Weapons. Hay and to his surprise, Wanderer's Ore.

"I never seen so much myself neither," an old man, bent of back and gray of hair, said.

Memories of the isle and the ships going up in an explosion of blue spark and flame flashed through his mind. But he hadn't seen the stores of ore before they exploded, only the terrible after-effects. If the Horned King was stocking it and they were heading to a port no less, it didn't bode well. None of it boded well, but the screams and scent of burning flesh refused to leave him. Even as the older man waved the air.

Lin blinked. He was waving at Lin.

"The ore I mean. You seem different from those other marked ones."

"Marked ones?" Lin narrowed his eyes and it dawned on him what the man meant. "You've the Sight?"

"I see the markings if that's what you mean."

Matching his pace to the man's was easy, though those marching behind him cursed at the lack of haste. Lin looked over his shoulder, concerned that the grumblings might result in worse than wagging tongues. The last thing he needed was to get spotted because he had a soft spot for the elderly. He'd blame that on Denro if he got the chance. Pael too. The fact that he'd seen the man's hat— or what he'd assumed was the man's hat— and not the man didn't bode well.

"The other's with the markings. Have you noticed a pattern in their movements... Or a structure to their command?" In the few hours Lin had been among the forces, he hadn't. Of course, there were those antlered untethered, looking idiotic, but there didn't seem to be so much a structure as there was organized chaos. True to the one soldier's words, the camp had the untethered and less likely to defect at the edges, with the newly inducted and abducted at the center of the force. Lin would wager that was where the Horn King and his main outfit were as well.

The man's wet eyes looked at him, suspicion plain across his wrinkled expression.

"I'm *not* with them. This isn't a test." He hoped he sounded earnest.

"Well... I don't know that I'd call myself an observant man, mind you. But—" Before he could finish the sentence he sprawled to the ground, catching himself on his palms but shooting up a spray of dirt and groaning as he did.

An untethered, stocky, and squat compared to most he'd seen, stood there with a black-bottomed foot hanging in the air. "Get up and stop slowing the ones behind you. Or you'll have worse than a kick, old man."

Lin stared, fists clenching. He tried to steady his heart. And it took everything in him not to form a Blade.

"Problem?" The untethered turned its cruel eyes to Lin.

Of all the untethered Lin had ever seen, none had ever looked so plump, their face so flat. Almost like a pig. They had a small set of horns, far shorter than most, with that same ghostly green glow at their base. Stringy, short braids of hair fell on either shoulder. All together, it was the ugliest untethered Lin had ever seen.

Worst of all, not one person slowed their steady march to help the older man up. They continued forward, one woman even going so far as to nearly step on the man as he struggled to climb to his feet.

Lin shook his head and swooped down, grabbing the man despite his protests. Walking him upright and allowing him to lean on Lin while others pressed around them proved to be a challenge, shoulders jostling and knees knocking against the both of them. There were too many people. Too many villages attacked and absorbed, too many untethered not caught in the once inescapable clutches of the Ferrucium.

When Lin risked a glance over his shoulder, the pig-looking untethered was gone from view. "I slowed you with my conversation. I'm sorry."

"I'll be fine. I can walk. Not the first time I've fallen. Won't be the last. Important thing is to get back up and all that. I could've been kicked down without you, not sure I could've gotten back up without you, so thanks. Names Mirl, by the way."

Mirl.

"Ease your breathing. I won't let you fall again." A promise easy to make when he was holding the man up, but even without Aemun's spirit haunting his mind, he doubted himself. Since Lyre he'd failed, over and over. Saving Mellyr had been the one thing he'd done right, that and somehow convincing the council to reconvene regarding the Accords.

Mirl didn't reply and they continued forward in silence.

Lin was still eager for answers, but with the pig-like untethered having already noticed him, he didn't want to draw more attention.

Three sharp, nearby horn blasts sounded, and the rumble of hooves carried through the ground. Riding atop steeds that looked stolen right from Ferrucium stock were three gray-skinned, muscle-bound untethered. All three were topless, Inlays shining along their limbs and torso. Only the smallest of the three, a woman, bore the haphazard Stitches that most untethered had. Not one of them had a full head of hair, but they each had a collar of bone and Binding around their necks, obscuring Velkath's Sigil along their throats.

Lin tensed up and Mirl must've noticed as he whispered, "Keep moving, lad."

In the hands of the smaller untethered was a head, torn flesh flapping like banners on the parapets of a gray stone keep. An untethered's head. With antlers sticking from it in uneven directions. *They'd found the group they'd dispatched.*

Lin forced himself to look down as they rode past. The entire force had undercutting scents of sweet, rusted iron. But the stench was choking, unbearable from the passing trio.

"You asked if there was structure?" Mirl said, his tone low and forced. "The ones without any bones, they seem to be foot-soldiers. Weak-minded infantry, mostly kept in line by the horned ones. Those are the ones like the flat-face bastard who kicked me. They corral us… And them. Treat us like we're no better than those crazed fools."

Mirl winced as he sucked in a deep breath. "Anyhow, beyond the horned fuckers we have the collared ones. Leaders— think like generals in a Duke's militia. Haven't heard them speak, but you can tell by the eyes they're sharp as a honed blade. Maybe ten of them overall? Hard to tell, as they don't come to us often."

"And they report directly to the Horned King?" Lin asked.

Mirl nodded and waved Lin off. He limped on his own for a few steps then cursed under his breath and nodded to himself and picked up his pace. "A God reborn, for all the rumors. Thought any of the Six were meant to be faceless, but they say he's from before the Six. Old as the stars themselves."

"We'd have heard of him if he was."

A grunt of agreement. "Unless he hadn't wanted to be known yet. They say he doesn't sleep. Don't eat real food. I even heard he doesn't bleed from the first few captured."

"Everyone bleeds," Lin said. "But who was the first captured? Duke Errond's men?"

"Not just his men, but him. Saw the signet on his finger and all before they sent him into one of the villages a ways back. Hadn't seen him again."

Lin's heart sank. Of course, having a ducal signet didn't mean he *was* the missing duke, but it was possible. Hope was such a frail thing, but part of him had wanted to believe that the Horned King was just a power-hungry duke. That would make any explanation that much easier. Surely the truth was an easier explanation than the man— the untethered being a reborn God.

Lin was nearly knocked off-balance as the same pig-faced untethered from before shouldered into him. While he kept his footing, he did bite his tongue and for that alone he had to keep from slicing the squat creature into pieces.

"You— All of you— in this pocket. Keep up. We've come to a village and require probers."

Even seeing an untethered, with wild, unorganized Stitches and all, speaking so well made Lin uneasy. He knew all untethered had been human once, many of them possibly even Binders like himself, slipping from sanity. But they were monsters. If not for their appearance and workings of crude magics into their flesh, then for the vile acts they committed.

"If this goes well, I'll earn my mark and true name. So if you're thinking about causing trouble, I'll kill you now."

Mark and true name? Lin didn't know what that meant and didn't care because if he had it his way, all the monsters would die a horrible death. He ignored the untethered and kept his head down as he walked alongside the other thirty or so individuals in what the untethered had called a pocket.

At the forced pace, the pocket ended up reaching the front of the columns before the sun fully set. Mirl's face was twisted into a grimace and he shook his head to himself as he stared at the monsters. It seemed the fortunate ones were those who didn't have the Sight. They likely thought the untethered were just sick, mad people.

The faces Lin saw spoke of pain and hardship. Compared to those he'd been walking among, these people had the worst of it. All of them wore Bludwieves and even the most human-looking of them had Stitches worked into their arms and torsos.

None of the expressions of those near the front looked remotely kind, friendly, or concerned for Lin and his group as they were marched to stand at the lead. They'd truly been broken down. Was that what this exercise was meant to do? Break the will of those forced to take part?

Off in the distance, marked by a string of lanterns and painted by the dying sun, was a short stone wall. Homes laid behind it, a small village wedged between wide hills and a stretch of forest to the east. Not one village on their path could be safe. Not one town could possibly withstand this force without a resting army there.

Lin thought to Watchlake and the guards there, but even they would likely be overrun. Maybe Wellgrove could withstand an assault, but Lin frowned at that. There just weren't enough fighters.

"Why is *he* with *them*?"

Lin tried to keep moving forward with Mirl, but a Weft chunked the ground in front of his foot, spraying up dirt and grass.

Mirl tripped, regaining his balance as he continued forward. A young man who hadn't spoken filled in Lin's place, helping the aged man steady himself.

"Him?" Pig-face squealed.

"Why are you being herded, child?"

Child. The voice had been deep and rattled Lin's confidence.

Lin forced himself to relax and took a good look at the speaker. It had been too long since he prayed, but seeing the Horned King, pale flesh robed in gray cloth, standing not more than two arm's length away from him made him consider it.

He'd been so focused on the village and the faces of the broken surrounding him, he'd missed the tall, horned bastard.

Up close, the bastard was even taller than Lin first thought, forcing him to crane his neck to look up at the man. *If he even was a man.* Scars lined his torso, sheening with a bluish crystalline hue. Where the other untethered had actual antlers piercing their skulls, the large, many pointed horns coming off the side of his head were an extension of the crown he wore. His crown— Gods— it was like a circlet of starlight. Clearly, it was wrought from Bindings, but the shade was such a pure golden white that it stung the eyes. Similar to the Blade the monster had formed when taking the soldier's head from his shoulders. It was anchored to his head by Thorns, verdant and bright. A Stitch carved across the side of his face, from cheekbone to above his eye, more a normal hued Binding than anything else.

Lin hesitated, then took a knee. "I— I didn't want to cause trouble."

"Rise. Not all of us have opened our true eyes. Come here, beside me. The village of Tiska here, they've yet to put out their offering." One arm swept lazily across the length of the stone shroud. "Without an offering, the stone shroud is as useless as stones stacked by a child."

Thankfully Lin's knees didn't shake as he rose. One of the nearest untethered, average in appearance, blew a large horn as they approached the short wall. The others pressed forward, urged closer to the wall by the untethered at their backs, and handed weapons by one of the tall, collared untethered near the front. A general of some sort, according to Mirl.

Lin glanced at the Horned King from the side of his eye. He could end it all here right now. Couldn't he? Prove to everyone gathered that he was no God, for Gods couldn't bleed.

"Do you think me cruel for demanding tithes?" The Horned King asked.

"No," Lin said.

"Do you think yourself a hero?"

Lin chanced a glance at the tall man again and froze. His bright eyes were trained on Lin's. "I— I don't know what you mean."

"Long ago. Another lifetime ago, I vowed to never be put into a position that would see me fall again. As a child, I learned to study others. Watch them. You carry yourself like you think you might make a difference. And if there is one thing I detest more than anything, it's people who think themselves special. You are a child of mine, like all the others here. Nothing *more*."

Lin went down to one knee as a Weft, sharp and bright, cleaved the air where his neck had been. The pig-faced untethered behind Lin hadn't been so quick. They, and several people including Mirl, fell to the ground. Lifeless bodies crumpled.

The Horned King towered over Lin, looking everything like how the One should've if it had a face. A true monster. "Watch what is to come and if I feel your eyes on me again, I'll remove them."

There was no doubt the untethered meant the words, he spoke them so passively as if stating the sun was downing. Seeing the bastard removed any doubt about whether Velkath Reborn was simply the missing duke. Many of those scars and Stitches looked far too old to be from a recent untethering.

Lin didn't dare look up at the monster, instead watching the events transpiring at the border of the village. Sweat beaded into his eyes, but he didn't dare move. Not yet.

Tiska, was it? A small, peaceful village. One Lin traveled through before meeting with Aemun and Margaret.

The Alderman had appeared, back straight, shoulders back, chin up. The man, a few years younger than Denro by the look of it, appeared ready for war. When he spoke, his voice was clear and booming. "Days ago, we made our offer."

The bone-collar wearing untethered who had been handing out weapons turned and nodded at the Horned King.

Lin nearly followed the untethered's gaze but kept his head locked forward. He could fight the king, fight all the untethered, but it wouldn't go well. He'd wanted to meet with Tylle or find Pael before engaging in a fight. And the surety the Horned King spoke with sent knots writhing through Lin's guts.

"They didn't survive. We require another," the collared untethered called back.

Lin grit his teeth.

"You monsters!" A woman behind the Alderman screamed. Her words devolved into a wail as she collapsed, held up by two or three other citizens.

With the torches flickering, and the sun nearly set, the mass of an army pulling up to the lone village must not have been fully visible. Even so, fear and worry played across the line of faces staring back over the stone wall.

Stone shroud. Lin shook his head. What a load of shit. He knew the things weren't good for keeping anything at bay and this... This proved it.

"And if you get another offering, you'll leave all of them alone?" A child's voice, wavering and pitched, called from the village's side of the wall.

The Alderman paled and looked as if he might fall over. "Tyson!"

"Yes," the Horned King called loudly. "Though, any who would wish to join our clock are still welcome."

Like a blur, the boy vaulted the wall. He couldn't have been older than ten passings and approached the army with his head held high. Taller than little Leo, but just as brave. He turned back and waved at the Alderman. Likely his father. Now that he was closer, his tear streaks were visible but he smiled through it all.

"I'll see you soon Pa—" His voice died, crushed like his throat in the grasp of the Horned King. Shouts and gasps sounded from the villagers, but not one of them crossed the stone shroud. The boy kicked weakly, flailing like a caught fish.

"Your offering is accepted. Next time, don't think to argue with a God."

Lin wanted to look, but couldn't bring himself to do it, not after the warning the Horned King had already given him. And especially not knowing where this was likely going. He shut his eyes and clenched his fists as sounds like the snapping of branches and embers popping filled the air.

Then there was a painful stretching silence followed by a thirsty, gulping sound. Screaming came from the village. Indignation. Fury. Pain. *Horror.*

Lin tensed and started to rise, but a hand held him in place.

"Need to lay lower than a sow's sagging teats." Pael's familiar voice was soft and easy.

Despite how much Lin had hated the diminutive man for taking a shot at Mellyr, he was sure there wasn't another person he'd be happier to have by his side at a time like this. At least among those still living. Lin relaxed and nearly turned to look at the man, stopping as the hand on his shoulder squeezed in warning.

"Don't look at me. The next part will be dragging bodies from those who resist. We'll do it together along with the others they ordered to the front. Then we can talk."

Daring Hate

"I feel bad for the next fools who think to invade Danica. The natural features that make it so hard for Danicans to leave the peninsula give invaders the same challenge on entry."—Belanisian smuggler who refused to give their name.

Flies had taken the place of the steam tendrils that had drifted from the sad, flattened bread bowl the gruel had been slopped into. When it was fresh, it tasted like wet dirt. Now that it had cooled, it resembled a grainy stone. However long ago the army procured the bread, it was well beyond the point where any sane person would think fit for consumption. The flies twitched around, landing and darting away anytime Lin shifted.

While moving the corpses, Pael had briefly explained the composition and layout of the Horned King's army. Lin's guess had been correct. Recruits, unless they were Stitched before arriving, were forced to swear Uethes or die. He'd waggled his finger to prove he didn't have a Bludwieve himself. Pael claimed there were at least a thousand Danicans ensnared, with half as many untethered in fighting condition. No small force.

Collectively they'd settled down a good span southward from Tiska. No villagers had joined in the pressing army, but the Horned King didn't assault the place, instead ordering his soldiers more to the west.

There didn't seem to be any reason as to what villages were consumed and which were left, but Pael had his guesses, none of which he shared as they moved the corpses left by the Horned King's Weft.

Now, Pael was pressed to Lin's back, the two of them sitting and facing opposite directions.

"Do I want to know why we moved the bodies into the camp, and not out of it?"

Pael grunted.

Between the thought and the cool night air, a shiver took Lin. "I knew—"

"Shhh... You're too loud." Pael put his elbow into Lin's ribs. "Don't hear anyone else talking, do you?"

Pael had a point. Only an occasional soft muttering carried through the encampment.

His whole life he'd never seen so many untethered gathered. Shifting. Sitting. *Speaking*. It was like watching wild animals play dice. Even now not far, some worked Stitches into their flesh. There had to be more than simply five hundred of the creatures.

"I can't believe he drank that child's blood. I knew the monsters killed people, but..." Lin's stomach turned. Better that he die before fully untethering if that was even a remote chance.

Pael's back shifted as the man sighed. "Far as I can tell, only the big bastard does that nasty work, but... Yeah, it's about as bad as it gets. But speaking of a child, I'm assuming you got that little one of yours back?"

"I did. After all the trouble I went through, I ended up leaving her with the Scholars. I thought she'd be safe." Lin set the bread bowl down, not wanting to force down any more bites. "But this force... there's only one place on Danica worth anything in the direction it's heading."

Pael shook as he coughed. "There were worse places you could've left her. But if you're here, I'm assuming you met with Grovetender. He sent you alone?"

Lin stared up at the stars and the slow rolling clouds shrouding them in intervals. "Carine and Jun were with me. We encountered scouts, I guess. Killed them. Then when we saw the full force they wanted to retreat— they *did* retreat."

"Smart of them."

Lin dug his elbow into Pael. The older man's side was surprisingly solid. "I saw her and I couldn't help myself."

Pael stilled and it took him a long moment to reply. "Little Tylle, you mean?"

"Yeah," Lin dropped his head and stared down at his Bludwieve. "I wish I knew what she was playing at. But that big bastard, he's had someone working from inside Grovetender's people. Had to of, cause the moment we crossed into Northern Ladrica, he was on us. And since then, she hasn't strayed far from him."

Dirt lined Lin's nails and he picked at it, moving from finger to finger until he ran out. "She wouldn't do that. Betray Erias I mean. When we got to Wellgrove, she made it clear how much he and his people mattered to her."

"I've known her and her sister for a long time, boy. Something changed in Tylle when Margie left for the Ferrucium. She got big into the old ways."

"So either she saw this man and assumed him to be a God when she was younger... or she saw him now and thought the same." Lin scanned the camp, the few cookfires dotting the army fading out, one by one.

"I don't know. I hope she's playing at a bigger game. Playing her part. Getting in close. The bastard cares about the old ways or at least the image of them... No denying that. But at my age, I've seen enough betrayal to recognize shit from honey. And something doesn't smell too sweet about all this."

Lin chuckled and considered just how much he'd missed the braggadocious man.

"Either way, my ass is starting to itch and I haven't slept well in days." Pael yawned, accenting his point. "Think you can watch over me while you ruminate on how Tylle's likely betrayed us?"

"Sure, but only if you can think of a reason why the bastard is moving south."

Pael grunted and curled up behind Lin. He looked awful. Dark circles under his already dark eyes and without his wide-brimmed hat, the wrinkles along his brow were doubly pronounced. He'd always been dark, but without the hat, his pate looked burned from the sun's kiss.

Tylle learned the old ways from someone. Maybe she needed to be saved— or maybe the captives needed to be saved from her. It didn't matter.

Alone and awake, his mind drifted to Denny. She'd have snuck in with him. Likely would've looked at that horned bastard too despite his threats of eye-gouging. Lin licked his lips. Thoughts of the single shared kiss and his failure brought burning tears to his eyes. He should have taken her offer to go with Mellyr. But then all these people, what would've happened to them?

Lin shook his head and stared at the dirt between his legs. No. Leaving Danica to deal with a fallout he helped cause, wasn't how Denro had raised him. Even if he, Denny, and Mellyr might live a quiet life somewhere else, the echoes of Danica would have followed them.

Lin was scared. Terrified that this was one battle they couldn't win. All he ever wanted to do was help people. Start a family. Then he wanted to remove his Stitches, and now? Now he was worried even with his Inlays, he was just a single man.

Admitting it to anyone but himself would be hard to do, but he was in over his head. He'd hoped the untethered threat was exaggerated, he hadn't expected them to be as structured and prepared as they were.

Could *Tylle* be working with him? She'd been robed in white and stood beside the Horned King, hadn't she? Since infiltrating the encampment, he hadn't seen her.

***

When the sky finally lost the stars, Lin stretched his legs. The camp surrounding him had come alive and what slop hadn't been divvied out for dinner was now being shoveled as breakfast. Rewarmed and just as bland looking in the early morning light as at dusk; Lin's appetite hadn't grown.

Pael woke at the second horn that sounded, grousing the entire time. Before the sun was fully over the trees the march had begun anew.

"Anyhow—" Pael mumbled. He'd been explaining what he'd learned since his people's capture. "I've seen a few of the ones with collars. Think like generals. Mean and quick to kill. There is a hierarchy no doubt, at the big bastard is at the top, pissing down on everything and everyone else."

"To think this was growing under the Ferrucium's nose this whole time," Lin said. They walked among other captures, some having their own chopped conversations.

"You'd be surprised the fools I've met who didn't know they had an ugly, uneven mustache," Pael cackled. But his smile looked forced. His eyes furtively glancing around.

"Well, I spoke with some who say they saw Errond's men get captured. Seems his holdings were the first to be invaded. So the silence from them makes all the more sense now. It seems Fallo was one of the first villages to fall— though there were rumors of smaller villages being raided when I was still just an Escorter."

There had been signs. Fewer children were recruited. More Ferrucium soldiers not returning. A rise in untethered.

Had Lin been blind to it? No. But with everything going on, he'd been too busy, too burdened to do anything about what he thought was a distant threat. If there was one thing he wasn't going to do, it was blame himself for this. If the Ferrucium had a better system, if the Accords, Tenets, or whatever name fit them best actually benefited his people instead of shackling them, then maybe the army of untethered could have been avoided.

Or maybe this was how things would've always shaken out. Trading one cruel ruler for an entirely new despot.

Pael nodded but didn't speak. His eyes rested on the shoulders of a mounted untethered. The thing, person, *monster*, looked unnatural atop the horse. With the antlers coming off the side of their head as if they were some sort of stag human monstrosity. Inlays lined its muscles, even across its back.

The green Thorns to ease their minds and halt their madness was one thing. If anyone could understand that now, it was Lin. But the horns? Made to honor the Horned King, no doubt. But that bastard only wore a headpiece, around his crown of Bindings.

Ahead, an old man fell causing the entire forced march to slow. "You there!" The untethered's voice cracked over the press of people. "Get up!"

Once the monster was far enough ahead, Pael said. "You mentioned Errond?"

"Yeah," Lin said. "We thought... You know, we considered that Duke Errond, as silent as he's been, might've decided to take advantage of the chaos. Name himself a King and all that. Or take the moniker Velkath Reborn."

"You know all those stories I've mentioned? The ones where I'm seducing and having copious amounts of—"

"Yes," Lin interrupted.

"Well, all of that happened across three separate stays with Duke Errond. The man is as stupid as he is hospitable. The sort of fool that you feel sorry for when you realize their heart is larger than yours might ever become."

"Maybe someone took advantage of his soft heart."

Pael nodded and flinched as another horn sounded across the midmorning sky. "Well, either way, he's around here somewhere. Look, I'm as brave as most, if not braver, but before I spotted you I was thinking about getting out."

They'd trundled past where the old man had fallen and where the mounted untethered still rested. Like a drunkard, the man leaned against two others. He favored his left leg, limping along.

Lin twitched. The untethered wasn't focused on the old, limping man. No their eyes were locked onto Lin. They had a gaunt face and strips of loose, knotted braids hung like a shroud over their horns. It was then that Lin noticed the collar of bone around their neck.

Untethered weren't pleasant in the normal variety, most looking sickly and frail, but with the horns and bone, the higher-ranked untethered looked terrifying. Having that creature's attention sent Lin's heart racing. But he nodded and turned his attention back to the march. He leaned toward Pael as a child, fully untethered by the flash of Stitches, rushed past him.

Thoughts of Leo flashed through his mind. Which led to more thoughts of Denny. *Denny wouldn't flee.*

"I can't leave. Not without talking to Tylle. Not without learning what the Horned King's goal even is."

"Boy, men, monsters, kings, or Gods. Not one of them amasses a force like this for a trip to the beach. This is beyond us. Plain as that."

A breeze picked up, welcoming against the sweat building on Lin. Perhaps they were coming closer to Wakewatch Lake. Swift as the wind, the child untethered rushed past again. A message runner, without a doubt.

"But Pael," Lin said. He kept his voice low as more marchers crowded in. Whatever was happening near the front wasn't entirely slowing their process but it was pushing many of the outer edges of the force in on itself. If only the Ferrucium soldiers and scholars had enough notice to take advantage. If their goal was Fentis, with its fields and hills before the city, the Horned King's forces would have ample room.

"Don't but me, boy. I haven't managed to live this long by taking fights I can't win."

Lin studied Pael's face. Dark circles under his eyes like burial plots, the deep blues of his eyes like flowers on the grave. "How did you know about Lucky Venya?"

Pael tapped his nose and smiled. "You don't get into my line of work and not learn about her."

"So you knew she was also the One Shadow, Wicked Tel'Myr?" Lin asked.

His brow furrowed in confusion, then contemplation, and finally, he shrugged. "A person can be loved and lucky, while also being hated and considered Wicked. I'm sure I've left plenty in the past who feel that way about me. So, as far as I'm concerned, Venya can keep my loving my dice."

Lin let the words sink into him. Venya had supposedly killed Vellia. But what if it was more complicated than that? What if Aemun had killed Margaret... But it was more complicated than Tylle and Aemun led Lin to believe. Lin shuddered. He hadn't thought about why Margaret had been killed in some time.

"I think I've missed you," Lin leaned over more and nudged the shorter man.

"Ha! Same, boy. Same." Pael's voice lowered and his eye twitched. He rubbed his head and took a deep breath. "Do you even have a plan?"

"Way I see it, they've message runners. And a command structure." Lin glanced over his shoulder and sure enough, the mounted untethered was among the crowd watching the marchers. Lin looked forward as their gaze started to swivel to him. "If we can find Duke Errond, that'll be a start. His men will likely still be loyal to him. Sow chaos when able. Lay low."

"But that doesn't explain how we're going to handle the big bastard or his generals if they notice us."

"I think... I think he's at least as strong and capable as a Nooseman," Lin said.

"And?" Pael said. "You survived a few of them."

Lin considered it. He had of course, but to this day he still hadn't faced a Nooseman one on one and beat them. At least not one trying to kill him. "Survived and defeated them are very different. But it should be possible."

"I don't like *shoulds*," Pael said as a woman beside him jostled past.

"Neither do I," Lin said. He averted his gaze as the mounted untethered pressed their horse through the crowd. Most moved aside to let the monster pass and those that didn't were moved. Some by the horse. Others by neighbors paying more attention and yanking them aside before they could be trampled.

Lin untensed his shoulders as the untethered moved so far ahead they became just another figure in the press. Something about the way that one stared at him didn't sit right. Or maybe it was how the creature rode a horse like it was still human. Lin traced a lone finger over his temple where he'd stabbed the single Thorn. The flesh was smooth, not even a bump to indicate the magic there, but he knew it glowed like a sick firefly.

Hope was a fickle thing. But it was hard not to think that perhaps he'd solved his problem. Aemun's ghost hadn't haunted his mind since working the magic and the only Sigils he'd seen were Stitched into the untethered. If he could survive all this, maybe he had stopped the worst of his poisonous blood.

Waist-high grass marched over and pressed flat in places, had become the new path forward. Dust and seeds drifted on the wind, the haze bringing many in the crowd to sneeze or cover their faces with what cloth they could. Those who were topless used the crooks of their elbows, but Lin had never minded the pollen from fields like this. He took deep breaths, reminded of better days And while the sea of grass was marginally more difficult to traverse than the stretch of hillside he'd joined them at, it didn't account for the slowdown.

Pael had drifted away some time ago, letting Lin know he'd be looking for the duke. All the better considering Lin couldn't recall what the man was meant to look like.

What snippets of conversation carried were over mundane things. Complaints mostly. The treatment of them all, the poor quality of food, and occasional, disgruntled muttering about taking a stand. But as the march continued, it was clear none of the lone mutterers planned to actually stand up to the untethered commanders. Anytime one passed by on horseback, Velkath's Sigil proudly displayed across their chests, antlers worked into the bone of their skulls, the mutterings silenced.

"All of you. Carry as many as you can. Less than ten and you'll get lashings." Ahead, the main cause of the possible congestion became clear as the army was forced to press in around the capsized wagon. It wasn't the largest wagon, but somehow both axles were ruined, apparently having been driven through a sinkhole initially obscured by the grass. It wasn't the only wagon either.

Barrels lined the nearest side of the tipped-over vehicle, pommels sticking out like a crop freshly harvested and sold at market. Hundreds of them if not more. Chances were all of those ahead of their little group had been given the same task. There were more than enough swords, good Ferrucium steel at that, to arm a sizeable portion of the gathered forces.

Some struggled to carry the required ten, blades dropping like overstacked kindling. Those who failed were whipped, lashed by tendrils of Weaves not sharp enough to normally cut, but swung like a cracking whip they split the skin.

Lin took twelve swords. He'd taken plenty of those Lash-like attacks in the woods near Wellgrove and had no interest in taking more.

Studying the weapons brought worry fresh to Lin's mind. Every single pommel had the familiar, Ferrucium shape, like a stretched-out needle's eye. All of them. How many soldiers had been captured or died to stock this? He slowed his thoughts. Surely not all of the swords could truly be from the Ferrucium. Unless they'd been slowly supplied over a long time. Lin shifted to keep his back as straight as possible.

"Don't stop until you reach the pyre at the crest of the hill!" Some voice called over the din of the crowd.

Lin frowned. The horizon was bare of hill and pyre, the sea of somewhat flattened grass rippling as far as the eye could see. Twelve swords. He had to carry them close to his body, flat so the edges didn't catch his arm and spark from the contact with his Inlays. More than one person bumped into him, their own load too cumbersome or unwieldy.

Any sane man wouldn't give his enemies weapons. It felt like a test, and as he carried the load, he felt like eyes were on him. Watching and judging.

Daring Blood

"Danica was the pyre— the hopes and dreams of most citizens the kindling and the desire for betterment the flint. When it finally caught flame, it burned until the corpse of what had been was no longer recognizable."—High Scholar Anya

When they said pyre, the untethered general had meant the burning outpost overlooking Wakewatch lake. What had once been a Ferrucium outpost, long since abandoned, was a pyre to the failure of the Ferrucium to protect its people. From where it rested, and as bright and hot as the inferno raged, it was as if the Horned King wanted to signal Fentis itself.

The forced march had taken all day. Lugging the stacks of steel uphill had seen more than one person stumble, slip, and hurt others as they tumbled down the slope.

Despite the cool night air blowing off the lake, the nearby blaze had brought a layer of sweat to Lin, and judging by the acrid scent, everyone gathered was feeling the heat.

"Drop the weapons and line up. You. Stand off to the side with those others." Lin blinked at the realization that the untethered leader— a woman younger than Lin— was speaking to him. Her hair was a tangled mess around the horns worked into her skull and the sun-bleached bone around her neck was off-kilter. The tip of Velkath's Sigil was hidden under the macabre collar, but the rest of it was visible through the tattered rags she wore. If there were only ten or so of these "generals", Lin had seen two now. Four if he counted the pair riding with the first.

Letting the weapons fall from his faltering grip and clatter against the rest in the pile might've been the easiest thing Lin had done in recent memory. The blades clanged as he tossed them onto the mountain of steel. He took his place alongside a column of about forty men and women. Each one of them was a soldier by their garb and how they carried themselves. Captured and made to work a Bludwieve by the dour expressions and the band of crimson twining on their otherwise unmarred flesh.

"Hot enough up there to light the heavens aflame," a younger man said. He wore a coat that looked muddied and sweat-stained with a ruined tunic underneath. A bruise the size of an egg was across his temple but he smiled warily when he caught Lin staring. "If it's all a great tapestry like they say, I mean."

"Grand," Lin whispered.

"Eh?"

"The Grand Tapestry, woven by the Six Faceless Weavers," Lin whispered. "If it's as they say."

"Right. Garth. By the by. Not that it's like to matter much."

While Lin stood there listening to Garth explain where he was from, how he'd gotten the knot on his temple, and why he thought calling it the Great Tapestry made more sense than Grand, the rest of the army covered the entirety of the sloping descent toward the waters of Wakewatch.

The raging fire, hotter than any Lin had been near before, sent black smoke writhing into the air marring the cloudless sky. Reflected across the waters far below, the fire was mirrored. And so were the untethered, though only one shone so bright as to truly stand out.

The Horned King seemed to materialize from within the flames, his pale skin blackened by soot and smoke but unburnt. His crown of bright Bindings shimmered in the roiling heat and he looked everything like the One. He raised a hand and several of the untethered who'd been lining up around the pile of swords began moving. Each one carried a blade near the flames.

"What many don't know about Wakewatch... it was home to some of the first ironworks of Danica. Even this decrepit outpost has an attached forge." The Horned King's voice boomed across the otherwise silent night. The wind didn't even try to compete and though the burning outpost made noise in its own right, it was as if the inferno had better sense than to cause noise while the tall man spoke. "*These* weapons are the tools of our oppressors!"

Sword after sword was flung into the flames. Then the Horned King moved. "While this group is sent to Wakewatch— the fools too proud to even have a stone shroud— the rest of you will witness the rebirth of a true Danican tradition. Our ancestors didn't fight with swords and armor as the northern army does."

There was no fear as he moved deeper into the flames. The shadow cast from him was long and terrible. No hesitation as he reached into the flames and pulled out a white-hot sword. He carried it, bare-handed with purpose, to what had to be a kiln, though amid the flames it was impossible to be sure.

The tinging blow of a hammer impacting steel shattered the unease. Garth flinched with each strike. One after another, sounding as if the metal itself wailed at the process. Lin closed his eyes. He wasn't dreaming. He wasn't a weapon being crafted. Those dreams— those nightmares— were behind him. A hot hiss sounded, like a nest of disgruntled snakes.

Before long the Horned King reappeared, backlit by flame, sweat rolling down his pale, Inlayed flesh.

"No longer will we be shackled by those beneath us. No longer will our people, true Danicans, wield the weapons of those who would bind us to this land." The muscles along his arm were corded and tight as he lifted the newly forged weapon, still glowing a warm red near the center.

Whoever this Horned King was, he certainly wasn't a blacksmith. The weapon's design was clear. Anyone who'd had to chop wood before could recognize it as an ax. But the head appeared too large and angled off the shaft in such a way to look overly cumbersome.

"Before Vellia, long may her star shine stitched to the heavens, wielded the first magicks, she wielded an ax. Come and craft the tools of our oppressor's destruction." His eyes, bright with Inlays, scanned the line Lin was a part of. "And send them now."

When the monster's eyes were off him, Lin felt he could breathe. Sword, ax, it didn't matter. Ferrucium steel was Ferrucium steel and the shape mattered less than the material itself. Though... It would be better if he wasn't being sent into Wakewatch. Not that he knew much about blacksmithing, but that could be a good thing if he wanted to cause issues with the creation of the axes.

But no. He was led down and around the large lake. It would take them running full-tilt to make it there at a decent time and the ferry which had taken him across not so long ago wasn't on this side of the water. Good thing.

"Can't mean... To make us... Run the whole way... Can they?" Garth kept up, but he gasped for air, cheeks a blushy red.

Lin ignored the young man. He had a choice to make and a decision he wasn't planning to make lightly. Fleeing now— without answers from Tylle. Without Pael and without saving any of the captured soldiers and citizens. Just thinking about it made Lin's stomach twist. Denny wouldn't leave anyone behind.

But the other option... Staying and feigning servitude until he was caught? He'd assaulted the Ferrucium but he was doing the right thing then. Or at least he thought he was.

Wakewatch clarified. The buildings were a sprawl compared to the distant, isolated steads that occupied most of Northern Danica. Despite the late hour, some lamps were lit, flames lighting various shopfronts. The homes would be southwest side, which meant they'd have to cut their way through if they intended to take the entire town.

As they grew near shouts sounded from some of the rooftops. It seemed the Horned King's little show wouldn't go unanswered. *Good.*

A man appeared, stepping from a doorway, clothed in gray and lit by a handheld piece of Wanderer's Ore. His other hand held a boltshooter and he looked fearful and furious at the same time. "We'll give you one chance to explain yourselves. Are you the group who lit the outpost on—" The man's throat was split by a Weft wide enough to show bone. It was a marvel his head didn't fall clean off, but he collapsed, choked gurgles escaping. The ore clattered to the cobbled stones, sparking as it struck.

Arrows fell from the rooftops like rain. *Good.* Lin was far enough back, and his vision enhanced well enough that he didn't need to fear the arrows. Seven untethered, antlerless but with Inlays and Stitches aplenty, charged the city. The leader of the assault, the same bone collar-wearing, One-loved one that had stared at him while on horseback, hung back. Their eyes seemed to scan the various roofs as the untethered they sent into the town scaled the buildings.

"The rest of you go. Show them their folly for standing against Verbanth's wrath."

As the stragglers caught up, winded and gasping for air, Lin rushed in. He didn't need the overly alert monster thinking he hesitated. Not if he meant to stay with the army and find a way to stop the Horned King. Plus, if he could get to people and save them before the others got to them, all the better.

Bells rang as alarms went out over the city. The sounds of screams and the chaos of it all reminded Lin of Wellgrove when the Noosemen descended. He never did find out what befell Duke Wellgrove, but Erias hadn't mentioned anything when they last met.

The screams of people willing, even eager, to hide in their homes scratched across the night sky from disparate alleys, leaving gouges of silence when they ended abruptly. But combat sounded too, from those brave enough to stand against the assault.

Lin rushed forward, glancing behind him and not seeing any of the untethered. Saving anyone would be hard, especially if he was spotted. So he slunk into the shadows of an alley and, using the technique he'd learned and mastered, stabbed Weft after Weft into the woodwork of the building to pull himself to the top.

While it was only two stories tall, it still stood at least as tall as the shopfronts where the assault began. On the horizon, the burning outpost was a sign of what would befall Wakewatch if something didn't change. As childish as it was, he'd harbored a hope that maybe Erias and Azhura's forces, what few remained, might be here waiting for the Horned King. Or at the least Carine and Jun would be waiting to take a stand. But no. Wakewatch was left to fend for itself. And based on the screams and blossoming fires, it wasn't doing well.

A look to the southwest showed newly lit lanterns and people fleeing the city. Good. Though, on foot, chances were they wouldn't be able to outrun any untethered scouts. Wakewatch was doomed. Rumors of war had been spreading since the Fall, but he was sure a town at Danica's heart hadn't expected violence of this magnitude.

Lin blinked back the tears. All these people. Jun and Carine had been right. He was just a single man... He couldn't stop an army like this.

A scream from nearby pulled his focus. He saw a pair of untethered moving in tandem, flesh bright against the dark backdrop of the city, as they raced down an adjacent street. A family fled from them. Two parents and three children, the smallest carried in the father's arms. Then one of the children slipped, tumbling to a sprawl and crying the entire time.

If Lin could get through this without being forced to attack anyone that would be a small victory. But... where the family had fled to was deep enough in the town to not be visible to the general on the outskirts. And the other untethered all looked preoccupied. If he could get through this having saved even one life without taking any... that would be worthy of being called a victory.

Lin sprang from the rooftop he was on, landing on the first-story shop beside it with a thud before racing along to where he'd last seen the fleeing family. The wood underfoot groaned but it was better than attempting to race along thatched roofs like what most of northern Danica had. Dropping to the street below allowed him to quicken his pace, a blur of Bindings flickering around a corner.

Screams.

Rounding the corner, Lin saw the pair of untethered creating Weft after Weft, the brittle-looking magic biting the cowering man's flesh without slicing entirely through. He howled with each new wound but stood his ground. His children and wife screamed behind him.

Anytime one of the monsters relented with the Wefts and drew near, the man would lash out to keep them at bay. He held a thin cleaver, the edge bloody. "Get back!" He cursed. "Back! Leave us be!"

A fresh Weft caught him across his arm.

"Let me have a turn!" Lin growled. He did his best to look as monstrous as the other two and judging by the renewed begging of the family, he managed well enough. Using his weight, he jostled between the two untethered, knocking the scrawny one on his right off-balance.

A glance around the alley and up at the overhanging roofs. *Nothing. No watchers.*

"I won't warn you again!" The tip of the cleaver shook and the man breathed heavily, sweat and blood wrapping him like a sick cloak. Odds were the man wouldn't make it. But Lin could save the children. The wife.

Behind the man, his family begged. The two children pulled at the tattered tunic hanging from him in strips. Was this what Fallo had seen before the fall? Before the families were slaughtered and strung about the buildings.

Standing between the untethered, Lin formed a Needle in each hand, jamming both into the ears of the untethered beside him. The scrawny one on his right twitched just out of the way, and the Needle, thin and sharp but not at all strong, shattered against the creature's skull.

As the one on the left crumpled without sound, the other attacked. So fast and fierce that it had to have been waiting for some sign of betrayal. Hissing curses came, but this one had their lips

Stitched. Lin pivoted to stand between the monster and the fearful family. "Go!"

Lin dropped his hand and let a Blade form, burning bright in the otherwise dark alley. The untethered lunged, claws scraping the air where Lin had just stood. With an upward slash, the arms were severed. Barely a spark erupted from Lin's Blade clashing against the poorly done Inlays. Ochre-hued blood pooled from the wounds, the scent of rust ruining the alley. Not that it had smelled well prior to the kill.

When he turned, the family was still there. Fear illuminated on their faces by the Blade. But none stared at the magic, only at him. "Run." He lowered his arms, letting the Blade disintegrate. "Head to Fentis. Others have already fled."

"This alley is a dead-end," The wife said. "And Able is too weak. We could hide. There is a cellar not far—"

"Shh Tanna. I'm not weak at all and this man had better," the man wheezed. " Recognize that. So move aside or be moved."

Bravado often tasted like sour milk, but Lin swallowed it. Odds were good the man would die running away and the last thing he wanted his family to see was a brave man. A hero. How could Lin find fault in that? The wounds along Able's arms were shallow, but many. And when he turned at the entrance to the alley his back was a mosaic crafted in blood. Shirt and flesh alike ruined.

Lin watched, following at a slow pace. As early as the night was, there had to be others he could still save. There had to be. He reached the alleyway's entrance and looked left, seeing nothing, then right to watch the fleeing family.

The silence had grown, eerie and heavy. Where were the screams, the joyous jubilation from the untethered, the fighting?

Lin checked his left again. He'd thought he saw movement for the briefest moment, like a large dust particle drifting past. Then a Weft, sharp and bright and everything a Weft should ever be when thrown by a Ferrucium Binder, took the Able's head cleanly from his bloodied shoulders. The man's corpse took a half-step before stumbling and collapsing into a flower planter, rolling and crashing to a stop. His cleaver clung against the cobbled road.

Tanna clutched the corpse, sobbing, screaming, cursing. Her children pulled at her—

Lin broke the crescent Wefts arcing for them, but it wasn't easy. It was like scraping stone with his fingernails or chewing on the edge of a sword. Weaker Wefts could unravel at a thought. Much the way the Noosemen seemed capable of taking control of the magic.

"I saw you and thought to myself... How did they manage to slip past him? I see now. I've watched you for a time." The scraggly-haired general stalked toward Lin from the left, Blade brandished in their left hand.

Fuck.

"I know." Lin stepped fully from the alleyway and bladed his stance. He'd already thought he was dying not long ago. Untethering. If this was his last act, so be it.

"Which is why you were careful and thought to kill them inside the alley. Clever. But not clever enough. What did you think one man might do?"

"Enough to make a difference. Your Horned King isn't a God." Exhaustion was a familiar friend to Lin and all the marching and slop hadn't done him well, but when he formed his Blade, it was as bright as a fresh Binding could be. Golden-hued like the moon itself had given him a sliver of itself.

"Never claimed he was. But what he will do is make Danica free."

"At what cost?"

The leader shrugged, shifting the glow from Velkath's Sigil across their chest.

"How much blood does freedom require?"

A sneer played across the untethered's face. "And how much blood have you spilled? You don't get to stand there after killing two of my soldiers and claim your hands are clean!"

Without warning two more Wefts flew toward the children who desperately pulled at their mother's skirts. Lin unraveled them, fingers and hand cramping. Then the general's Blade was at his side, sparking against the Inlay along his left arm. The untethered spun, slicing with their other hand. This. This was the caliber of monster that fell on Fallo. It was obvious from the timing of strikes, and the fluidity of movements.

But Lin had grown since Fallo. Learned and evolved. The untethered lunged forward, Blade ready to pierce through Lin's sternum.

Lin shifted his torso, hips aching from the motion, the flat of the Blade hissing as it scraped against the dark band that striped his chest. Bringing his left elbow down as he pressed his right palm flat along the untethered bone-thin arm, the arm popped, dangling loosely at the joint. He grabbed the monster by the horns and with all his force, flipped the creature onto the pavement. Steps sounded from behind, hurried, but before Lin could turn a tackle from his left sent him sprawling.

Garth wheezed, eyes full of fear as his brow bunched. A crease lined his forehead and his mouth trembled.

"Bind him." A rattle sounded from nearby, not quite steel. Bound Metal, the rolling-oil sensation unmistakable as it washed over him. Pain, sharp like the teeth of a hungry cat bit into his wrists, and nausea took him fully.

"Cowards!" Lin bellowed. He spat toward Garth and the other soldiers who'd come with him. Five in total as well as another one of the horned bastards.

"W-we... What would you have us do?" Garth asked, face red and tears fighting to stream down his youthful face.

"He'd..." The leader grunted as they were helped up, shaking off the soldiers who lifted them. "Mhmm." Their arm popped back... And it healed, the soft glow of cerulean lighting the area they caressed. "He'd have you all die. Ask another question like that and I will feed you your own tongue."

Garth cowed. Lin struggled as the world spun. What didn't these bastards have? Ferrucium steel. Bound Metal. *The dagger.* No. Anya had it safe.

Lin stared at Garth. It was easy to forget that many of the Dukes's soldiers had never seen combat. Hadn't fought untethered the way the Ferrucium had. Many of them didn't know that nearly all Danicans could Bind. "I want us all to live."

Lin was lifted by the chains, each manacle digging into his flesh at multiple points. Warmth leaked from his wrists and each jostle dug them deeper. "What now? Make an example of me?"

The leader, limping and followed by the soldiers, led Lin to the edge of the docks but remained silent.

The ferryman was dead, mouth and eyes open as his head hung from one of the bells that had rung when the untethered attacked. His boat burned, lighting the blood-stained wood and casting shadows across the dark water.

Lin was pressed to the dock, and forced to kneel where wood met water. Across the way, the outpost still danced with flame. But the army was moving. Coming in full force, some forced, some eager. Wagons rolled, staked untethered like grotesque banners unmoved by the wind. And the Horned King was among them, standing taller than any man should, heading for Wakewatch.

Disastrous Hope

"There is a game Danican children play called Gudladr involving several tokens and a board that can be scratched into the earth. Basic though it is, it teaches strategy. More children should play Gudladr if it means our next generation is raised to have more cunning and less fear." —Weaver Azhura

Chained and kept beside the water as the army marched in felt akin to being swallowed by the vast lake. The progress was slow. Those conscripted who hadn't been sent in to assault the town walked in, shock, horror, and disgust evident by most reactions. Even a good few of the untethered looked disturbed by the chaos and carnage. Limbs, much like in Fallo, were strung along the shop fronts like macabre decorations for some old, ancient religion. *Fitting, given the context.*

It was clear why he'd been placed here. The Horned King, freshly draped in clean gossamer robes, approached. Bright as a rising sun. Pale as the first flake of winter snow. Lin had watched him the entire time he sat there, the fear of losing his eyes diminished by the very real threat of instead losing his life.

But the man didn't walk. No. Velkath Reborn, the Horned fucking King, was atop a palanquin being carried like some sort of God. His flesh which had run greasy with sweat and soot from the flame was clear and clean and those who carried him were all marked with Velkath's Sigil across their bare chests.

His leaders, those with the bone collars, had already stalked the streets. They hunted.

And none of it mattered. Not the clean robes that looked soft as silk. Not the markings on the untethered who carried him, all of them with horns and the green magic jammed into their skulls. No. None of it mattered once he noticed *her*. Sheathed in a white shift at his side, Tylle was beautiful and just as dangerous-looking as the rest of the monsters.

Tylle.

Jealousy, hot and fierce as the outpost flames raged within him. Breaths came shorter, harder as the crowd dispersed, making its way through the streets to pillage and ruin any semblance of what Wakewatch had been.

Lin stared at her. At the cut of her neckline and the Sigil burning along the bones that showed there. The flesh. Her face was impassive, the scar at her jaw barely visible as she craned her neck to examine the ruin of the city. She looked everywhere but at him.

There was still a chance, slim as the space between her and the pale bastard, she was simply acting. Playing a part at something larger. Tears welled up and as he leaned forward, not able to plunge into the water but near enough to see the mess he'd become, he screamed. Rage and fury, all the emotions and frustration he'd tamped down for so long lighting like a blaze. His wrists stung and even feet above the water where he should smell the algae, moss, and fresh air from the wind off the surface, the stench of death that suffused the city didn't leave him.

Everything. That was what he'd given her. And for what? For her to sit there and ignore him? To look everywhere but at him. Calming wasn't easy and even the kick to his side delivered by the bone-collared leader who'd dragged him to where he sat didn't quell his fury.

Flashes of Denny's uneven smile made it worse. He'd said over and over it wasn't the thought of Tylle keeping him from having a life with her, but it had at least a bit. The thought of, 'what if'?

What if?

Lin looked up, exhaling as he leaned back. His breath fled him in foggy bursts.

Briefly, it seemed the Horned King's procession would pass by entirely, but once the main force had filled the alleys and roadways like spilled blood might line grooves in tiles, the palanquin came to a stop. It lowered as the untethered who carried it knelt.

It was baffling to think they'd been this organized. This capable.

"Why is this child restrained?" The Horned King asked. His voice booming, arms raised.

"He is not one of your children, my king." The commander said from the kneeling position they'd taken beside Lin at the dock.

There was no mistaking the King's expression for anything but rage. His thin lips twisted into a snarl. "All Danicans are my children, Rith."

"O-of course," Rith mumbled. "I meant that he was aiding those who thought they were too good to follow the old ways."

"I see."

Lin kept his stare at the monster's bare, ashen-gray feet. Each step brought the Horned King closer, a sweet scent like vanilla carrying with him.

"You're the one who wouldn't stop staring at me like you thought you could make a difference. Look at me now."

The Horned King stood near enough that a Blade formed from either of them would reach— but Lin being bitten by cuffs of Bound Metal meant the King had the advantage. His muscles rippled just from breathing, lean and taut as his body was. The Stitch along the side of his face accented his cheekbone, giving him a wild appearance to his eyes. Behind him, a host of untethered stood. Velkath's Sigil bright on their sternums. Antlers stabbed into their heads and hued with the green magic of stasis. *Copper.*

"There is something familiar about you." The King took another step forward, eyes narrowing, nostrils flaring.

Lin studied the man. The monster. The so-called God.

"I'd never met you before the other day. But I've killed plenty of your *children.*" Lin spat the last word mockingly.

Growls and hisses sounded from the untethered who had circled them— nearly ten in total, each with a crude ax of Ferrucium steel hanging from their hands.

"My lord," Lin added.

"Lord?" The Horned King shook his head and raised his arms. "I'm no wasteful Duke, ignorant as they are. I'm not a little lordling sitting north of the pass, scared of the shadows. I *am* the shadows!" His words accented like the clap of thunder. "If you won't call me God, save the titles. But no... I remember where I've seen you."

The Horned King grabbed his crown of antlers and lifted them from his head. "Several times I've seen you. Several times I've spared you. But no longer." He held the crown at his side, the many points sharp and brutal looking.

Without the crown, he appeared shorter. But the Stitches along his face extended up along his skull. His hair was shaved short showing the Thorns all around mingled with the golden Bindings. Like a garden of daisies planted around his temples.

Of course. "Outside Drekinsburg," Lin whispered.

"Perhaps the most recent time... but the first?"

Ice trickled down Lin's spine as he realized what the man was saying. *First time.* Flashes of monsters of a caliber he'd never experienced before. Waking up with a wound that would've killed him if Tylle hadn't intervened.

Lin pulled his eyes away from the Horned King, looking for her amongst those kneeling. Rough fingers grabbed his chin, squeezing and pulling his focus back. "You've received a new name recently, haven't you? Hero of the Fingers. A fitting title seeing as how we first met."

Each joint along his knuckles snapping and popping back on themselves. Then nothing as his arm had done the same. It was the first time he'd seen a Binding be taken over by someone else. "Fallo," Lin said though he couldn't move his jaw to put force into the word.

"Fallo," the Horned King agreed.

Then from the corner of his eye, he saw Tylle. Standing there motionless, holding the crown. Her dark eyes met his, her face remained impassive. Might as well have been wearing a Nooseman's mask for all the emotion he could read in her features. "Her," Lin whispered.

The Horned King smiled, showing unnaturally sharp, yellowed teeth. His breath smelled of rust and mint and rotted flesh all at once. "Her?" He released Lin's face with a slight push and turned to Tylle, raising his hand toward her.

If this monster knew him from then… There was no doubt he knew Lin and Tylle had traveled together. No sense hiding it and maybe, even if he'd die here, he'd have answers. "She— She told me she killed all the attacking untethered."

The Horned King's smile slowly dropped. He patted his muscled chest and ran a hand over his face. "Untethered. An ugly word created by our oppressors! But no matter the name, I'm still very much alive. To be lied to… To have a companion betray you… This hurt you feel—" The Horned King rushed toward him and slammed a palm against Lin's chest. " —Is a pain I wouldn't wish on anyone. But it happens."

"I never lied." Tylle's voice was like a knife through Lin's chest. "I told you I was more of a monster than my enemy. It isn't my fault you never asked who my enemy was."

The Horned King stood fully upright. "Truthful Vellyr would be proud." He shrugged, then frowned.

All around, the kneeling untethered hadn't moved.

If there was ever a moment Lin wished for Pael to appear and pull salvation from thin air, it was now. But the short man was missing. Lin cleared his throat and took in a deep breath. "I've heard you called many things now. The Horned King. Velkath Reborn. Who are you? Who are you *really*?"

The Horned King paced, reaching out and taking his antlered crown from Tylle. "Danica's hope. Rise."

Lin blinked at that. All the untethered around him rose but the way Lin had been forced to his knees made it impossible for him.

"Help him up," The Horned King commanded.

Rith moved at once, jerking Lin upright.

"Walk with me."

Murmurs spread through the gathered monsters, but all moved away for him. Tylle was gone, back atop the palanquin.

Wakewatch was a ruin. Bodies and limbs scattered, many drawn up and Stitched into crude approximations of Velkath's Sigil. "It is a brave thing you've done."

Lin pulled his eyes from the blank expression of a hanging man, limbs fully intact but body twisted so savagely that his back had to have broken from some great impact.

"I can't think of a single sane person who'd not want to stop this," Lin said, unable to lift his arms in the manacles, and pointed with his chin.

"We are of the same mind then." Despite the Horned King's long limbs, he kept his pace slow so as not to force Lin to keep up. His robes, long and flowing, trailed along the street. Grime and worse covered the hem and his lip curled in disgust. "Would it be that violence like this could be avoided.

"Danica is a carcass, long dead. Infested with parasites. Yet Ladrica and other nations still want the fetid strings of meat from the bones. We carve our way through the corpse, cleansing it."

The Horned King raised his hands.

"There is no way we're of the same mind!" Lin snapped.

"Aren't we? Does this slaughter enrage you? They ignored rules set out long ago. My version of the *Binding Tenets*. Every village we've cleansed. So it was alright for our kind, we Inlayed, to be treated as monsters? Persecuted and prosecuted? But when the power shifts, new laws can be ignored?"

"You are monsters!"

The Horned King spun, robes flaring as he grabbed Lin's chin with one large hand, the other tracing a line along Lin's temple, coming to a rest where the Thorn had taken root. A nail dug in, sharp and painful. "*We*, all of us, are not monsters. We are people with a proclivity for madness. It seeps into our minds, but you found the solution!" The nail dug in deeper. "Why is that the Scholars kept a potential cure to themselves in that ivory tower? Why are the Ladricans and Fentians and anyone with a "just" cause to do so all allowed to test our people?

"If we are to be monsters, let them truly find reason to fear us more than just our existence!"

A line of warm blood trickled over Lin's eye.

"I've been told you are flexible of mind. Do you truly not see your hypocrisy by calling *us* monsters?"

Lin couldn't form words. His temple throbbed and there was no doubting the self-proclaimed God's passion. But... It wasn't right. These people, all of them, were innocent. Even if the argument could be made that untethered were innocent— and surely some of them had to be— that didn't change the truth that the majority were violent.

When Lin didn't answer, the Horned King continued forward, stopping after several steps and waiting for Lin to follow. It was like a guided tour of the carnage. Every turn through Wakewatch's streets brought a new horror.

"You see death. But like nature, there must be decay for life to flourish. Those that escaped? *Good*. They will doubtless tell others and those others might heed the laws I've decreed. Hero of the Fingers. We are those who walked before. We are those who will walk after. And what those who fled left behind? Clothes. Supplies. I see food for those who've starved. Warmth for those who've frozen. Beds to sleep in, at least for one night. Just because madness once had a grip on some of our brothers and sisters, doesn't mean it still does. This is a war. And it's long been fought."

"But aren't there other ways?" Lin asked.

"Are there?" The Horned King slowed and turned, a pensive look on his Stitched pale face. How did the Fall occur? The first real sign of change across Danica in centuries. How did you and Erias's little band effect change; through peaceful conversation? Or your venture across the pass, hmm? Surely no Ladricans were harmed while you were there. No deaths occurred for you to achieve your ends."

"It's not the same! I didn't have a choice!"

A smile revealed his sharp teeth. His right eye bulged as his flesh pulled tight, the Stitches and scars across his face taut. "And neither do I. Though, if I did, this is still the path I would walk upon."

When they reached the edge of the southwest side of Wakewatch, Lin spotted the wagons. While the main force had come through to occupy and overrun the bustling city, the wagons had continued around the lake. They were still a ways off, but the cargo was clear. All the staked untethered rattled and bounced as they went.

"I want to ask at least once. One question, and don't think I won't know the truth of it." The Horned King stared off into the distance, his tongue licking his thin upper lip. "Will you join us? You are more akin to me and mine than the Scholars or Ferrucium soldiers. Afflicted by the blood poisoning as you've been.

"I could use someone like—"

"No," Lin interrupted. "I'm done being used."

The pensive look fell away as the monster smiled again and gently raised a hand. Lin flinched and pulled away. "You misunderstand. Either way, you will be used. I'll have you walk behind your sleeping brethren while you consider my question."

Lin had a curse ready on his tongue when three shadows erupted from behind the untethered-laden wagon and rushed toward the Horned King. His first thought was the trio were Jun and Carine, but they hadn't been wearing flowing black robes when they'd left, and there wasn't a third person he knew who might keep up with them besides Denny or Tylle. And one was dead and the other a traitor.

Untethered rebelling was where his mind went next, but seeing the glint of hauntingly familiar flat metal masks, Lin shuddered at the realization. Noosemen. King Lodram's assassins.

Before these new, cognizant untethered struck fear into Lin, it was these assassins who'd haunted his waking dreams. If untethered were the rot eating at Danica from within, then Noosemen were meant to be the physiker's scalpel.

One Nooseman was taller than the others by a head, and they rushed straight at the Horned King while the other two took off-angles to catch the monster in a pincer attack. It was a brutal strategy meant to not give the Horned King a chance to react and Lin wished his hands were free to assist.

A Blade formed in each Nooseman's hand. As swiftly as they moved it looked similar to the falling stars Lin had watched with Jun.

But what were stars fallen from the sky compared to the light of one still in it?

Golden white, impossibly pure, the Horned King's Blade formed flat at his side. If he was surprised by the assault, his expression didn't betray it. A crazed smile formed as he licked his lips. The taller Nooseman's Blade caught the Horned King across his shoulder. A diagonal slash meant to kill in a single strike.

At either side, the other two Noosemen flanking arrived and thrust the tips of their Blades at the monster's sides.

All three Blades exploded into sparks and were reformed by their wielders only to shatter against the Horned King's flesh again. Over and over, not a drop of blood spilled.

"Pale imitations. Did they tell you you were loved? Blessed? They lied. They always lie."

Lin flinched at the sudden ferocity as the monster parried the attack from his right with so much force the attacking Nooseman spun to the ground and skittered. The Horned King pivoted and spun, grabbing the leftmost Nooseman by the metal mask they wore. It crushed like a dry leaf, folding inward until metal shrieked and a dull pop sounded. The Nooseman's arms went limp.

"They send children in the place of men!" The Horned King screamed, tossing the limp corpse at the Nooseman still standing. It hurtled too fast to jump away from so the Nooseman cut down with all his might. Blood coated him in a spray as his ally's two halves crashed to the ground beside him.

From their movements, it was true these Noosemen didn't match the ferocity of the one-eyed Nooseman who'd attacked the Ferrucium. *Children.* These Noosemen had to be recruits. Newly forged members. Lambs to slaughter.

Shouts carried from Wakewatch and Lin fell to his knees as the Horned King spun to stare at the blood-soaked Nooseman. The one he'd sent stumbling earlier was struggling back to their feet, but their mask was skewed and blood streaked down their face. It was a young girl. Her eyes were hard and emotionless with no fear seeping into her cold features.

"I'll go at your speed, then at mine," the Horned King said. He shifted his weight onto his front foot and slashed diagonally. It was a mirror of the first strike the Nooseman had landed on him.

The attack was easily blocked, and the next, and the next, but with each attack the Nooseman was pushed back nearer to the wagons of untethered.

"You aren't blessed by the Six. You aren't loved! When you die, no one will remember your name because all of your comrades will be corpses beside you!"

This side of the Horned King was what Lin had expected when first seeing the untethered. Cruelty. Rage. A fury that he barely kept under the surface as he pretended to be a God. This emotion was something Lin could use if he ever found the chance.

The Nooseman whispered something unintelligible as his Blade was broken one final time and the Horned King's Blade took his head from his shoulders.

The last Nooseman screamed as she charged. She threw three Wefts at the Horned King in quick succession and he unraveled them with ease. But her true goal had been to stab him and this time she'd aimed the tip of her Blade at his eye.

Mask askew, breaths coming fast, the Nooseman struggled to inch her Blade closer. Her arms shook as she pressed forward against the Horned King's lazy block. Then the motes of light remaining from her shattered Wefts rained down like fallen stars. Tens upon tens of glittering, shining trails of light impaled her.

"None of you are loved."

It wasn't until after the three Nooseman were dead that any of the Horned King's people made it to where Lin had been taken. They glared at Lin. He glared back, but couldn't keep his eyes from the dead Nooseman for long. Recruits or not. Children or not, they were still coordinated and had been strong. They'd been Noosemen and the Horned King had *toyed* with them.

Without a word to Lin, the Horned King stripped the two intact masks from the dead Noosemen and handed them to the first two leaders who had arrived. "Wear them as penance for arriving late to my aid. Feel the burden these foolish children bore."

Disastrous Bone

"War comes for us all, same as death. Often it comes for us wrapped in the things we love, making us all the more reluctant to step toward it. But step we must." —Erias Wellgrove

The coarse rope chafed both Lin's waist and pride. It was bad enough having the Bound Metal manacles biting into him with every jolting step, but the tight rope rubbed his sides raw. If he walked too slow, he was pulled along. Too quick and he had trouble looking away from the staked untethered. Or the Noosemen, dragged behind the cart by a short rope.

Lin tried to keep his eyes on the sky but was tired.

The staked monsters had the bases of the stakes stabbed through the bottom so the gruesome poles stood upright like banners. Living untethered walked beside the wagons. If the bottom of a stake caught, they freed it. If a Noosemen's corpse did the same, they kicked it.

Children. Trained to be members of the King's Noose or not, the dead had been young. Lin's plea for the youth on the island meeting place was fresh in his mind. The next generations deserved better.

It had been two days since Wakewatch and being forced to march and tied to a wagon had left his mood fouler than he thought possible. He kept expecting Pael to appear and save him, but in the two days, he'd seen no sign of the man.

Everything Carine had worried about Tylle ended up being true. How could she have sided with the Horned King? Even as far back as Fallo? It was a cruel blessing Lin still had enough water within to shed tears as he considered it. But a seed of hope was blooming as if his salty tears had given it sustenance.

She hadn't really known Lin back at Fallo. They hadn't yet spent all that time together. Saved each other. And if he considered that to be true, he had to acknowledge the inverse. How odd was it that the untethered attacked Lyre the night they arrived? And that other random assault on the roadway leading from Creekside. What if it had all been because of her?

The wagons slowed, then regained a bit of speed.

"Terrifying, huh?"

Lin blinked at the soft voice. He'd been so focused on his pace and avoiding the corpses dragged in front of him, that he hadn't noticed Tylle slip onto the wagon's rear. The hem of her dress fluttered in the air just above the corpses, like a pale shroud for the deceased.

"But I suppose you saw them when you went north."

"Leave me alone." Lin's cheeks flushed. He didn't even mean his quick retort, and that was as embarrassing as admitting how hurt he was.

"You don't mean that," she said, like she'd read him.

Lin met her eyes before dragging his gaze away. "Maybe I do."

"Do you?" Tylle asked, pulling his eyes back with that simple question. She smiled that crooked, uneven smile of hers that was as rare as Denny's. And that's how he realized he was in far over his head. Not the Horned King. Not the armies both within and without wanting to destroy Danica. But because Denny deserved better than to be compared to this cruel woman. And he couldn't help but do it.

"I don't think I do," Lin said, deflating. "This the part where you tell me I've got the big, wicked bastard misunderstood? That he had a good reason to rip a child apart and drink their blood? Or that he isn't as big a threat as the Noosemen, despite treating them like playthings."

Tylle scowled and shook her head. "Some things have no sense. And some people, even Gods, will have their actions weighed against their worth and be found wanting."

"I don't understand. Pael told me... Told me you wanted me to deal with this not more than two months back. Why? If you'd been working with them all along."

He watched her expression, hoping for anything to give a clue to her betrayal or innocence. He couldn't help but stare at the slit across her chest that showed the top of her breasts and Velkath's Sigil etched into her flesh there. For someone who'd been wrapped and covered tighter than a wound, she sure displayed herself now. As gray and gaunt as she was, she was still beautiful. A sharpened version of what Margaret might've been.

Tylle looked beautiful in that gown, beautiful with her Stitches fully displayed. Beautiful in general. And that made her dangerous. Though, he'd always known how dangerous she was.

"Are you familiar with the tale of—"

"No." Lin forced himself to glare at her. He quickened his pace as the rope tugged around his waist. Across the vast hillsides, the forced march was slowing. But not the wagons. Whatever the orders had been, they'd been forced to continue. Nothing good could come from transporting these untethered. Unless the Horned King meant to free them from their stasis and even that seemed a poor decision. "You don't get to tell me a tale. You don't get to sway me with a story of Vellyr, Verbanth, or Virt. Tell me *your* tale!"

Tylle shifted and crossed her legs, a frown bringing wrinkles to the corners of her mouth like a carrion bird eager to feast on the now-dead smile. "I thought meeting him might sway you."

"Because I was swayed so easily by you?" Lin shook his head. "You thought me so weak-willed?"

"I thought you so understanding. But then you rushed to Ladrica and I was sent to investigate for lack of others." Tylle ran a hand along one of the Bound Metal stakes at her side and shuddered at the touch.

"And I'm glad I went. Rescued the family you couldn't care less about! Learned the truth about Wicked Tel'Myr too!"

"Venya," Tylle whispered.

"Funny, you didn't tell me the truth about that tale."

Tylle shook her head and stared up at the sky for a long minute. Her neck extended, and the sigil across her chest burned brighter. He'd spent so much time wishing to see her, and now that he did the thought disgusted him.

When she met his gaze again, her eyes glistened. "If I had, you might've drawn parallels to Margie and I that weren't meant to be drawn. But if my simple stories and teachings brought the truth closer to a single person, I did my job as a priestess of Vellyr."

Lin couldn't control the tremble that took his fists. A fire, that same rage that had burned from him when seeing her beside the Horned King on his palisade, rose hot through his core. And then it petered out. There was so little fuel left for the furnace. "I... I sacrificed *everything* for you. Everything."

"You can say and think what you want about me, but you don't get to do that. I never asked you to Inlay yourself. I never told you to do anything. You chose to follow me!"

"And it still wasn't enough to fix Danica!" Lin went on, ignoring her counter. She had bloody well ruined his life, so far as he was concerned. The way things stood with him tied to a wagon full of frozen untethered, he would've been better off dying in Fallo.

Denny flashed through his mind. The soft, gentle brush of her lips. The smile she rarely shared. "The Ladricans pulled back and received the order from Lodram himself to stay their hands until the council meeting. But me? I'm... barely holding on because of you! I've untethered, damn you! And you sit there... Smiling while you betray *everyone* who actually cares about you. Pael, Erias, me!"

Tylle slipped from the back of the wagon and easily leaped over the nude corpses. She grabbed the rope around Lin's waist and yanked him forward. Her hand blurred as she slapped him. "You speak as if I owe you something! As if I caused you to slip into madness. I warned you how real of a threat that was!"

Lin spat the blood from his lip, pink spittle staining the front of Tylle's white dress. With his head hung, he stared at the tall grass tickling his shins. "You owe me many things. An apology for one."

"Oh... I'm sorry." She shook her head. Her eyes glistened and she looked away. "Sorry, you never once bothered to ask enough about me to see where my heart lay."

"With monsters." Lin jutted his chin at the distant palanquin the Horned King sat upon.

"I thought after the Fall, after all this time, you'd have stopped using such small-minded labels. He *is* Velkath Reborn. The blood of Gods runs through his veins."

"Aemun too apparently. But he bled like a gutted pig. You saw to that." Lin was ready for the slap this time and ducked, the flat of her hand connecting upside his head. It ached, but not nearly as badly as his mouth throbbed. "So does Mellyr. And King Lodram allegedly."

Tylle pulled away, hands shaking. Her thin lips had drawn to a tight line and she shuffled through the grass, back to the wagon. "I shouldn't have struck you."

Lin couldn't fight the chuckle that surfaced. "I've been through far worse since we last parted."

"Speaking of Mellyr..."

"No letters, no check-ups, no nothing, and now you want to ask about your family?"

Tylle sighed and seemed to notice the stain on her dress for the first time, rubbing at it with the back of her hand. "There was no need to check up. I knew she was with you. And that you'd keep her safe. I'd hoped... Rather foolishly that you'd bring her with you."

Lin froze and the slow pull of the wagon nearly brought him to his knees. He stumbled, legs numb, realization crashing around him like a wave. But he needed to stop making assumptions. He needed to put thought into words. "Why?"

"Because as you just said, she has the blood of Gods," Tylle said. Her voice soft and light, carried on the wind like a dandelion's seed.

The terrible image of the Horned King's blood-stained face and robes tore through Lin's mind. "You can't mean what I think you mean!"

Tylle didn't react, her face had returned to that same placid expression she'd borne when he first laid eyes on her. "What is it you think I mean?"

"You'd give *her* to him."

"Nothing so monstrous. When she comes of age—"

"Not you too!" Lin interrupted. "You'd give her to that monster? Everyone wants to marry that fucking *child* to someone. You're no better than the Scholars or King Lodram! I'm not the same man you left at the docks!" Lin twisted in his manacles and rushed forward. He'd wanted to give her the benefit of the doubt. But that had burned him from the outset at Lyre and he was done trusting her.

Done listening.

He was almost to her when her foot caught him in the sternum. Air left his lungs as he crashed to the ground. He tumbled and twisted, dragged through the grass like he was one of the corpses in front of him. A stench wafted from them, sour and rotted. His manacles dug into him, chafing his wrists as he tried to right himself.

Lin tried to get his feet under him, but the grass stalks were too slick. At least he wasn't scraping his backside raw, but as it continued, a fear settled in him. She might leave him to be pulled.

"Slow the wagon!" Tylle called from beside him. A handful of untethered had surrounded them now, two of them wearing the Nooseman's masks.

When the wagon finally stopped, Lin noticed Rith. She wore a strange smile on her gaunt face.

"Lift him," Tylle ordered.

Whatever rank Tylle had within the Horned King's forces, these monsters listened to her. Truly jumped at her commands.

When he was upright, the wagon started rolling forward again. Tylle had already started walking away but turned to look over her shoulder. "If he tries to run, break his legs. Lin, listen, you'd be better off if you were the same man you'd been because whether you like it or not, I haven't changed. But consider the truth, you're only alive because Velkath Reborn wants you to be."

Lin nearly fell again as the rope grew taut and pulled him off-balance. The handful of watchful untethered remained nearby, talking among themselves.

Wrapping his head around everything proved difficult when he couldn't stop thinking about Tylle. All the little moments, all the betrayal. What if she *had* killed Margaret, then killed Aemun to keep his silence? Or what if Aemun knew something about Tylle that she hadn't wanted him to share? Lin had been naive back then. So why were they heading to Fentis? The big bastard claimed it was to make the scholars pay... but why else?

Tylle had given Lin the answer. Or an answer at any rate. *Mellyr.* But she'd lied already, or willfully obfuscated the truth. How could he be sure that was *really* what the Horned King wanted? Tylle wanted Mellyr out of the tower. Easier to take. Not to mention all the other secrets she'd kept— Lin blinked. He had his own secrets now. *The broken dagger.* If he could get his hands on it, he'd be able to slit the Horned King's throat with ease. Didn't matter how Inlayed his damned flesh was.

***

Lin stretched his legs in front of him. He'd thought the days of blisters were behind him but the forced march had brought some to areas of his heel he hadn't expected. He stared at the conscripted groups working off to the side. Ladders, or things very much like ladders, were being assembled. If he'd had any of those when scaling the Ferrucium walls, he would have had a much easier time of things.

Not every person forced to serve was a Binder and Lin kept doubting the effectiveness of the forced Bludwieves. He hadn't witnessed anyone resisting, but if they did, would the Bludwieves harm them?

Lin chewed the inside of his cheek as he watched them work.

Several familiar faces were among the forced laborers. Garth, the young man who had caught him by surprise in Wakewatch. Mirl too, toiling away deftly with a length of rope. But the most surprising among them was Pael. Lin didn't glance his way too much, but when the man wiped his brow with the back of his hand, he winked at Lin. With any luck, he had a plan.

As a force, they'd been moving non-stop for days. Doubtless countless of the captured would be dead from the strain of it. And if not from the forced exertion, then from the untethered killing them when they couldn't keep up.

Getting an accurate count of the troops was hard, especially since his movement had been restricted to the rear of the slow-moving wagons. But his general estimation hadn't changed. A hundred hundred all totaled between the untethered and the captured citizens.

He'd spotted three more bone collar-wearing leaders, bringing their numbers nearer to ten, and the two who had worn the Noosemen's masks as punishment skulked near the rear, never far from Lin.

What villages they'd passed looked abandoned. A sight that had replenished some hope that had sloshed out of Lin over the past few days. Attacked and ransacked was one thing— but these villages had been left tidy, but barren. And between the stretch of land between Wakewatch and the Tower of Fentis, there weren't many steads. Which meant this last leg would see supplies hampered. Carine and Jun could have gotten word to Duke Elmore.

Lin shifted, wincing as the toothed manacles bit against the scabs along his wrists. Sure this army was vast... But a good number of them were forced into service. Most of them should be happier dying to break their forced Uethes than to serve that fucking monster. There was no way he was letting the Horned King get near Mellyr. He'd die before he allowed it.

"Here." Garth stood over him, an uncorked waterskin held out toward Lin.

"If my arms were free, I'd knock that out of your hand."

A flush rose to the young soldier's sunburned cheeks. He ran a hand through his greasy hair and frowned before a smile broke across his ruddy face. The swelling around his eye had lessened. "But since they aren't, how 'bout a sip? Look I feel real bad, but they'd ordered us in... And I'd just seen Clive lose his head to one of those..." He waggled his fingers, "Magics you lot do."

Lin pulled his legs underneath him and settled into a kneeling squat. His first instinct was to tell the young man, who looked every bit like a full-blooded Danican, that he likely could do the same magic. Then the thought of taking a Weft from the bastard held his tongue. Worst-case? Sure. But he also didn't want the idiot overdrawing on his spul and leaving Lin feeling responsible.

"I'm not thirsty." He licked his lips at the lie.

Garth shook it, water within sloshing. A lone drop trickled down the side, like the waterskin was weeping for him. "You sure?"

Another sigh shook Lin and he stared at the long, thick ladders that had been moved to rest among the wagons. Tall enough to help scale the tower if need be. Pael was gone. Odds were the man was responsible for the few decommissioned wagons before Wakewatch and there would continue to be issues. *Maybe.* "Why did they have you building ladders?"

"Dunno," Garth said. He looked like he was trying to puzzle something out but gave up halfway through. "Like I said, I'm sorry for tackling you. So here. I'll set it here and if you decide to drink it later, then good. And if you leave it here to be trampled and lost, that's fine too."

"Fine, give it here."

Rith, the gaunt commander, only gave him water twice a day. So Garth's waterskin was like a spigot blessed by the Six as the cool water poured. Lin guzzled it, belly swelling and aching, and when Garth finally pulled it away, water dripped from Lin's chin and ran down his chest.

"How long... How long were you a soldier?" Lin asked.

"Who said I was a soldier?"

Lin nodded at the young man's boots and the ruined coat he still wore. "And you told me they'd attacked when you were with Duke Errond's men. Up by the outpost?" Lin clarified as confusion wrinkled the young man's expression, the knot on his temple exaggerated from the motion.

"Ah." Garth leaned forward and shook his head. "Not a soldier. Not anything anymore but a survivor. Really can't say much more for my own safety... You understand I'm sure. What I can say is I was taught how to fence by my brother's father and this is *his* tunic."

A horn bellowed. They'd become less common over the last day or so. Either they were sending fewer scouts out, or fewer scouts were returning.

"You there, come away from that man. You know they told us to watch from afar." Not Mirl, but another older, weary-looking man.

"You're right as always," Garth said, a sad smile on his face. "Hope they don't take my head for this."

Lin stared after the young man as he made his way back to the shade between wagons where more of the lumber for ladders rested. Was the man trying to get killed? *Perhaps*. Lin licked the edge of his mouth and exhaled. He'd grown used to the manacles, even when they irritated the scabs, but the flesh around the scabs had become intolerably itchy and stiff.

Of all the things that dead bastard Aemun had done, working Bound Metal into his flesh had been one of the strangest. It had consumed his flesh and the way his arms itched, there was a good chance it was doing the same to him now.

As the sun retreated, the encampment came alive. The dour mood hanging over the forced march like a funeral shroud lifted. There seemed to be someone playing the pipes far off in the distance accented by a steady drumming. A celebration.

"Up." Rith's brittle voice clawed at Lin's ears. "Or have you lost the will to walk?"

"Where to now?"

"Our God wants a word with you." Rith sneered.

"Does that upset you? That *your* false-god wants me more than he wants you?" Lin didn't struggle as the untethered lifted him wholly by his armpits, though the bitch's nails dug into his sides and as close as she was the scent of rust wafting from her was overpowering.

"It is that witch beside him— She has his ear and you have her attention. But do not mistake attention for love or kindness."

A lesson he'd needed when he met Tylle, not now. Though, a reminder never hurt. Lin wished he could rub his chest where Tylle's boot had connected.

All through the camp, different sections seemed to be crafting various things. More of those ladders, though some of the operational wagons— four that Lin could see— had been converted into rolling towers of sorts. Ax's were being doled out to anyone who could take them, at least three brave fools who thought to attack their captors were quickly killed without hesitation but Lin was sure there were more. It was a large force after all.

Lin had assumed the wagons with the untethered were near the front, given that they hadn't stopped moving over the last two days, but as he was led south through the sprawling, chaotic encampment, he saw the tip of the Fentian Tower. Maybe he'd misjudged the size of the Horned King's forces after all.

Tylle and the Horned King sat above the others who surrounded them. The palisade was used as a lounge with cushions stuffed like bloated clouds and rugs with designs like tapestries pulled from a duke's walls. Given that Duke Errond's holdings had been overran, it was a very real possibility.

Rith led Lin past the rows of antlered untethered, their eyes lingering on him. As if he were a chicken being shown off to a pack of foxes. Lin counted five of the collared leaders and at least twenty of the ones with just antlers. All the wildest of the untethered sat silently, staring at the Horned King. Mad, save for a Thorn stuck in their temple. Their intelligence too far gone to be saved by magic. Or so Lin assumed.

A chill had taken the air and a storm loomed on the horizon blowing the strands of knotted, thinning hair that most untethered had.

"Join us," The Horned King said. His voice was confident and booming.

Lin didn't have a choice as he was led like a dog by the rope about his waist before being forced to kneel. At least there was a pillow. He stared at Tylle, his jaw tight. Then he glanced at the big bastard and couldn't help the smile that broke across his face.

Lounging as he was, the Horned King had his legs spread and damn him if it didn't look like even his nethers had Inlays of a sort. Glowing as it was down there. Denny would have finally seen something that might impress her. Lin settled into the cushion, shaking his head and taking advantage of the comfort after days on hard ground.

Between them was a low, wide table with several wooden cups that had curls of steam fleeing them in undulating waves. Scarlet vines, like those he'd seen outside that one village wrapped the edge of the table. The leaves, bright like Bindings, sounded like muffled laughter as the wind blew them against each other. Centered on the table was spiced meat of some sort coated in pale flower petals. Trussed up, it was likely a hog cooked over a spit and coated in butter and other thoughts that brought Lin to the edge of salivating. Then he recalled the way the Horned King had swallowed that young boy's blood and he looked closer, a sickness rising in his throat.

It was a hog. Meat charred in places with onions and potatoes in the tray around it.

Chunks of flesh had already been cut away from it, and many of the surrounding leaders chewed, while others of lower stations conversed. It looked everything like a celebration, and perhaps to them, it was.

Lin glanced at Tylle, then looked away as the Horned King grinned. Every time he thought he was over the feelings that had stolen months of his life, the longing and hope that she'd wanted some small thing to do with it, a new surge of pain buckled his heart to remind him. As soon as that thought occurred, guilt stabbed him for not accepting Denny's feelings for what they were.

"Days spent walking behind those that walked before... Walking behind those who wore masks and pretended at power. Have you reconsidered? Will you see us as the brethren that we are?" A shadow danced behind him, cast by the grand set of horns on the crown he wore. The Bindings along his temple, gold and green, were bright against the darkening sky behind him.

"I don't know who you are. What you are. Are you a God? Maybe. But I knew a set of Gods who turned out to be falsehoods given to our people from Ladrica."

Rith twitched at Lin's side, but the Horned King raised a single hand, what looked like grease dripping down his wrist. Slowly, he licked the viscera from each finger, eyes burning into Lin.

When the big bastard nodded, Lin continued. "Then… I learned of Velkath and his kin in more detail than I thought possible. Only to learn they too weren't *truly* Gods. It may not be in my lifetime. You may overthrow the world as we know it. But in time…" Lin fought through the tightness that had grasped his throat when he looked at Tylle. "In time, you will be shown to be a fraud like the rest. If you can bleed, you aren't a God."

"Ha!" The Horned King barked. Then clapped, slow and steady, his hands glistening. Hesitantly, others joined. "You are a good speaker. Not as eloquent as some I've met. But you speak from your heart. Do you think you could make me bleed? Prove to all my followers that I'm not Velkath Reborn?"

The crowd grew still and Lin shifted on the cushion. Weak as he was, he doubted he could actually fight the man. *The monster.* He'd single-handedly beaten three Noosemen. What chance did Lin have? But… if he could prove this man for a fraud, wouldn't that be worth it?

Lin glanced at Tylle. Her thin lips were drawn into a line and the scar along her chin shone silver from the dancing firelight.

"Undo my shackles and I will show them the charlatan you are."

Tylle, naturally pale, looked sickly. She gave the slightest shake of her head.

"Rith," The Horned King said.

With a boot to his knees, far rougher than necessary, the Bound Metal shackles were undone. When Rith moved away, chains dragging, Lin fell forward onto his palms. His arms ached as much as his wrists and the wounds were gray and flaking. Reaching for his spul proved futile, numb as his core was. Nothing was there. Not even when he formed a focus to find the other magics within him.

"We should all commend this man's bravery. Many of you look at him with scorn. Revile him. He is what you should all aspire to be. Even weak, he yearns to fight. Starved, he hungers for battle. Betrayed, he still seeks love. Stand when you can, Hero of the Fingers." The Horned King rose to his full height and slipped off his robes, baring his flesh. Inlays lined all his limbs and the wrapping he wore around his loins barely contained the light from his Bindings, let alone his manhood.

With steady hands he removed the crown of antlers, setting it in Tylle's lap. He raised his long arms to the crowd and most bowed in reverence. Those who didn't bow lowered their heads and traced Velkath's Sigil in the air.

As he walked the edges of the palanquin, his Stitches were clear. There. He had a wound along his side and face that had been healed once. Clear as day the way the flesh, as statuesque and stone-like as it appeared, was puckered like a scar. Not to mention the way his right eye bulged with the Stitches along his brow and cheekbone.

Lin rose on unsteady legs and at a gesture from the Horned King, the table was scuttled away. Tylle didn't move. Didn't even look at him.

"If I am an example of what they should be... They should look to you and see something they should never become."

A pensive look crossed the Horned King's expression before he nodded. "None could come close to the heights I've reached, lest they fall."

Never, in all of Lin's life, had he seen a man so large move so quickly. Unless of course, he considered the attack in Fallo. But he'd been less traveled then. And the Horned King moved as quickly as Denny despite being as large as Hugo, if not larger. His meaty, pale hand gripped Lin's neck in an instant, lifting him before slamming him into the palanquin's base, a crack resounding from the impact. Then he was lifted back up, stars in his vision matching the blurred ones in the sky above.

The Horned King could kill him now, send a Weft through his throat while holding him.

Lin grunted, dangling while his skull throbbed. Somewhere in the crowd, Pael was likely watching and thinking him a whole fool.

The crowd cheered and the Horned King spun in a circle, showing Lin off like a fish caught but not yet descaled.

Lin lifted his legs and hooked one over the Horned King's shoulder, the other tightening around from the other side. A shift from the momentum didn't so much as move the bastard off-balance, but his grip loosened just enough that Lin could suck in a greedy breath. Using his hips as the focal point, he tried to twist the large man's arm.

Something shifted— Lin as he was slammed back into the palanquin. Spots danced now and shrapnel of broken wood stabbed up from under him. He didn't have to win the fight; he just needed to prove that this man was no God. A little blood.

Lin extended, straining his arms and hips in an effort to torque the man's limb. It was like trying to bend a blade of Ferrucium steel. Slowly, he felt the man's muscles give and his rigid arm start to bend. All he needed was— The world flashed as he was lifted back into the air. But he wasn't held solely by his throat anymore, no the Horned King had shifted to use the other arm and had grabbed him from his waist holding him nearly horizontal in the air. Any sense of tension he'd had on the monster's arm was gone. Upside down, the world looked odd. Tylle didn't look at him, instead staring at the crown in her lap.

"I'm sure you thought... 'I don't have to win. I simply need to prove he isn't untouchable.' Tell me, did this work out the way you'd hoped?"

It was a funny thing death. He'd expected it to be softer. Like a velvet cloak, or some soft tapestry. No, it felt so much like broken wood that when Lin blinked his eyes open to see his cheek resting against the bloody floor of the ruined palanquin, he wasn't surprised.

Night was fully upon them and the Horned King's face was lit by a nearby flame. Tylle sat there in her sheer robes, chest alight with Velkath's Sigil, cheeks flushed as she drank from a golden goblet.

Lin tried to stand, but his hands had been reshackled. *Mercy.* Is that what everything amounted to? Was he at the mercy of these monsters?

"Our hero awakens." A crunch, much like the sound of a dog gnawing open a bone, followed the words and Lin narrowed his eyes, trying to make out what the Horned King held.

Bile rose at the realization. Raw meat— tendons and all. Blood soaked the monster's chin and chest and he smiled as he chewed. Lin shifted his feet, both there. Hands, both bound. He twitched staring up at Tylle, wondering how he'd been so blind to everything. All the time they'd traveled together he'd been worried about whether he was a monster for having the Stitches and not whether *she* was the real monster. Despite everything he'd been taught telling him she was at the minimum, heretical. *Fuck.*

Lin blinked away his tears.

"Oh... I see. Ha. If you think I'd sully myself with bits of you, then you're a fool. No. You're far too lacking."

The Horned King flicked his wrist and the hunk of meat he'd been holding landed wetly against Lin's face. A small hand, only stringy tendons and torn flesh gripping the thin bones. Lin gagged, pushing his face away, trying to roll.

"Tomorrow at sun-rise we will finish our march on Fentis. You'll be led to the front as an example. Perhaps they'll surrender seeing their 'hero' so defeated."

Disastrous Hate

"Without war, the world would stagnate. Danica was wanted for a variety of reasons but truly, it was the sort of peninsula a man might build an empire from, if only given the chance." —King Lodram

The Tower of Fentis caught the light from the rising sun, alabaster material glowing more like a string of hazy, opulent pearls than true stonework. Atop the walls and along the tower, ballistas rested. Aimed and pointed inward toward Danica itself. Behind the port, the sea sparkled like wet Wanderer's Ore, shimmering as it rippled from a steady breeze.

Behind Lin, an army built on all the hate and destruction of northern Danica stretched out until it disappeared over the nearest hill. Even during the Fall, even when he'd assaulted the island off Ladrica's coast, he couldn't recall a larger gathered force.

If Lin was the Horned King, he'd first send in waves of the captured villagers and soldiers. Those who had taken the Bludwieves and not railed against the slaughter of Wakewatch or the villages before it.

A sole comfort was that in all the moving from point to point, nobody looked like a familiar face from Lyre. Which meant Nebra had a chance of being safe. *Hopefully.* They'd hit Fallo and Drekinsburg and... Lin shook his head. He'd never understand what it all meant. Why it had all happened. Stone *fucking* shrouds.

Maybe the big bastard really was a reborn God. Maybe he upheld old traditions to sway the hearts of people like Tylle, or there was some deeper, older magic at work.

Lin sucked in a breath of the crisp morning air, shifting with his Bound Metal manacles to look again at the fields separating the Horned King's army from Fentis. He smiled. Trenches had been dug out, palisades lined atop them.

Somehow, someway, news had reached them. Jun and Carine, likely.

And at the gates of Fentis, so far away that even with improved vision, he struggled to make out the exact numbers, a veritable host stood at the ready. The Scholars' banners twisted in the wind.

Like the sun being covered by the clouds, Lin's smile faded as he was pushed forward. Alongside him, the two wagons of staked untethered rattled along.

As odd as it was, not having Aemun's snide remarks at various thoughts had left him feeling lonely. He hadn't noticed as much when in the company of others, but now? Lin was alone. Pael was hopefully alive and well somewhere in the gathered force causing mischief. Tylle had all but guaranteed she'd thought nothing more of him than a tool to be used and discarded. *Denny.* Denny still haunted him. But at seeing the defiled bodies of the untethered rattling along beside him, he understood what Carine had meant. Denny wouldn't have wanted that, even if it would have stayed her death. Wouldn't have deserved it, most importantly.

Lin maneuvered his arms to itch at the scabs of gray flesh that had, over the last few days, flaked like bark falling from a tree. It left his arms raw, and the wounds smelled of infection. His Inlays had grown heavy, but this time he recognized the feeling. The lack of whatever it was in his blood powering the magic. Iron. Spul. *Spite*. Though, he had plenty of the latter.

In his condition, the chances of vaulting the trenches, clearing the fields, and escaping to the Scholars seemed slim. They said he was to be used as an example. Lin looked back up at the staked untethered and shuddered. Would he be impaled? Skewered and kept alive by that strange combination of copper and Bound Metal?

A chorus of commotion sounded from the western flank of the army and one of the leader type untethered, mercifully not that cold bitch Rith, shouted for silence.

While the gathering of Fentian scholars and whatever force for protection they'd drummed up hadn't gained a response from the leaders, the fleet sitting in the port, hidden at first by the rising sun painting the sea with light, elicited shouts and orders.

A young message runner, possibly the same one from days ago, rushed back the way he'd come. Inlays glowed along his small frame.

Ladricans. Or Free Nation ships. Or Elodians. From this far, it was impossible to tell. But with all the Fentians' outward focus directed this way, hopefully those ships weren't attacking the port. The fleet had to be Ladricans. They'd been off the coast last he saw them and easily could've beaten Lin here from the Ferrucium.

"You're with me." Rith's voice sounded forced like her throat had been crushed and the words crawled out from the ruin. She'd snuck up on him. Not that it was a hard feat to achieve when he was gazing into the distance trying to decide if it was a coiled serpent on the ship's sail or not.

Ungently, Rith pushed him forward, the two wagons with staked untethered the only other accompaniment. All the others stayed back— far enough away so archers and ballistas alike couldn't rain fire down on them. The driver of the nearest wagon slowed the mounts, then climbed up and began waving a large white flag. It snapped in the wind, loud and aggressive across the field.

Behind, hundreds of hundreds lined up, axes in hands, Inlays across flesh. It made Lin's stomach twist thinking about the number of lives ruined by the untethered. *By untethering*. And his was no exception.

Dry grass crunched underfoot. From where he stood he could nearly make out the tree he'd rendezvoused with Pael and Denro under. Rith led him by the arm and two untethered flanked on either side. One held a large standard that the wind grabbed and flared out. It revealed Velkath's Sigil stitched with golden thread across a black background.

Three figures approached from Fentis on horseback. One bore a flag of their own, though, much smaller, but all three were donned in the robes of scholars— two white-clad initiates and one dark-robed High Scholar.

Despite being a soldier all his life, this was a new sort of waiting.

At the Ferrucium they'd been trained in combat. War, far less so. Blades of grass and stalks of the itchy type swayed with the breeze and the flag continued snapping. This was far from the world of escorting and a piece of him longed for those simple days. But there was no going back. Even if the world refused to recognize the independence Danica deserved, even when the Horned King tasted defeat, the Danica that existed before the Fall was gone with the winter. Everything else was just growing pains.

Even if Lin met his end here, he'd done everything he could to live a good life. To do what he felt was right and just. To light the path forward. Saving Tylle only to be betrayed by her later hurt, but he wouldn't change how things had unfolded. It was brief but he'd found a family. The time spent on the road growing, the time spent in the tower learning— Lin sucked in a deep breath as tears blurred his vision. The time spent watching Mellyr grow. He wouldn't change a single moment of it.

"Realizing the futility of fighting *His* coming reign?" Rith asked. She'd brushed her hair aside, parting it around the antlers protruding from her temples.

Lin sighed. "Thinking."

"Surprised you can after the beating you took."

"Hmm." Lin shook his head and closed his eyes. If he was to die, he'd die picturing the things that had made his life worth living these last few months. Not listening to the gravel-choked voice of a monster with less sense than teeth.

"Leave us for a moment."

Lin squeezed his eyes shut tighter and shook his head.

"Your orders mean nothing—"

Lin peeked from one eye to see Tylle glaring at Rith. Her robes, sheer and silken, rippled in the wind behind her, draped across her hard physique.

"My voice is the voice of Velkath Reborn."

"Last I checked, you were a priestess to another *God*. Tell me, do you change loyalties as easily as you change faiths?" Rith frowned as she asked the question.

Lin raised his brows and smiled at that. Who needed Aemun's ghost when Rith had a tongue as sharp as a dagger?

Tylle's jaw clenched, scar stretching, and then she turned her back on the leader, eyes scanning the approaching trio still a ways off as they navigated the trenches. "Lin, please step this way."

He considered ignoring her out of spite, but as far as his options were concerned, he didn't have much else to do. When she tsked and walked to the side without him, he followed.

Still a dog to her whistle. No. Lin shook his head, not able to go much further than three long strides away from the wagon, tied up as he was. It didn't matter what she had to say. He'd do what he needed to. Even if it meant killing her. At the isle, his conviction had wavered. But there was no way Denro wouldn't want him to fight tooth and nail to get himself away from his current predicament. No way Anya wasn't staring from wherever she was, wondering what the Horned King's intentions were.

"Here to tell me to accept my fate?" Lin asked.

Her eyes bore into his, the shades of light brown like a topaz striking in the early morning light. Her dress's hem rippled in the wind, grass stalks brushing against her shins.

"Or feed me some tall tale of Vellyr and have me believe this," Lin jutted his chin at the bustling army of monsters, "Was for the people of Danica? What of Roge and Jules? The old woman who tied your braids. What of when we rode together after I saved your life? After I lied for you regarding Aemun? Took the blame so you could continue to earn good favor with Erias and Azhura since you refused to leave!" He'd started yelling and he didn't care. Every moment of indecision, pain, and rage had built to this.

Tylle looked at the ground, then reached for his hands. Lin jerked away at first, but she grabbed his wrist with one hand and rubbed his Bludwieve with the other. "I'm sorry you were tangled up in all this. Truly."

Lin wanted to pull his hand away, wanted to rip it free from her grasp much like the tenuous hold she still had on his heart, but he couldn't. Tylle squeezed, caressing his fingers, and after a long, painful moment, he gripped back. Even now, she attempted to use him, didn't she?

"How can you apologize, when you're still poised to betray me?"

"I never betrayed you!" Tylle hissed.

"If trying to recruit me to join that monster, and lying to me all that time wasn't betrayal, perhaps I don't know the meaning of it."

"Betrayal is watching your sister bleed to death giving birth to a child she shouldn't have bore. Betrayal is watching the people of your land turn on themselves because of lies banded about by foreigners! Betrayal is what—"

"Witch, finish up with your plaything, the tower rats are nearly here." If the wind was stronger, spit would've accompanied Rith's words.

"Betrayal is what? What you did to Erias and his people?"

Tylle pressed something into Lin's hand as hers dropped to her side. Aside from a twitch of her lip, her face had grown still. "Everything I've done has been at his orders. And it kills me to know how many suffered so that the many might thrive. But that is what it means to make a difference."

Lin couldn't tell if she meant Erias or the Horned King, but it was easier to assume the latter in the position he was in. Like a signal of their doom, a series of bursts from horns bellowed out across the field as the trio from Fentis drew nearer. He watched Tylle walk away, back straight, single braid down her back like a length of rope that might form a noose.

He hadn't noticed it at first, as focused on Tylle as he'd been. But she'd slipped him a knife. Small and likely only good for cutting rope. It might've even been the same blade as the one he'd cut those strips of cloak for to cover his Stitches back before Creekside. He didn't look at it much, not wanting to alert Rith or any of the other nearby untethered. Maybe Tylle meant it to be a reminder. Or maybe she'd thought to give him a way to end his own life before the Horned King could do whatever it was he meant to do with him. Whatever the reason, it wasn't as if the dull blade could break the shackles.

Rith stood, hands on her hips, glaring at the approaching Scholars. Tylle was gone, fled back to the lines of unwilling warriors. Already Lin had seen pockets of men and women killed for refusing to march. Whatever the Horned King claimed, his path wasn't for the betterment of the Danican people.

The big bastard was giving a speech, clips of it barely reaching Lin. Promises of this being the last battle. Freedom to follow. Words that no real leader would ever think of muttering.

If there was a single reality crystallized over the last passing months, it was that there would always be another battle. Another war. The war on the untethered the Ferrucium claimed to be waging for decades, all while the rot of the Horned King spread in the shadows. The Ladricans and their desire to control Danica. Surely, no matter how this battle shook out, someone would move in to deal with the victor.

Lin shifted and turned his back to the bone-wearing leader.

Rith's attention was far from him and the rope tying him to the wagon was nearly cut through. He sawed back and forth. Glad to be forced near the front, all things considered. If there was a chance for him to get across the long stretch of field, it would be when all eyes were elsewhere. As the final few strands of rope began to give, a worry settled at the back of his mind. What if, after everything, this was what the Horned King wanted? Him to run across the field only to be cut down by the approaching trio. Or be taken in the back by bolt or Binding?

With a final furtive cut, the rope fell to the grass. Lin rushed to Rith who turned to face him. Bound Metal manacles caught her cheek in a cross-body hammer blow, then he took her back as she reeled. He was taller, weaker currently but with enough mass to lift her regardless. Inlays made a person stronger, but they didn't add mass.

Rith kicked and clawed and any behind them paying attention would notice something was amiss, but the Horned King's voice still carried on the wind and odds were those closest to him wouldn't give much care to see the gaunt monster killed.

The two nearest untethered, the one with the flag and the other, were facing away and a good four to five long strides away. But they could turn at any moment.

Lin was glad to have saved what spite he had, using it to barrel Rith nearer to the advancing trio who'd just cleared the trenches. Pushing her forward and pulling chains tight around her neck simultaneously proved challenging. The bone collar, a jaw or pelvis of some beast, dug into his chest painfully. She managed to plant a foot, stalling his momentum enough to flip him over.

From his back, he rolled as a Blade, colored like a dying sun, stabbed where he'd just been lying. It seemed a bad day to be a stalk of grass. Worse day to be Rith though, as he managed to trip her in her scrambled haste. He climbed atop her, wrestling to stay on top without her Blade opening him like a fish.

The magic of her attack sparked against his manacles as he stabbed downward with the tiny knife. *Fuck.* She caught the knife in her black ruined teeth. He pushed down with all his weight, her Blade slashing across his side in a line of heat.

Lin heaved. Heaved again. Then shut his eyes as the pain at his side grew too fierce and the sound of cracking teeth too awful. Blood covered everything, himself included.

When he looked up, the two nearest untethered were approaching, led by two other bone-collared leaders still wearing the stolen Noosemen masks. A glance behind revealed an unfamiliar junior scholar, a soldier wearing ill-fitting colors of Wellgrove, and one of the High Scholars in their dark, night-sky-shaded robes.

Rith choked out something. Lin left the knife in her mouth and rose to his feet. He was done being used.

Twenty long strides. That's all it would be to get to the Fentian trio. Twenty, coverless strides across uneven terrain with an army of soldiers and monsters at his back. Nothing more, nothing less.

The two mask-wearing untethered rushed to close the distance. Lin didn't look at them as he turned and stumbled. Rith's hand clutched his ankle. Dying, but not dead.

Wefts cut into the ground around him, sod and chunks of earth erupting into the air.

Shouts and cries carried from the large force of untethered, but Lin pushed forward. If there was ever a moment he wished to be as quick as Denny, it was now. His strides ate the distance between him and the now worried-looking trio, as he raised his manacles to show he was a prisoner and not a mad untethered.

As he made it to the midpoint, he hazarded a glance over his shoulder and flinched in horror as a Weft nearly took him in the throat. He swung his manacles up and caught the magic against the Bound Metal, sparks erupting in a flash as the impact sent him skidding on his back toward the Scholars.

He made it to the midpoint, the two masked untethered crashing toward him. And behind, towering over them like the god he claimed to be, was the Horned King.

Disastrous Blood

"The world is far larger than Danica, and so too are the horrors. War would've come eventually, be glad there was a hero to fight for us." —Duke Errond

All the air had been knocked from Lin when he landed and it didn't seem eager to return as he kicked into the field to push himself away from the untethered.

The masked untethered, leaders with their bleached bone collars around their throats like the hinged jaws of some great serpents, sprinted. Basic untethered looked like nightmares made manifest, but these bastards with their antlers and masks terrified Lin. Blades formed at their sides and it would only take them a moment to close the distance Lin had managed to make.

Behind them, the Horned King walked forward at a measured pace. Slow, methodical. More untethered leaders rode on horseback across the staggered lines of troops. They were divided into columns, the conscripted flanked on either side by untethered. At a distance, the distinction was nearly impossible to note.

There'd been a hope, slim as it was, that seeing a shackled, beaten man kill one of the leaders would spur some courage among the captives. But perhaps too many deaths had been doled out for that hope to blossom into something more.

Lin crawled along his back, then spun to right himself. The trio approaching from Fentis looked ready to fight. "A-Anya! High Scholar Anya! Denro! It's me. Lin! Lindel!"

A Weft bit the space he'd just been in and sent chunks of earth colliding against his back.

"Hold!" There was so much force, so much expectation in that single word, that Lin nearly stopped his frantic crawl. But it had been the Horned King's booming voice and he'd been talking to his leaders.

Lin inched forward and when he noticed the pale, terrified expressions on the Fentian representatives, he glanced over his shoulder. Blinking away sweat, breaths aching in and out, he froze. He couldn't help himself.

The Horned King had stepped in front of his leaders, his crown, bone and Binding, looked brighter somehow and his robes fluttered gently in the breeze. Inlays glowed along his flesh like lightning breaking across a white-cloud sky.

If Lin hadn't seen some of the horrors the monster enacted, it was easy to envision him as a king. Though, to the bastard's credit, the one other king Lin had met didn't inspire confidence or at least obedience as this monster did.

The three scholars were to Lin, lifting him.

"Run!" Lin bellowed.

They didn't move and held him there limply.

He screamed. "Now!"

The two juniors looked at the High Scholar robed in deep blue, eyes searching the woman's stern face. "I—" she started.

Lin wasn't there to discuss why three scholars standing in an empty field in front of the Horned King and some of his top untethered was a terrible idea. He shouldered past them and sprinted. Everything ached, even his teeth. He couldn't save them, and he wasn't in a position to convince them if they were of a mind to speak with the monster.

A stretch of trenches and debris separated him from the forces armed and waiting afield under Fentis. Lin gritted his teeth and pressed on, manacles biting and stinging with every jolt forward.

"Hero!" The Horned King shouted, raising both his hands.

Looking meant death. Looking meant slipping and falling and... Lin looked over his shoulder anyways.

The Horned King's voice, loud and steady, could've carried to the top of the Fentis Tower. "Listen, Fentians. Danicans. Scholars and soldiers and those who claim neither. I *am* Velkath Reborn. Cunning in my ways. Wrathful in my lost brother's name. Wise with my knowledge. Truthful with my words. Mournful of those we've lost. Dull in my urge for violence but wicked if pushed to be so.

"Long have we, Danicans, been oppressed. Kicked while down. Treated as less because of our superiority. If you surrender, there needs not to be bloodshed. Three times I've sent requests for peace, three times you've rejected my pleas, slaying a child of mine. Let this not be the fourth!

"Give me the child that is mine by rights!"

Lin narrowed his eyes at that. *Three times?*

The wind whistled, the Horned King standing over Rith, grass stalks shifting from the breeze. With the cliffs to the southwest, the wind chopped intermittently. Tylle had to be somewhere near him, as close as she'd kept this entire time, but Lin couldn't see her amid the crowd. He looked at the army beyond the trenches. Lined up with weapons drawn.

"*Hope.* A fragile, frail thing constantly broken by those in power. Bone. Like hope, often broken, all because we are more powerful than *they* want us to be. Hate. Festered and fetid, growing within every Danican, ready to spew out. Blood. The only thing that will be left of all those who oppose us.

"What will it be?" A smile spread across the Horned King's face, forcing his right eye to bulge large in its socket, his Bindings shining like light caught in the bead of dew on grass.

Lin ran. The scholars dumb enough not to heed him wasn't his responsibility. He needed to get as far from the king as possible. His strides were shorter than usual, but he still tore at the stretch at a pace he couldn't have managed before Lyre. A cramp knotted his side and he nearly tripped.

A series of horns bellowed from the east. Another set, tinny and metallic as opposed to the carved bone that the Horned King's troops used, echoed behind the first.

Cresting over the slope, a band of untethered on horseback, ten plus by the looks of it, were being routed by a cavalry bearing the whipping banners of the Ferrucium. Twin-headed birds displayed bringing a sense of pride to Lin as he stared.

Screams of pain erupted from behind Lin. A lance of pure gold impaled the High Scholar and sent the two junior scholars tumbling to the ground from panic. Her back was to Lin, but he hoped she didn't look surprised. All the robes and crowns couldn't hide the monster the Horned King was.

Struggling, the High Scholar seemed to be grasping at the Blade ineffectually. Then she was lifted, kicking vainly as her feet dangled above the ground.

Shouts carried from the direction Lin was heading. A man stood there in armor, waving his arms and yelling at the top of his lungs. Lin's blood thrummed in his ears. Get here? Is that what the armored man was screaming?

Lin slowed as a fresh cramp tore through his side and threatened to take all the air from him. He looked over his shoulder. The High Scholar's robes were ruffled by the wind and she looked like a banner as blood and vitals spilled out. Her weight shifted her down the sharp edge of the light.

Chaos erupted as the High Scholar's body crumpled, her sucking, gasping heaves doing nothing to close her wounds. Two Wefts cut Lin's way, he spun around the first and the second would've caught him in the shoulder if he hadn't thrown himself to the ground.

He was so close. The trenches were just out of reach. The soldier who'd been waving at him rushed his way, sword in hand.

Lin dragged himself forward. Then firm hands lifted him and he was half carried, half dragged by the soldier. The man smelled like oil and sweat and breathed just as hard as Lin.

"Fuck, they're coming!" The soldier cursed.

Lin shuffled forward, past the barricades.

The Horned King hadn't moved— it looked like he was speaking with the dying High Scholar, but it was hard to be sure. His two mask-wearing leaders had charged, though. Leaping and bounding in ways that shouldn't be possible for a normal person.

"Covering fire!" The soldier screamed.

At his command arrows tore down from the Tower, bolts too, though fewer and slower. The two scholars who'd been beside the High Scholar hadn't moved. If they weren't dead yet, it was too late now.

"Told them not to go out there. Can you stand?"

Lin nodded and leaned against the barricade. There wasn't time to catch his breath, wasn't time to ask questions. The way he saw it, the two approaching untethered were worse than Noosemen, even if they wore the masks.

"We can't hold them here," Lin gasped.

"We have to," the soldier said, patting Lin's shoulder and examining the manacles with a disappointed look on his face.

Another soldier approached, saluted curtly, and said, "Duke Elmore— the Binders are ready."

"Have them loose everything they've got as soon as they're in range. Form the bulwark."

"Sir."

Lin blinked at the realization.

Duke Elmore continued. "Time isn't our ally in this. A Ladrican vessel waits in the harbor, but I've heard no assurances of aid. The cavalry fielding now will do some good, but horses never fare well against Binders. Especially untethered."

Lin raised his brows at that. He looked like the average soldier, save for the iron armor he wore, but he was far from the only man wearing it. A far cry from the ostentatious clothes Duke Wellgrove had worn the singular time Lin had seen him. "Y-you shouldn't be on the front lines."

Elmore nodded. "I'd have it no other way. I wasn't able to aid Errond's lands. His people. Warning got to us in time but even those under my banners have already suffered. Until my eastern Danican counterparts arrive, my men are all that separate *that* from the good people gathered within Fentis's walls."

Well-spoken, calm, and with sharp eyes. It was a wonder he hadn't played more of a role in the Fall. Locale played a part of course, but perhaps he was too earnest to have orchestrated what Erias thought needed to be done.

Arrows continued raining down and soon Wefts joined in the flurry.

"The Scholars have a broken blade, it can cut through these. I need it!" Lin said.

Screams from the field carried and the sound of clashing steel rang through the air.

Elmore gave word to someone, a message runner by the looks of it, and nodded at the approaching untethered. "Get inside. We'll hold them back. Monsters, the lot of them." He cast a kind, apologetic look toward Lin. "No offense."

"No—"

One of the masked leaders landed just against the barricade, Blades sparking to life in their hands. Arrows stuck from their chest leaving bloody trails obscuring their Inlays.

Elmore flinched away, bringing his sword up to block an attack that didn't come as the monster lunged for Lin.

A wall of soldiers pressed forward. Some wore armor, but most were in thick cloth gambesons or simple boiled leather. But it wasn't their armor that caught Lin's eye, but the shields they carried. Not Ferrucium steel but *shields*. Something Danican soldiers— Ferrucium soldiers didn't bother with. If it wasn't Ferrucium steel, it wouldn't be enough. And yet they pressed forward, forming a wall between the other soldiers and the palisades. Spears hovered over their shoulders and it seemed that Elmore, if he'd been in charge of the defense here, and formed a tight barrier between this section of Fentis and the killing fields beyond.

Lin hesitated as he was jostled back out of the way. Right now, he *was* in the way. He needed that dagger for his manacles and to kill the Horned King. He turned to run, pushing through the press of soldiers when an Inlayed leg crashed down into Lin's shoulder.

The soldiers around him screamed in horror as the other masked untethered vaulted into their midst.

Something in his shoulder popped and pain raced through his arm, but Lin forced himself up and took the untethered's mass atop him. He struggled to push the monster's hips down. They were too close, too pressed in by the bodies of the soldiers for the monster to make use of its superior strength. Wild strikes and lashes of Wefts raked Lin's arms, but with the help of the soldiers around him, he pressed the chain connecting his shackles into the creature's throat, squeezing and smothering despite the snarls until a click sounded from the bone.

Exhausted, Lin clambered to his feet.

Mud and blood coated him and when he looked over his shoulder past the wall of soldiers holding back the masked untethered, the Horned King still stood motionless at the center of the chaos. The Blade he'd forged withered into a cloud of dusty motes, drifting away on the coastal breeze. His army hadn't moved either except for the force that had turned to fight the approaching Ferrucium troops and fear rooted in Lin's guts. *Why?*

Duke Elmore had stepped back and was observing, shouting orders at his men. He could tell the shield wall wouldn't hold. Especially not when more monsters broke across the field. The trenches would help slow them, but still. Bodies were beginning to pile on this side of the barricade as the barely held back untethered sent Weft and Blade wherever it spotted an opening. It bled, the stab wounds glistening with rusted blood, but it was very much alive.

Aiding Duke Elmore and his men would make the most sense, especially as the arrows had slowed their rain at the realization that the opposing army wasn't attacking en masse. Lin fought his instincts. His mind screamed at him to rush into the tower and protect Mellyr like a starved dog might a bone, but that wouldn't do anyone any good unless he had the dagger.

Lin smashed his heel into the untethered's stolen mask several times just to be sure the creature was dead.

"We need to—" Lin's voice was drowned out by a screeching that carried through the air like the rending of steel. One by one, like grotesque leaves falling in an orchard made of corpses, the staked untethered collapsed to the ground, freed from the Bound Metal that held them in place.

Alone, just in front of the falling monsters, the Horned King raised a single hand.

Duke Elmore pulled at Lin's shoulder, but Lin couldn't take his eyes off the scene unfolding before him. Forty or more of the monsters shakily stretched to their full height. More screeching carried on as the other wagons released their burden. Then the guttural howls came. Howls that sent shivers down Lin's neck.

Finally, the duke stopped trying to pull Lin and backpedaled to the gates. *Good.* Lin knew he needed to flee but his legs wouldn't heed him.

Blood dripped from the monsters' many wounds, a wildness to their erratic movements that proved they were the type of crazed untethered Lin was accustomed to before the term became a blanket that didn't quite fit all those under it. And as the Horned King's hand dropped, they charged forward. A veritable swarm of gangly, Stitched flesh monsters. Bands of magic thick and crude across their limbs as they charged. Each of them gave the Horned King a wide berth, tearing across the field toward Lin and the wall of shields as fresh horns trumpeted out from Fentis.

Arrows and Wefts rained down anew.

Lin shifted where he stood as the wild untethered threw frail, sickly-looking Wefts. Most disintegrated before even reaching the barricades, but the last thing he needed was to be swarmed and eaten alive by those still with teeth. He still had scars on his shoulder from the last time one of the mad bastards bit him.

Ahead, just across a wide trench separating the front lines from the rear, Duke Elmore waved.

Hairs on the back of his neck rose and Lin shifted to the right, tripping on his own feet into a roll. A Blade, impossibly long and bright occupied the space he'd just been standing. How the Horned King was capable of such Wievings didn't make sense. *Blood and Binding.*

Lin clawed at the dirt and lifted himself, running as hard as he could. Sweat had crept into the slash at his side and stung cruelly. Just past Elmore, a scholar with large eyes nervously waited. Pale and trembling, they clutched something to their chest. A sheath of bone and wood. They shut their eyes and shuddered as more horns blew.

More soldiers, clad in Elmore's colors of gray and blue and armed with spears and shields, formed a secondary, or possibly third line of defense. Lin had pressed through so many soldiers, he could no longer be sure.

"H-high S-scholar Orson," the pale scholar muttered.

"Is dead. Killed by that monster and we'll be the same if you don't take that dagger and cut these manacles." Lin held his arms out expectantly but the terrified scholar didn't move. Didn't even fully open their eyes.

"Give me the blade."

Grunts came as the untethered crashed into the barricades and soldiers holding the shields behind. Screams, howls, and terrified cries sounded from behind.

Lin stood over the junior scholar and took the sheathed dagger, bending back the scholar's trembling fingers. If all the junior scholars were filled with fear like him, then those inside had no chance. They'd lost before the battle had even begun. But the more he thought about it, the more he realized how true Pael's words had become. They'd been at war all along.

Flesh slammed against shields and the sick crunching of bones breaking against the sharpened stakes that jutted from the fortifications was impossible to ignore.

"Run," Lin growled as he unsheathed the odd-colored dagger. It cut through Bindings with ease. Crumpled Ferrucium steel. Surely it would do something to the Bound Metal. Lin frowned as screams sounded from the front. But what if the Bound Metal ruined the dagger somehow? Simple stonework had shattered it back at the island.

The junior scholar hadn't moved but their cream-colored white robes were already stained. "Will *this* break the Bound Metal?"

"I don't know, I don't."

Fuck.

Lin sucked in a breath and as he placed the edge of the dagger against the left cuff of his shackle, sparks hissed. Sparks from the metal tearing apart. Heat spread then burned his wrist, the hairs along his arm curling up and adding the stench of burnt hair to the foul odor of combat.

Then Lin was knocked from behind. Untethered had climbed over— and more than that, the full army had begun marching. The dagger flew out of his grip as he stumbled, bouncing dully in the trench and coming to a rest right where a group of soldiers retreated. Elmore was between them being carried by two men. A thick, steady line of blood matted his hair to the side of his head.

Lin tried to get to the dagger, but the crazed monsters were upon him. Weft and claw-like strikes coming from all directions. A flash of light and Bolts, large as boulders, rained down from the walls overlooking the gates. Jun. It had to be Jun up there.

The Bolts struck true. They scattered earth, wooden fortifications, and untethered alike.

Crazed untethered clambered through the destruction, stepping on the corpses of allies and enemies alike. Pressing in behind the first wave of untethered, those who'd been converted joined, pushing their way to the fray. Fear and fury danced across their faces. Conscripted or not. Forced to fight or not, these men and women had chosen their side.

Lin growled and, wincing, clawed his way to where the dagger had fallen.

Dirge of Hope

"We all wear masks. We all hide behind them. War rips off the masks, showing everyone who we really are."—Gritt

Between the press of bodies, stench of untethered, and chaos of battle, Lin's head spun. It was hard to imagine this was truly what Aemun had intended when he first assaulted the Ferrucium. As much as he'd learned about Aemun, there was no telling what the man had hoped to see play out. He'd wanted to flee and let the chaos play out and if death counted as fleeing, Aemun had done just that.

Lin caught a boot in his back and someone tripped heavily across his shoulders and landed with a cursing grunt. The dagger was there, just out of reach. He dragged himself forward, scrambling to his knees, then his feet.

Behind, quickly approaching the defenses, wagons that hadn't been sabotaged and left in the fields on the march rolled forward following the surge of advancing bodies. Rickety ladders rattled atop them.

Too many. The chokepoint they were defending couldn't stand. Not as things were.

From both sides of the assault, Wefts and Bolts sailed through the air. In a fray like this, the Sight was as much a distraction as a boon. Sightless soldiers died, not seeing the death sailing for them.

Lin pressed to where he'd last seen the dagger. The earth was churned to mud here, and a drizzle had started making the terrain slick. He stumbled, was jostled, and struggled to keep balance as the wall of bodies knocked him askew. It was impossible to tell if it was the blood loss from his wounds, the Bound Metal ruining his senses, or something else altogether, but Lin felt like he couldn't regain his balance.

Yells. Orders. Banging of drums and horns. *Chaos.*

Lin was shouldered to the side. He'd been tripping a lot recently and had attributed it to the uneven terrain. But there was no doubt that keeping his feet straight was a struggle.

Screams of terror rippled through the entrenched soldiers defending the vast entrance of Fentis. Plenty of times Lin thought a Binding looked like a thread caught in a ray of sunlight. But from where the Horned King stood, it looked as if the sun itself, fresh and brilliant, crested the hill.

A Weft that spanned the width of the trenches, the largest Lin had ever seen, sliced through the air. Something so large shouldn't move so swiftly. But it did.

Lin tumbled face down atop a pile of bodies. Wood, dirt, and what he presumed were limbs, pelted his back. He rose and spun in time to catch the gleam of a twin Weft cutting the same trajectory.

The second attack was so sudden that Lin was caught by it. He jerked the manacles up and his wrists screamed, bones straining, flesh tearing as the Bound Metal manacles dug in from the force of impact. And the Weft was sliding him back. Pushing him with so much force that his legs caught on the pile of corpses he'd just fallen on.

His arms would break before the manacles— at least that's what it felt like as everything strained.

A gruff voice near his ear shouted from behind, but between the pulse thrumming in his ears and the fray all around, he couldn't make out the words.

Something solid like a wall pressed to his back. Hands gripped his shoulder. "We've got you! Hold!" The same voice, clearer now, shouted.

Not that Lin had a choice.

If the Bound Metal gave, weakened as it was from the dagger, Lin would be cut right in half. Metal shrieked and hissed, the light from the Weft blindingly bright.

"Dagger!" Lin screamed.

"Dagger?"

"Broken dagger!" Lin couldn't say more than that, even speaking those simple words nearly broke his concentration. He tried to unravel the Weft, but it held. It felt like trying to bend Ferrucium steel with his fingertips.

Pressure behind Lin subsided and he slid back. His knees nearly buckled. Everything in front of him was washed out. Shouts rang unintelligibly from behind. One thing about a Weft this sized, there was no doubt the Horned King had injured some of his people. Even if those he'd sent in were the fodder, those crazed untethered who'd lost themselves long ago, and the scared conscripted men and women who'd have died if they didn't charge in. *Cruel bastard.*

A tap on his shoulder and a redoubling of the pressure on his back. "This it?"

Lin craned his neck but couldn't see anything. Metal screeched as his manacles grew hot and bent inward, tearing at his flesh more and more with every passing moment.

"Dark as the ocean at night, broken—"

"Give it to me!" Lin hadn't thought about the handoff. Lin couldn't move his hands and the man, brave as he seemed, wasn't rushing to move from behind Lin.

"I can't!"

He couldn't. Lin knew it. The man knew it too. But he had the Sight. "You need to take the dagger, hold its edge against the magic, and cut it, right between my arms. Get good and close!"

"I might owe you dinner after this!" The man screamed, wrapping his arms around Lin.

The Weft sliced in half as the man's shaky hand cut forward.

Lin smiled but then watched in horror. The two separate sections continued on either side of him. In one fell swoop, many of the protectors were eviscerated. Torsos cleaved as easily as the dirt. Scholars. Soldiers. Not all of them, but enough that another wave of attackers would easily breach the front of the city.

Dust and debris settled, and through the smokescreen, the Horned King cocked his antler-crowned head to the side. Surprise plain on his ghoulish face.

There was no time to mourn the losses. Not when a force the size of the Horned King's army was steadily pushing forward. But to the east, the full force of the Ferrucium and what looked to be the ducal militias was drawing nearer. Flanking and routing the far side of the Horned King's forces. Somewhere out there, Carine was likely moving in. Not that Lin thought she'd stand a chance against the Horned King, but the more fighters of her caliber they had, the better things would go.

"Dagger," Lin said. Turning, surprised to see Duke Elmore with his head wrapped by a bloodied red cloak, Lin stretched his arms out. "Cut these."

The manacles shrieked, twisting on themselves and sloughing away, leaving his wrists raw, bloody, and gray-toned. Most of his forearms, including his Inlays, had the pallor of a corpse.

Do you really think you can stop this assault, Escorter?

Lin froze. He blinked and looked around the battlefield. No sign of Velkath's Sigil. No stray Bindings in his periphery. But he'd heard Aemun's ghost. Even if it was a whisper, he'd heard it.

More soldiers and scholars had moved in to take the place of those killed or injured by the Horned King's grand attack. They wore a mix of colors and resembled a scab forming over a wound.

"Don't take this the wrong way, but are you alright? There's triage setup, but with that last assault, I'm not sure we've enough defenders."

"I'll be fine. Heard a ghost. Give me that and get to safety." Lin took the dagger and licked his lips, wiping his brow with his forearm. "Send me honey-caps if you can. I'm sure some scholars have something if you ask."

Duke Elmore, along with the other men who'd kept Lin from being pushed back rushed away. Terrified-looking scholars, robed in the white of junior initiates took their place. Denro was somewhere in all the chaos. Anya too. *Little Leo.*

Arrows continued peppering the land between the ruined trenches and the Horned King's advancing force.

Lin turned and brandished the dagger. This was what he'd hoped for. A chance to make the big bastard bleed. Lin might be weak and wounded, but one cut from the dagger, Venya's fucking dagger, could ruin his Inlays.

Despite the chaos. Despite the haunting echo of Aemun's voice and the feeling that something was missing within him, Lin smiled. And across the field, past the fray of fighters, the Horned King raised his head.

Lin charged, wound at his side pulling painfully. Without some of the palisades, it was easier, but more of the Horned King's army stood between them than allied forces. So Lin dashed, slit the throat of an untethered slashing a Weft toward him, and stabbed up into the side of one of the conscripted while the man was fighting a Scholar.

Light as a feather and terribly sharp, the dagger was like a shard of black, oily glass.

A Weft flared to life and flew toward him but Lin cut it with ease. The dagger, broken as it was, felt odd to wield. The weight was off, but it did the job, and then some. One of those Ferrucium steel axes arced his way and the head clashed with the dagger. Any other blade would break from that sort of impact, but something about the dagger and steel seemed otherworldly. The dagger sank into the ax head, cleaving it, and Lin followed up with a stab to the jugular.

A weapon like this in Denny's hands would've been a sight to behold. But she was gone, and Lin did his best. He wasn't fluid. If anyone watched his progress, they probably saw a wounded, limping man moving as quickly as he could and killing any monsters in his way as he did.

They'd see a tattered hero.

When Lin reached the Horned King, he noticed for the first time Tylle standing two steps behind him to his side.

Lin sucked in a breath, forming a focus and feeling his spul. The azure thread of magic was slow in surfacing from the depths it was hidden in, but it did emerge. Like a taut bandage, Lin covered his side. Flesh puckering together, though the hue of magic was closer to black like the healing he'd done across his chest. *Not good.*

Not good? You've thought some silly things, Escorter, but look what that slender-boned bitch has done? Betrayed you. Ever wonder why she offered me my life simply to take it anyway? Vengeance—

Lin screamed as he charged forward. As soon as he'd pulled the thread of magic, Velkath's Sigil had danced into his view. Drifting away when he chased it with his eyes.

A Blade, normal in size compared to the ones the bastard had made before, flared to life. And the Horned King moved to meet him. Dagger bit Blade and the magic was swallowed, dispersing into threads of blinding light. Lin moved in, slicing up, but the Horned King danced away. Wefts flying from where he'd just been.

Lin rushed forward, quick decisive cuts sending the Wefts sailing off in pieces. He stumbled as Tylle moved in front of him. She was as quick as he remembered, punching across her body and pivoting when Lin avoided it. Hesitation meant death. She may have given him a way out of the—

The Horned King grabbed Tylle from behind, lifting her with one arm by her neck. She twisted in his grip, dress flowing, legs wrapping around his arm.

Lin stepped forward, looking for an opening to stab the bastard. The Horned King backpedaled, then formed a Weft at the base of Tylle's neck.

"No!" Lin screamed involuntarily.

But Tylle had somehow gotten her neck free of the man's grip. Thin needles stuck from the monster's wrists and his fingers looked slack as she hung upside down from his arm.

One of the bone-collared leaders rushed into the melee, either stupid or unaware of what Lin's dagger was capable of. They had a Blade, burning bright in the dust of battle, and Lin sliced it and their throat at nearly the same time.

Tylle stabbed dual Blades at the Horned King, looking to sink into his exposed side. It looked like the muscles under his flesh were alive as he tensed and the Needles shattered. Tylle fell to the ground into a roll and the Horned King moved to chase, but Lin cut him off.

"You're a brave little monster aren't you?" The Horned King asked.

Monster? Lin smiled and tightened his grip on the dagger. Tinny horns sounded and bolstered his hopes. "This is the part where I'd say I only see one monster, but you've brought so many of them it wouldn't make sense."

"Ha." The Horned King shook his head. "Venya's dagger. I was under the impression it was lost. Rare metal. That thing can cut the threads that bind us all."

"I know what it is." Lin forced out. "Figured it's a good way to prove you can bleed."

With a shake of his head, the Horned King rolled his arm where Tylle's Needles had stabbed into him. "Gods don't bleed. Tylle. I don't do second chances. But I'll make an exception. You allowed him to cut his rope. When we were fighting just now, you went easy on him. Do you really care so much for a worthless would-be *hero*? If you can explain to me why, I'll spare you."

Tylle stared at the ground, her jaw clenched. When she looked up, there were tears in her eyes. "I think he is a good man. Take the tower. Take Danica. Spare him, please."

"That depends on him. Lindel. Hero of Vellia's Fingers. Will you stand aside? Give me that dagger and let Danica come into the rule of Velkath Reborn?"

Lin listened to the battle. The thud of projectiles. The hum of Wievings sailing through the air. The chaos. He shook his head. Of course, freedom had a cost, but this wasn't right either. All he'd wanted was to allow Denro and Erias, and now after meeting the man, Duke Elmore, to speak to the world. "What're you after here?"

"Here? Fentis and the Ferrucium are so very similar. They deserve judgment just as the Ferrucium did."

"And Mellyr?" Lin asked. He watched Tylle's expression.

"Who?" The Horned King narrowed his eyes, turning to Tylle.

"Margaret's daughter. Aemun's daughter. I know you have plans for her!" Lin spat.

A twisted smile formed across the monster's Stitched face. "I am the nearest thing to a God this sad world as seen since Vellia first learned of the tapestry. I am... I am vengeance. Retribution for all the Danicans treated as monsters."

"You plan to marry her? Bring your bloodlines together?" Lin asked, brandishing the dagger. Tylle hadn't moved but was tense.

All around, the fray continued pressing in.

"I am Velkath Reborn! I'd never sully myself by wedding a child, despite the villain you'd paint me to be. Though I do desire her blood and with it, Danica will never fear being shackled again."

Lin's stomach turned. He couldn't let this monster get Mellyr. "The world powers won't rest with you in charge. You're no God. No hero. You are everything they fear. Powerful and cruel and if you think taking possession of a child will change that, you're also a fool!

"Ladrica. The Free Nations. The entire world will be at your throat."

The Horned King's muscles rippled as he shrugged. "So be it." He growled the words and his grin faded. "I've lived so long as

Velkath Reborn, I wouldn't remember my first name if it were spelled out for me. But one thing I do recall is my Uethe. And I swore to serve with my life, and you, with your flimsy Uethes and bonds, won't stop me."

Lin stared at the tall monster of a man. It was like he noticed for the first time the fact that the big bastard had a Bludwieve of his own. Bright as a gash across his ring finger. Like it was some twisted hierarchy and even he, a self-proclaimed God, answered to someone else.

But who?

The Horned King formed a Blade in each hand and crossed them, right eye bulging as the Stitches along his face grew taut. Then he rushed forward, two long strides eating the space between him and Lin.

A horizontal slash saw the Blade caught by the dagger fade into sparks, while the second Blade nearly bit into Lin's shoulder from a vertical strike downward.

Tylle stepped in, Wefts flying from her hands. More untethered, antlered ones with axes swarmed now that the crazed untethered had all been exhausted.

"To think a priestess of Vellyr would side with swine." The Horned King stepped in, shoulder-checking Lin and sending him stumbling off-balance. He spun, anticipating Tylle's counter-attack and nearly took her arm, but left her with a deep slash across her arm that stained her white gown crimson.

Lin righted his stance.

Whatever reason the pale bastard had attacked Tylle, whatever reason Tylle had chosen now of all times to side with him, none of it mattered. As they'd fought, they'd turned. And Lin could see the front of Fentis overran despite the defenses. Smoke curled up from within the city itself. What Lin wouldn't give to be with Denny again. As sporadic as she fought, she took chances. Made opportunities. Tylle was skilled, no doubt, but she didn't help make openings.

The Horned King tilted his head and shook it slowly. "Tylle, Tylle, Tylle. You of all people should've known how foolish it was to stand against me."

There were plenty of things Lin was tired of. Aemun's voice, which he'd thought gone. The increasingly frequent flashes of Velkath's Sigil. All signs that despite his best efforts, he was once again untethering. But there was nothing worse than a bully. And God reborn or not, the Horned King was cruel in his taunts.

"Tylle told me of you. Mentioned you might be swayed to the cause."

Lin still couldn't form a Weft. Nothing came when he tried to draw on his spul. At the center of his being, extending to his extremities, was a permeating numbness. So he stepped in, ducking under a wide diagonal slash, and stabbed up. He'd been aiming for the heart, but as he pulled the dagger out of the bastard's stomach, he smiled.

A backhand from the monster's long, strong arm knocked the smile from Lin's face, and he went rolling into a corpse. He'd expected worse. But it was worth it, getting a stab into the bastard's guts and making him bleed.

Lin's stomach dropped.

The Horned King wasn't bleeding. Without even dropping one of his Blades, a crystalline-cerulean line formed across the wound and sealed it.

"This is your hero, Tylle? This is the man you'd risk everything for, as opposed to me, a God?"

You barely bested me. Only defeated that Nooseman wraith with aid from others. You thought to take on a God and walk away alive?

Lin rose to his feet and watched in horror as Tylle looked from Lin to the Horned King and finally rested her eyes on Fentis. A flurry of Wefts exploded out from her and she was gone. Fleeing. In all of his thoughts, even the ones he felt wholly betrayed in, he never pictured her as a coward. And yet, without a look back she ran away.

The Horned King lunged to give chase, but Lin managed to get in front of him, dagger brandished.

"All that means," Lin pointed his dagger at the Horned King's wound. "Is that maybe you've already been bled enough? Maybe you're some sort of bloodless monster. But you're no God."

It was a theory Lin had considered for a while. Who wouldn't work the blue magic of actual healing when they could? The Horned King had full-on Stitches. Along the side of his face and across his gut. This man, for he was undoubtedly a man, had been severely wounded before.

"She is a betrayer. Betrayed you. Betrayed me. I wonder... What is it she's running into Fentis for?"

Lin knew the answer. She was rushing to Mellyr. Maybe to save her, but more than likely, to do the same thing Pael had attempted back when the Ladricans took her. *Shit.*

Dirge of Bone

"There are no sides in war. Only a list of things you can and can't sacrifice." —Tylle

Lin moved to chase after Tylle, and the Horned King was on him. A stab. A slash. Lunges powered with so much force that despite Lin having the dagger and destroying the Blades as they formed, he was bullied backward by the sheer presence of the Horned King.

He destroyed countless Blades. But every time he caught one, and the blindingly bright magic evaporated, a new one was back in its place just as bright. So quickly, Lin could've believed he hadn't destroyed it at all.

The Horned King crashed forward with both Blades as Lin barely dodged away. Weak and wounded as Lin was, death itself hounded him. So close. Each errant strike nearly the end.

Then the big bastard slashed a cross into the air, the Blades leaving Wefts in their wake. Lin brought the dagger up to block. But it seemed the Horned King had adapted well and early to the way the dagger cut through the magic. He took three surging steps forward following the wake of the Weft. Swinging forearm as much as Blade, pushing Lin to block then dodge. Only for another follow-up to see him eviscerated.

Lin was acting on instinct, but the Horned King was hounding him like a hunting dog cornering a fox.

He stumbled, taking a broad shoulder to his chin and falling back. He kept the dagger clutched tightly, but the Horned King was upon him, and the bastard was smiling.

"Even Venya's cursed dagger couldn't stop me. Yet you think I'm not worthy? I've given everything to this cause. Friends, if they could be considered that. My life, if what I had before could be considered that. Take solace in knowing that I *won't* remember you. History won't remember *you*. You were only ever an insignificant blood-tainted monster."

Lin tried to raise the dagger to block the Blade angled for his throat, but there was no contact so his arm overextended.

The Horned King had also expected contact judging by how he stumbled. Someone had taken control of the big bastard's Blade and unraveled it. A feat Lin thought impossible. Or maybe he really was just that weak now.

Thudding steps carried over the chaos of the fray. Soldiers still fighting despite the front gates being breached.

Carine rushed forward like a bolt loosed from an alley-piece and Jun careened towards them from the direction of Fentis itself. Swathes of monsters fell before them.

"We aren't losing another one!" Jun howled. He was covered in blood, his top tattered and Inlays across his muscles rippling as he ran. The madman even had the gall to grin as he charged toward the Horned King. Lin winced at the man's words. Of course, he meant another friend. But it was Lin's fault he was where he was. No doubt about it. They'd wanted him to leave the army alone.

Carine looked bloodied herself, but she moved like she wasn't wounded and she'd fared well enough against soldiers in Ferrucium Steel, so Lin assumed it was from those unlucky enough to have gotten in her way as she aided the assault from the east.

"Untethered have overrun Fentis. Crazed ones, but more with those damned antlers than not. I was launching Bolts and saw you." Jun stood over him defensively as Lin struggled to his feet. "You look terrible."

Lin nodded. "Feel about as good as I look."

Carine attacked the Horned King like she'd been waiting her entire life to unleash a severe level of pain on someone. But the Horned King kept up, parrying blows, sweeping back then lunging forward. And he was gaining ground.

Jun slipped in and together, both with Blades formed, they attacked the Horned King.

Double-Blades moved where only one rested. Lin blinked struggling to see clearly. Twin Juns, Carines, and Horned Kings fought like mad. Someone jostled him from behind and he saw it was a bloody, dying untethered gnashing black teeth at him. He drew the dagger across the thing's throat, ending its death throes.

Lins's legs ached, nearly unable to move, and every breath felt like it came shorter than the last. He raised his hand and studied the tremble of it. He just needed time. A little time and then he could aid them. Greedier breath followed greedy breath and tears burned his eyes. He needed to move. Needed to save them.

"You two," The Horned King bellowed, "Are like a poor man's shadow of the King's Noose. You work together, but not in tandem. You are Inlayed, but you. Aren't. Chosen!" A Cocoon of Wefts surrounded him, forcing both attackers back as the magic swelled and unleashed around him. Chunks of sod sprayed into the air.

Lin covered his face with an arm, cutting stray Wefts that cut the air toward him.

An explosion of dirt and debris kicked up and for a terrible moment, Lin thought one of the untethered leaders had joined the battle. But when he blinked past his blurred vision, his heart jolted. Then rose as impossible hope struggled against what he knew to be true. Denny had arrived. Hair less wild, more curled. Thinner, but taller. The differences in appearance sunk the foolish hope Lin had conjured. Where Denny was missing a whole arm, only this woman's hand was gone. And while they looked like they could be sisters, Gritt didn't have the crude Stitches across her face.

It was like a stone had been planted in Lin's gut, and then the traitorous organ had been thrown into the ocean. He'd watched Denny die. Heard her last words. Tried everything to keep her alive and still failed.

Gritt danced across the battlefield with poise as a slew of Wefts erupted from the Horned King. There was a flash of something across the woman's face but Lin didn't know her well enough to be sure what it might be. Doubt? Fear? Relief? To him, she looked to be in disbelief, but as she pivoted to avoid the lethal arcs of light capable of cleaving limb from torso, he truly couldn't be sure. Her arm was tight to her body in a sling, but she moved as if she hadn't been bedridden from the Bludwieve at all.

Jun formed a Bolt, launching the compact, heavy magic from the Horned King's blindspot, but it fizzled out, unraveling before it reached him.

"Little Gritt," The Horned King said. He cocked his head to the side and a smile spread like an infection across his pale face. Gritt froze for a split second and the Horned King's leg connected with her side in a strong, sweeping kick.

Lin expected the force to send her sailing, but she planted her feet and held her position, grabbing the bastard's leg and squeezing with her good arm. Jun approached from behind, a Ferrucium steel sword gleaming in his hand, likely scavenged from one of the many corpses.

Gritt tightened her grip, face reddening from her strain. "You should be dead. Dennick *swore* you were dead."

"Seems Dennick lied." The Horned King shrugged and the muscles along his thigh strained as he yanked his held leg free and spun, Wefts following in the wake of his movements. If Lin had any doubt a focus wasn't necessary to form magic, it would've fled at seeing this monster move. Every single motion sent a sharp, deadly arc through the air.

Jun barely blocked the follow-up kick aimed at his head, steel ringing as it clashed with the Horned King's Inlays. The Weft that followed bit into Jun's neck at an awkward off-angle, grazing the bald man and sending him spinning away.

Carine hadn't reapproached, instead keeping back and working to unravel any Bindings the Horned King formed. Her fingertips were bloody, each straining motion to unravel the magic slower than the last.

Screams carried on the wind from Fentis and the smoke rising from the city seemed thicker. From the east, the troops long in coming had fully arrived and had cut a wedge into the side of the Horned King's forces. But all it did was send more of the army surging forward into Fentis.

Lin took an unsteady step forward. Heavy as his limbs felt, they finally listened to him again. The Horned King was being harried by Jun and Gritt. Lin moved quicker and quicker until he was limping as fast as he could and he leaped, dagger aimed for the bastard's neck.

It felt like he was weightless as he dangled from the Horned King's grip. Jun, Gritt, and Carine rushed in, but as Lin studied the monster's flesh, he saw no blood. No sweat. His skin was pale, bright, and unmarred. Even the hand that choked him now, the same hand that had reached into the kiln to forge the axes, was unmarked aside from the Stitches and Inlays.

"You're no god!" Lin croaked out as she took the dagger and ran the broken, jagged edge across the big bastard's bicep.

Blood like tar bubbled up from under pale flesh. It looked like the moon itself had cracked and let out all the wettest shadows of the world.

Surprise, recognition, and rage all flashed across the Horned King's features until his right eye bulged and he shook his head while gnashing his teeth. Light swelled in Lin's periphery.

The Horned King dropped Lin and clutched his arm, the wound sealing with the blue-crystalline magic.

Lin hit the ground hard, rolling to a stop near Gritt. Dual Blades formed and the Horned King stalked forward, batting away Jun and Carine with a strike each.

"Run to your daughter!" Gritt spat. "The assault may have breached the Tower. Go. It seems this ghost needs to die again."

Lin struggled to stand, let alone run. His knees wobbled as he rose and it felt like he'd been stabbed in the gut. But Gritt helped him up and formed a Blade of her own, leveling it at the approaching monster.

Even knowing it wasn't Denny, seeing her here *hurt*. It sent a resonating ache through his bones that not even being dropped could mimic.

Lin held a hand to his side, wishing the pain away. When he pulled it away, his palm was wet and warm, Lin realized he *was* bleeding. The Horned King probably stabbed him while he was hanging in the monster's grip, now that he considered it.

Your daughter? You failed to keep Margaret safe. You're useless, not that such a thing is new to you, Escorter. But now, you plan to die here facing that monster while Mellyr is ripped from the sad caretakers you left her with?

Lin licked his lips and clutched the dagger tighter. He had failed Margaret, a truth that would haunt him his whole life. Mellyr deserved a normal life— all the children of Danica did. But as he was, he didn't stand a chance against the Horned King.

Had he managed to catch him off guard? Slightly, yes.

Never had he felt more like a coward than when he turned and limped away. The Horned King rushed toward him, but Gritt clashed with him, and the sounds of fighting carried from behind. All around, the fields surrounding Fentis were chaos, and Lin moved as quickly as he could through the fray. Avoiding stray attacks and killing those who were untethered or wielding a Ferrucium steel ax.

He wasn't a coward. He was untethering. He needed to see her one last time.

Once he made it to the base of the Tower, he spotted the doors open with bodies from both factions crowded up like gruesome decorations. Lin looked back, the slight slope allowing a better vantage. The trio still fought the Horned King, but the monster was pushing them bit by bit towards the Tower. His movements even seemed to be growing more precise, more powerful. Or perhaps he hadn't started waning, but the others had making him look all the more proficient.

Bells and horns and screams carried through the city of Fentis.

Guilt racked Lin. He could've stayed. Tried to get another surprise attack on the bastard. But as he touched his hand to his stomach again, still feeling the slick wetness of a weeping wound, he knew the odds wouldn't have been good. Lin formed a focus and tried to heal the wound. A stench like that of fetid flesh carried up and the wound had closed but was black and necrotic around the edges.

Lin limped into the tower. More corpses lined the grand hall. Reflections of the dead were everywhere, polished stone floors slick with the blood of defenders and attackers alike. White robes of junior scholars were tattered and ruined, stained a deep brown and more than one High Scholar joined them.

Screams resounded off the stonework, but so did the clashing of steel and the thudding impact of bodies slamming. The grinding of wheels on stone and a rumbling underfoot had chased Lin into the tower, and he was sure that even if the Horned King was stopped, his mass of untethered would swarm Fentis entirely.

This... This was an assault that put the Fall to shame.

"L...Lindel!" Gronccio's soft voice pitched and the man, covered head to toe in blood, pulled himself away from the press of bodies lining the wall. He had a gash running from his collarbone to his navel and limped as he moved. "M-many of the High Scholars have retreated up— the... Duke Elmore's men are defending the way up, but there are too many untethered. They swarm like ants."

Lin grunted. He moved to leave, heading to the only stairway he could recall, but Gronccio clutched at his arm.

"I owe you an apology. There were many questions you asked... And I could've answered. Many times I considered—"

Lin pulled the heavy-set man toward him and forced their brows together. "It will be fine. I forgave you long before you considered you might want forgiveness."

Slamming his head against the junior scholar's hurt, but getting slowed by him would've resulted in death. Not that Lin was in the prime of his life now. Either way, he had a better chance without the man, and in the chaos, there was a good chance the soft-spoken man would pass for dead among the corpses. That was practically what he'd been doing already.

Lin lowered the unconscious man to the ground and rolled him onto his side, making sure the gash was visible.

Heading to the stairway meant running from the sounds of combat echoing through the halls, but as weak as he felt, a silent stairwell was the better option. He found more dead untethered at the entrance, mad bastards with their rusted blood pooling at the bottom of the staircase. He warily stepped over them and began the slow walk upward. Every other rotation the slitted windows drew nearer to eye-level and the destruction in the northern fields grew more apparent.

Like a blood-red tide, the soldiers of the Ferrucium had carved into the meat of the Horned King's army. Bone and all. Lin stared for a long moment. Spotting the Horned King was easy, as tall and imposing as he was. Jun, Carine, and Gritt were all still alive, but they'd given up so much ground that they were past the trenches and nearly into Fentis proper.

There were still so many attackers. Maybe half were still afield, not knowing how many were fighting in the tower or sacking Fentis. But that half still greatly outnumbered the Ferrucium troops who'd arrived.

If they couldn't find a way to kill the Horned King, Danica as they knew it was finished. He wanted Mellyr. Wanted her blood. Lin shuddered, terrified at what that meant.

Conscripted soldiers, forced to fight and bear the Bludwieves were dying left and right. Those who tried to turn on the untethered were torn apart by writhing threads of crimson magic. Lin looked at his own Bludwieve. Recalling the time he'd felt the sharp pain when confronting Aemun. Bludwieve. Uethe. After everything, some Bindings still didn't make sense. Or perhaps Erias was simply more forgiving in his desires than the Horned King.

"Move aside or— Lindel?"

Lin's pace up the twisting stairwell had dramatically slowed and he looked behind him, surprised to see High Scholar Anya, robed in the deepest hues of the night sky. She held her hem up and sprinted up the stairs. Viscera speckled her face and she slowed, if only to place a shoulder under Lin.

"Left a trail of blood like a snail, haven't you?"

"Eh?" Lin shook his head, then noticed the wall he'd been leaning on for support. A smear of blood streaked the stonework from the wound at his side. Seemed he hadn't healed it after all.

"C'mon then. We have someone who wants very badly to see you, I think."

Dirge of Hate

"Verbanth was a fool. If he'd truly been 'Vengeful' there wouldn't have been a bit of Ladrica left." —Duke Wellgrove

"Should've known you'd be in the thick of it. Even a scholar buried in the tomes could've seen that coming from over the hill."

It hadn't been long since he'd last seen Anya, but it felt like a lifetime. A lifetime since he'd hoped he might not be untethering, but was sure he had been. A lifetime since seeing and holding Mellyr. A lifetime in a span of days so brief compared to all the rest of his life, but so much more rewarding.

Anya had helped carry him up the winding staircase, and now they'd exited, heading down a long, familiar hall reserved for guests of the scholars. Even from where they were, far removed from the fighting, the sounds of clashing steel harried them.

Despite not seeing the battle continue to unfold, it was hard to imagine Fentis wasn't overrun. Even if the combined forces of the Dukes and the Ferrucium routed the Horned King's army fully, they'd been too late to stop the progression into Fentis proper. Screams and howls wound up the central shaft. Steel on steel rang like a smith's hammer, and explosions much like those at the isle shook the walls.

"No choice," Lin muttered. He kept his eyes down, as that was the only way to keep Velkath's Sigil at bay for any extended amount of time. Given a chance to breathe, he did so greedily, then pressed fingers into the tender spot at his temple. He'd had suspicions when the Horned King had harmed him there, and now, as the world around him unraveled, he knew he was right.

Lin pulled his hand away, free of fresh blood. There was no humming fuzz of magic, no sensation of the Thorn that should be buried there. The Bound Metal manacles kept him from noticing, but there was no doubt now that his Thorn had been snipped.

"Nasty knot you've got." Anya grabbed his chin and lifted his face, forcing him to stare at her. "How did it feel? Your eyes I mean?"

Lin blinked at the thought. "Hurt worse than most things I've done."

"Has it helped?"

Lin grunted. It had for a time. Or maybe he'd made himself think Inlaying his eyes had helped. Anything to keep his mind off his inevitable madness.

Anya rapped her knuckles against the thick mahogany door three times, and it opened before the fourth. She pulled Lin in, moving aside the Ferrucium steel sword pointed at her chest with the back of her hand.

Lin hadn't been sure where she was leading him. He half-expected to be in a room with all the council members composed of High Scholars, but only three junior scholars stared back at him.

Well, two junior scholars and one white-haired man wearing robes nearer in color to ash from a fireplace than cream white.

Denro grabbed him before Lin could react. In such a short time, the senior soldier had already risen within the ranks of Scholars. Of course, he had. Lin squeezed back as hard as he could. There was so much he wanted to tell the man. Of Denny. Of Tylle. Of the Horned King and what he'd seen. Tears stung the corners of Lin's eyes.

"You've Inlayed your eyes..."

"And still I feel blind," Lin whispered pulling away. "At this rate, you'll be a High Scholar before the war is over."

"Unfortunate, the passing of High Scholar Orson, but she understood the risk of parlaying with a monster who razed towns and pillaged the north as Jun described." Anya's lips drew into a tight line and she nodded toward the dagger. "Were you able to cut him? Soldiers came in demanding the dagger and I knew it had to be you."

"Once." Lin eyed the other two junior scholars, wondering what luck they'd had to be away from the battle. Not that the battle wasn't coming to them. "But he's coming. Jun and Carine and that Nooseman, Gritt, they're struggling to keep him back. I've never seen a Binder like him. He's a monster."

"If he'd be believed, he is a God reborn," Denro said with a laugh.

Lin shook his head, hating that he felt compelled to disagree. "You haven't seen him up close. He might be. He moves quicker than any Nooseman and is far faster than a common untethered.

Even his leaders, seem made of sterner stuff. He drinks the blood of *children*."

Speaking of... Lin scanned the room and then saw Mellyr, standing on her own against the rail of the crib. There was a range of emotions across her tiny face, then she scuttled back, falling to her rear, soft whimpers coming from her.

"Shhh," one of the scholars said. "All's well littling. All's well."

She fears you. Azhalia fears you. And can you blame her?

"No," Lin snarled.

"Lindel... Are you unwell again?" Anya whispered.

As if Lin had ever *truly* been well.

There had been so much that happened, to say he was well in any context would be a lie. But what she clearly meant was, are you untethering again?

Lin touched his temple. "I could feed a hundred more leeches and I don't think I'd ever be myself again. But good news, if it's my blood that poisons me. I seem to be losing it."

Anya stared at the bloody fingers he'd pulled from his side. Her large eyes unblinking in the dim light of the room, then she nodded. "Leo. Rush to my chambers. Not the lower ones, the upper ones, and bring back three vials of what will look like ink to you. Quick as a blink."

Lin blinked after the figure that had rushed from the room. He hadn't even noticed the child. Everything ached, even his teeth. Wanting to go to Mellyr, but not wishing to disturb her as she was quieted down by the scholar, Lin stumbled to the balcony.

"Do you truly mean that?"

Ignoring Denro's question should've been easy, especially considering all the time the man had kept him in the dark and did the same to him months ago in this very room. But when Lin looked up at the man, he couldn't keep it in. Lin was the errant ember, burning and ruining everything he touched and now Mellyr didn't even recognize him. "I do."

Smoke hung heavy in the air, the northern side of Fentis aflame. "The ships," Lin said, noticing for the first time that two of the sleek Ladrican ships had docked.

"They've yet to aid us, but came into the harbor a day ago," Denro said, his voice sounding hollow— broken in a way.

Anya shook her head, running a hand over her scalp. "It is impossible to tell if they plan to aid us, given the past alliance and circumstance of attackers, or if they hover waiting to swoop down on what remains."

Lin slapped the balcony's railing. Odds were they were behind this somehow. Behind all of it. Someone had aided Aemun. Lin wheeled and stared at Anya. He hadn't forgotten how odd it was that her ship hadn't been targeted by Royce. That she'd recognized the dagger— sent him north to Ladrica in the first place. "Denro, do you recall the game we played?"

"Hmm?" Denro moved to stand closer, running his hand along the crib as he came to stand between Lin and Mellyr.

"With Pael. When we guessed what reason Ladrica might've wanted to steal Mellyr away. Well, what reason would Fentis have to instigate war?"

It felt like someone smacked the side of Lin's leg, and when he looked, he noted Leo standing there expectantly, hand out with three tiny stoppered vials. Either Lin had gotten shorter, or the boy was sprouting up quickly under the watchful eye of the scholars.

"As much as I enjoy a puzzle, I can assure you tha—"

Anya cut Denro off with a single raised finger. "Do you hear that?"

Lin turned, pulling back into the room and taking the stoppered vials from Leo's hand. Nothing. He heard nothing save the sounds of combat carrying on the wind.

They stood in silence for a long drawn-out moment before the door creaked on its hinges. Leo rushed behind the door in an instant, a dagger in his hand and a grim look on his youthful face.

Like a shadow slinking, Pael scurried in, shutting the door with a soft click behind him.

"Pael!" Lin said, thankful the diminutive man hadn't been lost amid the battle.

Pael had looked bad before, but now he was a ghost of a man. His clothes were tattered and he had scrapes along the right side of his body. Sweat, blood, and worse coated his top and when he noticed Leo behind the door, he barely reacted. He grunted and slid against the wall, shaking his head. "Did what I could, but too many of them. They've got Ore ready to be launched into the city. Putting out the normal fires with water will just make the Ore eat at the surroundings worse."

Anya glared. "Do you still think to ask why the scholars might have a hand in this?"

Lin ignored her, unstoppered the vials, and downed the first one without answer. It didn't prove anything. How many disparate threads had Aemun been weaving there at the end? "He's here for Mellyr. Wants to take her blood in him."

Denro bristled and his knuckles tightened along the crib's rail. "Why?"

"Bloodlines. Aemun's family dates back, apparently, the bastard really did have the blood of Velkath in his veins. And now this monster wants what's left of it."

Lin's tongue stung from the inky concoction. Grit irritated his gums and when he burped it tasted overly metallic. Without waiting, he uncorked the second and downed it. Heavy lines of fluid dripped down his beard, stinging where it reached his skin.

"If someone else were to drink of her blood, would they stand a chance?" Anya asked.

Lin glared at her, tossed the second vial to shatter against the tile underfoot, and uncorked the third. "I'd kill anyone that tried."

"Wait!" Anya started.

But Lin consumed the contents of the third vial and played with the glass, looking at himself in the hazy reflection. Breathing felt forced and aside from the immediate cramps taking his guts, a knot formed at his center. Never had his spul felt so tangible. So accessible.

"Anya, Pael. Pael, High Scholar Anya, and her companion Little Leo of Ladrica," Denro said.

Pael raised his brows but didn't move or respond. His eyes were wide and he stared off into the sky beyond Lin.

"The Dukesman responsible for infiltrating and freeing the pair of you? Among *other* things?"

"His list of crimes is far longer I'm sure, but I've no doubt things would've been worse if he hadn't infiltrated the Horned King's forces, destabilizing small things in the encampment." Lin put a hand to his stomach and winced at the sharp pain.

"And how did he know to come to this room?" Leo asked. Even his voice seemed deeper than the last time Lin heard him speak.

"Blood. I followed the blood."

Some men are measured by their crimes. Others by their virtues. Others by action and fewer still by inaction. What will you be measured by, Escorter? Besides your failures.

"Hiding up here was never my plan," Lin said, staring at the faces of all those gathered. "I came to... I came to see Mellyr one last time. And now I've seen her and she's seen me and I can't let the Horned King get to her. Even if all of this stemmed from Aemun's plotting or the Weavers' many failings. Denro.

"If I don't survive, there is only one man I can imagine raising Mellyr to be not a queen, not a ruler, but a good person. A wonderful person. You. And Anya. Thank you for giving our people a chance. Even if blood had to be shed to see it happen."

"Pael."

"Save it," Pael muttered. "You aren't dying today. Think. You don't *need* to fight. We have our backs to the sea. We flee. The lot of us. *Rebuild*. Do you think Erias is out there, fighting? We did everything we could."

Lin shook his head and walked over to the old man. "I don't know you half as well as I'd like. But I know you're trying to feed me shit to keep me from dying, all while having no intention of giving up yourself."

Pael stared at Lin, his dark eyes searching for something, then looked away. Gaze averted as tears welled into the man's eyes. "Have you seen yourself? Maybe Anya won't call you off, maybe your old friend Denro thinks he has no right, but fuck that. You look worse than… than…" Pael's words choked as a shudder rocked his lithe frame. Any witty comparison dying on his lips.

"I look worse than a Belanisian whore without wine beforehand?" Lin offered, steeling himself.

"You're still not good at those. And a smart man wouldn't be caught dead with a Belanisian whore, with or without wine." Pael wiped his cheeks with the tattered bits of his sleeve. "But I meant what I said, boy."

Leo's cheeks had turned red and so had Anya's when Lin looked up at her. He rose, feeling every bit of the last span of months in his bones. But the twisting knot in his gut had calmed and he felt rejuvenated, at least a bit. Denro had been silent since introducing Anya and Pael and now he stared down at Mellyr, avoiding Lin's questioning stare.

"Denro," Lin whispered.

"Trouble follows you the same way it followed your father and mother. Trouble follows you and you always seem eager to meet it. We will… When the time comes… Raise Mellyr together. I've no doubt about that. Because I know you wouldn't willingly let me lose another of my children. Would you?" It wasn't what he said that hurt Lin, but in the spaces between the words. Each unsaid thought a corpse left on the road to get where they'd gotten.

"I wouldn't," Lin lied.

Denro knew it too. Obvious in the way his shoulders slumped and his wrinkled face scrunched up. Everyone in the room could likely tell the lie for what it was, painted across Lin's body in each scar, Stitch, and smear of fresh blood. His wasn't the body of a man who could ignore trouble. From the bite he took to his shoulder back in Lyre, to the snapped and reformed digits of his left hand.

Lin raised the dagger marveling at the broken, black edge. All those awful dreams of being a broken, reformed blade. In a swift motion, he slit the Bludwieve that encircled his ring finger. He wasn't sure what he'd expected, but the ends fell away like it was a simple scarlet string cut down the middle. It drifted into nothingness like fading embers.

"This might be the key to saving any of the captured Danicans from their forced Uethes." Lin flipped it and held it by the broken tip, pressing the hilt toward Anya.

"It *might* be the key to you surviving this. Or *they* might depending on how this all goes." Anya raised her chin to the balcony and Lin turned.

Running like they were chased from the docks by a horde of untethered, despite the opposite being true, was a large contingent of fully armored Ladrican soldiers. A figure cloaked in black with a sleek metallic mask led them. A Nooseman.

Lin stared, gripping the dagger so tight it was a marvel it didn't slip and cut him. As impossible as it was to be sure, Lin had no doubts it was the Nooseman who'd been responsible for killing Denny. It was in the way they moved, even this far away. So far above the skill of the three children who'd attacked the Horned King.

Pael groaned and rose to his feet, a grimace causing him to look far older than the old man should. "I hear shouts from up the hall and some vibrations. Something big is coming."

The junior scholars, silent the entire time, moved in unison to stand beside Mellyr's crib. Both bore daggers and grasped at vials strung around their necks. That gave Lin pause, but it didn't matter now. It was a matter of perspective, really. Sure, they carried Danican blood around their throats like crude jewelry, but at least they weren't drinking it. Lin shuddered and looked away when he noticed them notice his staring.

Lin pressed past the scholars, reached in, and brushed aside Mellyr's hair. Waves with a slight curl she'd gotten from her father. Pale skin from her mother. Her eyes, large and blue, pierced into him. He held his breath, terrified that she might cry, but then a single, tiny hand reached up for him.

As gently as he could, he grasped her hand. Kissed it. Leaned in and kissed her on her brow, frowning at the smear of blood he left behind when he pulled away.

Before more tears could take him, he stood upright and wheeled toward the door. From the hall, clambering shouts and snarls carried, accented by the slamming of doors. Over and over the intruders made their way from the grand staircase.

Lin took the dagger in a fighting stance, a Blade colored like a peeled orange flaring to life in his left hand. "Anya."

"Hmm?" She'd straightened her back, both hands leveled flat at the door and revealing thick bands of fresh ink along her arms where the silver scars had once been.

"I'm sorry I didn't help you rewrite the lost tome like I'd planned."

"There is still time."

"After," Lin whispered.

"After," she agreed.

Dirge of Blood

"Seduction and war are too similar. Whispers here. Light touches there. And that's not mentioning the pain during or after."—Pael Hollander

Leo lay flat against one side of the door, Pael on the other. Seeing them so near each other, the comparisons were clear, but so were the distinctions. Leo was clean and pristine in his white initiate robes, Pael dark and worn in his near-rags. Both held a dagger, but Lin would've been happier to see either of them with a bolt-shooter near the balcony further back from danger.

Lin moved as soon as the door opened. Shrapnel flew inward and three horned untethered bearing bone-collars around their necks stalked in. All bore Velkath's Sigil on their chests, temples glowing with the green glow where antlers melded into flesh.

Denro gasped, Wefts flying lamely from him. Not remotely sharp enough to cut through the Inlayed flesh of these monsters.

The untethered in the lead, a heavy-set one by untethered standards, dragged an unconscious junior scholar by their hair. Or perhaps the junior scholar was dead with the amount of blood pooling under them.

In one sweeping arc of the dark dagger, Lin cut away the Wefts forming to harm his allies. He stabbed with his Blade, envisioning the intense power the Horned King was capable of. His Blade did spear the leader, but it wouldn't go beyond the traditional size he'd grown used to forming.

Then his Blade unraveled, stolen from him by one of the monsters. Lin stumbled as the tension from the magic evaporated. He slashed forward with the dagger, pivoting.

The big one in front, wounded as he was, managed to lift the corpse of the scholar into the air and blocked Lin's dagger strike.

Lin was knocked back as the corpse collapsed into him. His back struck the wall, thudding violently and Mellyr's crib erupted with cries. What Lin wouldn't give to have Julius's power of sleep if only to calm her.

When Lin freed himself of the corpse and rose, he rushed forward. Denro had taken his place and seemed to be holding his own with the untethered. The other two leaders, keen and tough as they seemed, were dead. Deep gashes across both throats showing bone. Pael and Leo crowded the untethered's back and then the room was awash with light. A blinding light so sudden, so bright that Lin couldn't be sure if it was still shining or if he'd been blinded.

Lin staggered forward, a firm grip clutching his throat and lifting him. The first thing he saw was the crown of Bindings and the over-taut flesh Stitched on the right side of the monster's face. The Horned King's eye bulged as he grinned. He tried to stab forward with the dagger but the monster caught Lin's wrist and held it in place, muscles barely straining.

"To think how much trouble you've caused." His grip tightened and stars flashed through Lin's vision. "To think how little you've truly achieved!"

But Lin *had* achieved something. A black line was carved around the monster's forearm. Scabbed now, but a wound inflicted by Lin.

"Wait!" Anya's voice came muffled from the side. She was out of Lin's line of sight and turning his head was impossible.

Lin kicked, leg catching the big bastard in his side, over and over again.

"What it seems like you don't understand, what none of you understand, is that you have no say in how this unfolds," Anya said. "Ladricans are coming. Fighting back the untethered. If you think they'll cede Fentis and the tower and the child to you, then you're mistaken."

A gruesome, blood-stained smile stretched across the Horned King's face. "What men can truly cede anything to a God? Especially when it is mine to do as I please in the first place. Everything you've thrown against me has failed. I am the pinnacle. I *am* Velkath Reborn. And all of you have been judged unworthy. Especially you." The Horned King directed that last part at Lin.

Lin's arm holding the dagger trembled as he tried to keep the blade from being turned on him. But it came, inch by inch until the broken tip trembled in front of his eye. He gripped his wrist with his other hand and used his legs to brace against the Horned King's side. Moving his head away was impossible and his left hand did nothing but slow the process. With his throat constricted, he couldn't even scream as the edge found purchase, stabbing in. A hoarse, crushed scream came out then the world shifted as he was thrown to the ground in front of Anya.

"Your Hero is a fool."

"My hero is a better man than you'll ever be," Carine's voice carried into the room.

Lin lifted his head and stared at the hilt sticking out from his left forearm. If the weapon had a full, unbroken blade, he'd have lost an eye. Instead, the bones on the left side of his body screamed in a dull throbbing sensation, and pain and blood seeped from the wound equally.

"Good thing I'm no mere man," The Horned King snarled.

Anya had shifted to stand between Mellyr and the Horned King, Leo at her side looking like he'd pissed himself. Not that Lin blamed him. Pael was nowhere to be seen, but the untethered that had thrown a corpse at Lin who Denro had been fighting looked as if his throat had been recently slit. Denro sucked in heavy breaths and kept a hand to his side, blood staining his fingers.

Jun arrived just behind Carine, blood painting him a brackish brown over his shining Inlays. He'd gained a slash across his eye, and the meat around the socket was bruised and swollen. Then, rushing past both of them, Gritt crashed into the room with a howl. She formed dual Blades, thin and frail compared to the Blades the monster before her could conjure.

Even in the cramped room, the two fought like they were in the open field. Blades lengthened and shortened at will. The Horned King seemed desperate to take control of Gritt's magic, but hers held, never looking close to unraveling.

Mellyr shrieked and even the junior scholars looked ready to cry, terror taking any color from their faces. One sidled away along the wall, muttering and shaking, then tried to flee the room. An arcing slice from the Horned King's Blade caught the scholar across the middle of their back and would have taken Jun across the chest if he hadn't blocked it in time.

"All of you are tainted. Ruined by generations of beliefs pressed into your skulls. Pressed into your souls!" The Horned King screamed as he pulled the Blade back, then lunged unexpectedly into Gritt's side shouldering her to the ground. "With these hands, I'll correct the course of this failed ship. That is my Uethe. That is my destiny!"

Destiny.

Lin blinked and fought back bile as he pulled the dagger from the sheath his arm had become. He shook his head, wincing as the blood refused to slow. Like he had so many times before, he formed a focus. Hued like the light shone through sapphire, the magic of mending flared to life, puckering the flesh closed under its gentle kiss. But the glow of his Inlays didn't return and his arm felt heavy and unrespondant.

Moaning as they went, the junior scholar tried to crawl out of the door, hands clutching at the broken shards of wood.

A distant rumble sounded, then a staccato barrage followed. Outside, the sky flashed in bursts of violet and indigo. *Wanderer's Ore.*

Lin was upright, but his legs trembled. Velkath's Sigil flashed every time the Horned King's Blade clashed with one of the others. He couldn't pull his eyes from Mellyr, face red and tear-streaked, blood smearing her brow.

In a flurry of motion, Anya scooped Mellyr into her arms, clutching her tight, hand resting gently on the back of her head. When she turned her eyes burned into the back of the dying scholar. "She is what you want, no?" Her voice trembled as she raised it.

Denro moved to stand beside her, Ferrucium steel leveled toward the Horned King.

"Swords are for the conquered!" The Horned King spat.

A kick centered on her sternum saw Carine fly into the far wall, crashing into a dresser. Jun was there in her place, punching and slashing in a steady rhythm, but his Blade unraveled at every clash and his knee gave a sick pop when the Horned King caught him with a crunching kick while pivoting. As he dropped, the monster's Blade, which had shifted to be thicker at the head like a One-whispered axe, chopped diagonally down, and aimed for his throat.

"Wait!" Anya screamed an ochre Weft pressed to Mellyr's throat. "I know what she is. Aemun, her father, left a letter. I know... What her potential means to those who want power. But right now... she is a child. Nothing more. And if I kill her... You lose. You'll have come all this way for nothing."

Lin stared in disbelief. Pain and rage and fury painted the room a darker red than even the splatterings of blood.

"Do it. I don't want her. Just her blood, even if I must lap it from the tiles after you've slit her little throat."

Anya's hand trembled, more rumbling shaking the tower as thicker, darker smoke r up to the balcony. Then the Weft shattered into motes of light. Mellyr squirmed to escape Anya's grasp.

Gritt stepped in, forcing the Horned King's Blade away from Jun's throat. Her hair had come undone, a wild mess of tangles. She didn't move like Denny. Not in the odd, natural rhythm Denny had possessed, but she was swift and accurate in her strikes. She parried a hard overhead strike with one Blade, the other cutting across the Horned King's torso. No wound or gash where she'd struck him. All of that to land a blow, and nothing.

How many times since Lyre had he been on the backfoot? Too many. He'd learned long ago that fighting these monsters head-on never seemed to work, but he'd gotten confident after Ladrica. Cocky in thinking that he could match them even though the last Nooseman he'd faced nearly killed him and *did* kill Denny. Every wound on his body reminded him how wrong the thought was. But how had he survived Dennick?

Lin worked Weaves, low and tight in the doorframe. He used bodies, desks, and chairs to make a web of sorts as Gritt fought the Horned King. Even after all the fighting, the monster hadn't broken a sweat. When the Snare was finished, Lin felt exhausted. Whatever was in the vials, he'd felt like he burned through it too quickly. Then again, he'd lost plenty of blood.

Pael had likely run, given the situation. He'd have a better time helping others if he'd managed to get out alive.

The Horned King spun, Wefts flying in all directions like golden petals blooming on a flower. Most hit walls or furniture, sending papers and chunks of stone flying into the air. Some connected with Lin's Weaves, clashing before slicing through them. A smirk twitched on the monster's face. "Rarely these days am I impressed. But you've managed it."

"Why?" Gritt spat. She'd begun breathing harder and harder and her arms drooped.

"You always had questions, didn't you? Incessant little chirpings of a baby bird not ready to be thrown from the nest. I don't need to explain my thoughts or actions to any of you. You, the best that Danica had to offer, were found wanting. Time and time again. I'm impressed by all of your ineptitude!"

"Aarrghhh!" Jun screamed. He'd worked a Bolt, compressing and shaping his magic until he flung it like a spear.

The Horned King's eyes went large, the right larger than the other, as he brought his Blade up to deflect the attack. Like a poorly tempered sword, it shattered. The Bolt took him in the chest and sent him stumbling back.

Lin readied. He wasn't sure how the monster would be caught in the Snare, but he'd hoped one of his companions would send the big bastard into it. A Weave caught his ankle and he teetered for a second.

"Childish—"

But Lin cut him off as he tackled the man. As strong as the Horned King was, the momentum was too much. His hands brought sections of the wall with him and together, Lin and the Horned King teetered on the balcony. The thin rail groaned as it began to twist from the combined weight and force.

Lin had stabbed on impact, dagger raking into the man's abdomen in savage, brutal arcs. Perhaps this was the rage Tylle had felt when attacking Aemun. Perhaps this was the culmination of all the pain and anger and confusion Lin had bottled for the last few months.

"Jun, again!" Lin called.

Denro yelled. The tower rumbled. It felt like a hand tried to grab his shoulder. The Horned King twisted, slowly righting his balance despite his large size.

The force of the Bolt crunching into the middle of Lin's back sent the railing crashing away and together he and the Horned King slipped from the balcony.

Dying Hope

"Hate and hope. Pain and pride. War and worry. There is freedom, when you allow yourself to fall." —Duke Errond

Lin hadn't considered the next step. All he'd wanted to do was get the big bastard as far from Mellyr as possible. And now, as he plummeted clutched to the Horned King and a sickness writhed in his guts, it all felt so dramatic.

This was it.

The Horned King continued fighting. Despite the many slashes and stabs Lin had managed to inflict, the bastard still found a way to wrap his large arms around Lin and squeeze. He stabbed Lin with tiny Blades and slashed him with Wefts.

Below, still a good distance away, the port city burned. Red flames mingled with unnatural purple ones and worst of all, explosions still erupted from the buildings. Rain fell in sweeping sheets, the seaborne wind blowing against the port city. But projectiles of Wanderer's Ore didn't diminish from the water, sizzling and burning all the brighter.

Above, much closer but quickly distancing, faces stared in horror as Lin and the Horned King twisted through the air. From this angle, Gritt looked so much like Denny. Curly hair waving in the wind. No Stitches across her face, of course. But, still.

Lin winced as the Horned King's Blade bit into the wound at his side. Lin tried to stab again, but the Horned King trapped his arm and held it there.

"You small, insignificant, tainted-blood fool!" The Horned King howled.

A laugh came unbidden and, despite the sick feeling in Lin's gut from the fall, he smiled. The only people who'd called Danicans tainted-blood were from Ladrica. Not that he'd survive to tell anyone where the Horned King seemed to be from. *Arrogant bastard.*

"You think this will kill me? I've survived worse. I've done worse. I'll—"

Lin couldn't hear the monster's vile words a scream was pulled from him. The Horned King twisted his arm in that powerful grip of his. But the motion had sent them spinning and Lin saw what the monster didn't.

Like an eye of glass, the ceiling to the auditorium Lin had awaited the High Scholar's decision rushed up. The Horned King hit first, Lin crashing into him, and then the air fled his lungs.

The world was silent save for the shattering of a thousand glass vials. No, the world itself broke. Then bit by bit, in flashes of bright Bindings, it rebuilt.

Despite the shattered skylight doing its best to break Lin's bones and slash flesh, it was clear they'd managed to crash through to the floor of the auditorium. Lin's head swam and everything hurt. He was wrapped and tangled in a rich fabric, banners that had run from the top of the ceiling to the edge of the seats. Ruined now. They'd cushioned his fall, but not enough. Not nearly enough.

Injured, it made sense that his breath caught in slow clicks. The air didn't want to leave him, for it had the sense to know it would struggle to return. Tears stung his eyes as he stared up at the shattered opening. All those fragments and fractures in the ceiling. He'd shattered it— shattered himself trying to be something that, maybe, he never really was. So busy trying to fit the mold others cast of him, that he broke in the process.

Lin groaned, tried to roll over, and gave up. He couldn't feel his left leg at all and the pain he did feel shooting up his left side convinced him to stay in place. Jun's Bolt had propelled him forward, but it also took a chunk of his flesh as payment.

Glass littered the floor, a wide expanse that looked as much like a coliseum as it did an audience chamber. It crunched underneath him as he breathed. Or it was his ribs making that noise, as a dull click sounded with each forced inhalation.

Blood, thick and black, dripped from the edges of the broken skylight. Lin laid there for a long moment, listening. The explosions outside calmed and eventually ended altogether, and even the terrified screams of citizens stopped. He knew he hadn't lost his hearing as he could still hear the clicking when he breathed. Small comfort. Aemun's ghostly chiding was silent. Maybe it'd been crushed from the fall.

But what he really listened for, and what he eventually heard, was the steady grunting breaths of another person in the room. Hope had been there, buried under all the pain. Hope that with that fall, as injured as Lin was, the Horned King would be worse.

It took everything in Lin to roll to his side, fragments of sharp glass catching his palms and digging in. His left arm screamed where Venya's dagger had stabbed into him, and he couldn't close his hand into a fist.

He couldn't untangle himself from the ruined banner, so he lay there and looked up.

Suspended like a doll on taut strings, the Horned King was impaled through in four intersecting places, skewers made of Wievings holding him in place. Somewhat like Velkath's Sigil, if Lin squinted. Bit by bit the magic faded, lowering him as it weakened. Black, rust-flaked blood seeped from his wounds. His gut was a mess of blue-hued swathes, but many of the wounds refused to seal, weeping out his insides. One leg hung low enough that his foot rested on the ground.

Amid the broken shards and debris, a black gleam caught Lin's eye. He pulled himself along. Standing up felt near impossible, numb as his body was, but he managed to kneel on his right knee and painfully kick off the soft fabric that had rolled around him.

Getting to Venya's dagger, then to the Horned King as he hung there, likely wouldn't be possible.

"What now?" Lin tried to shout, but the pain in his ribs doubled and the words came out whimpered.

"All you've done is bought them time."

A fair assessment all considered. It felt like, if Lin slowed down to think about things, that's all he ever did. But maybe, that was all a man like him was good for. Buying people time. Giving everything he had in him *now* so that others could win *later*. Of all his battles and victories, each a struggle, he'd never been the hero. Not the way people seemed to view him. Though... He'd be lying if being named the Hero of the Fingers hadn't felt earned, in a way.

"Maybe." Lin squeezed his eyes shut as he forced himself upright.

One of the Wievings keeping the Horned King blinked out of existence, causing him to droop lower to the ground.

Lin forced himself up, squeezing his eyes closed at the pain, and stepped forward, dragging his numb left leg. Sprinting was out of the question. "I know you're not Velkath Reborn. Maybe a descendant, like Mellyr, but not truly a god."

"You know nothing." The Horned King snarled. Another of the Wievings faded, leaving only his arms held spread.

"I know, like all the untethered under your control, you have a Bludwieve. I know the only place I've heard the term tainted-blood is from the lips of the Ladrican King. I know—" Lin nearly passed out as he stooped down to pick up Venya's dagger. Even more of the strange black blade was broken. A fingertip's worth of the material was left on the hilt.

"You. Know. Nothing!" The Horned King's right eye bulged and bloody spittle flew from him. Without waiting for the last two Wievings to fully fade, he ripped his left arm free of the one suspending it.

"Gritt recognized you." Lin limped to where the Horned King was as the man freed himself from the final Wieving.

Even after all the fighting and blood loss, the man still formed a Blade so pure and bright that it could have been forged from a star. Maybe his spul was endless. Maybe it came from drinking the blood of children. Maybe someday Mellyr might reach his prowess.

"Even if I die here, I've fulfilled my uethes. I did all that was asked of me. I... I will not be broken *ever* again!"

"It's funny..." Lin whispered. "I feel the same." Looking at the Horned King was hard, only because the magic lining his flesh warped, twisting and writhing like serpents just under his flesh. They twisted, coiling into Velkath's Sigil.

"Ha... hahaha," The Horned King's throaty laugh bounced off the walls of the audience chamber. "You really have gone mad though, haven't you? Didn't even realize it, I bet."

Lin narrowed his eyes and stared at the ground between him and the big bastard. If he lunged, he might be able to reach him. "Realized what?"

"That I took the copper from your mind."

Lin shrugged. He'd assumed. Then he lunged, pushing off with his right foot as hard as he could.

Instead of grabbing Lin, the Horned King moved aside, slashing Lin across the back as he tripped past and crashed to the ground.

"Over and over you surprise me. But you're done. The child's blood will be mine. And even if all else fails, Ladrica will have more than enough reason to take control of Danica. The Free Nations and powers that be can't deny them after this."

Lin blinked. His consciousness was fading.

Someone was running. Many someones, by the sound of it. Good. They'd get here in time to kill this bastard. Or maybe they were more of the intelligent untethered coming to find their fallen king.

Everything screamed as he was kicked over, rolling to a stop against the raised seating where the High Scholars would sit.

At least from this angle, Lin could watch Gritt and... an actual Nooseman, mask and all, rush towards the Horned King.

Lin's suspicion from earlier was confirmed as the Nooseman grew closer. Only one part of their mask had an eye hole. The Horned King spun as they drew near, splitting his Blade into two, but the hue went from moonlight to the color of wheat.

Gritt was far slower than her masked counterpart, but her assault was still swift. She got into his range and cut horizontally with her own Blade. As the Horned King parried, the Nooseman did the same from the other side. Together they pushed the monster back, his movements slowing.

A hand grasped Lin's shoulder and he flinched, both from the pain and surprise. "Tylle."

Her face was bloody, and her hair was matted to her temple. It looked like she'd lost a bit of her ear and her white dress was in tatters, displaying more flesh than was modest for anyone other than an untethered. But, what was she now, if not untethered?

Worst of all, he couldn't look away. He wanted to watch Gritt and the Nooseman continue to push back the Horned King, but his eyes were locked on Tylle's. Had she always known it would come to this? From the moment she saved him? Tears came easily and he struggled to grab her hand.

Without a word, she took Venya's dagger. Her fingers were like steel as she uncurled Lin's weak grip on it.

Lin closed his eyes, waiting for the stab from the short weapon. Three pained breaths, then three more. When Lin opened his eyes, Tylle was gone. Slinking silently behind the Horned King. Flanking him, Venya's dagger in hand.

Watching the Horned King fight, moving fluidly despite his injuries, it was easy to see why he might be mistaken for a God. Tall and strong. Cunning and wise. But the Nooseman was having none of it. And the wounds they were delivering to the Horned King were piling up ten-fold. Slash after slash. Almost like the Nooseman had something to prove to the monster.

What now, Escorter?

Lin blinked away the flashes of Velkath's Sigil and frowned. Maybe it was better to die now before the madness fully took him. He'd wished he'd seen Nebra one last time, but at least he'd kissed Mellyr goodbye.

Tylle had managed to get fully behind the Horned King before he noticed her. He spun, taking a Blade across the back of his knee for his maneuver. The attack likely severed a tendon the way the man fell to his knee. Quick as that, the Horned King had Venya's dagger sticking out of his skull. Gritt blocked his counterattack, saving Tylle's life in the process.

As a trio, they stabbed the monster, Blades easily piercing the man's flesh despite his Inlays. Even when he collapsed, it still didn't look real.

Lin couldn't hear them, but Gritt was telling the Nooseman something. Then, she pulled the finger-length dagger from the bastard's skull.

They approached Lin, dagger in Tylle's hand. Gritt and Tylle barely made eye contact with him, but behind the mask, the Nooseman stared. Gritt handed the Nooseman the dagger and they crouched near Lin.

"I... I'm sorry," the Nooseman said in his odd pronunciation. In one quick motion, he severed his Bludwieve with the edge of the dagger. "For your friend." When the Bludwieve shriveled away, he set down the dagger before Lin and slid his mask off, dropping it to the side to clatter on the stone.

A handsome man, with a strong jaw. He appeared healthier than most Binders, but his right eye was a mess of scar tissue where there wasn't a gaping hole.

Even if Lin wasn't injured, reaching the dagger in time would have been a struggle. He clenched his jaw and slowly leaned toward it, surprised that the one-eyed man hadn't moved to stop him. His fingers brushed the blade, just out of reach. He struggled to lean forward more and Tylle stepped to his side.

The hilt scraped stone as the Nooseman pushed it towards him.

Gritt grabbed the man's shoulder but he raised a hand and didn't take his eye off Lin's eyes. His throat bulged as he swallowed like any words he might've tried to utter in that dialect of his were stuck in there, choking him.

"You took her," Lin wheezed. "What is he to you?" Lin grabbed the dagger. His hand wouldn't stop trembling no matter how hard he tried to control it. Everywhere he looked, the walls, the blood, the Inlayed eyes of the Nooseman, he saw fraying versions of Velkath's Sigil. And a deep cold, starting where his spul resided, was creeping through his limbs.

"A friend," Gritt said softly. She clenched her jaw, jutting in a way so similar to how Denny would that nothing in the world could convince him they weren't related somehow. And that hurt even worse. Children were ripped from Danica to be trained, to be used as weapons. It *hurt*.

All of the rage. All the fury he'd had over the last few months hadn't just gone away. Sure it bled out of him with the pain and blood, but it wasn't fair. None of it had been fair. What now? Was he really supposed to be a stoic bastard and let his hate and anger die with him? One look at the silent tear the Nooseman across from him shed was the only real answer he needed. If there was a Grand Tapestry, he hoped to find Denny up there, woven in all her glory. And maybe someday he'd see the others too.

Lin hung his head and shifted to push the broken dagger back to the Nooseman. "If you see any of the scholars again, give them this. Please."

"Give it to them yourself," Tylle said.

Lin sucked on his lip for a second, wincing as he shifted. "No. I won't be climbing back up those stairs. Tylle?"

She hovered over him, her presence practically bristling.

"I'd like to sit by the sea. Like we did that day at the Ferrucium. There is plenty of fighting left..." Lin winced as he sucked in a breath. "But it won't be for me. If you'll take me, you can leave and help whatever side you've chosen to help now that this big bastard is dead."

Watching the Nooseman and Gritt move together, taking the dagger, and leaving the large echoing audience chamber felt odd. Especially considering they did so holding the detached head of Velkath Reborn, the Horned King, He-who-decidedly-could-fall-again. Whatever name he wanted to go by.

Tylle stared at him, looking every bit as awful as he felt. "We didn't sit by the sea then. Not really."

"I'd like to now, though. I'm going. With or without you." Lin coughed, sucked in a deep bone-breaking breath, and hoped for once that he might understand the expressions flickering across her face.

"They might be able to—"

Lin shook his head. His spul was spent. And he knew there was a limit to what the magicks were capable of. And even if it weren't for the breaks of flesh and bone, there was something more sinister broken within him now. He felt it in the way the air ran across his skin. In the way how Aemun's ghost had silenced but still continued to whisper, just outside of earshot. Steady and haunting.

Without her help, he rose, glass and debris crunching under his right foot as he dragged his left. Then she was under his arm, painfully so, helping him along.

"What about Mellyr?"

"She saw her mother die..." Lin wheezed. He couldn't finish the sentence, not the way words refused to come. But doubtless, she knew what he meant. Mellyr didn't need to see all her parents die.

"And Denro? Pael? If they're both still around?"

Lin didn't reply. No need to. Tylle likely didn't care. Fake worry from a woman who hadn't bothered to let Lin know anything. Not when it mattered at least. Besides, he'd said his goodbyes to them already.

If Gods were good, there'd be no delays moving through the city. No Ladrican soldiers looking to make a name by killing the corpse of the Hero of the Vellia's Fingers.

"You don't..." Lin started, then shook his head. Every other step the world blurred and he mumbled, "You should smell like wildflowers."

Dying Hate

"War never ends. We just pass it along. All you can do is hope you lit the path for those who follow." —Tylle

There was a small mercy in the way Tylle dragged him without word, as they trudged slowly through the streets of Fentis. Through half-shuddered eyes, Lin saw the peaceful port city turned into a war-torn spectacle. Blood and worse ran in the streets, stones slick with it where it was fresh, and sticky where it had the time to dry. Sometimes both as rivers leaked from piles of corpses, freshly made tributaries feeding into lakes of older origin.

It wasn't that Lin had grown attached to Fentis itself. The last time he was here for any extended amount of time he'd been a prisoner. But the devastation? Unwarranted. An argument could be made the scholars were complicit in keeping Danicans in the dark, but so were other Danicans. Aemun had learned all he had from somewhere, likely Weaver Azhura. And the Ferrucium had done little to prepare the people for this outcome.

They should have made it clearer how ineffective things had become.

But even as Lin thought it, he knew that couldn't have been an option. To tell the Ladricans that things were any less than handled would've meant worse for Danica. Likely. Though, Lin wasn't sure what could be worse than this.

Lin nearly tripped and Tylle shifted her weight, carrying him more than dragging him now. Another mercy. He couldn't help staring at the scar along her jaw. There were more questions he could've asked if he thought they'd had time for small talk. Now, he didn't feel he could talk. Not well at any rate.

As they made their way deeper through the ruined guts of the city, Lin was sure he couldn't have made it alone. Eventually, his energy would have failed him and he'd be just another corpse on the side of the alley. A single man among the multitude. Hundreds at a guess. Easily more. Not even considering the untethered troops that joined them. Poor bastards.

Smoke hung in the air overhead, but either he'd lost his hearing or the explosions had finally stopped. He imagined the latter, considering he heard every heavy, gasping breath of his as much as he felt it.

Part of him, a small part, wondered why Tylle had agreed to take him to the water. Not when there was doubtless more fighting to be had. He'd given up trying to understand her when she'd given him the small knife taken from the pack recovered at Fallo. With any luck, he'd find some answers at the water.

Luck. That was a funny thing. Lin craned his neck, wincing at the action. The tower stabbed into the horizon, diminished by the obscuring smoke, but still grand as the sun fought through the haze and clouds.

When Tylle's steps thudded on wood instead of stone Lin nodded weakly at the side of the pier. Several more ships waited in the depths of the water, some Ladrican. Others not. Who they were mattered less and less as Tylle lowered Lin to sit. He expected the cry of sea birds to carry, but none called. Scared away by the explosions likely, but it wouldn't be long before they realized how much fresh meat lined the streets. Planters of flowers traded for piles of Fentians.

"Why the water?" Tylle asked.

Pulling away from her to sit down was difficult for a variety of reasons. Paramount was how the numbness on the left of his body had spread and now his right foot refused to do as commanded. Second was the sticky pull of fabric from the blood dried between them as Tylle held him.

"Huh?" Lin couldn't take his eyes off the steady crest of water that carried under the pier. The storm had passed, but like the battle, left its mark.

"Why the water, Lin?"

For the slapping of waves. And the simple fact that it felt right. In all those early nightmares where he was a blade, breaking, he'd been doused in water. Why not again? One final time, dunked to let his anger hiss under the waves.

Tylle stared over her shoulder at the tower.

"You can go," Lin muttered.

"I'd like to stay."

Lin wheezed and shifted to rest his head on her shoulder.

Tylle's shoulders were lean and not nearly as comfortable as Lin liked, but a dying beggar could hardly choose the final place where he might lay his head.

How many times had he wished to go back to the docks behind the Ferrucium? To do things over again? He'd wanted to run away with her and Mellyr.

"I... missed... you. And..."

And he hated her. There had been such a profound longing for what could've been that he hadn't seen what was there in front of him.

"And?" Tylle's voice had grown soft as velvet.

"I hate you."

Tylle grunted.

Lin felt lucky she hadn't shrugged, as bony as her shoulders were. "Why... Did you do it?"

"Betray you?"

"Betray... Him." There was no answer she could give. No closure that could make any of the pain feel better. But an explanation would be nice if not appreciated.

"Can I... Can I braid your hair?" Tylle asked. "You'll probably have to lay back on me."

Lin sighed, which hurt, and nodded, which somehow hurt worse. Likely her damned shoulder digging into his cheek.

With a hand, she kept him upright as she shifted around to hold him, slender strong fingers taking his shoulders and leaning him painfully back into her. She still didn't smell like wildflowers, but it would be impossible to say this wasn't more comfortable.

Lin eased into her, eyes catching a lone seabird circling high above them. Round and round it went, like a knot.

"Venya... She fell in love. She was tricked and fooled and eventually killed her sister. This you know."

"Aemun, he tricked my sister. Then he killed her. My mission was a simple one. See if I could bring her, her child, and her consort into Erias's good graces. Things quickly fell apart."

Lin winced as he chuckled. To say things fell apart felt like a slap in the face of everything they'd gone through after Margaret's death.

"And then I met the untethered in Fallo. Part of me wanted to believe what *he* was saying. Velkath Reborn. Imagine. One of the Six true Wievers coming back to save Danica.

"It would've been amazing. If he'd really been here for our people. There were too many small decisions along the way to explain it all, but eventually, Erias and I agreed that I at least needed to see what the monster's promises were all about. Investigate the untethered problem and see if there was any merit to siding with him. By the time I was among him and his people, it was clear that leaving alive wouldn't be an option. So I bid my time. Lean further back. Please."

Lin eased back, letting any remaining tension in his back go. He barely felt the pull at his tangled, matted hair. Maybe that said more about his state than Tylle's skills, but it was hard to forget how deft her slight fingers were. "You... Would've betrayed Erias. If the promises were sweet enough."

Tylle grunted. High above, the bird continued circling, lazy, dizzying spins.

"Do... Do you think Margaret and I might've been friends?"

"Maybe."

Lin coughed. "I'm sorry I couldn't save her."

Pressure on his scalp, a kiss perhaps, but Lin couldn't be sure. "We both failed her."

"But I... I saved Mellyr."

"You did."

"Why is it... Why is it we see Velkath's Sigil when we untether?"

"There are many different ways a person might go mad. Sights. Voices. But I've neither seen nor heard anything."

"I've been hearing Aemun's," Lin whispered. "I thought I could fight it."

"If things had gone a bit different. Maybe. But it takes us all. Us fighters anyways."

"Eventually," Lin said, voice distant to his ears.

"Eventually," Tylle agreed.

Lin wept silently, eyes drifting from the sky to the sea. At least he hadn't become a monster. Not the way some did.

Tylle shifted, hands leaving his hair alone, and wrapping him in a tight embrace from behind. Shallow breaths came and went. Eventually shouts sounded that he couldn't entirely make out. He didn't care to hear them really. It all sounded like excess buried underneath the waves. Drowned.

While Tylle held him, he thought of *her*. And he knew it was her he thought of because her name hadn't needed mentioning.

If they could just sit by the water forever.

Forever.

Steps, screams, sobs, and shakes.

Stitches belonging to an uneven smile.

Silence.

A Dawning Tapestry

Three months nearly to the date of the last meeting to discuss the Danican Accords, the second meeting was held. Despite the damages to Fentis as a whole, thanks to the assistance of the Ferrucium and the Free Nations, rebuilding wasn't just possible but quick. Countless lives had been lost, buildings damaged, and the state of Danica changed forever. It hadn't been easy, painless, or even enjoyable, but along with the other Fentian Scholars who'd survived, rebuilding and regrouping had been more than possible.

And now the meeting was being held in the same room the Horned King had met his end. *Temmin*. A rogue Nooseman, by all accounts. It was fitting the Ladricans had a role to play, seeing as how everything wrong with Danica seemed to stem from their overinvolvement. A fact that hopefully, the gathered committee might recognize.

The halls were empty, everyone that mattered already inside the expansive room. No trace of the battle as Denro stepped into the room. Aside from the hole left by the shattering of the skylight.

Denro carried Mellyr strapped to his chest in a sling of sorts, Rosa, a junior scholar at his side. Mellyr didn't like the carrier, kicking and fussing. Sitting meant Mellyr might try to wriggle free, so he stood at the back of the steps, watching the impassioned speaker talk.

Gritt, the former Nooseman. Her voice carried well, though some of that was the design of the room. The acoustics were good for lectures, debates, and of course sentencings.

Denro stared up at the skylight as Mellyr grabbed his beard. He hadn't planned to let it grow out, but as busy as they'd been, he hadn't the desire to trim it. Besides, it seemed High Scholar Anya liked it, the way she'd twist it when they were alone.

Applause pulled Denro from his thoughts, and he looked around to see more than one person standing.

"What did she say?" Denro whispered.

"I... I'm not sure. Something about the need for stronger controls on Danicans, but with more freedom. Education opposed to training," Rosa said, her voice hushed and somber.

Denro's brows shot up and he nodded. A fair stance for someone like her to take. A shudder racked him as he considered what sorts of training the Nooseman might've been subjected to become the weapons— the people they were now. Six knew the Ferrucium hadn't been kind to their trainees.

Mellyr looked around, clapping with an excitement she likely didn't understand.

Quiet blanketed the room as Anya stepped into the center where Gritt had been speaking. She raised her hands to aid in the silencing. "Our final speaker is also from the north. King Lodram if you would."

Denro couldn't decide if the man looked as old as he'd expected. His hair was white and short to the scalp, a modest circlet of Bound Metal as a crown. Kind. That's how he looked. But as he stood from his seat, hands trembling, lip snarled, the snake showed his fangs.

"Yes, yes, yes. Let's applaud the words of a known oath breaker. Someone who swore fealty then deserted Ladrica in its time of need. Months ago, lest all of you gathered have forgotten, our council was assaulted by some unknown enemy. *And* a tainted-blood.

"How convenient, that the monster that came to our isle, disrupted the meeting, has died." He slammed his fist into his palm. "How convenient, that when we have such a momentous decision at stake, the Scholars of Fentis are attacked, aided by the traitor dukes, and now seek sympathy from the compassionate minds of those gathered here"

"I can sympathize," His voice rang out. "I can. Southern Ladrica has been oft beset by the wicked monsters. Yet, it is our name whispered as the culprit?"

An aide had moved to stand beside the king, keeping him upright as he trembled. Whether age or rage was to blame, Denro couldn't tell. But he saw where the king was going. What lines of thought he wanted the other gathered leaders to walk along.

Mellyr let out a string of nonsense and Denro smiled. "Mocking a king is cruel work Melly."

"Whispered because we were victims ourselves of lies? Led to believe that the Nooseman named Temmin was dead so many years ago now that it baffled us to believe him alive.

"All this has proven to me and my people, is that we've been too lax with those who could wield these strange magicks. Too lax with the Elodian Empire and their wraiths. Too lax with the Danicans and their untethered. I... I am entreating, humbly pleading, that you consider ratifying the Danican Accords. I agree with the sentiment of stricter controls. But I've no doubt that education, slipping of knowledge to these fiends, is what caused all this to begin with. If you won't think of us, all of us, and our plight, consider the plight of your children to come!"

A grand speech, all considered. Denro frowned. He wasn't sure what the right course was himself, but he knew that all those people couldn't have died for nothing. He'd said his peace after Erias Wellgrove and Duke Elmore and had garnered far more grumblings than applause. But, everything that had happened aside, there needed to be a better path forward.

Denro looked up, noting Anya scanning the crowd. Her face was as impassive as always, the slight wrinkles at the corners of her eyes exaggerated by the lighting leaking in from the hole.

"As we always do, we will take it to a vote," Anya said.

To be alive at a time of such crucial import couldn't be understated. Denro had done things, seen things, being complicit, and conscious of certain actions that might have led to this. Rescuing Lin as an infant. Teaching him combat and compassion. Making studying people into a game. Denro wiped the tear from his eye, Mellyr reaching instinctively for his hand.

The vote wasn't open to all the scholars. Only the High Scholars, leaders of the Free Nations, the Ladrican King, and the voice of the Emperor in attendance had any say. Erias Wellgrove and Weaver Azhura were in attendance, but the debate to let them or any of the actual dukes vote ended in the Danicans being allowed to speak, but not cast votes in the outcome. Some Danicans might disagree, but Denro agreed with it. Whatever the outcome, it couldn't be said that Danica won the vote from sheer numbers.

Denro could still remember watching Lin fall, unable to stop the Binding sent into his back to push the Horned King over the edge. He'd expected to come into the auditorium and find both Lin and the monster dead, but that hadn't been the case. Amazing, a person's capacity for survival when they had something to fight for. To protect.

To see the fighters compelled by the Horned King's Bludwieves realize they were no longer tied to him, and turn on the untethered they marched alongside. The battles hadn't ended, not on that first day, but it had turned from that point.

"I can take her if you need a moment," Rosa said.

Denro wiped his cheeks again and smiled. "No. No. It's okay." He kissed Mellyr's brow, her tiny fingers fussing with his beard. He watched as the votes were cast. Seven hands in favor of ratifying the Accords to cede control of Danica to the Danicans. Five opposed.

Cheers and yells. Glee and fury. Denro watched the king specifically, a vein visible even this far from the man like a grub writhing within a rotted log.

Too much stimulus for one tired man and his excitable baby. Denro left the audience chamber, Rosa following like a shadow. Ready and able to help with Mellyr should he ask of it. But he never asked. Lin had entrusted her to him after all. And besides, he didn't have much else to do when High Scholar Anya was otherwise preoccupied.

No matter how much time had passed since the battle, it was still hard to imagine they'd cleaned all the blood from every crevice. Every nook. But they had. Or at the very least, they'd managed to hide the traces of gore.

Denro took the long way to their rooms. These days he always took the long way, just to see the progress on the tapestry. One entire month had been spent simply convincing the various isles of the Free Nations to send the correct reagents for the colors to dye the materials.

The room was empty, but it looked like the majority of the weaving was finished. Denro's breath caught and he covered his mouth as he took it in. Comparable to the piece at the Ferrucium, if not a breadth smaller.

He moved further into the room. A cot had been set up in a corner. That Tylle woman had been sleeping and taking her meals in here, eager to finish the project. Now, she was nowhere to be seen. Likely watching the council.

Denro narrowed his eyes and ran his hand along the fabric. He hadn't the first idea how a loom worked or why all the threads and bundles looked so out of place strung up, but he recognized Lin, and that was all that mattered. Though, they'd made him a bit tougher looking than Denro thought he should be.

Mellyr cooed and Denro lifted her a bit in her strap to get a better look. "That right there, was one of the most foolish, brave men I'd ever met. He would've broken this world apart to keep you safe," Denro breathed the words into her curls, blinking to fight back the tears.

"Instead, he broke himself."

Denro turned at Pael's voice. The man had been slinking about the tower the last few days, no doubt eager to stick a dagger in the King's throat if things went poorly.

"He did," Denro said.

"But look at us, two old soldiers, making it to the end of the battle."

Denro shook his head. "I doubt the battle will ever truly be over. But today marks a good start."

"He looks a bit mean there, no?"

"Better mean than weak, I guess." Denro sighed and then scanned the room. "What now for your people?"

"True. Lin wasn't weak. Stubborn and in over his head. But I've met weak men, and I don't think he was one of them." Pael limped forward. "I'm so used to things going bad, I hadn't actually considered what we'd do if they didn't."

"Same."

***

Denro rode through the forest, one of the only patches northward that hadn't been wholly ruined by the Horned King's army. Even years later, the reforestation was slow going.

Mellyr rode just in front of him on her own pony, five years old and already a better rider at her age than Lin had been.

"Take it easy," Denro called. *Please.* Always pushing boundaries. Always ripping away on straights just before the path curved. It made Denro uneasy.

"Okay!" Mellyr called back. Simple as that. No fussing or fighting. But, of course, she didn't slow.

He'd been fortunate enough to have never *really* met Aemun. In passing perhaps, but he had a feeling she'd earned that streak from him. Or maybe the mother, if she'd been anything like that priestess Tylle. Denro could still see her gripping Lin's body on the dockside, cradling him like some precious cargo, worried the waves might come and take him. Weeping.

Even as she pushed her pony, Denro eased his pace. They'd come this way every year since the Accords were ratified and though this was the first year Mellyr was allowed to ride alone, she knew the path.

In fact, just around the bend she was so sharply racing to, was Lyre. Such a small secluded village, it was a marvel the Horned King's forces had left it alone. Though, if they'd come from Fallo, and pushed due south, it was easy to understand how it might've been missed at that final march seeing how westward it sat.

Every year Denro visited Lyre, it became larger. By a child or two. Word had quickly spread that it was a safe place for those who longed for the wilderness of northern Danica, and that had brought families and refugees.

Denro rounded the bend, Lyre coming into view. Around the village, the stone shroud looked well-kept. An old superstition and one the Horned King had played into. Children, near enough to Mellyr's age, walked along the wall, inquisitive eyes bright in the early hours. Screams sounded, joy. They likely recognized Mellyr and no doubt would want turns on her pony.

Two new homes had been built along the western side of Lyre since his visit a year ago, and chickens and goats walked freely through the city center. As Denro had assumed, the children were eager to speak with Mellyr, commenting on her pony in squeaky excited voices.

"'Ello," Alderman Pryor called. Denro had recognized him on his very first visit based on Lin's somewhat mean-spirited, if not accurate, description. And the man had been as accommodating as Denro had hoped he would. "That time o' the year already?"

Denro's legs ached as he dismounted and he nodded at the gray-haired Alderman. "Nebra still tolerating the children?"

"More than ever. But... Sometimes she spooks them the way she protects the... His stones."

"I'd like to think she loved him as much as he loved her. I'll be about it then, mind keeping an eye on Mellyr? She'll come when she's ready. I still don't think she fully understands."

"Course I don't mind. All the little ones love her. Oh... And the priestess is here already." Alderman Pryor straightened the rope he wore tight around his chest, the little bell attached jingling as he did.

Denro nodded. He figured someday she'd stop showing up, but she hadn't yet, and seeing as she was Mellyr's kin, it didn't seem right to fight it.

Despite its growth, Lyre was a simple village. The Physiker's home sat on the east side, still the largest building, but behind it sat a field where they burned their dead.

Denro stepped into the House of the Six. Alderman Pryor was also the resident holy man, and the House was empty, save for the pews. Depictions of the Six were crafted in stain-glass at every window and hanging at the back of the church, was Lin's tapestry. They didn't worship him. Nothing like that, but it felt like a fitting place all considered and Alderman Pryor was more than willing to put it up.

For four years it had hung there, honoring Lin. Four years Denro had come and prayed to whoever would listen, that Lin was in a better place. That Danica would continue to see reformations in the right direction. Already, they'd seen progress. Trade with the

Free Nations, and open conversations with Elodis and Ladrica, though the latter was often in more terse terms.

When his prayers were finished, he rose and left the House with a second look at Lin's tapestry. Of course, everyone who knew Lin and saw it thought he looked a bit severe in it, but he'd been a good man. And it still hurt thinking how he wasn't still with them. An aching longing for the conversations they couldn't still have. He'd been cruel to Lin after the Fall, pushing him away. Anya told him he couldn't blame himself, but Lin had needed support and Denro hadn't done enough.

It didn't help learning from Carine and Jun that he'd suffered the loss of someone he held dear, right before the events of The March, as they'd begun calling it.

The fields behind the Physiker's home were thick with spring grass. Even the patch where bodies were burned seemed to be growing in, fresh and green. Wildflowers were in full bloom, purples and reds like the colors of a sunset vibrant against the verdant sea.

Mellyr's scream of excitement conjured a smile as the little girl noticed the lean woman sitting by Lin's stone marker along the stone shroud. She ran, light hair bouncing in the wind as she rushed and squeezed Tylle in the sort of hug that only a child could give.

"Little one," Tylle said, smiling and pressing her brow to Mellyr's. "You've gotten so tall!"

"I have. And I've been riding on my own. And reading my letters. Oh! And I even braided my hair myself!" Mellyr happily showed off the braid she'd done, which wasn't the worst he'd seen, and Tylle scooped her up and spun her.

"Well done!" Tylle laughed.

Denro gave them a moment, watching at a distance.

"Den-roooo!" Mellyr called.

Denro waved as he approached. Her grin as she was spun showed several missing teeth and was an easy reminder of how old she'd gotten in a blink.

"Can I braid your hair, little one? Show you how it's done again?" Tylle asked.

Mellyr giggled and squirmed as Tylle set her down.

Denro nodded at Tylle and made his way to the stack of stones.

"Did you already look at the scary-man?" Mellyr asked, her voice lowering as she stared at the grass.

Denro frowned and knelt in front of the stacked stones. "He was a good man." A piece of him hated Tylle. For what she'd caused. For how Mellyr fawned over her while dismissing Lin. The priestess hadn't wanted Mellyr, Denro knew that much.

"He was a hero," Tylle said as she dragged Mellyr over to the stone stack.

"*He* saved *me*," Mellyr said, sounding every bit like she didn't believe it.

"More than just you. So, so many people. Me too." Denro bunched up his brow, giving his best scowl. "Am I a scary man?"

Mellyr's giggle almost made it hard to be upset with her. One tiny finger poked Denro's nose, pushing it in. "No. You're never scary."

"I could tell you a story about Lin," Tylle said.

Mellyr's eyes got big and she wiggled free from Tylle's grip. "You tell the best stories!"

There was no sense in arguing with either of them. Patience is what it would take. "I could tell a better story. You know, nobody would've believed it if I told them a Ferrucium Escorter helped shape our world into something better. A simple, silly, stubborn Escorter."

"How?" Mellyr asked. Her attention was already drifting, eyes studying a butterfly that had landed on one of the nearest, scarlet-hued flowers.

"I think he felt he was an ember... And at the end... He wasn't afraid to burn."

Tylle smiled and grabbed Mellyr's hand. "Ready for me to do your hair?"

Mellyr wouldn't understand. Not for a long time but it was Denro's place to teach her, watch her, and see her become someone Lin could be proud of. She hugged Denro and whispered. "That *sounds* scary."

Tylle took her away, leaving Denro in peace to have his moment. He was sure she'd fill the child's head with all sorts of fanciful stories about Lin. Was probably the reason Mellyr thought he was scary. That and the tapestry.

Once they were gone, he turned and faced the stones. The prayers in the House were for Lin and the others lost, but this? This was for him. "I...I went through Wakewatch the other day. And I saw... I saw a woman with hair curlier than a sheep's. I'd never seen the like. And I saw a tree you would've struggled to take your eyes off of. It seemed a type of mold had grown under its bark, maybe related to honey-caps because it *glowed*. Odd right? Mellyr, she's already a better rider than you."

Off to the side, Nebra, white-faced and healthy-looking chewed on grass. "And... Pael is still being a bother. Won't stop visiting me. I think he's lonely. He replaced that silly hat of his with a bigger one if you could believe it. He looks like a mushroom. Oh... And...."

The End

To everyone who has made it to the end of Lin's journey, thank you. This book was the hardest to write because, like most readers, I didn't want Lin's story to come to an end. But all journeys conclude. All paths end.

Even if you die holding the torch, you've lit the path for those who follow.

Please consider leaving a review, telling friends and family, or mailing your local government so others can also fall in love with this series.

The Crystallium Depths

If you enjoy my writing, please consider looking out for my next project— Cracks of the Deepest Black, book one in the Crystallium Depths Saga, an epic multi-POV fantasy inspired by my love for Final Fantasy, the Legend of Zelda, and authors who've inspired me along the way. Enjoy a short sample of chapter one.

Graham exhaled and blinked, praying the sweat on his brow would stay from his eyes. A futile thing to pray about considering how rolling beads already threatened to drip down. The Crystal before him, far larger than he was, shimmered with the light roiling off it. He swallowed, gagged on the lack of saliva, and then looked down at his boots to avoid the stare of Artificer Xand, the Crystal Master.

"We don't have all day. Best to act like you've been here before," Xand called. The ancient man stood directly beside the blindingly bright crystal. His features were starkly lit, a hooked nose that could rival a crow casting a long shadow across the stone floor from his side profile.

Graham grimaced. Each step closer to the crystal seemed to draw out more moisture from him. It was the entire reason Xand had the complexion of sunned leather more than man. And he'd forgotten his goggles in his morning rush.

"Where are your goggles?" Xand asked in that squawking, gravel-choked voice of his.

"I-I couldn't find them. And I didn't want to be late." Graham squinted, blinking so much that Xand's expression shifted in still, captured moments.

"Being late is preferred to being blind. A lesson I'm sure you won't repeat lightly," Xand chuckled. "Here. Crystal upkeep is a serious business, which means extra goggles. Extra gloves, extra *precautions*. Wouldn't want a sliver of the thing making you into a Cryst, would you?" As he spoke, he ran his hands over the numerous pockets built into his dark apron and pulled out a set of thick, black-lensed goggles.

Graham took the goggles in his gloved hands, ignoring Xand's comment about turning Cryst. He never could understand why the older generation disliked the concept. Having the power of a Crystal at the tip of his fingers couldn't be that bad. He frowned and looked at his hands. At least he'd remembered his gloves. As warm as the Crystal was, at least it was the Crystal of Light and not of Fire, as missing any protective wear would've seen him unable to enter, unable to earn much-needed pay for the day.

Xand's gloved hands trembled. Only slightly, but both of them noticed it, and both acted like they hadn't.

The goggles slid onto his face, blanketing Graham's vision in a comforting shadow. A *soothing* shadow. Even with the goggles, bathed in the aura of the Crystal of Shadow, looking directly at this particular Crystal wasn't possible, not if he wanted to keep his vision once he reached Xand's age. But they helped ease the developing tenderness.

They also helped keep the beads of sweat from dripping down, though at the cost of the lenses fogging.

"Have your rag?" Xand asked.

Graham nodded. When he noticed Xand wasn't looking at him he gave a soft, "Yes sir."

"And it's treated?"

"Yes. Yes, of course, sir." Graham shuffled and reached into the largest pocket in his apron, pulling out the alchemical solution-soaked rag.

"Of *course*," Xand chided. "As if you hadn't just told me you ran late and 'couldn't find' your goggles. Hmm. You do the top down today. My back is telling me I should avoid the staircase." He'd pulled out his rag and started running it over the bottom portion of the Crystal, starting at the base where it fused with the stone underneath.

Graham moved to the metal stairs that spiraled up around the far side of the Crystal. Each step shuddered with his weight, and once he reached the top, he waited motionless until the stairs had settled. From what Xand often said, the staircase was as old as he was, if not older, and hadn't been replaced. Ever. He stared up at the ceiling and wiped the crystal with wide, concentric motions.

It thrummed under the rag, warming the cloth despite the protective oils and herbs it had been soaked with.

The entire process, between the two of them working, took only the slimmest sliver of the day. Xand had an apparatus that told him precisely when the sun rose, and that was when they began. Then, they moved the various items into the Crystal's light. Panes of glass for lamps, metal rods for batons, and raw ore. All of which excelled at capturing the aura from the magic crystal. All manner of tools and sundries that, more often than not, only the nobility could afford. Well, nobility and the military anyway.

"You'll need to get quicker," Xand said after they'd finished and exited the Crystal care room. Snow crunched under his boots, and the wind whipped playful flurries through the air.

The sun, which was little more than a faded orange stain, was already setting. Not because so much time had passed but because their home was practically perpetually devoid of the sun. As the year stretched on, so would the time the sun hung overhead, but even the longest day was a blink compared to other parts of the world. Parts that Graham had only ever heard of.

"I know," Graham said. His voice was hoarse, and it was painful to talk. "I don't know how you do it."

"Experience mostly. But you're sharp if a pinch careless. You'll do fine on your own."

That was the unspoken truth between them. Xand was old. And sooner or later, death came for everyone. Crystal Master or not. Good man or not. And Graham wasn't ready. Not for the role he'd inherent or the old man's death.

Definitely Not A Secret
!You Found A Secret!

Okay, clearly this isn't a sword hidden behind a waterfall or a chest stashed on the other side of a hollow wall, but you've made it to the Secret Scribes page! The Secret Scribes are an affiliation of independent fantasy authors who write varying subgenres of fantasy. If you've enjoyed this book, please check out some other great authors and their titles below.

Alex Schueuermann- The Odyllic Stone
Bella Dunn- The Dreams Thief, Blood and Dreams, The Sorrow of the Wise Man
Bill Adams- The Godsblood Tradgedy, Lady Drakeslayer, The Tenacious Tale of Tanna the Tendersword
Damien Francis- The Tome of Haren
Dave Lawson- The Envoys of War, The Pawns of Havoc
E.H. Bradley- The Ranger, The Veil
L.M. Douglas- Gharantia's Guardian, Gharantia's Fury, Gharantia's Fate
L.N. Bayen- The Wingspan of Treason

R. A. Sandpiper- A Pocket of Lies, A Promise of Blood, A Claiming of Souls

R. E. Sanders- Demon's Tear, A Path of Blades, Tann's Last Stand

Sean O'Boyle- The Ballad of Sprikit The Bard(And Company)

And more titles to come!

Printed in Dunstable, United Kingdom